Books by Billi Jean

Love's Command

I0598597

Running Scared
Safe in His Arms
Catch Me If You Can
Trusting Love
Come a Little Closer, If You Dare
The Promise of Love

Sisterhood of Jade

Silver's Chance
A Spartan's Kiss
Midnight Star
Golden's Rule
Sorcha's Wolf
Eternal Embrace
Claiming a Demon's Heart
Gambling on Trouble
Hunter's Promise
Keeping his Heart

Anthologies

Into the Spirit

Keeping his Heart

ISBN # 978-1-78651-341-0

©Copyright Billi Jean 2016

Cover Art by Posh Gosh ©Copyright 2016

Interior text design by Claire Siemaszkiewicz

Totally Bound Publishing

Published in 2016 by Totally Bound Publishing, Newland House, The Point, Weaver Road, Lincoln, LN6 3QN, United Kingdom.

Totally Bound Publishing is a subsidiary of Totally Entwined Group Limited.

Sisterhood of Jade

KEEPING HIS HEART

BILLI JEAN

Dedication

Sometimes we have to step outside the box to actually see clearly.

Chapter One

Jamie gazed down at the city of Seattle, unsure what drew him here. His assignment was simple. At least he'd thought so at first. Find Elsa Wentworth, a former human, possibly Lykae raised outside the pack, and now a Vampire. Or, a wolf-vamp cross breed.

Find her. Watch her. Report in. Easy.

Not so much.

She wasn't here. He'd realized that when he'd first pulled into town. But there were other immortals here. He watched two of them talking in an alley behind a club. He stood on the roof, trying to come to terms with another dead end. She moved. *A lot.* Being a few steps behind someone wasn't what he was used to. He'd found pictures of her on traffic cameras, department store security tapes and parking lot videos. Not once had he been in the same town, at the same time, as the elusive Elsa Wentworth.

It was almost laughable. It *was* impressive. She was young, very young if he had to guess by the photos. But they never were good for judging age, not in an immortal. He folded the black and white print of her and replaced it in his pocket. He didn't need it. He could picture how her blonde hair had fanned out around her head, her face almost square to the camera, just a tad off so that she was staring, startled, off to one side. He wasn't sure what had frightened her in the picture, only that something had.

The music filtering out of the club drew his attention back to the here and now. It grew in volume every time someone entered or left the bar. The men below him didn't move to go inside or to leave. They were arguing. One was a Vampire suffering from the never-ending bloodlust that came with killing his victims. The other man, Jamie wasn't so sure about.

He broke away and threw his arm out. With a few more heated words, he pointed toward the town. The Vampire misted, as if he'd been ordered, disappearing from sight but not scent as he headed in the direction indicated. The man didn't go back inside the club. He stood with arms crossed, head down, contemplating either the concrete or whatever had been said to him.

The Vampire House in this town had been eradicated by Aidan, the king of the Vampires. There wasn't even a building left where the Vampires had once lived. Jamie had walked by today, amazed to see the ground bulldozed under. Squares of new bright green turf now covered the park. There were even cherry trees meandering along a manmade stream lined by a thick expanse of flowers.

It was a park now, named *Aidan's Way*.

Jamie had smiled at the name, getting the message loud and clear, even if the Vampires had not. He was betting on them understanding quite well.

He gathered himself and leaped from the roof, landing quietly on the road. Immediately the man spun, lifting an arm in a warding gesture.

"I mean you no harm. Settle down." Jamie kept his hands open at his sides as he straightened to his full height.

The guy took a few steps back, seemed to realize that the move proved him a pussy, and stopped. "What do you want?"

Jamie had him pegged as less than a year in the immortal world. There wasn't a chance he'd seen battle. Not with the innocent face and wide-open eyes.

"Who were you talking to?"

"A man, no one important."

"A man?" Jamie laughed. "My guess is he was your maker. Am I right?"

No response, but no aggression either at the slight. *Young, possibly less than six months turned.*

"Did you know turning Vampires was against Aidan's laws?"

Still no response, but the guy gave his head a slight shake to get his dark hair out of his eyes. It was either wet from the constant drizzle, or greasy. He smelled clean. No stench of blood clung to him. If he'd sampled recently, it wasn't within the last twenty-four hours. He smelled *too* clean.

"Who are you?" he asked, stepping away. He was elegantly dressed, as if he'd come from a black tie affair, but without an overcoat to protect his suit jacket, which was getting soaked.

Jamie walked closer until only a few feet separated them. "My name's Jamie. What's your name, kid?"

A brief wait and a clearing of the throat, then he said, "David."

"You're new to this world."

Another hesitation, then a nod.

"Tell me, if that wasn't your maker, who is? You're new to Vampire. What were you before?"

The guy licked his lips and nervously glanced down the alley. There was something off about him, a clinical smell as if he'd gone and washed at a hospital. It didn't add up.

"He's gone. I can scent him. He's back in the city, near the bay. Why not talk? I already assured you I won't kill you."

A feral light brightened his eyes then was gone so quickly Jamie wondered if he'd imagined it. "I'm just a guy. A Vampire—"

"You aren't *only* a Vampire, you're more." Jamie drew in a deep breath, walking a circle around him. There was something there, something... He almost thought not right, but dismissed it as quickly as it had surfaced. The man wasn't a Death Stalker. He was alone, and that stench was difficult even for the mages to hide.

"Explain the more."

Again, the man shifted nervously. "I... I'm not sure what you mean."

"Are you French?" There was something there, not an accent but *something*. A quick shake of his head was the only answer Jamie received. He let it go. "Look, I don't know who you are. He wasn't my maker, just...someone I know."

"How many Vampires call Seattle home?"

"Just a few."

"Do you know them all?"

Eyes widened when Jamie drew closer, he stuttered, "What?"

"Do you know all the Vampires in this area?" Jamie stepped closer and watched his eyes. He was going to try to mist, or run. Not allowing that, Jamie reached out and drew him closer by his neck. "Do you know what happens to a Vampire when they run from a wolf?"

David tried to shake his head but Jamie tightened his grip. "They die."

The guy nodded, or tried to, but ended up making a lot of gurgling noises.

"A girl, fresh Vampire, young, a dancer," Jamie said watching his eyes shift to the side, then back at him, only to shift away again. *Nerves or something more?* "Was she here recently?"

"N-name?"

"Elsa."

This time his eyes did register something. Jamie just wasn't certain what. "I think so. I think I've heard of her. I never saw her. She hides. She's good at hiding," he added quickly when Jamie frowned.

"Why would she need to hide?"

"I'm... I'm not certain."

"She's gone now?"

"Yes."

Just what Jamie had thought. "Any idea what direction?"

"No, no one could ever —"

"Find her. Yes." Jamie thought about what he did know of the girl. She was newly turned, less than ten years. What would she do? "Did she have friends? Vampire friends?"

"She knew very few. She was a loner."

Like me.

"Human friends?"

David tensed. His eyes narrowed as if he'd never considered such a question.

Jamie had. Over the past few weeks, the urge to find her had gone from a mission to an obsession. Every glimpse of her, every hint of her scent, drew him. He was worried about when he did find her. *Will I lose this urgency? The constant anxiety? Or will it grow?*

"She did have a human friend." David nodded, eyes flashing light. Did he sense how much Jamie wanted this information? "Bobby something. Simon, I think. He was in her dance troupe."

Jamie didn't ask how the guy knew that, or even for more. It was enough. And what if Bobby Simon was her lover? It was good that Jamie had dropped the hold he'd had on David's throat. If he hadn't the Vampire would be dead. Jamie's fists clenched. If this Bobby had sampled her pale pink lips, his days of doing so were over.

* * * *

Three weeks later

Elsa woke, freezing so badly tremors shook her bones.

She also hurt from the top of her blonde head down to the tips of her newly painted OPI Alpine Snow toenails. The shivers rippled and grew, making her gasp as pain-filled joints shouted in misery. One quick survey showed she wasn't at her hotel in Paris, or her new London flat either.

Or, wait, the hotel. Paris. The show... *Tool and Masters.*

Images, none clear, clouded her vision until she blinked them away.

An unfamiliar forest surrounded her. Dirt and leaves piled up and fell around her legs as she shifted. Giant pine tree branches hung down to the ground and concealed most of the wilderness from her, as well as protecting her.

9

There wasn't a close scent of anyone nearby. So, however she'd gotten to where she was, she was alone now... which meant no spectators. Misery does *not* like company. Whoever said that it did obviously *hadn't* truly ever *been* miserable.

Taking a steadying breath, Elsa slowly stood. Wincing at the feel of her bare feet on the rough ground, she pushed aside some of the pine needles. Every muscle protested, but she limped along until she got the branch up and away.

Stars shimmered brightly. "Holy crap." There was no moon lighting the lush forest, but she didn't need it. "I'm in the wilderness?" No lights, no sounds, no...people — at least for miles. The clouds moved aside and a waxing gibbous moon shone down over the horizon like a postcard.

Slowly, testing each muscle as she did, she took another step then another, sucking in a painful breath as her body protested. At least the ground was softer under her bare feet away from the tree roots and she consoled herself that it wasn't the middle of winter.

Mountains were etched across the skyline, along with an endless expanse of trees. She was on a hill, she assumed, since the forest fell beneath her, then rose again across from her. Behind her were more trees, going upward, and when she moved aside branches, she saw peaks behind her.

Nothing was familiar.

The cry of a wolf ripped through the silence.

Not just any wolf, either, but a *Lykae* in wolf form. She would never forget the sound of that cry. Never forget the panic, the tortured fear, or the result...

The instinctive jump to race off was only hindered by stepping on a sharp rock. Hopping up and down on one foot, she cursed herself. *I'm not wearing clothes. Worse, I'm covered in dirt, and...blood.*

Quickly, she cleansed herself with a thought, similar to taking a very, very fast shower, but without water. Assured that no blood remained to draw him, she tied her hair back with a band. Clothes followed, along with a sturdy pair of her boots. The boots slipped on painfully over her damaged feet.

Being a Vampire had its benefits—calling things that belonged to her was something she'd stumbled across when she'd forgotten her car keys one night. But that kind of power didn't help in situations like this. It wasn't as if she could call herself back home…or to her dingy hotel room in Paris. She hadn't mastered the instant movement from one place to another. Not yet.

Run. Find safety. Blood oozed into her eye from a cut stinging her forehead, but she wiped it off and tried to gauge how long she had until the wolf arrived, even as she took off.

Two minutes tops.

The only protection available was the town in the distance. At least there she would be surrounded by people. She'd have to bet on him behaving himself around crowds, which wasn't a great plan.

As far as she knew, the wolf pack didn't allow switching to their animal form, but this one was racing toward her on all fours. That kind of behavior really shouted that he didn't follow rules, so the 'no doing things in front of humans policy' was probably not something he obeyed either.

The forest was difficult to maneuver through. She had to dodge branches, duck under half-fallen trees and jump over rocks in her path to escape. She should've turned to mist, but that took energy and right now she had to save that for a last resort.

As she raced along, the worry over where she was, and, worse, *what* had been done to her tormented her. Blood still eased from slices along her neck. More dripped from her forehead. She even had blood welling from wounds on her palms and feet. Each step jarred cuts and bruises that should have healed immediately. Maybe because she needed blood *and* food, the process was slowed.

Just thinking of blood made her ache for it. Food was important, but not like the need for blood.

Behind her she sensed *him*. A second later, he broke through the trees.

She sucked at estimating.

Maybe misting would be better. She didn't do it, though, unsure what exactly would happen if she was this weak and...got stuck. *Maybe I'd be mist forever, or just fade away, no longer me.*

Thinking hard never slowed her down, but she calmed the craziness running through her brain and concentrated on pushing herself. With a burst of speed, she leaped upward and grabbed a tree branch, swinging down to do the same on another tree.

Jane, I've turned into Jane. Only that guy is so not Tarzan.

He raced after her, silently for the most part. Once in a while, he let her know he was still there. She'd hear him scrambling up a hill. Or once, he barreled right through the undergrowth. *Is he playing with me?*

When she reached a clearing she didn't pause. She landed in the middle with a leap and ran through the waist-high grass to reach the trees. *So close. Just there. If I can make it.*

"Stop!"

She glanced back, not quite believing the wolf thought something like that would *ever* work. He was big. Like all of his kind, he was also rangy and broad-shouldered. He clearly believed she would listen, because he slowed and shouted again.

"Stop running!"

There wasn't a chance of listening to *that*, so she took the only option she had. She misted, jumping. As she did so she soared through the air on a smoky cloud of her essence. The Lykae lunged, shifting to wolf as he did. He snapped his teeth around where her foot had been. He got a face full of the cool wind.

Bastard *tried* to bite *me*? She was quick to heal, but come on, that would still *hurt!*

He snarled. Even in mist she shivered. A growl like that was really just cussing, but wolves truly possessed an impressive sound when angry.

Elsa pushed herself higher into the trees. He slowed. Surprisingly he shifted from his wolf to a man again. Tall, dressed in black with a long, leather trench jacket, he could have stepped off the Matrix set. She caught her breath. He was rough around the edges, but in that handsome, drop-dead gorgeous way she liked. Rugged. His jacket wasn't sparkly new, but broken in as if he'd owned it for centuries. His hair was short, a dark brown or maybe black—it was hard to say from far away. Lean, mean, and absolutely knew it, was the vibe he gave off.

Why does he stare right at where I'm invisible?

Perhaps she wasn't hidden from the senses of a Lykae as she had assumed. Not if his steady regard meant anything.

It was also odd how he had clothes on after shifting back and forth to wolf.

She'd kind of assumed that wolves tore their clothes up when they changed. In wolf form, he was a large, tawny and gray wolf, only much, much bigger. As a man he was dressed pretty well, but he wouldn't stand out. Other than his looks, she amended as he walked closer. She wondered if he could call his clothes to him like she did. Or when he shifted from wolf, which was like a blast of light, the clothes were just…there.

Anything is possible in the world. She knew that first hand.

"Come back down. I mean you no harm."

Other than nearly biting my foot off, he must mean.

Elsa had no issue with the pack. Not any more than all immortals. Her lack of feelings, one way or the other, didn't stop them from hating her. It was a lesson she'd learned early on. Once bitten, twice shy and all that.

As she hovered, he settled his hands on his hips and canted his head to the side. His jacket spread out behind him, revealing a weapon on his hip. All in all, it was pretty hot. Even she could tell he was used to it working.

Too bad for him she was immune.

The headache and *entire* body ache pretty much ruined

the chances of her heart racing over his sexy glower.

Still, she settled on a nearby tree branch, too weak to stay in mist any longer. If she pretended to want to hear what he had to say, she could buy herself some time. She materialized.

"Good. Now come down." He waved to the ground as if she might obey.

Elsa snorted, but kept it soft instead of laughing in his face. Immortals were arrogant, some more so than others. There was no need to offend him. Not yet.

"I like it up here." She gripped the branch at the scratchiness of her voice. She touched her throat. Pulled her hand away. Blood smeared her fingertips.

"Did you do this to me?"

"Me?" His indignation was clear, so she guessed that was a negative.

"Then do you know who did?"

"You don't remember?" He walked to the base of the tree, seeming to size it up for something. *Gonna knock it down? Maybe he has an ax?* After a heavy exhale, he stood there gazing at her, arms folded across his chest. She was at least ten feet above him. High enough that he couldn't jump and reach her in one lunge. That fact didn't reassure her when he continued to stare at her.

"Would I ask if I did?"

He shrugged a shoulder and turned his gaze to the forest.

"Where are we?"

"France."

Paris. The show. Bobby. I left him again, didn't I?

"What do you remember?"

"Paris."

The wolf rubbed his forehead and waved an arm to encompass the forest. "Does this look like Paris?"

"No. It doesn't. Thank you for your keen observation. Who are you?"

He turned stony silent.

She mimicked the Sphinx as well. After a few torturous

minutes, when she considered hitting him with a pine cone, he sighed.

"Jamie."

No last name, but that didn't matter. Most of the handful of immortals she'd met so far hadn't offered a last name either. This one was different, though. Jamie might be… decent. He was still full of himself. But no more than any other handsome man — who could also turn into a kick-ass wolf whenever he wanted.

"I'm Jamie O'Connor."

Shocked, then pleased, she smiled. "I'm Elsa Wentworth, nice to meet you."

That didn't seem to be what he wanted. "We need to talk."

Over the past ten years no one had wanted to talk. Immortals all wanted things. Like her, to do things with them. This would then lead to her becoming part of *something* — usually their gang. Not one immortal she'd chanced upon had ever wanted to simply *talk*.

This one had shown up moments after she'd woken up alone in a forest with no memory. That meant he was doubly *un*trustworthy. Hello? Serial killers *were* those guys next door. And they all looked normal — decent. She knew it now.

She began to merge deeper with the shadows of the tree, keeping her mind still so that he couldn't see her, but he also couldn't *sense* her — or, in his case, *scent* her.

"No. No more running. I'm here to help you, not hurt you."

She kept hidden, climbing to the branch below her as quietly as she could. Walking carefully down it to another tree, she watched Jamie. He stayed where he was.

"I'll simply find you again."

The last time she'd had no memory was when she'd been hurt — by a wolf.

And even though what Jamie had said might be true, she still trusted no one.

Jamie might find her again. But she knew how to run. She

was good at it. Better at it than she'd ever been at ballet. And she'd been second only to the prima. Fearing for your life gave you an ability that daily dance lessons for fifteen years couldn't beat.

"I'm getting a kink in my neck." Jamie rubbed his shoulder and his neck with what she thought was a bit of an exaggeration. She'd only been in the tree for a few minutes. "Discussing this would be easier if you were down here."

He might not have been able to see her, or hear her moving, but he wasn't giving up. And he wasn't yelling and shouting profanities at her. He hadn't even drawn a weapon or jumped up after her. He was strong—if he'd wanted to be up there, he would have been.

Get answers. Find out what happened to you.

She wanted to, but hesitated. Jamie was...attractive. He was dressed in worn jeans that highlighted his powerful legs and a plain forest-green T-shirt that stretched tightly over his well-developed pectorals. The coat merely added that touch of dangerous, as if he wore it to disguise the weapons. He probably did.

She'd bet he had several hidden away, and knew one of them would be a sword of some type. Every immortal man—and many women—had swords. She'd once wondered why, then figured out that they were silent, and worse, *after* they'd destroyed their opponent—they could then dice them into bits.

Still knowing all that, she couldn't stop staring.

Hots for a man? After all this time?

She shook her head. Still, her gaze landed on his silky mane of dark hair. The moon made it shine, revealing a slight curl along his collar. The temptation to touch the softer side of him tingled along her fingertips. This wasn't a lifetime of pent-up sexual desires, it was...more. She felt as if she knew this man, and was confused by him.

Get answers. You can always run.

She eased out of the shadows. Immediately, his gaze pinned her right to her new spot. The intelligence, mixed with arrogance, gave her second thoughts, but she could be brave *occasionally*.

"I'm not coming down. You could sit over there. But I don't know you..." She thought that was true, but wasn't a hundred percent. There was something about him that made her hesitant about saying that out loud.

"No, you don't know me, but I know you. If I go sit, will you come down so we can talk?"

"No. I come down when I can't scent you on the air. And how do you know me if I don't know you?"

He quirked an eyebrow. Seemed to realize she was serious, and frowned. He opened his mouth to say something, thought better of it, and exhaled. But he did saunter to the tree stump and sit down. "You're a dancer, right?"

She snorted. "Please, don't waste my time. You didn't find me out here tonight because you liked the show."

"The show was good."

The show was *great*. When she'd finally been unable to stay away from Bobby, her only real friend, she'd knocked on his door. Instead of blasting her for coming back to life — and not telling him — he'd been overjoyed. Of course she'd not let him know she really had died and really had come back to life. As a Vampire. Instead she'd said she'd lost her memory — it seemed an okay lie — and had just recovered. Within a week, he had her dancing again. But not ballet. She would never dance ballet again. Tool and Masters, the kings of rap, were Bobby's new gig. He'd not only found her a place, but showed her there was more to dance than always striving for something she could never be — the perfect ballerina.

"I found you, earlier tonight, tied to a cross and being bled dry."

Snapped back from her memories, she shook her head. After an attack, and when she was lacking blood, her mind often...wandered.

"Say that again?"

"I found you tied to a cross and bleeding. Near death. I

got you down."

A goose walked over her grave at his words. Nothing, no memory of anything came to her. No matter how hard she tried to force it. It was like sleep walking but doing things when you were... Things that you couldn't remember — at first.

His gaze was steady, but he could be lying. Immortals were tricky. They had reasons for everything they did. If he took her down off a cross...he'd want something. *Or maybe he put me there and he's lying. Toying with me.*

Mouse in a maze running from the cat.

It'd happened before. The one other Lykae, *Nolan*, she'd met had been all smiles and chatter. Right up until he'd turned into a monster. She shuddered, recalling how she'd sensed something off with him. At that time in her life, she hadn't known what it meant.

Now she knew. *Danger.*

Jamie didn't give her that vibe. He gave off an entirely different one...

"You really are good at the silent thing," he grumbled. "I didn't harm you. I didn't know anyone else would either. I was tracking you for a while. I took a break once I *actually* located you in Paris. When I returned, you were gone. Vanished." He sounded frustrated, even to her. "At first I assumed you'd gotten the drop on me. You like to hide, right?"

She nodded, too shocked to do more. *He's been searching for me and hasn't been able to find me.* For some reason that made her kind of...proud. *The big bad wolf was stalking me and little old me gave him a run for his money.*

His dark eyebrows drew together over his nose, deepening his frown. "That was my second mistake. I held back and waited, assuming you'd show back up. But then I realized that maybe you wouldn't drop your friend — Bobby, right?"

Bobby was her *only* tie to the past. Her only friend. He'd be worried.

"So I went to your room."

"You went into my room?" She was impressed, then scared. If he could find her room, then he was good. She'd gotten a dingy place far from the other dancers. Don't bring danger to the door. Not when that danger might suck her friends dry.

A shrug met her question. "Of course."

"What did you find?" she asked, unable to stay silent.

"A mess." The growl was followed by, "And the scent of witches."

It was hard to believe he was being so open with her. At the same time, why make it up? Why fake the frustration he clearly felt at losing her, right when he had found her? But why look for her in the first place?

"I tracked them and found you the way you are now." He tilted his head again to meet her eyes. "You don't remember anything?"

She hesitated. What if he *is* the one who did this?

In the end her silence must have answered.

"You were outside a witch's house. The cross was in the center of their back yard, out of sight of the drive. No houses were near. They had positioned the house well away from the closest village." He had a nice voice—deep, strong. But it was also a bit harsh and clipped as if he were unused to saying more than was necessary. The way he relayed the details... *Impersonal.*

"They were performing a ceremony. Draining you. Murmuring spells that seemed to inflict pain. I judged you weren't volunteering. I killed the witches. Then I pulled you down."

"From a cross."

"An upside down one if it matters."

It mattered. "And then what happened?"

His dark eyes flickered to light then back to dark. "That's when you decided to wake up and lose your cool."

Was he...impressed? "Lose my cool?"

"You hit me with a pretty good left hook, and ran off before I could pick myself up."

Stunned, Elsa stared at him, then down at her hand. There was a mark there. She'd heard of such things. *A fight bite.* They could get infected. Human mouths were dirty, but... He wasn't human, and neither was she. *Still,* she examined her busted knuckles, *I hit hard.*

"I hit you hard enough to knock you down?" she asked, just to clarify.

"More like you caught me by surprise, but yeah, you could say that," he muttered.

"I'm saying that," she whispered, admiring the cuts and scrapes now, and unable to hold in the smile.

"Glad to know you're remorseful over hitting a man trying to save you."

She waved that away. He wanted something or he wouldn't have *gotten* her down. "Oh, that I am. But why were you searching for me? I mean, who *are* you?"

"Me? I'm no one." He folded his arms and leaned against the tree. Long legs out in front of him, crossed at his boots, he appeared the model for a lazy, no need-to-hurry guy. *Then what is the tension I can see in his shoulders and neck?* "Just a tracker."

That means he was hired to find me? "So, who hired you?"

"No one hired me." He snorted. "Are you coming down from — ?"

"Why were the witches after me?"

"Not sure. I thought you'd know."

She'd had drinks with a few witches in the club, but they hadn't spiked her drink. That kind of thing was hard to do. She was a Vampire. She could sense when someone meant her harm — now that she knew what a shiver down her back meant. Poisons weren't very effective anyway. She'd had a spiked drink — a human one. It had tingled, pissing her off. She'd back-handed the guy clear across the dance floor. Then run.

"So you can't remember anything since when? The show, or even that?"

"I remember the show." She left off the 'duh', but it was

there. He ignored the sarcasm pretty well, so she went on. "I remember going out celebrating. Paris was our finale. We had six months off after. We were drinking. There were some witches there, but they only talked to me for a little while and left me to my friends."

"The humans."

The way he said that made her tense. Most immortals she'd met didn't like humans. It was okay, since most, if not *all*, immortals she'd met *she* didn't like. She wasn't fond of many humans either, but some were irreplaceable. *Gotta get to a phone. Call Bobby. Explain…something.* "Yes, my human friends."

"Did you share a drink with the witches?"

It was silly to stay in the tree. He obviously wasn't going to hurt her. The branch was digging into her butt, anyway. She jumped down, landing softly. Jamie didn't move, but he studied her steadily. His expression was inscrutable.

"You're good on your feet."

"I am a dancer," she muttered.

"You have blood on your jaw. Is it a cut?"

Before she knew what he was doing, since she was now rubbing carefully with her fingers at her jaw, he took her hand and tipped her head to the side. When had he stood, walked over? He was…fast. Impossibly so. *And I thought I was safe…*

"Don't."

He dropped his hand, his eyes flickering from light to dark. Something inside her coiled in anticipation. A breath left her as she noted the golden color. Wolf? Or…

"I won't hurt you. You are cut. You're still bleeding."

"So are you." There was a long, bloody gash on *his* left cheek, traveling down his jaw and on to his neck. It looked as if he'd turned his face away and gotten the full amount of damage from a blade. Or claws.

Mine?

She fisted her hand at her side, unsure why she wanted to touch him there, soothe the spot with her…

21

She stepped back, putting distance between them. Took in his broad shoulders, his tense handsome features. Handsome? He was…beautiful. A warrior out of the storybooks. Rugged, slightly rough, he radiated power and something she'd never had. Self-confidence. This male didn't doubt himself. She bet he'd never known fear. Never felt that clawing feeling inside when you knew you were being followed with nowhere left to hide.

He lifted his hand and touched his jaw. "It's nothing."

It was still bleeding, but it didn't ruin the beauty of his face. Neither did the coarse bristle covering his jaw and upper lip. It wasn't the kind of facial hair some guys cut in on purpose to their face. This was there because he hadn't had time to shave.

She wasn't sure why she thought such a thing. Maybe because his dark hair wasn't styled so much as it was a reckless mess of sexiness. The no-nonsense, tough exterior to this man was probably bone-deep. It was reflected in the way he roamed his eyes over her face, neck, then wrists, to finally land on her neck again, as if categorizing her wounds.

She'd bet he could list them. And do it in that impersonal tone. Unaffected.

It was nearly impossible to stand still so close to him. In the past ten years, she'd not been near others, especially immortals, and none so attractive. Only he wasn't a man, he was a Lykae, and that meant dangerous. She couldn't pull away, though. Maybe because he didn't mean her harm, there was none of the sick feeling she'd experienced from another, much nicer — *at first* — wolf she'd met.

"The neck wounds haven't healed, either."

The dissatisfaction in that sentence was clear. It was almost as if she was too frail, and, of course, she'd not heal properly. She was about to jerk away. Stopped. Stunned as he reached out again and traced something lightly along her cheek. His fingers, she realized. It sent a shock through her. When it did, their eyes met, indicating he'd felt it too.

His attention was suddenly focused on her.

Blood scented the air. His blood. Her gaze pinned on his throat. His pulse beat a steady, warm draw. She blinked and focused desperately on his face. Her fangs tingled. *Blood.* She needed it. Had to replenish. Already the headache was building.

In an icy tone, he said, "You need blood." His eyes had darkened ominously.

It was true. And it was way too much to deal with on top of everything else going on. She took two steps back from him. "I am fine. I don't drink from immortals."

"Just humans?"

She scanned his face, unsure if the censure in his tone was there or imagined. His expression gave nothing away.

"Not talking about this with you."

"Then tell me this, did you sense anything?"

"Before I woke up naked in a forest?"

He squinted at her. Did his high cheekbones flush? "Yes."

She shook her head and moved farther from him. She'd never been so tempted to sample blood from someone before. Always it was simply to survive. Mostly she took blood from blood banks. The unusable blood was stale, but it was substance. But she'd learned that she wanted to live more than she wanted to die. The first time…had been difficult.

"Why do you care?"

"I don't. I want to know the facts."

Why did it sting that he didn't care? *It doesn't matter.* "So you can what? Help me find them? I thought they were dead?"

"They are. But there were…others."

"I don't go *after* people, if that's what you're thinking. I don't go get revenge and all that." *No, I just kill.* "I don't think this was from the witches at the club. They were young, and most witches I've met are cool." She dabbed at the stinging wounds on her neck. "Obviously not the ones that did this, but I didn't sense something off with them."

23

"And you can? Sense something evil?"

"Yes."

He nodded, again giving her the impression that he was checking off boxes on a list. *Am I passing? Probably failing miserably.*

"So they sat with you then left?"

"Yeah." She dropped her hand. Both of her wrists were tender, with marks on them as if she'd been tied up. Or hung on a cross.

"What else do you remember of that night?"

She wanted to snap at him that it didn't matter, but as he spoke something stirred. A vision of a beautiful woman with flowing blonde, curly hair floated closer. She was wearing a light green gown, as if she'd been to Cinderella's ball. The image disappeared like smoke when Elsa pushed to see more. A memory of Bobby talking with a woman—two women—came to her. It was gone in a haze of smoke, then replaced with a painful slice along her wrists. Jerking backward, she blinked, trying to bring the forest back into focus. Jamie stood closer, his frown deeper now. His blood made her empty stomach twist. *Gotta get away. Gotta go.*

"You remembered something?"

"There were two witches?"

"Yes. Two."

Nothing more came to her on the second witch. Then there was an image of cobblestone streets. A wide river. Wetness slipped along her fingers. Had she trailed them in still water? A sharp dig along her ribs. Lying on her side, hard bench under her hip.

Nothing else, especially no image of Jamie. She tried to force more, a face, anything, but other than that brief glimpse of the blonde witch, nothing else would come to her. The loss of memory sometimes responded to seeing what and where she'd been.

"Take me there."

"They're dead. I killed them. Set their house on fire."

"I want to see for myself."

His gaze sharpened. "That's not a good idea, it's not safe."

"I thought you killed them—"

"I did," he said, or more like growled. She got the distinct impression she shouldn't argue with him.

She lifted her chin. For some reason, she felt it important that she do just that. Even as she gawked at herself, she snapped, "Then it's safe, or else you didn't do a good job."

Expression bemused, he canted his head to the side. "Did you just...insult me?"

She stepped back. Only because it was hard to be taken seriously when a person towered over her... "If you killed the witches, then it's safe. If you didn't..." *If the shoe fit...*

Before she could sense what he was about, he took her hand in a firm hold. His speed was stunning. That electric shiver happened again, but so did her stomach-clenching reaction.

She struck fast, hitting him in the throat. The jab must have hit with just the right amount of force. His hold loosened a miniscule amount. She had just enough time to register his shocked expression before she broke free. His wolf flashed in his eyes. Fear shivered through her, even as something else clawed its way to the fore. Stunned, she could only stand as he walked closer.

Fooled again. Fooled again.

Please, don't want to kill him...

Jamie was stunned. He wasn't used to the sensation. She'd surprised him. So slight he could circle her waist with his hands, she still stood up to him as if she'd found him lacking.

The thought was insulting. She questioned him. Refused to answer his questions. All the while staring at his neck, clearly wanting to drink from him.

Wolves had an inbred distrust of Vampires. Even he had it. Not with her. For some reason the idea of her wanting his blood... *No problem.* He'd pull her on his lap, sit her down on his aching cock and bare his neck.

He gave himself a mental shake. "I won't hurt you. But you can't go back there."

No response. No lessening of her tension.

She was unexpected. But he *should* have expected this. After staring at her pictures for months, to be standing so close to her, his brain didn't seem to cross that reality bridge very well. Last night had been...a blur.

The instinct had roared in him. His wolf had burst free. Taken over. Not since he'd first been turned had he lost his control. That was centuries ago. The scent of her blood — her pain — on the air had maddened him. Even before he'd reached her, he'd been in a killer rage. Once he'd broken through from the trees and seen her, all thoughts had fled. He'd launched himself at the witches. Killing them before they'd even had time to register that he was there. No battle plans. No assessing the area. No thought at all. Other than free her. Punish whoever had touched her. Harmed her. *Kill. Kill. Kill.*

The blood from the witches still marred his clothes, probably his face, too.

And Elsa...questioned what he'd done? Questioned his advice? She was new, so damn new to this world. Fragile in ways that he could barely comprehend. No matter she'd survived ten years. He knew those years had been filled with fear. Could feel it, how it had soaked into her very being. Fear, and unhappiness, loneliness all radiated from her. She was weak, needed blood, but was so naïve that she truly didn't see the danger she was in.

He wanted to shake her. At the same time he wanted to hold her. Comfort her. Bare his neck for her. For some reason he did none of those things. His wolf was high, warring with him for control. *Again.*

Impossible situation. She had merely questioned him. He'd done the same to her, doubting her abilities.

"You can't go there. Again, it is not safe."

She lifted her chin. "I *am* going there. And just in case you missed the memo, I don't know you, and the jury is undecided if I *like* you. Or even trust you."

His shoulders went back. He was a warrior. She was a child compared to him. She was certainly acting like one, even if her rounded hips and lush, heavy bosom indicated she was completely, absolutely full grown. He tensed as his cock swelled. Inner shake of his head. *Not happening. Not with her.*

She'd struck him. Hit *him*. Once he could see. She'd woken, confused, hurting. But now? It was unacceptable. He'd told her he would not harm her. And she'd hit him.

Why did that seem so...wrong? He'd been hit harder — her small fist had barely registered. But the fact that she *had* hit him stunned him.

She was weak.

She was small.

She was possibly the most beautiful woman he'd ever met. She also had no understanding of how dangerous this world was. Dancing with mortals? On stage? In front of millions? She might as well have waved a red flag at a bull. Her sexy body, an immortal body, gyrating to music that sent out a sexual tone — it was like dangling a virgin in front of a room full of mages set on calling a demon.

She needed to understand her situation. All he had to do was get her to safety. Back at the compound she'd be secure. Then maybe he could see about testing the attraction between them — in his bed.

He reached out to take her hand and end this nonsense. Her expressive gray eyes lightened even more, then flashed back to dark. She raised her lip, revealing her sharpened fangs, and tensed as if to strike again.

Stunned, he felt as if she'd hit him with a frying pan in the face. She...would attack him?

Instead, she bolted. One minute she was there, staring daggers at him, then gone. So fast he was left flat-footed, staring at where she'd been.

"Elsa!" His chest tightened. She was going to the house. She'd see...*what I can do.* Jury's out on if I even like you.

She'd…be horrified. She still thought like a human. Probably had never seen blood — outside of what she drank.

For some reason that made his heart race. Not with pride, to show her how he could protect her, but with panic. *What will she think?* That intensity in her eyes. There had been anger there and something more. *Fear.* She feared him. *What will she think when she sees what I can do then?*

He tore off, racing as fast as he could. For some reason, he wanted to be there, to see her face, to reassure her he'd never turn that rage on her.

Even as he thought it, his worry grew. Deep inside, he wasn't certain he wouldn't hurt her. Wasn't that the problem? Why he felt so off kilter with her?

What if I don't know when the wolf will rise? She affected him. Her scent, her eyes, her body drove his almost more than his wolf.

Worse, what he wanted from her was something he'd never faced. He wanted *her*. Not merely for a night, two maybe three, then back to the trail again.

Elsa. He wanted…something *more*. His wolf was in complete agreement. So that meant he shouldn't pursue her. Not if the wolf won over again. Her slim body, covered in blood, her eyes closed, body limp. *What if I caused that?*

He stumbled. Struck again by last night. *I didn't have control.* Did she cause that? What if I lose control *with* her? He analyzed his feelings, his thoughts, and still he couldn't say. Didn't know. Undecided, he punched a tree. *Go after her? Or leave?*

Another punch didn't bring an answer.

She's alone. Unprotected. Weak. At the witches' house. There was evil there.

He focused in the direction of the smoldering cottage. Over the mountain, down the steep cliff, and through a stream, he knew he'd find it. And her.

Elsa all golden-haired, the kind of hair that was rich with color and hung in waves of curls down her back to brush against her hips. Winged brows that arched naturally over wide-set blue-gray eyes that shifted to darker slate when upset. Heart-shaped face. Full, kissable lips. Delicate jaw line with a chin she raised more than she should.

Never see her again? Leave this spot and let her go?

He fisted his hands until his knuckles protested. His chest heaved as if he were preparing for battle. His wolf checked in, more than ready to take over if he couldn't get them to where *she* was. *Protect her. Control myself. Seduce her maybe... Then take her to Aidan. Visit. Keep my distance, but keep her as mine. Just until this obsession passes.*

Chapter Two

Elsa misted so fast that even she was impressed. Inside, she was...confused. Turbulent thoughts raced in circles. As fast as her frantic heartbeat.

He should never harm her. Never glare at her like that. Never...

It felt...wrong.

He felt...right.

But not right. Wrong. *Don't know him. Don't want to know him. Want his blood more than anything in this... No. Don't want his blood.*

He'd yelled something, but she hadn't put meaning to the words. She couldn't. Her mind was whirling. Her heart a loud drum in her ears, blocking sounds. She caught the scent of smoke. Instantly her instincts shouted, *Find who harmed you. Remember. Protect yourself.*

She followed the trail. *Calm. Focus.* Something is wrong. The wind soothed her. The mist she'd shaped her essence in eased her. Slowly, her thoughts returned.

Listening to the forest, she picked up no sound of pursuit. Jamie was out there, though. He would come. That odd wrongness resurfaced. *Who is he?*

Focus. She scanned the high mountain forest and found it. It was far, much farther than she'd have believed possible. *How did I get to the other side of this forest? Over those mountains, even?*

She had no answer. A blank wall met her every attempt to force the memories. Hovering over the smoldering house, she let the effort go as useless. Next waking would be soon enough to bring back the horror of it all.

And it *was* horrifying. Below her, the small cottage still sent plumes of smoke in gray clouds on the wind. Two dead witches were sprawled in blood near a still-smoldering cross. Both were hideous, but superimposed on their haggard faces was a vision of two young women. One was the ball gown-wearing blonde. The other wasn't familiar. She was dressed in black with the image of someone much, much younger shimmering over her dead body.

A few feet from them she found an unknown Vampire. She was young and small, at least what was left of her.

Elsa took her solid form again and rolled the body over to pat down her clothing. She wore a leather biker jacket, burnt and bloodstained, and a short skirt. Her shirt was ripped and torn, half exposing her breasts. Next to her, Elsa found a small token, like a medallion or coin. On one side someone had carved *Forever* in script. There was a silver necklace attached to it, and for some reason the chain felt… wrong. Elsa dropped it and rubbed her hand on her jeans.

Whoever the Vampire was, she wouldn't rise any time soon. Her head was a few feet from her body. If the witches had abused her, they'd done much more to this Vampire than they had to Elsa. For one, her stomach was clear of slices, while the other woman had razor-sharp gashes along her torso. Worse, the abuse wasn't something a woman could do to another. And nothing like that had happened to Elsa. She'd know.

Feeling nauseated, Elsa snatched up the medallion and pocketed it, just about to rise when she tensed, realizing Jamie had already arrived.

"She was dead when I arrived."

At Jamie's words, Elsa stiffened, but she didn't leap up like a frightened rabbit, even though he'd scared her. She hadn't scented or sensed his arrival until right before he spoke. He could move much faster than she'd thought possible. She wouldn't underestimate him again.

"Why did you try to stop me?" She didn't turn, but could feel him glowering at her all the same.

"It isn't safe here."

She stood and faced him. She got the impression it was more than that. The horror left behind was disgusting. Someone had abused the Vampire. It was clear by the dirt under her nails and the marks on her arms that she hadn't been willing.

"You were angry."

"You hit me."

"So? Did it hurt?" What was she doing? *Baiting a bear...* "You shouldn't try to force your way on others."

His eyes had flared wide at her sarcasm but narrowed at her advice. *Didn't like to take it, but dished it out?*

"You're wounded, weak, and need to rest. You don't need to see shit like—"

"Please," she snapped. Those things she already knew. It wasn't his business to remind her, either. "I've seen worse at a *Rocky Horror Show*." *I've done worse.* "But you're right. And guess what else? I don't *need* you telling me what to do. Don't all Lykae hate Vampires?"

If her response surprised him, it only showed in a steadier, cooler expression. He crossed his brawny arms and leaned against the only post remaining in the house. She half-hoped it would come crashing down, him following in an uproarious tumble on his ass.

It held. His gaze remained trained on her. Like prey...

"At one time, yes."

"At one time?" she repeated. "Like today you don't but yesterday and for the last two *thousand* years you did?"

He halfway smiled but it was more a sarcastic lift to his lips. "So all this carnage doesn't bother you?"

"No, I'm glad they're dead." She didn't glance at the witches. "I only wished you'd burned them to extra crispy."

Appearing bemused, he canted his head to the side. "I still can."

For some reason she smiled. Laughed. "I guess you did good enough."

He seemed to like her compliment then, a second later,

scowled. "I thought saving your life I'd get less, shall we say, animosity directed at me for being a *Lykae*."

Okay, that was just wrong. Owing someone was bad, worse still when that someone was intelligent enough to know it. And arrogantly staring at me like I can't walk without help.

I did break away from him. She eyed him and guessed he'd let her.

"I don't *hate* Lykae. I've just never met one I like." An image of another wolf, with similar eyes, rushed up from where she'd buried him. She shoved the memory away and focused on the man standing in front of her. "You grabbed me. I hate being grabbed."

He quirked an eyebrow. It was a sexy expression, and one he'd done before. She wondered if he knew how panty-dropping it was. Probably.

"I didn't realize. But the first time I *grabbed* you, it was off that." She followed the direction of his arm to the upside down cross—or what was left of it. The fire had burned slowly but steadily, until only the support beams and brick arches for the doorways remained.

"Why didn't you burn this whole place down?"

"I thought I'd let the daylight do its work and come back when it was clear of…evil."

There *was* evil here, something sickening like rottenness she could feel hiding, just out of sight. They had brought her here to do what they'd done to the young Vampire.

"I don't understand. Why would they do this? And what were they *doing*?"

He shrugged a shoulder. It was hot, simply because when he did, the move outlined the muscles of his shoulders, pulling the leather jacket tight across his biceps.

"Witches are hard to predict. I try not to guess at what they were doing, or what motivates them to do what they do."

That answer didn't satisfy her. People didn't just snatch people for no reason. Even human serial killers had reasons. The witches… They had to have a reason. If they were doing some kind of ceremony on her, where were the runes, or…spells?

She walked over to the cross and touched the blackened, still-smoldering wooden beam. Nothing. No memories surfaced and the fear didn't diminish. There was more here than she could see.

"They were strong, huh? To put this up on their own, they'd have to be." The posts alone were enormous. They were as big as railroad ties. Both pieces together had to weigh a ton. The ground was soft, but they would have had to dig down pretty far to get the cross to hold upright, then with her on it… "It can't be easy to lift a thing like this with my weight on it too."

Jamie snorted. "Like you made a difference?" He'd followed her and come to a stop next to the cross. He crouched near the base to brush away at the piled topsoil. The scent of him tickled her nose. Fresh, clean, even under the dirt. The blood she savored. It was rich, dark, and it beckoned to her. She slammed her eyes closed, counting to ten, then opened them. "You add, what, ninety pounds soaking wet?"

She ignored the little, *very* tiny thrill that brought her. She had muscles from years of dancing. She wasn't heavy but she wasn't the classical emaciated, tall ballerina. Still, it was cool to have him think her so small. Until it dawned on her that he meant she was also *weak*.

"The cross would have been enormously heavy even without me," she said, not liking the way she was analyzing him and everything he said.

"Magic. They are witches." He stood, clearly dismissing her concerns.

"Then why use this?" She picked up the charred and frayed end of a rope she'd noticed lying beside the cross. There were several and she guessed they were set up to use to draw the cross up using a pulley system.

"And this?" She touched the roughly carved wooden pulley and a flash of someone's face—a boy—rose in her mind. She turned and scanned the woods. There, near where the forest was the thickest with undergrowth, she spotted a half-hidden shack. It blended with the trees so well it was nearly impossible to make out. Even the roof was the same material as the forest around it.

"Don't move. I'll see if he is still there."

"Hey," she protested, grabbing his jacket. "I found him. I'll go. He smells afraid."

"You can *scent* him?"

"I *am* a Vampire."

For some reason that made Jamie narrow his brown eyes and draw a deep breath. *Why is it so fun to bait him? Because he shouldn't think me weak. I am weak!* He sighed heavily and gestured, sarcastically, for her to go ahead.

"Be my guest."

Jerk! She bit back the retort, since she had insisted. He was the bigger and probably the better person to go check out the boy — or whatever it was — in the shed. Still, for some reason she wanted to show him she was…*fierce? Me? Fierce?* She almost busted up out loud. Barely keeping it in, she walked determinedly forward. *I might not be fierce, but I can be brave. People can smell weakness in this world. Being bold is the only way to survive.*

Jamie was arrogant, but she shouldn't let him bother her so much. Most immortal men were. It was probably impossible not to be. What with their strength and size.

She cast a glance over her shoulder. He was watching her to the exclusion of all else. Hands loose at his sides, he still gave the impression that he was prepared for anything. He didn't say anything but he did cant his head slightly and a knowing, really condescending smirk followed.

He really thinks I'm too chicken! Jerk!

Once again biting off a snarly remark, she faced the mysterious shed. There was no feeling of dread, as if danger lurked. No instinct flared. Just…a need to help. She studied the feeling as she examined the low walls and small door. Whoever was in there was either small, or the place was spelled and hid its size.

"I don't mean you any harm. Can you come out? That guy won't hurt you either. We wanted—"

A huge amount of rustling, then quiet made her pause. She waited a few feet from the shack. Slowly the door, a small two foot by two foot square, opened a crack. She could sense him more now, but didn't have a clue what to say.

"He's not too trusting." Jamie stopped at her right, and crossed his arms. Again she hadn't heard him come up beside her. It worried her, but she had other things to think about. Like why she could almost feel that electric current coming off him even without him touching her. Like how hard his muscles bulged—even under the long jacket he wore. Or how the wind seemed to love to play with his dark hair.

She sidestepped away from him.

He didn't appear to notice. "Kid, come out. We're not going to hurt you. The witches are gone."

"More will come." The door opened a fraction wider. "They are many."

"Yeah? Well, I'm sure we can handle however many they bring." Jamie's gaze hardened.

Elsa wasn't so certain of that. She also wasn't too keen on the 'we' Jamie put in that sentence, but kept it to herself.

"Come on, you're not afraid of us, are you?" Jamie crouched close to the ground and rested his arms on his knees. His head came to her chest, nearly her chin if she were honest. God above, he was big.

"We won't hurt you. Come out. You already have our word. Come."

Surprising her, the door opened wider. After another pause, a young boy crawled through.

She bit her lip. Jamie hissed out a breath.

The boy half crawled, half hobbled toward them. He dragged chains with him. He stopped a foot away and stayed on his hands and the balls of his feet. His little body was tense, as if he'd spring into motion at the first sign of movement. Particularly from Jamie.

Jamie didn't move. She got the sense he was staying perfectly still to not frighten the boy. Her degree of respect for him went up. Inside, she felt an acceptance of his behavior. As if he'd done well—for the first time.

The boy shifted his body backward but didn't flee. He was dirty, which might have accounted for the lack of scent. Shaggy hair, the color hard to decipher because it was so matted, hung in his eyes. He wore a ragged shirt and some kind of jeans maybe. His scrawny arms were covered in layer upon layer of dirt. There was a fresh red mark on his cheek, and ugly yellow and purple bruises on his upper arms, as if someone had shaken him. He drew his eyebrows down and tensed his little muscles, getting ready to run. His feet were bare and dirty, and, for some reason, made her heart ache.

"I'd offer to clean you, but I'm not sure it would work the way I do it. How about this guy gets you a room with a bathroom or something? He can probably break those chains too."

The chains were huge. Unnecessarily heavy, she thought. He was a boy. But the grimy cuffs were three inches wide and an inch thick, attached to chains that were at least a half inch in diameter. They had chafed so badly there were scabs all around his wrists. It was as if he was a dog and the shed his doghouse.

Jamie nodded and stood, holding out his hands by his sides when the boy tensed to run.

"Just gonna get those off. Let me see them." Jamie spoke quietly but with authority. The boy sat and held up his hands.

She blinked and stared at Jamie for some kind of answer. "What—?"

Jamie cleared his throat, she thought nervously, but walked to the boy and didn't give her anything more. She hoped he didn't expect that kind of obedience from her. Or maybe he did and what a disappointment.

"That's good. Now, just let me see them."

The boy turned completely docile. She scanned the area, reminded of the threat that more witches were coming. Dawn was still a few hours off, but she was tired. The time seemed to reinforce the idea that she'd slept part of the night.

Maybe I hit my head and passed out.

She ignored the thought. Soon enough she'd know. Right now she needed blood. She was thirsty. No one was near, not even wildlife other than some squirrels and a few field mice.

"Not coming off yet, but I can break this." Jamie took the chain in both hands, a few inches from the boy's left wrist, and strained. The metal screamed like a cat with its tail in the door, but gave with a suddenness that made the boy flash a grin. The expression was magical, transforming the dirty little bugger into one super-cute kid. He was quickly sober again. He nodded to the other chain, holding his right arm up expectantly for Jamie.

"All right, I got it." Jamie did the same to the other. The boy erupted in a jump and dashed to the house, then back. More on all fours than on two legs, but he was obviously glad to be rid of the chains.

"Lykae?" she guessed.

Jamie stared at her, expression unreadable. Finally, he nodded, but only when she thought the silence had reached an unnecessarily awkward degree of weirdness.

"Well then, I guess I'll leave you two—"

"Not a chance. You need to stay," Jamie began, standing taller.

She knew he was just warming up, but halted his reasons with a raised hand. Even the kid sat again, watching her like a puppy. He really was a cute boy.

"First, I'm thirsty. Unless you two are volunteering, I need to go. Second…" The boy covered his neck with both hands. She laughed and shook her head. "I never drink from children," she told him. She turned her focus back on the bigger problem. *Jamie. And I never take a nip of his kind either... Tall, sexy dark strangers with broad shoulders and...*

"Second, I don't want to go with you. So I won't be going with you." It was close to a lie, because she did kind of want to go with him. The urge frightened her, so she decided it was best to get some distance. Whatever draw she felt might be because he'd rescued her. She needed space to process.

"I did take you off that cross and save your —"

"Yes, and I think you throwing that in my face two times *already* made that permanently clear to my brain cells, so I got it. I'll hafta owe you." She shrugged. "Maybe someday I can repay you." Dubious expression from him. "But for *now*, I can't. I don't want to join your team, or, gang, or pack or...mission?"

"I want you to come with me, to meet Alrick, the King of —"

"I've heard of Alrick."

His scowl was deeper now, making a cute bunched-up wrinkle between his heavy eyebrows. "Then you know —"

"I know I don't want within a hundred miles of him."

The boy was sitting between them. She couldn't help but smile because he was swinging his head back and forth as if they were playing tennis. It was kind of fun sparring with Jamie like this, especially because it appeared to *torture* Jamie.

His expression said he was pondering some kind of action she wouldn't like — if the way he tensed his jaw meant anything.

"The boy needs to see Alrick more than I *ever* will. Wait." She paused and frowned, remembering something he'd said. "Why were *you* following me?" *Was it to take me to his pack? I haven't done a thing to the pack...*

Except that one time.

Jamie stared at her, his wheels turning. She didn't

interrupt. She waited. The boy began to shift, though, going from rocking back and forth to admiring his new bracelets, minus the chains.

"I wanted to talk to you."

"You were following me to *talk* to me?"

At his hesitation, then nod, she gave him the wide-eyed bullshit look that deserved. "There *are* coffee shops for that."

"Not for what I needed. Plus, you were harder to find than I could have guessed."

Is that surprise or respect in his tone? She nervously tugged her hair until she realized she was, because the boy copied her. She dropped her hand.

"You should get him a haircut along with some clothes. Probably some food, too."

Jamie seemed to consider that, then said, "I'll talk to you about it while the boy cleans up."

The boy perked up at that and stared hopefully from her to Jamie.

"He likes you," Jamie said that as if it should have some impact on her very real need to leave.

She stepped away from them both. "He shouldn't. I have to go feed. I'll look you up after, okay? Promise." Lie. But he didn't know her well enough to realize it. The longer she spent near him, the more weird things seemed okay. Like brushing his thick brown hair off his eyes or like touching his jaw where she could see a trace of blood still lingering on that gash.

They weren't.

They shocked her. But more than that, they...intrigued her. *Would he like that? Me touching him*?

The idea that *he* might was as frightening as the idea that *she* would.

While she was having a mini-battle over her attraction to him, Jamie shook his head and anchored his fists on his hips, his frown right back on.

Obviously he wasn't thinking along the same lines as she

was.

It was a determined, manly type pose straight from the movies. Only, it was also very common in the immortal men she'd met. They were used to being strong and listened to by others. At least the ones she'd seen from a distance, which meant the ones she got away from as soon as possible. She pegged Jamie for old. He had that chauvinistic vibe going on under the sarcasm.

"Elsa, you have no idea what you're getting into. Why not stay? At least until the memories return?"

"Thanks, but no thanks. But I will find you once they have returned. How's that?"

"If you survive," he muttered when she started walking away.

The boy surprised her by taking her hand, before she knew he was even there. She stared down at the dirty little guy, guessing his age to be somewhere around ten, maybe nine.

What would it be like, to be alone, out here, with witches, at such an age?

She'd been eighteen, nearly an adult, and much more mature than most of her age group. Dancing all her life had always left her as an outsider. That, and being adopted by Maria and Leo, choreographers and ballet dancers themselves. She'd always *felt* different—now she *was*. Extremely different.

But she survived because she had at least Maria and Leo there until she'd lost them to a car wreck on her sixteenth birthday.

This guy had no one. Well, he had Jamie—for now.

"Stay." The one word surprised her. She'd figured he couldn't talk, what with all the crawling on all fours going on.

"Uh, dude, I'm a Vampire. I don't hang out with wolves."

He grinned, revealing a chipped front tooth that seriously gave him a cute smile. He also had sharp, slightly bigger than an average baby canines. Also adorable.

"But you are."

She blinked, glanced up to see Jamie's frown deepening and back at the kid. "I am what?"

"A wolf."

"Uh, no. I'm a Vampire." She repeated it slowly, so he could understand, "*Vampire.*"

Jamie snorted. She stared at him. He shrugged. "Go on, you're doing great."

"*They* knew. That's why they had you on the cross. To drain the Vampire, and hope that the Lykae would rise to the top. *He* wanted it that way. To see if it worked."

"He?" she whispered, but it came out as if much, much quieter than a whisper because her mouth was suddenly dry. She swallowed.

"Yes. He wanted to see if you were strong."

"He who?" Jamie asked.

"Their master." The boy pointed to the witches.

Jamie walked over and bent, picked something up and growled. He cursed, but it came out all garbled like a growl. "Balrick," Jamie snapped, turning to hand the piece of paper to her. A note. Under the dirt and mud, and she hoped not blood, she found his name. "If he wants you, then you are in serious trouble."

We will need to find out if she is strong enough. If she is, she will be useful. If not, do what you will with her.
Balrick

"Uh, how do you know I'm the *she* in this note?"

Jamie chuckled. "Lucky guess?"

"It could mean her," she reminded him, pointing to the girl.

"It could. It could also mean Madonna, but since you were on that" — he pointed at the cross — "it means you. It also means you stay with me so I can help protect you."

Decision made. Done deal.
Right.

She backed away. Even she'd heard of Balrick. Insane was the nicest thing she could say about him. Lykae, brother to Alrick, now a half-Vampire, or whatever, he was one seriously dangerous, and, worse, sick, individual. If he wanted her, for whatever he thought was useful, well, she wanted as far from that as possible.

She dislodged the kid's grip, gently, and did what any Vampire with half a brain would do.

She ran—or, more precisely, she misted outta there. She couldn't shift her body instantly from one location to another, but used what she had. She caught the fastest updraft and put as much distance as she could between herself and the super-sexy, out of her league macho-man and his cute sidekick.

Hiding is always, always much better.

Chapter Three

Jamie sighed.

The boy squatted with his hands on the ground, close to his feet. "She's fast."

"Yeah." She was also good at hiding. But that was before. Now, well, he had her scent. Even if she did the hiding in the shadows thing she'd done earlier tonight, he could still locate her scent. The urge to run after her was nearly impossible to deny. But when he'd been standing near her, he'd never felt so *right* in his life. Now? Now, he wanted to find her to protect her. He would too, but first he had to figure out what was going on.

"She's afraid."

Jamie considered that. She probably was. Part of him was relieved to know she had the good sense to *be* afraid. The other, the one that wanted done with this mission, wasn't thrilled that once again he was left to chase after her. Only that wasn't exactly true.

He considered the spot where she'd been standing, arguing with him, and realized she was more fascinating in person than she had been the past few months tracking her. That was saying a lot.

Worse, he wasn't certain that was okay, especially since he'd become obsessed with every glimpse of her he'd been able to find. That hair, the length and thickness of it... What would it feel like, in his hand, trailing over his chest as she rode him to orgasm?

"What will we do now?"

Jamie blinked. *Caught fantasizing? Focus.* "We go get you cleaned up. Then *I* go get her."

That seemed to satisfy the kid. It caused a tense tightening along Jamie's muscles. He wanted her. The strength of that desire didn't fade with her trying to get as far from him as possible. If he read her right, that draw wasn't one-sided either. He stifled the thought, and the memory of her enchanting face and long blonde hair. *Focus on the boy. Feed him, clean him, get him somewhere to rest.* Elsa could be helpful with all the things a child needs. *Would she be a good mother?*

"What's your name?" His voice came out a little harsh, but the kid didn't seem to realize it. *What kind of torment has he endured that a Lykae barking at him doesn't make him blink?*

Tilting his head, the boy examined him, or maybe thought about the question. The small frown deepened and his eyes shifted over Jamie's face. There was doubt there, but a need to trust that the boy couldn't hide.

"Mine is Jamie."

"Keiner." The boy said it with a German accent, pissing Jamie off. The word *keiner* in German translated into *no one, nobody, nothing.*

"I think that's a mistake. First, you're not German, are you?"

The boy shook his head, but didn't seem certain. The confused expression didn't lift as Jamie squatted so they were more eye level.

"Then why would you have a German name?"

A shrug and duck of his head.

Naming someone wasn't in his plan for the night. Neither was suddenly being thrust into the position of caring for a child, but the boy couldn't be called *Keiner.* "I'd say you were a brave, strong boy. A little wolf, so we'll call you Faolan."

"Faolan," the boy whispered, then louder, "Faolan. I'm a wolf."

Jamie nodded. The boy was more, but for now, the strongest scent coming from him was wolf. He pulled out a pack of jerky and handed it to the boy, who accepted it with a smile. Standing again, Jamie assessed the area, still sensing no one. He got a fix on Elsa, though. She was fast. But she didn't seem to realize, yet, that he could follow her no matter where she went. Her scent was sweet and clean. Like a breath of fresh air. It was odd, since she was a Vampire. They usually smelled of death, even the good ones. Her scent settled him, as did the knowledge that he could find her anywhere she hid.

"Eat. I need to make a call. Then we go get a room. You have to walk. Two legs. Practice while you eat."

The boy stood immediately, a little hunched over, so Jamie straightened his own shoulders. The boy did a military stance. Eyes narrowed in concentration, he walked in a circle around Jamie. It was more than he could say for Elsa. Assured *he* wouldn't go far at least, Jamie pulled out his phone. He dialed Alrick.

"You lost her?"

Jamie squinted up at the half moon and answered, "She's quick."

The boy smiled, his mouth overflowing with jerky. But he followed when Jamie found the trail he needed. They started down it. The boy raced on ahead, then stopped and glanced back. Assuring himself Jamie was still there?

Jamie nodded and Faolan took off again at a fast scamper. Alrick was drilling what sounded like a pen against his desk. It was a tell, one his king displayed when truly getting worked up. No doubt the man's leg was bouncing too. Alrick had a lot on his plate. Jamie could suddenly sympathize. Taking care of a boy thrust upon him seemed an insurmountable task. That, and keeping his hands off Elsa.

Impossible.

"And?" Alrick snapped.

Jamie respected Alrick, but what he was getting the pack into might cause even more of a stir. Then discovering Balrick was alive — *and* a Vampire now, too? Oh, and siding with the enemy to create changelings that Balrick could then use to overthrow Alrick?

"I found her with two witches. They were performing a ritual. I killed them. We found a note. It could have been written by Balrick. She took off when we read it."

"What? What kind of ritual?" Alrick demanded. Something sounded like it had fallen to the floor, possibly shattering on impact. Another brush of his arm, knocking everything off the desk?

Jamie winced. Most likely. For some damn reason Elsa was important. Jamie was beginning to get how vital she was to him. He felt like he couldn't breathe. Like he was walking when he should be racing after her at all speed.

But why was she significant to Alrick? Jamie's fangs tingled in warning. Alrick hadn't found his bonded. Did he believe *Elsa* his?

The boy tilted his head. He was back on all fours, watching Jamie from a log spanning the trail at shoulder height.

No. If Elsa was Alrick's, he'd be here now, not Jamie.

Relief eased the pressure to break the phone in his hand.

"Jamie? What the fuck are you doing? I told you to find her! That was months ago. Now you tell me she was... She was —"

"She's safe now." Jamie motioned up with his hand and the boy immediately rose. He did it slowly, not losing his balance on the narrow tree. It was comical, but Jamie didn't smile. No need to encourage the kid, he was like a puppy already. He'd been with witches for a long time, but appeared to be fine.

"I found a kid too. Boy, probably eight. He's with me. Wolf. Maybe more. He's —"

"Wait, wait, wait a goddamn second!"

Again, Jamie winced. This time the boy startled, scurrying back to Jamie with a worried frown.

Jamie patted him on the head. "It's okay, he does this a lot." Unfortunately Alrick's temper hadn't eased with age. Lately Jamie wondered if the king wasn't losing his mind.

"Who— You found a *Lykae* boy, with two witches, who were doing a ceremony on Elsa?"

47

"Right. They were draining her, trying to make her wolf come out. All on Balrick's orders." Silence from Alrick, so Jamie continued walking and asked, "I thought you had him tied up with the immortal council?"

"He is."

Jamie nodded for the boy to hurry on ahead. The kid did as directed, but cast a lot of worried glances back at him until Jamie caught up.

"I think you need to come in." Alrick sounded tired. "Balrick is still being questioned, so he isn't free, but this sounds like a horror show. It was supposed to be a simple mission. Find her, watch her, and bring her in if in danger. Now you have a boy and no Elsa."

He had more than that. He had several months' worth of research on Elsa, from following her. All of it painted a picture of a very lonely woman, attempting to retain her humanity in a world where such ties could kill her — permanently, too.

He also had her, just not at the moment. "I can bring him in, and pick her up on the way."

"What? You said she's gone!"

Jamie shoved a branch aside and ducked under to find Faolan waiting for him on top of a boulder, next to the trail. "I didn't say I couldn't *find* her."

Alrick cursed a few times, then seemed to attempt to settle down.

"We're following her. I'll get the boy cleaned up then bring him in, with her," he repeated slowly. At times like this, it was best to keep calm with Alrick. Jamie recalled that his other brother, Derrick, a man Jamie would have at his back any time, thought Alrick nearing his time. For a Lykae, there was a point when the wait for normalcy, family and a life with his mate was crucial. If so, Alrick had hit it. What would happen if he didn't find her? Jamie believed he'd leave — hand over the rule to Derrick. Alrick had never hinted at such a thing, but Jamie could see things others within the pack didn't. Alrick followed Derrick and his mate Samantha with his eyes, assessing, always plotting and planning. Did Elsa fall into those plans somehow?

Alrick stayed silent but sighed heavily.

Jamie hated to remind his king of the facts, but he did. "We knew this wasn't going to be easy. She's good at hiding. It was just luck I ran into someone who knew she hung out with humans." He'd sent in his encounter with the Vampire, David, in Seattle. Alrick should have read those reports. If he had, he should know that Elsa had been difficult to find, which was good. It meant that no one else could find her either.

But someone *had* found her.

The show. If there was one way to broadcast your location, it was to go on stage, in front of thousands, and dance with one of the biggest rap singers in the business. Any immortal watching would have recognized her as a Vampire. Some might have caught her wolf scent as well. It was there, subtle and light, reminding him of something remembered, but forgotten. *What?* Something that stirred his chest.

"True. I didn't anticipate that. She still thinks of herself as a human?"

"No. Not that." He remembered how open she'd been about needing blood, which had been her idea of a joke. She hadn't hidden that she was a Vampire. That said, she'd either learned that Lykae could tell a Vampire when they saw one, or she simply didn't think she could hide it from anyone immortal. Both were true. The humans she knew, though... It was possible she still wanted to *be* human. The thought worried him. There was more going on here. That ritual...

"I'd say she isn't ready to say goodbye to her past. I found her dancing with two famous rap singers. She's young. If she was changed ten years ago..." Jamie couldn't believe it even as he said it. She'd seemed too level-headed for such a change to be so recent. "She would have been seventeen when she was bitten." He could barely say that out loud. The things he wanted to do to Elsa weren't PG rated.

A sigh was all he got, then Alrick said, "Our lives are all bloodied by our pasts. Yours. Mine. This boy's. Who is he?"

"I don't know. *He* doesn't know. They had him chained in a shed. I think they used him for his strength." Jamie considered the rope attached to the cross. The boy could have hauled that up and down using the pulleys.

"Could he be Balrick's?" The weariness in Alrick's voice was apparent. His brother had done evil things. Things even the worst of the Vampires had never accomplished. Separated the pack. The factions were growing. Jamie didn't understand it himself, but some felt Balrick was stronger and possessed a clearer vision for the future. Alrick forbade switching to their wolves, but as far as Jamie was concerned, what his king didn't know wouldn't hurt him. Others should do the same, and still owe their alliance to Alrick. He was the king for a reason. His brother was not, for reasons as well.

Jamie studied the boy but couldn't guess who his parents might be. Other than Alrick and the few warriors he drank with when he was back at the compound, he didn't know many others. Of those, only Ranger, Markee and Alex could claim they knew him more than casually. Derrick he respected. But the warrior had been missing for most of Jamie's immortality. None of those men had offspring. Derrick wouldn't allow *his* boy out of sight.

"I don't know. But even if he is, does it matter? He's alone now."

"Of course. And Elsa?" Alrick prompted.

"She's survived this long, so we knew she's developed well, even for her size."

"She's small?" Alrick guessed.

Women were always smaller than men. But Elsa could pass for a teenager if she wished. She *was* a teenager. She'd just *been* one for ten years. He didn't want to give it to Alrick straight, but there was no other way around it.

"Yes, she's small. And weak, but she finds ways to compensate."

Alrick murmured, "She's smart."

It wasn't a question but Jamie answered anyway. "Yes, she's very intelligent."

She was more than that. He'd dragged her off the horror of being bled dry and burned while in her sleep. Only to have her waken—at dusk, of course—and go bat shit crazy on him. She'd been half dead and not the Vampire kind. Blood and filth had covered her from the top of her blonde head to the bottom of her small feet. If she'd been dunked in a bog she wouldn't have been dirtier. He'd been unprepared for her strength. But after such an ordeal, she'd landed a blow that threw him off. Then she'd run. *Caught off guard, or... well placed punch?*

"She doesn't recall the witches."

"She will." Alrick sighed heavily. "Vampires that suffer trauma like that often take a few nights to remember. But they *always* remember."

That sounded like personal experience. Jamie was certain it was. Jamie was a youngster compared to his king and he'd been a part of the pack for over three hundred years. Jamie had earned enough respect from his king to become his tracker. But that role fit him. He was a lone wolf, more comfortable away from people than he was as a member of the pack. Always had been. But now... He studied the boy. The kid needed someone to take care of him. Jamie had no idea what a child needed, outside of needing someone who did.

Alrick must have drummed his fingers on the surface of his desk because the echo carried through the phone line. The boy startled next to him and eyed the phone curiously.

"Vampires always remember, sometimes far longer than other immortals. Now, in her case, she's young, and you weren't the one to hang her upside down. So that gives you something."

Jamie shifted his shoulders. Now that he'd met her, he wasn't at all sure he should continue with Alrick's plan. *What would Alrick think if he knew all I wanted to do was hold her close and hear her heartbeat matching mine? Then make love to her for weeks – possibly longer?*

"Where will she go?"

Shaking the worries aside, he focused. No way was he informing Alrick that he wanted to sink his cock and fangs into the mission.

"There are towns nearby. She might have gone to one of those. I'm following her now." The boy stopped on the trail leading toward a town and waited for him. "*We're* following her now," he amended. He got a toothy grin for that, then the boy was off again, more on his hands and bare feet than running on two legs. "The boy's smart and not showing any sign of having been tampered with. Outside of being filthy dirty, he seems…normal. Not bitten— Born," he clarified.

"Ah, well, if he is then he's not someone we're missing. I'd know, we'd *all* know," he muttered. "But whoever he is, he's going to need protection. We're resilient. You should know that. He'll be better off here, with us. He has no idea who he is?"

"None. He's not very talkative, but we'll see once he eats and cleans up. He's…pretty wolfy, Alrick."

Alrick laughed. "I imagine he is. Does he run on all fours?"

Jamie chuckled at the kid's antics. He reminded Jamie of a dog that had been chained so long it couldn't bear to stand still. "Half and half. You've seen this before?"

"Of course," Alrick murmured. "Make him walk. Does he shift to wolf?"

"Not that I know of, but that means nothing. I met him half an hour ago."

Silence, then Alrick sighed again. "Elsa. Go and see that she is safe, then move her. Get her to listen. I don't care how, but she needs to be protected. If they want her this bad, then there is something we're not seeing."

"There's a lot we're not seeing." Like why, right when he'd located her, someone else had as well and had taken her? There had been the scent of Vampires in her room. Vampires *and* witches. The other female Vampire was a mystery too. *I should never have left her side once I'd found her.* "What does Aidan say about the Vampires in Paris?"

"He's in contact with them. They report no Vampires near where you are. So either they are lying to him" — Alrick made that sound doubtful — "or the ones who helped take her, are on their own."

Jamie felt as if something were missing. Why a dead Vampire girl? Why take such young Vampires and kill them? "It's very similar to what Hunter discovered with Markee in Alaska. And Balrick. That note was his."

"Was it old? It had to have been, he's been locked up for weeks now."

"I have it, but it's hard to say. It's not like he left a date."

Alrick snorted. "Right, well, I want to see it. I'll have someone examine it. Keep an eye on Elsa. If you have to, take her to a safe house. There are no coincidences. They wanted her for something, and testing if her wolf would come to the surface... It's too similar to what Balrick was up to in Alaska. I'll have it added to the list of questions we have for him," he muttered. "But for now watch her closely, Jamie. I'll get hold of Circerran. She'll want to examine the area."

"I dealt with the witches."

Alrick laughed. "Yes, I'm sure you did, but where there is one or even two witches, there are often more. The covens in Europe, especially Germany and France, are dangerous. Be careful."

"I always am."

"Contact me when you have her somewhere safe."

"I will." Jamie ended the call and scanned the forest, considering his options. There weren't many. Bring her in and leave her with the pack. She wasn't safe out here. She wasn't safe alone. She certainly wasn't safe if Balrick's friends wanted a piece of her, or her.

How am I to convince her of that?

He reflected on that as he took off toward her location and still hadn't come to a conclusion when he neared the small town.

Chapter Four

Elsa's entrance in the local pub caused a stir. She ignored the mouth-watering smell of human blood. Focusing on being normal, she ordered a pint and some bread, cheese and a chicken dish off the menu.

The blonde, rosy-cheeked barmaid smiled big at the choice. Elsa guessed she did well with her limited French. Minutes later a mug of beer the size of her head was delivered, along with a plate of crusty bread with whipped butter on the side. Both proved delicious, but not as salty-sweet as the scent of the barmaid.

I'm in the Alps. I feel like I landed in some Swiss movie... Soon *girls with braids and aprons will mince in wearing wooden clogs.* Instead *I'm in a run-down ski lodge with a bunch of locals. Obviously this wasn't a big resort draw.*

"Is there a phone I can use? I lost my cell."

The girl smiled again and waved to the back of the bar. "Here, you can use this. Are you English?"

"American."

"Ohhh." She leaned closer. "I want to go to America someday."

Elsa didn't even try to resist. She slung her arm over the bigger girl's shoulder and walked with her to the back of the bar where she'd indicated the phone. "I can tell you all about it. How about over a pint?"

The girl was about to say yes, but as quickly as Elsa could, she mesmerized her, something like when you wave a laser around for a cat. It's in the eyes. Something Vampires possess that catches and holds a human's attention. She kept her focus on the image of sharing beers, and moved closer, as if to whisper to her. Two girls talking, nothing more, in case someone else entered the corridor. Gently, she drank from the girl's fleshy shoulder. She was careful to take onlya little. The impact hit harder than the trembling of her limbs. *I was starved. Then why didn't I hit Jamie up for a sip?*

The thought disturbed her. She'd never lost control and took blood from someone if she was in a bloodlust. But the worry was there, buried deep.

Careful still of the girl, she lifted away. She wiped her mouth then erased the puncture marks with a swipe of her tongue. Assured that she hadn't been spotted, she broke the spell.

She also dropped her arm and picked up the old phone from the receiver. She stared at it. How do you use this to call a cell? Was that even possible?

The girl blinked rapidly, focused on Elsa's face with a frown, then smiled in confusion. "Here you are. You only have to dial the right country code. When you come back, can you tell me about America?"

Elsa nodded, and smiled at her new friend. *Of course. Just like a cell, only...an antique.*

"I can tell you anything you want to know. No problem. My name's Elsa."

"I'm Megan." She headed off at a yell from a customer.

Elsa punched in Bobby's number, thankful that along with quickness and super cute fangs, she also now loved numbers. She'd memorized his within seconds. The first call didn't go through. *Of course. Country code. Losing my mind. Focus.* She sifted through her memory to try to figure out the code. She got it after a few seconds. *Well, I'm not losing it completely.* She dialed again.

It rang this time. She waited. He didn't answer after four rings. Then his voice mail picked up. *Damn!* Swallowing her regret, she outlined how sorry she was, again, to leave but had something come up. Last time something had *come up*, she'd been bitten and left to fend for herself.

She added how happy she was he'd found such a hottie at the club. She bit her lip. Then blurted out she loved him and would see him soon. As soon as she hung up, the guilt felt like it rose up to smother her. Bobby was much more fragile than the façade of super gay man he showed the world. He would be worried, and now, sad that she'd come and gone once again.

I should just let him go. Let it all go. Soon he's gonna wonder why I haven't aged. Soon he'll be old and I'll be the same me I've always been.

She rested her head on the phone. *He'll also love to see me again, and next time I die, I'll make sure to stay that way – for him at least.* She laughed lightly and considered her options. Most people would be amazed that Vampires, unless they were insane, didn't live wild lives.

Hers was pretty simple. She hid well from others like her. If she couldn't do that, like lately, she just kept moving. The tour with Tool and Masters had given her another piece of time with Bobby. It had also shown her that dance was more... More than ballet. Something she'd never dance again. Tool and Masters had also given her a convenient way to move around.

Without the constant strain of being pursued for some crazy reason, being a Vampire was pretty boring. Well, except those first few years. Those had been hell.

And although she wasn't one of those insane Vampires, there *were* ones that were. And they *did* kill, and they did it often, too. People didn't want to know that their missing child, sister, brother, husband, whatever was gone by way of...well, myths. That's what she was now. A myth. Immortals were spotted all the time, but people told themselves 'nope, didn't just see that'. Once she got her legs under her, being a Vampire proved to be laughably easy. Fit in and no one believes the crazy person on the street claiming they spotted a woman drinking blood from someone.

She contemplated that as she headed back to her bar

stool. Once there, she wolfed down more bread and spread creamy cheese on it as if she'd been born French. She finished the enormous beer, ordered a second while she swapped stories with the tasty barmaid — Megan — and her two friends, Elwin and Tom.

Everyone was pretty impressed that she was staying close by, and even more curious about that than she liked. She waved off the questions and muttered, pretending as if she'd had too much beer. She was tiny and the beer was, well, enormous so being drunk would have been logical.

If only. Witch's brew knocked her on her butt, but she could down beer after beer until dawn. She might have to pee a great deal, but nothing else really happened. Sucked, but there it was. She was now *not* a cheap date.

On the way to the bathroom, she scored one of the boys, Elwin. She sipped much more liberally from him. He was topping two-fifty and could handle the blood loss. He tasted sweet, like beer, and after, she bought him a pint, just because she got a bit of a buzz off him. Curious if his friend would give off the same, she ducked in after him later on. She took as much, getting a nice buzz on from his blood. It wasn't drugs — it was pure, finely brewed German beer. They'd been drinking for days, she guessed.

It wasn't until the door opened and blew in a strong wind filled with Jamie's scent that she knew staying in the pub so long had been a miscalculation. She'd been trying to feel normal. After run-ins with near death, she often needed normalcy. But she'd forgotten the first rule in her new immortal life — don't linger in one place too long.

Jamie's found me. Why do I find that exciting? Not irritating?

He didn't come in, but she knew he was near. A woman walked in and blocked her view. Then, as if set free from his leash, the little puppy raced in, wearing some kind of oversized shirt and enormous pants he had to hold up.

"Whoa, what in the world? Who dressed you? A blind man? Geesh, come here." She quickly dragged him to the back of the pub by the phone and gave him a once-over.

Sure enough, he'd been cleaned up. But there were smears of dirt someone had missed. She tugged him into the ladies bathroom. He didn't protest, just gave her that toothy grin.

"You're a mess. Where did you get these clothes?"

"Jamie."

"Did he give you *his*?"

The boy shrugged. She tried to think of what she had for clothes and called a black T-shirt she'd bought before the tour and forgotten. It would fit. The pants, though. She snapped her fingers, startling the boy. She handed over a pair of very, very cool Adidas track pants she'd tucked away for winter. She gave his feet a frown. He was barefoot.

"Seriously? Why would he let you out like this?"

"The stores were closed."

Made sense, but still…

Running shoes, a pair of black and white, also Adidas, landed next to him, along with a pair of white socks. The boy's grin grew. He picked up the things and studied her as if anticipating something else.

"That's all I got until we can hit a store."

He nodded and started to strip. She turned around, only then realizing she'd not thought of…underwear. She considered the problem and dismissed it. Jamie could deal with that.

"You can't stay with me."

"You fed."

"I… How do you know that?" She turned the hot water on.

"I just do."

She sighed. Maybe he did just know. She grabbed a towel and cleaned his face. He squirmed.

"Are you under a spell from the witches?"

"No."

"Your arm is better." She got the dirt off his ears and pushed his light brown hair away from his eyes, then used soap there as well. Heavy footsteps outside the bathroom made the boy stop squirming. *Jamie.* A shiver of anticipation at seeing him again made her stomach dive to her toes. No, not getting hot all over for a sexy werewolf!

Faolan grinned.

She frowned. "He can wait. He should have cleaned you properly. From now on you need to be clean. *Clean.*"

"Okay. Are these your clothes?" He pinched the shirt outward so he could read the lettering. It said "I'm not short, I'm fun sized" across the chest. Blinking, he gave another dazzling grin. *Really, could he be cuter?*

"Yes."

"They smell of you."

She didn't know what to say to that, so didn't respond. "I can't stay with you. Jamie is your kind. He can take care of you, or better, take you to a woman who will take care of you."

A snort from outside the door was so clear the boy smiled.

"He doesn't have a woman."

"How do you…? No, scratch that, I don't want to know. So…" The thought that Jamie was single shouldn't have made her heart rate speed up. She patted the boy's hair into place then arranged it into a scruffy mess. "There. Now. What are you doing here?"

"Where are you going to sleep?" he asked instead of answering her.

"In a musty old coffin in that old abandoned cemetery outside of town."

He wrinkled his nose at that.

"So, still want to be best friends?"

Jamie knocked on the door. "He really is too old to be in a women's bathroom."

She glanced at the door then the boy. "Do you have a name?"

"Faolan."

"Uh, Fowling?"

He laughed. It was the sweetest laugh she'd ever heard. "Faolan," he said. "It means little wolf."

"Ah, got it." She studied him. He was pretty cute in her

clothes, and they fit too, which was weird, but okay because she was a size small. The pants were a bit long, but that was the way boys wore their clothes. "You're upright, off all fours for a while? You're safe from the witches, the other witches?"

"Yes. Jamie told me to stand straight. He took the metal off my wrists. See? The witches are not near us. I am with Jamie now."

She snorted this time. "Sure you are. He's going to drop you as soon as he can." She had Jamie pegged for a lone wolf—an *ancient* one, too. She opened the door and tried to ignore the sexy impact of seeing him again.

But God, it was…impossible.

He was even hot leaning on the wall next to the door. He'd cleaned up, putting on a dark T-shirt and dark jeans, minus the tough guy leather jacket. The thin T-shirt fit him, not too tight over his chest, but pulled mouthwateringly over his biceps. Such flimsy cotton wasn't meant for guys like Jamie. The fabric clung to his pectorals, giving her a pretty good guess as to how firm the flesh was. He'd even shaved.

Not able to help herself, she focused on his whiskey-colored eyes, regretting it immediately. "Already called to have someone pick him up?"

"Not at all." She got the feeling Jamie's denial was way too defensive, which pretty much nailed that he'd wanted to, but now wasn't going to. "Faolan and I can walk you to your musty coffin."

"I can walk myself, thank you."

"Been busy, have you? You look better." It wasn't exactly a compliment so she shouldn't have gotten all giddy over it. Faolan slipped his hand in hers and somehow her brain cells turned back on.

Been busy? Drinking blood, he meant.

"I've been very, *very* busy, thank you." She brushed by Jamie without touching, which was hard, since he took up nearly all the hallway. She also kept the boy's hand in hers.

It was odd, but it felt nice.

"He's almost as tall as you," Jamie muttered, following her.

She straightened her shoulders and tried to stand taller. "I am five two, which is average." Her height was one reason she had always struggled in ballet. Dancers were meant to be lithe, slender, delicate, not—

"For what? Tree fairies?"

"I really don't like you." She pulled out money to pay for her meal, without looking at him again. It was a lie, since just standing in his presence was sapping her ability to think of much, other than him. Or wonder what he was thinking. Or what he *thought* when he looked at her. Or what he kissed like... Felt like when he did...

"I paid. We need to go. There's going to be—"

"You paid?" She turned and stared at him, something she'd told herself not to do. He shrugged big, powerfully built shoulders. Casual-like. But he seemed suddenly focused on the two boys sitting at the bar she'd shared blood and pints with. He lifted his lip, revealing an amazingly sexy fang. Her stomach clenched in want.

"You drank from them?"

Was that a growl? She bit her lip, suddenly happier than she could remember. Jamie turned his head and his eyes glittered dangerously. *Jealous?* She batted her eyelashes, then whispered, "Yes."

He focused back on them with a stony stare. His chest muscles rippled and his biceps bulged. If she had to guess, he was battling the need to pound the men to the dirt.

Her stomach did that odd nose dive. If she had to pick which was stronger, her pleasure at his obvious jealousy or worry over the boys, she'd have a hard time. Worry for the boys won out, especially when he tensed as if to go toward them.

"We should go." He didn't move at her suggestion, but she did. She waved nervously to get Megan's attention. The barmaid smiled big at her.

"He paid for you. He also ordered food." She handed over enough boxed to-go food for a family of ten. Jamie leaned in and took both bags from Megan. "Oh, you're a handsome one, aren't you? Did your mamma dress you better than dada?"

"Oh my G—"

Jamie's heavy arm landed on her shoulders, silencing her. All along where they touched, her body tingled as if he'd rubbed his feet on the carpet and touched her. *All* over. She fit perfectly. *If I turn my head I could bite his pectoral.* Something about that realization thrilled her. She turned slightly and her breast pressed to his side. His muscles hardened, but he didn't move away. She swore he held his breath, though. She knew she did.

Faolan ducked under her arm on her free side and smiled at them, then the barmaid. Elsa felt as if she'd been shoved into a movie, and any moment now The *Sound of Music* would blare… Wasn't that in Austria?

Nuance, this is insane!

She tensed, ready to run. *I'll just slip out from under Jamie's arm, wiggle away from the boy…*

"Oh, can I get a picture of you three? Such a beautiful family!"

"No, no pictures," Elsa began, feeling trapped. "We should go—"

"One picture won't hurt." Jamie handed his phone to the girl.

Before she knew what was happening it was done. Jamie had his phone back and was ushering her, arm still over her shoulders, toward the door. Faolan jumped away and scampered ahead of them. Deserting her with…her dessert?

Jamie caught the door as it swung and his pecs bunched. Would he like it? When she sank her teeth in?

She stumbled. He caught her, the door, and the food. He could probably do anything. As soon as she got outside, and the door closed behind him, she spun away. *Can't catch my breath.*

Why? Because I wasn't breathing. Oh right, I don't need to. Still...

"What was — ?"

"You seem stronger. The wounds are healed."

She touched the scarf she'd put on to hide the marks on her neck. "What was that all about?"

"No need to draw attention to yourself. A beautiful woman alone. It's remembered."

That wasn't what she was talking about. And he knew it too. She stalled over him calling her beautiful. *Does he really think so?*

"I meant what was — "

"We really should head out." He shoved his brown hair out of his eyes, just like she wanted to. "Others could have seen you go in there alone and think you are. It's not safe."

"Really? So some big" — she was about to say *sexy guy* and instead grumbled — "*dude* shows up and, presto, I'm safe?"

Jamie seemed to think that wasn't worthy of an argument. "We should go."

"I already told you — "

"Elsa, I found you." He settled another frown on her. *Like all the others weren't enough?* "If I can find you, so can other people."

"I can always hide. I can go now. This won't happen again." She waved off the witches. *What you don't know won't hurt you.* Until she remembered what happened... She *never* peeked under the bed to check for monsters. Clearly, Jamie threw the bed on its side to kick ass.

"This?" he repeated. He made it sound as if she'd just uttered blasphemy. "This isn't something random. It was a damn *attack*," he warned, then seemed to get his temper back down. Again. *What happens when it blows?* "Why won't you simply let me help you?"

The sudden drop to nice guy floored her. *And they say women are moody?* "Because it's never simply *help you*. It comes with strings. What's the catch?"

Jamie toughened his stance. "Can't a man want to help a

beautiful woman?"

Again with *beautiful*. *Something is up.* "No."

He actually grinned that time, but ducked his head so she couldn't enjoy it. Man, she was kind of happy about that. His smile was — stunning.

He lifted head with a serious expression again.

"I need help with the boy."

That went without saying. "Obviously. You let him run around *barefoot*." She threw her arms out, then centered back on him. He was distracting her. "What else?"

He anchored his hands on his hips again, and even though she'd seen it before, she still went a little weak in the knees.

"I'm certain you can find a woman to help you out." She gave him a head-to-toe examination, pretending a lack of interest in all his assets. "Or anything else you might need. But I'm not on that list."

He cocked an arrogant eyebrow and stalked closer.

The danger with pushing Jamie O'Connor, she discovered, was that he pushed back. She felt a little like prey. He slowed when he got within touching distance.

"Why aren't you included in that list?"

"I'm immune." *Lie, but he is a little too full of himself.* "Is that so?"

She forced a laugh past numb lips, encouraged when his frown returned. "Yes, sorry."

"Humor me, would you?" he muttered. "It won't kill you to stay with me for a few days. Just until we know why you were taken and what they were up to."

The chance to respond slipped away because he stepped closer, cutting the ability of her brain to work properly. In the distance Faolan was still playing in the fountain, getting his clothes all wet. But Faolan was removed from the nerve-racking way Jamie was staring at her. She couldn't step away. She didn't want to. No one had ever stared so single-mindedly at her before. Not when she was human, and definitely not since she was...well, a blood-sucking Vampire.

"I thought I *was* humoring you." She was pretty proud of herself when his frown grew. "You know, if you want me to help you with the boy, you really need to be nicer."

"I bought you dinner."

She smiled and shrugged. His attention shifted from her lips to farther down, and stayed there. She didn't dress to show off, but she did have breasts. Something that had caused her no end of grief as a ballet dancer. She never would have made her rise to prima ballerina. Not with her height and breasts beyond an A-cup.

Feeling oddly emboldened by his attention she leaned forward so he glanced at her face, not her cleavage. "And? I guess we're even then."

"Even? How do you figure?"

"I charge for the view. And you've had more than a dinner's worth."

"I can't believe you just said that."

She couldn't believe she just *did* that. The way he stared at her, then her lips, seemed to say he wasn't upset as much as he was intrigued by it either. He stepped nearer, following her when she backed away. She stopped, sure he would as well, but he moved closer. His amber gaze flickered from her eyes to her lips, then her eyes. She thought he might kiss her. The idea caught her breath. In a daze, she recognized that he was lowering his head, tilting it just so, and she almost let him. *Let him? I want this.*

First kiss. First. Kiss.

She was just about to lift her head to meet him halfway when something startled her.

A small scent carried on the breeze. She froze, her hand clenched in Jamie's jacket. *When did I do that?*

She dropped her hands and spun, frantically searching for Faolan as the scent became undeniable.

There! Foalan was outlined by the lights brightening the fountain, but he turned, an anxious expression on his small face. Then it was too late.

She was just about to lift her head to meet him halfway

when something startled her.

A small scent carried on the breeze. She froze, her hand clenched in Jamie's jacket. When did I do that?

She dropped her hands and spun, frantically searching for Faolan as the scent became undeniable.

There! Foalan was outlined by the lights brightening the fountain, but he turned, an anxious expression on his small face. Then it was too late.

Chapter Five

Ancients.

Elsa scanned the deserted surroundings, not seeing anyone, but she knew they were there.

"Elsa, calm down—"

"Quiet!" The scent, like rich, dark, well-aged wine if you mixed it with something else a bit spicy and…well… ancient, settled closer. Would Faolan be okay? Would Jamie survive this? Ancients were dangerous.

"Elsa. At last. Do *not* make a run for it."

Me? Why me? Why not Jamie? He was old, he was big, he was already digging a hole in her plan to ditch him.

She stepped farther away from Jamie, not wanting him harmed in this. He'd saved her. *Did I thank him? No, he was too busy rubbing my nose in it. I will. If we make it…I will… with a kiss.*

Focus. Focus. She played relaxed, when every inch of her body had turned to icy cold, 'man am I in trouble' mode. "Me? Run? Why would I do that?"

"Elsa, it's okay." Jamie tried to move closer. She stepped away again. There, in the shadows, a man stood, partially hidden under the eaves of the opposite building. She measured the distance from him to Faolan. He was safe. For now.

"Don't run," the ancient repeated.

"I wasn't going to. This place is great. Popular, too. The beer is awesome—"

"Enough." It wasn't a shout, but it was a direct snap of his voice. It made her fear that whatever he was planning on doing to her was not going to be good. Fear had never served her well, though, and neither had backing down. "I have searched for you for —"

"Really? I can't remember seeing you —"

"Silence! Come here at once. You are in danger."

Her chin came up at the tone of command but so did her stubbornness. *Enough of this. Why is everyone thinking they know better for me than I do?*

"Eat my mist, ancient." She used a trick she called shadowing to throw herself into the darkest corners along the buildings. Immediately, she was down the street before the three elders even gave chase. She heard Jamie laugh. He said something to the ancients. It sounded like 'she is going to leave you in the dust, old boy'. Couldn't be. Jamie wasn't proud of her, he obviously thought her incapable of surviving. That was why the almost-kiss. *Blindsided by a kiss and I'll be your baby? No way, Jose!*

The wind carried the sound of Faolan yelling her name, but it was already too late. She was gone.

She was good at this, at least against those from her *century*. She could feel the pulse of anger coming from the one who had shouted orders. Oddly enough, humor from the other two. She left them in her dust, misting *into* the ground. It was something she hadn't known she could do until a few years ago.

The vibration of a thud was rewarding, as was the curse that followed. So, maybe they couldn't follow her this way. She stopped that thought and concentrated on the shit she was in. Getting all happy before arriving home safe was the dumbest thing people in those horror movies ever did. Up ahead, an opening broke up the earth then plunged down deeper, instead of going along steadily. She followed.

Moving through earth was like flying, but in a thicker substance than air. She heard worms crawling. She sought them out, following their path as she circled the town. They won't expect me to leave again. *Will they?* She headed east toward the cemetery she'd flown over after leaving Jamie. At the entrance, she broke away and went deeper. They'd expect the cemetery. After another long ways, she broke free in the forest. She was far to the east of the town, much closer to where she'd met Jamie than she'd realized.

Jamie, did you rat me out? Call in reinforcements? If so, why Vampires?

She was still wary, even as she sniffed the air.

No way is it that easy.

Seconds later a bolt of lightning crashed down on her head. Or close enough that she felt the burn along her face.

"Cheeky, but don't move, little one."

Since she was still holding her stinging face, she wasn't planning on moving anywhere, at least not yet. "That was my cheek, you jerk!"

"That or your ass. Now, don't run again."

Okay, not good. She scanned the area, and knew they were alone. No, wait, maybe two of them?

How fair is that? Nothing is fair in love and war. She knew that was true about war, but love?

Keep him talking. Big jerk, ancient, he'd like the sound of his own voice.

"How did you know where I'd go?" He was hiding, much as she did, but so concealed all she got was his voice. It was enough. If he'd talk again!

"I guessed."

The sarcasm did it. Everyone seemed to think her weak, and apparently stupid, too.

She launched upward and spun into mist, heading right for where he stood, in the deepest, darkest shadows. Instead of misting above him, she whizzed *through* him, something that freaked most immortals out. It seemed to do the same to the Vampire. He shouted, stumbled backward and fell on his arrogant ass.

Ah-ha! So you didn't guess that, did ya?

She didn't wait around to see him rise. Or laugh too hard. She shot off, heading into the forest, deeper this time. Jamie was there. So was little Faolan, running in her brand new Adidas that never had fit because they'd been too small. He was probably getting dirty all over again.

What have I done to deserve this kind of attention? And why do I care if a child gets dirty? He probably likes dirt.

When she was clear of his scent, and everyone else's, she switched to a wolf and took off at a pace that tore up the soft turf. By the time she had covered several miles that way, she was panting and unable to run a step farther. She switched to a mouse and found three other mice deep in a hole underneath a log. They squeaked a lot in mouse talk but after a while, they simply huddled around for warmth, she hoped they wouldn't try to eat her.

There she stayed, cold, frightened and feeling as if the *world* had been turned upside down.

She turned her brain off and concentrated on sleeping, grain, and the warmth of her companions. Thoughts she hoped a mouse would have.

She woke from a doze to a wolf outside, snuffling amid the brush and causing her mouse-mates no end of worry. They skittered all over the place, anywhere but near the loud, scrabbling sound of his claws digging up the tree to reach them.

He didn't succeed. The sunrise was nearing, so she merely out-waited him just like she had the Vampires.

How had these people found me?

* * * *

Jamie watched the sun sink beyond the horizon. Elsa was stubborn. And had a sense of humor, or a death wish, unlike anyone he'd ever met before.

When she'd misted right *through* Bryson, *he'd* nearly fallen on his ass laughing. Bryson had struggled to his feet. Jaxon had laughed so hard that the Vampire was forced to hold onto a tree or else collapse. Aidan, though… Aidan hadn't been amused. Jamie had an idea kings rarely were.

Alrick never was.

Jamie should have backed off and let the Vampires

have their way. They obviously thought, since she was a Vampire, she was one of them. He'd argued that he could guard her, and since she knew him, she'd come out when they were gone. Aidan had spoken with Bryson and they'd come to a decision. For now, they'd agreed, she was to stay with him, but if he lost her, again, they would step in to ensure her safety.

Jaxon had met his eyes once, concern clear in his frown. He hadn't said anything, though, as he left. Jamie had been with Jaxon on a few hunts. Bryson as well. Both were strong and capable men. Either could have secured Elsa, but the thought of her with either of them, especially Bryson, the *un*mated Vampire, had set Jamie's teeth on edge.

She didn't belong with them. She was Vampire, that was obvious, but he also knew she was much more.

Right now, though, she was a mouse.

Faolan gave him a sleepy-eyed frown. The boy thought he should have gotten her to come out. He'd not said it, but it was there. Jamie admitted Faolan looked better in his new improved Elsa T-shirt, with the cute as heck-like writing on it. Now, Faolan could pass as any other kid. Elsa had fixed his hair, and found dirt the kid had missed.

It was clear whose side Faolan was on. *Elsa's.*

Jamie was tired from days with no rest. The tree roots dug into his back. He wasn't used to taking care of someone, least of all a boy. Or a woman. Not that Elsa seemed to think she needed taking care of.

Still, even exhausted, he found himself conflicted. He wanted to try. Just the thought had him frowning and watching the boy play in the dirt. Faolan was at ease. He'd slept, curled up near Jamie, his arm thrown out, his small hand resting against Jamie's thigh. Jamie had covered him with his jacket and rested his head on the pack, so he had a pillow. The bruises were gone. There was a healthy glow to his skin. For some of the day, he'd been happy to sit near Jamie and wait for Elsa. It was clear the boy felt safe with him.

Elsa, though... It was going to take more than saving her life or buying her a meal to earn her trust.

He smiled, remembering her laying the trap of her perfect breasts right under his nose. He'd fallen for it, for her, and been shown exactly how smart she was. All that made him want to do was test her in ways he doubted she'd ever experienced before. Just the thought had his mouth watering and his body tightening. He stopped that before it got out of hand.

"Well," he sighed. "Maybe she'll come out now. It's dusk."

Faolan crawled over to the pack and cleaned his hands like Jamie had taught him. He even rubbed the cloth over his face. Preparing for Elsa's inspection? After, he picked up the box with the meat pies. The kid avoided the vegetables, but had done pretty well on the other foods. He also kept glancing at the tree, obviously wanting Elsa. Jamie wasn't sure on children, but he thought the boy needed...love. Elsa gave it to him freely.

Jamie frowned and studied his hands. *Would she turn that so easily on me?* She'd held her breath for his kiss. He swallowed and got to his feet. There was no use fighting this attraction. If she returned it...

"Maybe if I ask her, she'll come out?" Jamie paced the little clearing. "What do you think?"

The boy smiled wanly around a mouthful. "What do you think?"

"I don't know. Elsa," he called. "You need to come out."

It was a long shot. She could just turn to mist and leave again. If so, the chase would be on much like before, but with this little guy.

But where could she go? She needed to get back to London. If she could shift, cutting through space in a heartbeat like some Vampires, she would have done that before, when Aidan was after her.

She had a place in London. Not a good one, but he'd found it.

There was also Seattle, but he thought she would avoid that city. He wasn't certain why, but he doubted she'd return there.

She'd have to start over again. No doubt she could, but he had a feeling she was getting tired of that. Ten years... It was a long time to drift from place to place. *Worse than centuries?*

He shook off his thoughts. "You can come out now. It's just me, and Faolan." He waited. The longer he did, the more he wondered if she'd simply stay a mouse forever. "Faolan saved you a few sausages. Maybe some meat pie. I hid a loaf of bread from him." She'd eaten a full meal last night, along with more than a few beers. She'd also sampled three people's blood. None of them were aware of, or even seemed to mind, the donation. The two men he'd wanted to rip to pieces.

She came out of her hiding spot, shifting from the mouse in a blur of gray smoke to herself. He must have been holding his breath, because when she stood before him, he let it out in a long sigh.

She didn't appear pleased. She was wearing a small, brown leather jacket this time with scuffed riding boots and faded black jeans with a gray, low-cut sweater and what looked like a few other T-shirts under it. A pale blue scarf covered the gentle rise of her breasts, but he still glimpsed the delicate flesh. She had high, rounded breasts, the kind that would fit his hands perfectly. She also possessed the sweetest, blondest hair he'd ever seen on a woman. She wore it parted in the middle, but it caressed her high cheekbones and when she blinked, sometimes it caught in her long eyelashes.

This wasn't his first good eyeful of her. He'd had her inches from being kissed last night. He'd dragged her off a cross. He'd spoken with her. Yelled at her. And shared a laugh with her. All that left him in a rush. *She's more beautiful each time I see her.*

It might be a Vampire thing, the beauty, and the delicate

appearance that drew him. Whatever it was, it had him completely. But it shouldn't. He was a wolf and most of the pack found strength the most attractive feature for a mate. Life was hard, and the tougher both were, the longer they would survive.

All he knew was that she was the most beautiful woman on the planet. And standing there, with her blue eyes pinned on him, all he wanted to do was have her rush into his arms, so he could stop the panicked racing of his heart.

If only life were so simple, like the fairy tales of old. Instead, she gave him a minute or less inspection, then dismissed him.

Faolan got the smile he wanted, and the hug. "You got dirty again."

The boy grinned up at her as if she hung the moon. She probably did. "Did those mean old Vampires scare you?"

"No. They weren't so bad."

"I'm sorry I left you alone, but you had him. I figured he could handle you."

"I missed you." Faolan hugged her tightly around her neck, making her laugh and almost topple over. He had to keep his feet firmly planted and not rush to make sure she didn't fall. "Are you going to stay with us?"

Jamie held his breath. She grumbled something and stood again. "Eat your vegetables too, you won't grow tall and handsome if you don't."

Faolan's eyes widened. Jamie fought a laugh as the kid quickly ate two pieces of the broccoli he'd avoided like the plague. At least his hands were clean. Jamie had purchased some hand wipes in town and now had a backpack as well. He'd stashed away things they'd need, but they'd have to restock before too long. The boy ate a lot more than Jamie had anticipated.

Elsa turned back to him with an impatient glare. "Did you sic those ancients on me?"

He tensed but couldn't stop the rough retort. "Where do you get your ideas? Why would I—?"

"Okay, so, what do you want? No, please forget that, I know what *you* want."

He highly doubted that, since he didn't know anymore what he wanted. At the inn, he'd nearly kissed her. If not for Aidan he would have. And he had an idea she would have kissed him back. It'd been there, unspoken in the way she tipped her head and rose on her tiptoes to reach him.

"What does *everyone* else want?" She seemed more than a little angry. Before he could respond, she settled her hands on her hips. "You really didn't sic them on me?"

The aggression in her tone made him smile, but he bent his head to hide the reaction, sure she wouldn't appreciate it. Women didn't have the same sense of humor as men.

"Is something funny? Because, you know, some day it will be you they're after, then we'll see if it's funny."

He considered that, but didn't see the comparison.

"And, why are *you* here? A wolf, when those Vampires were older than China?"

She'd lost much of the fear she'd displayed last night when dealing with him from the treetops. If she'd even had any after the first few minutes in his company. He wasn't certain that was wise. There was still something about her that made him want to be as far from her as possible but at the same time, close, so he could ensure she survived.

While he was lost in thought, she stared at him. She had the ability to make him worry what she was thinking about him — something he never concerned himself with. She could also do silence unlike anyone he'd ever met.

"I didn't sic Aidan on you. Do you know who he is?"

A sullen nod was all he got for an answer.

"He wants you to talk to him, much as Alrick wants to talk to you. You're a Vampire and a Lykae." He held up his hand to stop the instant denial. She opened her mouth, shut it and lowered her pretty eyebrows in a scowl. "Whether you like it or want to admit it, you are. Do you know what the Immortal Council is?"

"Yes."

"Do you know what a Death Stalker is?"

"Yes."

He smiled, then handed her the bread he'd wrapped in a towel to try to keep soft for her.

She shook her head and sat down on one of the giant tree roots. "I'm good. So, this is about what I know about the immortal world? The team players, and all that?"

"All that?" He lowered the bread.

"What goes on between the good and bad guys, that kind of thing?"

Faolan scooted over, closer to her. He was good. He did it slowly, but she zeroed in on him and took a sausage from the greasy wax paper. Immediately the kid was next to her, touching his side to hers. The boy needed the connection. Maybe any kid would need the attention after living in a shed, but Jamie worried it was a wolf thing.

"So, bad guys and good guys. Changelings?" she prompted. "Monsters made from people who don't sign on with the bad guys?"

The way she spoke confirmed how new she was in this world.

"How long ago were you bitten?"

She balked at that. He saw the non-response in her face as if she'd shuttered out the light of the sun. He thought she'd tensed to stand, but the boy leaned on her a little bit harder and held up the mustard. She glanced at Faolan, rolled her eyes, but dipped her sausage in, before taking a small bite.

"Not something I want to talk to you about. Next question."

"All right. How have you survived?"

She choked on her bite and glared. "How have you?"

"I'm part of a pack that no one messes with."

"Fine. I move around," she offered.

He knew that. She could hide as well. What she'd done in the tree last night... It'd been impressive, even if he had still known she was there.

"Next question." She ate delicately, as if she had all the

time in the world. She did, he guessed, because she certainly didn't feel like she should go with him.

"How did you mist…into the ground? Aidan had never seen that before. And that, I have to say, was something to watch. He hit the ground. Really, hit it." He didn't bother to hide his smile, especially when she returned it.

"I know." She laughed, then covered her mouth and giggled. Her blue eyes danced, sparking. "And that big one? He fell over when I went right through him."

"Bryson." Jamie had seen that too, but hadn't stopped to rub it in the big Vampire's face. Jaxon had done that for him. They shared a laugh and she handed him a sausage when he bent to get one. "I didn't know you could do that. I've never seen it."

"I know, I'm full of surprises." She glanced at his eyes, then away, smiling secretly. If the boy hadn't been watching, he might have kissed that secret right out of her.

"They can't do those things you do," Faolan blurted.

Jamie straightened and ate his sausage. He was hungry, he realized. *Why didn't I eat before? Because you were too torn up over Elsa sleeping under a tree.*

Elsa smiled, not taking the boy seriously. Jamie wasn't so certain she shouldn't. Jamie bet the boy believed Elsa could walk on water. She probably could. Vampires walked softly, barely making a sound when they chose. But the boy knew things.

"How do you know that, Faolan?" he asked gently.

If he'd thought not to alarm Elsa, he'd failed. She stiffened and met his gaze with a worried frown.

Faolan was playing with a stick, more interested in the circles and loops he was making in the dirt than their conversation. "I heard them."

Jamie tilted his head. He hadn't discussed anything in front of the boy. "When? When did you hear them?"

Elsa's worry spiked. Having powers could be good, a form of protection, but he could almost hear her fear. Having something powerful when you weren't could be dangerous.

"When they were here. Aidan hadn't ever seen such a thing. He wants to see her, watch her, and ask her how she does such things. He wants to know what else she can do."

"Jamie?"

"I didn't hear him say that," Jamie assured her.

"He didn't *say it*." Faolan giggled. "He thought it."

"You hear people's thoughts?" Elsa stood, her expression becoming unreadable.

Jamie centered on the boy. Faolan shrugged, his focus on the ground. Elsa raised a hand and shook her head when Jamie reached out to take the stick from the boy.

"Faolan?" she prompted. "Kinda important. Can you answer us, please?"

Faolan squinted up at her through the hair in his eyes. "Only if I try."

A shiver of alarm ran through Jamie. He motioned Elsa to sit again. She did and he settled down across from them. So as not to alarm the boy, he touched Faolan's small arm as gently as possible to get his attention. "Can you read mine, if you try?"

Faolan grinned and shook his head. "No, Jamie." The way he answered made it seem silly that Jamie thought he could. Relieved, Jamie nodded.

"Can you read Elsa's?" Jamie asked, getting a wild-eyed glance from her. She dropped her eyes from his just as quickly. *My bank account to know what she's thinking.*

"No, only some of the old ones."

"The old ones?" he repeated.

"Only the *old* Vampires," Faolan clarified. The boy reached up and brushed at something on Jamie's jaw. "You're all hairy again."

"Only the old ones," Elsa breathed. She clutched his jacket. Jamie didn't think she knew it, but she'd done it last night as well. Her gaze went to his. "He can hear ancients! Jamie…that's… That's… Is that good or bad?"

Jamie smiled and lifted a shoulder. "It could be both." He

79

eased his answer by tucking a long curl out of her eyes and behind her ear. Before she could snap at him, he turned to Faolan. The sizzle of even that brief contact steadied him. "Can you hear ancient wolves, too, or only Vampires?" Jamie asked, scratching his jaw. He did need to shave again. Elsa's skin was silky soft.

Faolan squinted and tilted his head. "Only Vampires and very, very, *very* old witches. I've not met an old wolf." Big grin. Jamie responded. He wasn't too keen on knowing the mind of the oldest wolves. He'd bet it would be disgusting.

"Ew." Elsa giggled. "That must be gross."

Faolan laughed and, after a second, Jamie did too. *She's almost mirrored my thoughts.*

"What?" she demanded. "Who'd want to know what *they* think?" She laughed some more and ruffled the boy's hair. Faolan had puppy dog eyes for her, no doubt about it.

"I wonder why you can do this." Jamie had been worried over the same thing, but hadn't wanted to push too quickly. "Is it something the witches did to you?"

"I don't know," Faolan denied too fast.

Jamie opened his mouth to demand an answer. Elsa reached over and squeezed his arm. She gave him a frown too, no doubt a warning for him to go slowly. He experienced a shock again. She jerked her hand away as if burned, and gave him a questioning glance. Then she seemed to think better of it, and focused on the boy. Jamie let it go. There was much he had to speak to Elsa about, but now, the boy was the most important puzzle.

Faolan was paying a great deal of attention to his drawing, making Jamie's concern grow. If the boy could hear ancients and that got out…

He was about to stand when Elsa patted Faolan on the head, brushing his hair off his eyes when he stared at her.

"I can do things, too. Maybe it's okay. Right, Jamie?" He wasn't given time to answer, because she added, "I can do things I don't know I can, until I do them. Like my clothes and shoes. I call them to me, like… Once, I forgot my car keys and there was this disgusting Vampire hanging outside my apartment so I couldn't go get them. I just wanted them so bad they just, pop, appeared on the table in front of me."

A disgusting Vampire. Just to hear that she was in danger like that made his skin crawl. Faolan considered her story and nodded.

"So, maybe you have things you can do, too."

"Maybe, we can't be sure. Until we know more, it's best we don't let anyone else know about your gifts, Faolan." Jamie stood, uneasy with what she was saying. She was a Vampire therefore she could do the things she did. She was also a wolf, so perhaps that aided her to do things other Vampires could not. But Faolan was a boy, too young to be given such powers. If anyone discovered this about him, his life would never be safe. Maybe they already *had* discovered this about him and *that's* why he wasn't safe.

Elsa watched him now, her worry clear in her blue eyes, but she nodded.

"We should move out."

She frowned immediately. "Jamie, I think I made this clear, but I'll say it again. I'm seriously not going with you. I do better alone."

Jamie blew out a frustrated breath. Neither of them was safe, yet, of the two, Faolan understood that and, looked to Jamie to keep him safe. Elsa waited, her elbows on her slender knees, her blonde hair blowing gently against the delicate curve of her cheek. The picture of a relaxed, beautiful woman, without a care in the world. She was so pretty his heart felt as if she was squeezing it.

It pissed him off. *She can't seem to listen, or even see her danger.*

"Elsa, are you really this stupid?"

She slowly widened her eyes, but she didn't appear upset. Instead she actually smiled sardonically. "Not the last I checked, but go on. I can see you have something to say."

Something to say? Do I need her permission?

"You're safer with me. Everyone can see that and all you

can do is sit there pretty as a picture and pretend it's not true. You're *always* safer with other people. That's why Lykae have a pack. That's why Vampires have Houses, and witches —"

"Have covens, I know. But they aren't me." She stood and faced him head on. "My turn yet?"

Faolan moved aside, either out of the way, or to watch the show.

Having a woman, especially one as small and young as this one, stand up to him was remarkable... Shocking really. He expected her to back down. Nod, say he was right and maybe even, God help him he hoped not, cry.

Elsa did none of those things. She met him head on, anger for anger.

"I don't know what would have happened if I'd woken up on that cross. *Neither* do *you*. I continually shock myself, so you've known me, what? Twenty-four hours and already you know more about me than I do? I survive, that's what I do." She turned away, her back to him, and he thought mumbled, 'Even when I don't want to.' "But" — she turned back and jabbed a finger at his chest, blowing his mind with how much fire flared in her eyes — "I *have* survived, oh high and mighty Jamie O'Connor, and without you either. I might be young, but I am strong."

Strong? I can toss her over my shoulder and run a hundred miles without tiring. "You're not young. You're an infant!"

"At least I'm not acting like one!"

"You little —"

"Seriously, how old are you?"

"I'm over three centuries older than you, and old enough to know when I'm not as strong as I think."

"Well, that explains why your knuckles are still so scabbed over from dragging them!"

"You're not running any longer. I can find you. Wherever you go, I can find you. So, if it wasn't enough for me to save your butt off that cross, consider that —"

"Ahhh!" she screamed. "*Always* with the *cross*. You know

what? Reminding me of what happened, and how you saved my life, like *umpteen million times*, is *not* how you make friends."

Even angrier, he settled a stare on her that usually got him what he wanted. "I'm not trying to be your friend, Elsa. I'm trying to keep you *alive*."

"Well, you failed. I'm already *dead*."

Chapter Six

Jamie clenched his fists. Elsa had stormed a few feet away, leaving him standing without a clue how to respond to her. *I'm already dead.*

She was the most vibrant person he'd ever met. She wasn't *dead*. She was… *Hell, more alive than I've ever been.*

But not now. Now all the fight had just gone out of her, and he was still ready to go another round.

Fuck. I just shouted at a woman. And she — His attention snagged on her slim shoulders, traveling down her slender back to her rounded backside. He blinked. She was still there, not running. *But holy hell, I don't yell at women. I don't care enough to bellow.*

His heart felt clenched again.

There'd been something there, a break in her voice, a hint to some kind of emotion he couldn't understand when she'd spoken. *I'm already dead.*

He hadn't known her when she'd thought she was human — before she'd been bitten. Didn't know the girl that had probably been walking at night, after ballet practice maybe, to go get a bite to eat with friends, and ended up being some Vampire's snack instead. Only a Vampire hadn't taken her blood. A Vampire had *changed* her and her life.

But she *had* survived.

As far as he knew, very few humans lived. A change like that was excruciating. That she'd endured it, that she'd continued to exist as the beautiful, sane smart-aleck standing with her back to him blew him away. But it wasn't pissed-off anger coming from her now, it was something else.

Hurt.

If she still felt pain over her change…

Then she wasn't nearly as mentally strong as he was beginning to think.

He hung his head. Contemplated the ground, littered with fallen red and yellow leaves and brown pine needles. The scents of the forest were clean, as was her uniquely sweet signature on the breeze. Still sitting on the log, Faolan shifted, drawing his attention.

He was hugging his to-go box, eyes wide. Surely this wasn't the first shouting match he'd seen? Faolan gazed up at him sorrowfully, then at Elsa, eyes going back to Jamie.

He modified his approach. She liked Faolan, and just as clearly thought he didn't know what he was doing with the boy.

"You need to go somewhere, why not go with us?"

She blew out an exasperated breath at that. "Because I don't want to go *anywhere* with you."

"I'm sorry I yelled at you."

"I'm sorry I yelled at you, too."

All right, this is great. She's obviously a clear-headed woman. "Okay, so—"

"I'm still not going with you anywhere."

Forget clear-headed. She was stubborn as the day was long. *Calm. Play it easy with her, no more yelling.*

"We could work together on finding out why you were both taken. Protect Faolan together."

She frowned at that, obviously not trusting him. No doubt because he wasn't being exactly honest. "We would work *together*?"

"Yes. There's a town, farther over these mountains. We can go there, buy him some things. Protect him together, in case more witches do come after him. We can also hunt for clues. Anything we can to figure out who those witches were and, more, what they wanted."

She didn't respond, and for a while, he simply waited,

watching her. She fascinated him. It stung that she so easily didn't want to go with him. He wasn't used to the cold shoulder coming from women. He didn't bother with a woman who didn't want him. More importantly, he didn't bother with women who didn't want *sex*. Last night, when he'd put her under his arm, something had clicked. She fit there, almost like that was what his arm was for, to pull her in closer so she was safe.

Like she was his.

Only she wasn't his. He'd know. All the stories he'd ever heard about mates said he'd know. Even him, he assumed.

She reached up and tugged on a section of her hair, stroking it with one hand then another. She kept her face away from him, her shoulders hunched a little. She lowered her head, clearly debating what to do.

He'd seen her wait on a bus that way. It'd been on a traffic camera in London. He'd watched it over and over. When a bus had finally pulled up then away, she hadn't been standing there any longer. She hadn't been on the bus either. She'd misted, but had waited until the cameras couldn't see. She was smart like that.

"I need to go back to Paris. My things are there in—"

He shook his head. "Not any longer. The room was trashed. We'll get you whatever you need here."

She humphed at that, but finally asked, "How far is the town? You don't expect us to walk, do you?"

The relief he felt should have worried him as much as the desire he felt building. He shook that off as easily as a dog shakes off oily bath water. Not well at all. "I think it's not far. It has a lot of tourists, so stores, restaurants."

She didn't budge.

"I thought we'd see if Faolan can take his wolf form, first, before we head out."

She turned, stunned at that, staring wide-eyed from him to Faolan, then back. "Is that allowed?"

He smiled, but ducked in case she got angry again. She was so damn innocent. The draw of that, the knowledge that she was even more innocent in so many damn crazy ways, had to be what was causing this need to touch her. When he could, he looked up.

"Sure, it's allowed as long as you don't mention it to Alrick."

"I never want to meet Alrick, so no problem." She grinned and walked over, coming close again, like she had last night. This time he kept his eyes on hers. "To the town and maybe a bit longer. Just to see what we can find out about those witches. Also, we need to do some shopping. Faolan can't wear girl clothes, you know. It's worse than using the ladies room."

"All right." He worried, with her warm scent surrounding him, he would have agreed to anything to keep her close.

"I hope you have money."

"Why? How much can kid-sized clothes cost?" Jamie eyed the boy.

"Probably not a lot. But mine will. I'll need clothes, and since my room was trashed, just consider it the price for my help."

Faolan laughed and skipped over. Smiling, he stared from her to him. "She will need many things. Pretty things."

He was more than okay with that. For some reason his shoulders went back at the thought of giving her something she wanted. "Why am I buying? It's your life we're trying to secure, isn't it?"

She quirked an eyebrow. "I thought it was Faolan's?"

Belatedly, he nodded. "Right, Faolan's."

Swinging her hair off her face, she gave him a mocking smile. "So, can *you* shift to a wolf?"

The challenge in her gorgeous blue eyes wasn't to be ignored. Jamie grinned. A second later he was in his wolf form. But she was too, which left Faolan, who laughed and petted them. Her wolf was small, but well-defined and glossy-white and gray. The boy hugged her around the neck, petting her until she switched to herself again.

"Can you do that?" she asked the boy breathlessly.

"No."

Jamie took on his human form again. Elsa gave him an odd sweeping glance from his head to his toes, then blushed and turned to the boy. "You can't shift to wolf?"

Faolan shook his head.

"Then you can ride my back, and we'll run," Jamie supplied. For some reason that got a radiant smile from Elsa, as if he'd done something right, which felt damn good.

Faolan laughed. "I can run. I'm fast." He put words to action and took off with a wild, happy shout. The boy was like Elsa in far too many ways.

"He's too independent," he grumbled.

"He'll be fine. There's no one about."

"Is that so?" He turned to find Elsa studying him. A shiver raced over his shoulder blades.

Is that desire in her blue eyes? Or fear? He didn't want her fearing him, but maybe it was best.

"So you will play my boyfriend? Is that possible? I mean, don't you guys have a one mate policy?"

He nodded, suddenly unable to think of a single thing to say. *Boyfriends have sex with their girlfriends.*

He doubted they had week-long passionate fucking until their girlfriends couldn't lift a finger. Suddenly, sex with Elsa, long, hot and sweaty hours of fucking, was all he could think about. Intense, painful kisses until their mouths were tender, and his lips were bitten by her fangs, kisses.

"So? Who is going to believe we're a couple? I don't even think I *like* you."

Slowly, he grinned. She liked him or she'd have left immediately. She wouldn't have come out from her hiding spot. Or stayed and talked with him when Faolan was racing on ahead.

"You can pretend. And we date before we find our mates, Elsa."

"El."

He was never calling her such a simple name. *El.* It didn't fit her.

"Let's get this started, then." She took off, walking away from him without a glance, but he knew she was interested. A man could sense it, see the way a woman flushed and her eyes fell on him then skipped away. She was innocent, far more naive than she appeared.

He followed her, trying to tame the rush of anticipation.

Her sense of direction was good. He could take that off the list of things to worry over. Especially when she kept walking, the sweet rounded curves of her ass flexing with each step she took. She paused under an elm tree and he drove his eyes up off that gorgeous sight to stare into her beautiful face.

"Did you peek at me when I was naked, on that cross?"

He ducked his head to hide his smile. He'd just been admiring her ass, with jeans *on* it. But when she'd been on that cross he'd lost control of his wolf. His smile slipped. Her being naked hadn't registered past her being hurt. He lifted his head and met her inquisitive stare. There was a challenge there, in her expression, as if the woman in her were testing the man in him.

"I'm ancient. Do you really think you have something I haven't already seen a few times in the past three hundred years?"

"Three hundred isn't *ancient*. And well, of course I do." The challenge glowed as if she'd banked the sun in her eyes and kept it there just to use against him. "*Me*."

He laughed, caught off guard. Damn her if she wasn't right, though. Better, she didn't think him a Neanderthal.

She huffed, taking his amusement the wrong way. "I assure you, wolf, I'm something you have never seen, nor are likely to *see*." She walked over as she spoke and stuck out her hand. "We keep this business only. It's a deal only if you keep that in mind."

"Afraid you won't be able to keep up?" The words left his mouth before he could call them back. But once gone, he watched her eyes widen, then a slow, seductive smile lift her pretty pink lips. She'd done the same last night, pushing buttons on him he was certain she shouldn't be able to trigger. But she had. Easily, too. Now the need to have her, to sample the lips of this delicate—*appearing*—but smart-mouthed and hopefully strong woman was riding him hard.

She dropped her hand when he didn't move to take it. "Have you ever been with a Vampire before, wolf?"

He hardened at the sexually charged tension coming off her. Vampires were able to draw their prey not only with their eyes, but with their bodies and voices as well. Had she experienced sex with immortals before? *If she has then surely she's strong enough for me.*

"No?" she whispered.

He shook his head, too fascinated by her to stop whatever else she'd come up with.

"Then just be warned. If you wanted to mix business with pleasure, you'd have to dose up on the little blue pills and be prepared to pay the hotel for all the broken furniture, because when Vampires have sex, they don't stop until they can't lift a single finger, let alone anything else."

With that sexy tease, she smiled and revealed not only a dimple in her cheek, but her little canines he could just imagine sinking into his shoulder as he rode her to orgasm.

"So, should we start after him, or wait until he gets lost?"

It took a full minute for him to readjust his intelligence above the belt. By the time he did, she was already heading off after Faolan. Sweat poured from him. He knew one thing, and one thing well—when he was challenged. This woman had just laid down the gauntlet and had to know he was going to pick it up.

She cast him a questioning glance over her slim shoulder that even his knuckle-dragging brain picked up on. *She knew. She fucking knew. She wants me.*

If it wasn't for the boy, the woods, and the potential threats, he'd have proved to her just how capable he was of meeting that challenge.

"Try to keep *up*, wolf."

He shook his head at her tossing his words back at him, and followed, trying to gain his equilibrium so he didn't trip over his own feet. Or kiss her senseless.

Chapter Seven

I've lost my mind. I'm playing with fire, an entire volcano! Have you slept with a Vampire before? Who asked that? Was it me?

Aliens had obviously taken over her mind. But it wasn't aliens. He got to her with his superior attitude and *Mr. I Know How Weak You Are* arrogance. She *wasn't* fragile. And she sure wasn't backing down from showing him how wrong he was.

"How did you find me at the inn? I went to the farther village thinking you'd go to the closer one." Since she was so weak and all.

Jamie held a branch aside for her, like a gentleman. "I will always be able to locate you."

She froze. "Since when?"

He lifted one brawny shoulder—just like a man. Everything about Jamie was…manly, though. His hair, his clothes, his attitude. He didn't know how to act around a woman, or else didn't care to know how.

The problem was if he was a playboy used to women falling at his feet, then he was a no-go. If he was, on the other hand, a guy's guy, used to being alone, or hanging out with other men, and just didn't *get* that you don't repeatedly tell someone they were the 'little lady' and 'too weak to lift a finger' then well… Maybe she could teach him she wasn't. *And maybe then he'd be a go?*

"Since the other night."

She blinked, confused by just what night. Her mind was awash with Jamie dilemmas, not nights. Then she remembered her rule.

If he said a single thing about the witches and cross... "Oh."

He continued on, moving to walk ahead as the undergrowth took over the trail. He possessed that tall, big man thing—the fear of nothing because, well, nothing would fuck with him. He even walked as if he knew she'd follow. *Obviously, we're going to the same place.* He pushed another pine branch out of the way, and held it for her. "Careful."

From anyone other than Jamie it would have been courteous. From him she knew it meant he probably thought her too delicate to be able to push the branches aside herself.

"So you can find me no matter where I go?"

"Yes."

Not good. "What about if I go to another country, leave the continent?"

He held up another branch, and she ducked under, straightening after to wait. He wore one of those dark glowers men from BBC movies wore, the kind Mr. Darcy was famous for. Most of the time, that was, until he finally did smile. She wondered what had him so serious all the time. From what she could gather about him, he was a tracker... But that meant what?

"Yes, even then. Are you leaving?"

"Eventually. What do you do, I mean, for this pack of yours?"

"Do?"

She found Faolan up ahead, leaping from rock to rock crossing a stream. He certainly enjoyed his freedom.

"I'm a tracker."

"So you spend a lot of time with this pack?"

"Not really, no. I'm usually away, like this." He gestured to the wilderness around them and headed down the hill before her.

"Faolan seems fine, I mean, for being with those witches. Did you ask him how long he was there?"

"No."

She studied Jamie's posture and decided she was making him uncomfortable, so kept on asking more questions. "So maybe we should ask him. I mean that's kind of important." No response from Jamie, so she switched topics. "So what does a tracker do?"

He turned and, hands on hips, gave her his 'steady, that's about enough' stare. She smiled and walked past him, pushing a tree limb out of her way all on her own. She was just about to snap it back on him, when Faolan shouted.

Ice shivered over her skin. The next instant two women appeared near the stream.

Why always two women? What was up with – ?

Five guys suddenly materialized out of the woods. All of them were dressed in black, and, worse, wore the tattoo on their left cheek.

"Jamie, Death Stalkers."

"Get Faolan." Jamie drew something from his hip, and seconds later, it snapped into a sword. His amber eyes flickered to light, then back to dark. He took her arm and held her firmly in place. "Don't get involved. I'll handle this."

"You're joking. A sword?" She shook him off then caught his arm. "We go, we don't fight. Think of Faolan."

"I am thinking of Faolan. I fight. You go. As fast as you can, with him."

She scanned the forest. They were still hidden. If they ran. *No, no running this time.* "There are seven of them, Jamie!"

"Don't argue with me, woman!"

A full second that she knew they didn't have passed, then a laugh burst from her lips. "Woman?"

Jamie grabbed hold of her upper arm and squeezed, gently but firmly. "Elsa, for once, just do as I say."

"Elsa!" Faolan shouted.

She spun away from Jamie the Neanderthal. Faolan sprinted toward them, so frightened she could scent it. She dropped Jamie's attitude from her list of worries and misted to Faolan.

She scooped him up before she'd even fully touched down. "Trust me now, Faolan. We hide, it's just thinking of nothing, absolutely nothing. You can do it."

He nodded, but was trembling so hard it was difficult to tell if he really meant it. She set him down, not tired from holding him, but he *was* nearly as tall as she was. The spot was good, dark enough, deep enough in the forest to hide them visually. But she needed Faolan to hide his essence as well.

She checked in on Jamie to see the Death Stalkers walking toward him, as if they'd chanced upon them. If she could get to Jamie, maybe she could convince him to leave.

"Elsa, Jamie is not safe."

"I know, Faolan. I'll help him. But first, take my hand."

Faolan nodded. She moved him back, deeper in the shadows. From there, she watched Jamie raise his sword.

"That's close enough. What do you want?" he called.

One man was the center for the group. The others were spread out in an arrow formation, each as dangerous as the leader. His dark hair was combed ruthlessly into a part that reminded her of the fifties haircuts Elvis wore. The similarities stopped there. He was old, powerful, and clearly a Vampire. He didn't appear pleased with Jamie, but smiled cordially, as if introduced to a person far below his social status. He also scanned the woods, no doubt searching for her.

Jamie waited, confident and tall, but alone.

She bit her lip and moved Faolan back even farther into the underbrush. Faolan was silent, completely still except for his trembling. The grip on her hand was tight, indicating that his level of fear was still high.

"Just concentrate." She sensed him begin to disappear, not from her sight, but his scent and everything that made up Faolan blurred. "Good, that's it. That's it." He'd done this before, but now she got the impression he wanted her to blend with him. "I'm going to help Jamie, but we are not letting them touch you."

A spike of fear, then more of the nothingness he was hiding in.

"Want?" the man asked loudly. The question got her attention back on Jamie. "Well, our boy back, of course. His mothers were murdered just last eve. So tragic." He clucked his tongue. "But they've passed on and now he is alone. I will feel better when he is with us, his remaining family."

"Those witches were not the boy's family."

"No?"

"The boy is wolf. He stays with me."

"You?" The Vampire glanced at a redheaded woman by his side. She smiled, revealing what Elsa already knew — she was wolf. "I thought the boy was yours, my dear."

"He is mine."

At the woman's response, Faolan buried his head in Elsa's stomach, hugging her tightly now, as if she might hand him over. She stroked his back, merging them more and more with the shadows of the forest. She sensed the night creatures on alert near them, as if they too were waiting for something horrible to happen.

Jamie tossed his hair away from his eyes and suddenly laughed. "I doubt this bitch has ever spawned life."

Shocked at his language, let alone the insult, Elsa tensed. Faolan stared at her, worried, but slowly pulled back to gaze at Jamie as if he'd just won points with the boy. She nudged him, but when he glanced up, he shook his head firmly, frowning up at her.

Not his mother.

"You'll die for that insult, *half breed*." The woman moved forward, but the man stopped her, holding a hand on her shoulder as if in comfort.

"There is no need for this, Melinda. Surely we can solve this without bloodshed."

Elsa doubted that, seriously doubted that. The man had come armed, and every single Death Stalker with him stared at Jamie as if they'd have loved nothing more than to tear him apart.

"Boy?" The Vampire tilted his head. "Boy? Come here."

Faolan cringed, but tried to pull away. Elsa stopped him. She also covered his mouth with her hand and pulled him closer to whisper in his ear. "Don't you dare move. You stay here. Blend in, hide, and, no matter what, you don't listen to anyone but me, or Jamie."

He went wide-eyed, but nodded when she shook him just a little. She couldn't believe this was happening, that she was going to actually go *out* there, but she had to. Seven against two sucked for odds, but one against seven was worse. Jamie had saved her life. She could at least try to even that up.

The first step was the hardest, but at the quick scowl she got from Jamie from that single step, she continued on much easier. He really did think she was useless. She had survived by hiding, but she'd also had to fight a few times as well. And kill.

"Ahhhh." The man nodded respectfully and drew in a deep breath through his very large nose. "I see."

"What exactly do you see? Were you part of the 'hang me on a cross' crew?" she asked.

"Elsa," Jamie muttered, trying to shield her.

She stepped aside so he couldn't. "Zip it," she muttered to him, then faced the scary Vampire. "Really, what are you people doing out here, in the middle of the night?"

She'd stopped a few feet from them. Far enough to get away, close enough to show that she wasn't afraid. Of course that was a lie. She was terrified. The redhead stared at her with something close to hatred. Not sure why, Elsa stared around her for who would cause such an emotion, saw no one, and stared right back at the woman. "What is your problem? Have we met?"

She opened her mouth, but the man stopped her again.

"My dear Melinda is in mourning, as we all are, for the loss of our sisters."

They were all in black, but she kind of thought that was their style. "Sisters, meaning the ones that tried to crucify me?"

He tsked. "They would not have killed you."

"Tell the girl missing her head, she might believe you," Jamie said.

Right. Jamie was so cool. "So, what do you want? You're not getting the boy," Elsa added.

"The boy is ours." The only other woman of the group stepped forward. Somehow, she appeared much more dangerous than the evil, glaring redhead. Pale, with black hair down past her butt, she was dressed in leather from a high collar on her neck down to the tips of her toes. It had to be hot. She made Elsa's stomach roll. Jamie didn't appear to like her either.

"He didn't come when called." Jamie settled his feet wider apart. "I suggest you leave, now, while you can."

The man chuckled and his friends, after a weird non-response, did so as well.

"Who are you people?" she asked, not expecting them to hear or answer.

Drawing a deep breath and standing taller, the man, who wasn't very tall, bowed his head regally. He was the same height as the women. The man behind him towered over him so much that Elsa could see his entire ugly, pockmarked face.

"My apologies. I am Dario Black."

Elsa exchanged a glance with Jamie. He lifted an eyebrow, obviously not knowing the guy either. It was the strangest meeting she'd ever had.

"Okay, nice to meet you, Dario. I'm Elsa, this is Jamie. What else would you like, besides the boy we aren't handing over?"

Jamie tensed, but Dario smiled. "You believe he is one of the pack?"

"Yes." Jamie lowered his sword a fraction, but it was more menacing, not less. "Why did you have him?"

"I?" Dario touched his chest. "I did not *have* him."

"Bullshit," Jamie muttered. "What did you do to him?"

"I can see this is going nowhere, is it?" Dario asked conversationally.

"Pretty much." Jamie tossed his hair out of his eyes again and waited. For what, she didn't know, but kept her mouth closed. The tension was building, not lessening. The muscles in Jamie's sword arm bulged, but everything on Jamie seemed to swell. *His wolf?*

She glanced around the clearing, worried suddenly that they were stalling so someone else could swoop in and take Faolan. He was still where she'd left him. It wasn't because she could sense his aura — it was because where she'd left him she *couldn't* sense anything, not the trees, the grass, the bugs, or small creatures, nothing. A void, small and circular, caught her attention, nothing more.

He was good.

She was about to suggest to Jamie that they leave, when Dario dropped his hand from the woman's shoulder. At the same time, he smiled.

All hell broke loose around her. Faolan cried out Jamie's name in warning. She got shoved, hard, by Jamie and hit the ground. Jamie rammed his shoulder into a man as if he was a linebacker. Then, with his sword, he knocked the man back and away from where he'd been trying to behead her.

The redhead charged right for her. Elsa scrambled backwards, nearly fell — again — but caught herself and drove a punch into the redhead's stomach. The woman tumbled backwards, but landed on her feet half a dozen yards away.

Dario disappeared. She sensed him and the other, scarier woman over by Faolan's hiding spot. *Not good!*

Everything slowed to a crawl, every detail became crystal clear — but too late to do anything about it.

A Vampire tackled Jamie from behind. The disgustingly ugly guy caught her around the waist, dragging her closer to his horrible stench. Faolan cried out. The sound skyrocketed her panic.

She couldn't catch her breath. Terror paralyzed her, even as the man on top of her shoved her arms above her head. *Get to Faolan.* She gathered a deep breath and shoved outward, knocking the man aside enough to nail him with a slice down his ugly face. When he reared back, roaring, she managed to knee him in the balls. His bellow turned to a grunting sob. Then he came back at her, eyes red shot and trained on her as he gripped her throat in his meaty hands. He gritted his yellow teeth as he squeezed so hard she feared he'd break her neck.

The world narrowed to him. He had fangs, but unlike any others she'd seen. He wasn't a wolf. And he wasn't a Vampire. Soon, she didn't care. She struggled to get his hands off, but even as she did, he shoved between her legs, really terrifying her with the solid bar of his erection. It felt big enough to rip her in two.

"Ever been fucked by a real man, blondie?" He ground against her, sickening her further. "On your knees with your pretty arse up begging for more? Does your wolf make you howl like that? Beg for it?"

She nearly vomited. Instead, she swallowed it down and rammed her head into his. It worked. His hold loosened. She bit his arm, ripping through his veins and causing as much damage as she could. He went back to howling and tried to get away from her. She hit him with a hard punch to his temple and surged up, almost knocking him off.

Suddenly he was gone, his terrifying body flying through space to crash into a tree with a resounding crack.

Jamie stood, breathless and so fierce she feared she might be next. Immediately, another male drove into Jamie from the side. Jamie spun and stopped a sword stroke to his side. With a twist of his wrist, Jamie sent the guy's sword soaring end over end. The two went tumbling down, Jamie on top, delivering blow after blow. He was merciless and magnificent. *Fierce warrior.* A rush of possessiveness flooded her. But with it came the awareness that she had to get her fight on.

Melinda barreled into her and they crashed to the ground. A rock bashed into her temple. Her vision blurred. Black spots swam closer. *No! Focus!*

"Damn it, would you people stop throwing me down?" She snapped at the woman's arm, got nothing but a punch to the side of the head.

Anger turned the world a red haze. She slammed her fist into Melinda's nose, elated when something broke. She got bitch-slapped for it, but she grabbed red hair by the handful and used it to crash her forehead into Melinda's. The bones in her nose cracked further. Melinda screamed, but it sounded gargled.

Good. She is not getting Faolan!

Melinda tried to crawl away. Elsa didn't let go. They scrambled on the ground, both trying to gain the upper hand. A tree smashed into her back and she sprang to her feet. Melinda gained hers as well, dabbing at her nose with the back of her wrist. Her eyes went feral. Elsa beckoned her with her fingers.

"Bring it on, bitch."

Melinda screamed and attacked. She punched her in the stomach as hard as she could, then drove the flat of her hand across Melinda's throat. When Melinda gasped and doubled over, Elsa nailed her with an uppercut Ali would have envied.

Just like the disgusting guy with yellow teeth, Melinda flew backwards and down to the dirt. Motionless. To be certain, Elsa kicked her in the head. She just had time to gain her breath again when she spotted Jamie in trouble.

"Jamie! Behind you!" She dodged under the arm of the man coming at her, and raced for Jamie.

A cloaked man was easing up behind him, sword raised, ready to shove it into Jamie's back while Jamie fought off two men. *No time. No time.*

She misted to Jamie and knocked his feet out from under him. He fell hard, but missed being gutted by the Death Stalker. She rolled to her feet and aimed a kick she used in ballet right between the guy's legs. The Death Stalker went down. The other two backed away, eyeing her, the man, then her.

"Damn it, woman!" Jamie roared. He was tense, breathless and, oh Lord, was he gorgeous. Hair fallen on his forehead, eyes blazing amber, he was the picture of an angry warrior from olden days.

She smiled. "You're welcome. Now, can we go?"

Jamie wiped the blood off his mouth with his wrist and eyed the groaning man.

"Get Faolan, then we go." He lunged to her left, terrifying her, until he punched a man behind her. The man hissed and bared sharp fangs. Jamie punched him in the mouth. She thought one fang fell to the ground. The Vampire's eyes widened and he lost his shit. Jamie tackled him backwards, away from her.

"Go! Get him!" he shouted, while beating the hell out of the bloodsucker.

But… She held her breath, fearing for him. The Vampire broke Jamie's hold. Hissing now, he flew at *her*. She misted through him and turned. He followed.

"Elsa! Here! Again!" Jamie beckoned to her and she blinked.

Smart man.

She misted through the Vampire again and again, leading him in circles until he was closer to Jamie. He followed. She materialized at last, leaving him facing Jamie. He was all but salivating to kill her. Insane with it, he screamed at Jamie. She kicked him in the back — right onto Jamie's sword. It was sickening, worse because the sound was loud in the sudden silence.

Silence.

"Jamie —"

Jamie took her hand and scanned her face, for what, she didn't know. "Good girl. Now go get him. I'm right behind you."

She flew to Faolan. The frightening woman was there, but

it was Dario who held him. He was trying to shove a black hood over his head. He already had Faolan's small wrists bound behind his back. The terrifying woman dove for her, black hair like a fan behind her. Suddenly Jamie was there, knocking the evil woman aside as if she was nothing. She came back with a terrible scream, hitting Jamie. His head jerked to the side. Blood spewed from his mouth. The last man charged, tackling him hard. They tumbled out of sight.

She didn't know what to do. Jamie was in trouble. Faolan was in trouble.

Jamie rose to his feet, squinted over, found her, and bellowed, "Elsa! I've bloody got this. Go get Faolan, woman!"

She nodded and misted closer to Dario, trying to figure out how to stop him. When she materialized, he pulled a wicked knife and shoved it to Faolan's throat. The hood blocked her view of Faolan's face, but she knew he was terrified because she was. *Can't lose him. Can't lose him.*

"Stop!" She held her hands up. "Don't hurt him."

"Of course not," Dario panted. "Come with me and no one will harm him."

"There is no way I am coming with you. Let him go."

"You *will* come with me." He laughed and cruelly drove the knife deeper. "Or I will kill him."

"Shift, Faolan!" She took a step to the left so Dario would follow. If she could get his back to Jamie, maybe Jamie would see what was going on. She could hear Jamie fighting, knew by the sounds he was still alive, at least.

Dario didn't follow her. "He can't shift. He can't do anything I don't allow. Can you, boy?" He drew Faolan up closer and shook him in a macabre imitation of hugging him. Faolan struggled. She heard him whimper. *No. Can't let him go.*

Dario jerked him closer, digging the edge of his blade deep enough to draw blood.

"Decide now. He lives or he dies." Dario's fangs lengthened and he lifted his blade above Faolan's chest, ready to drive it into the boy's heart.

Behind her, Jamie shouted, "Elsa, get down, get down!"

Dario watched her, tensing his muscles to drive the blade in, a smile on his face as he glanced over her shoulder.

It was all she'd hoped for. She didn't think, she didn't process her idea, she dove forward, misting *into* Dario like she had with Bryson. But not fully. This time she used only her hand, then grabbed his still-beating heart and squeezed it tightly.

His eyes flew wide. He made a choked sound, blood bubbling from his mouth. The knife dropped from his hands. Faolan stumbled and fell to his side. Black stepped backward — or tried to, but couldn't. Not while she held the disgusting, wet mess of his heart. She misted her hand, but kept his heart, ripping it out and throwing it at their feet. He toppled like a tree.

She tripped over the uneven ground, would have fallen, but heard an unholy scream behind her, and spun in time to get floored by Melinda. *Why didn't I kill her?* All the air left her lungs. Black dots swarmed her vision. *Got to stay strong!*

They rolled. She used it, pushing harder to gain time to get her vision back on.

Branches dug into her, rocks crashed against her head, but she managed to fend the bleeding woman off as they tumbled down a hill. She got in one punch, to Melinda's nose again, then they fell apart. She scrambled backwards, trying to gain her feet. *Stay strong!* Melinda gained her feet first and drew a knife.

She could hear Jamie running down the ravine, shouting her name. "Elsa! Shift, damn it! Disappear!"

A God-awful roar sounded. She peeked behind her shoulder and saw Jamie tackled by a huge Death Stalker with gray-blue skin. *Demon?*

"I'm going to gut you, then him."

Elsa twisted back around, crouching at the ready. *No one is gutting me or Jamie.*

Melinda smiled, and licked her lips free of the blood. It was revolting, especially when she smiled, with her teeth all red stained.

"Then eat both of your hearts while they still beat in your chest." She drew another knife. Slowly she flipped it and held it between her fingers

Elsa tensed. Melinda turned and threw.

Elsa screamed, terrified as it spun end over end toward Jamie. He was trying to break free to reach her. It landed in his upper arm. Jamie growled, but pulled the blade free and drove it into the demon's chest. A second later, he threw the man off him. The guy landed on his feet, laughed and came back at him, knife still embedded in his chest.

That was all she could see before Melinda drew her attention back to her. She sprinted up the side of the hill. Elsa knew where she was going. *Faolan.*

She tore up after her, using the trees as leverage, then remembered she could fucking mist. She did, materializing by Faolan, but not before Melinda arrived. She was edging toward him, eyes on her. The boy was on the ground, curled into a ball, but trying to merge with the forest. He was doing it, but the poor thing was out in the open, not hidden in the underbrush like she'd left him.

"Stay away from him," Elsa warned. She was breathless, aching from head to toe, but she was not letting this bitch touch Faolan. She stood taller. *As if that will help.*

"He's not yours. He's ours. You have no idea what you've started. No idea at all."

"Back off or I will do the same to you I did to Black."

Elsa wasn't completely sure she was boasting. The thought of doing what she'd done to Dario made her stomach roll. Melinda sneered and drew closer to Faolan.

"Don't. I'm warning you."

Melinda suddenly dodged for him. Elsa caught the woman by the legs and toppled her to the ground. In the background she could hear Jamie battling, but she knew he couldn't help her. If he could, he would have. She knew it without question.

Melinda's knife went flying as they fell. She pulled another.

Always with the knives.

Rolling, Melinda brought it up to stab Elsa. Panic again surfaced. It was all Elsa could do to hold Melinda's hands with hers and keep the sharp tip away from her throat.

"When I kill you, I'm going to take him where no one will ever find him again," Melinda threatened, eyes crazed.

"Why?" Elsa grated, getting desperate because Melinda was slowly managing to ease the knife closer to her throat.

"Because I want to." She growled, and her eyes flashed. *Lykae!*

Elsa lost her grip. Melinda savagely drove the knife down. It narrowly missed her shoulder to stab the ground. The edge sliced along her cheek. The pain brought clarity.

Elsa misted her hand and did to the wolf what she'd done to Dario. Only she didn't waste time, she drove her misted hand in, grabbed and yanked Melinda's heart out. As soon as the woman fell, Elsa pushed her off and frantically turned away to vomit until she was weak.

Thankfully she heard nothing. No more fighting. Then her name, spoken quietly by Jamie as he helped steady her. He held her hair back while she continued to dry-heave. When she could stop, she turned away from the mess and rested on her elbows and knees, head to the forest floor.

Jamie surprised her by comforting her with gentle strokes of his hand up and down her back. "Are you unharmed?"

She groaned at the question and turned her head to shoot him a dirty look. "I'm fine. You got stabbed with a flying dagger."

He appeared surprised. "I'm unharmed."

His arm was okay. She sat up. Even the skin she could see under the bloody mess of his T-shirt was healing. The sight made her sick. She turned away, swallowing repeatedly. "I think I need to be sick again."

He squeezed her shoulder. "Go ahead. No one is here but

us."

"Faolan?"

"He's cleaning up at the stream."

She searched for his little brown head. Found him, crouched by the water, cleaning his hands and face. He was farther up, away from them, but then she realized he wasn't away from them, but from the bodies strewn around the clearing.

"They're all...dead?"

"Yes." He pushed a water bottle under her nose. "Here, rinse your mouth."

She took a sip, spitting the water out and repeating the process several times.

"Take this, it will help." He handed her a piece of spearmint gum, and took the water bottle. His hands were covered in gore and dried blood and dirt. She took the gum anyway, and, with shaky hands, took the blue foil off and quickly chewed the minty gum until it was all she could taste.

"Better?"

She nodded. "Did you kill—?"

"Yes."

"Is Faolan okay?"

"Yes. He knew them."

She hadn't asked, but had been wondering. "That woman wasn't his mother."

"No. She wasn't."

The reassurance didn't help reduce her worry for Faolan. "He even knew the Vampires?"

"Yes." Jamie studied her, then the forest around them. "It's quiet now, but you see now why we need to protect him. Why I need to keep you with us." He gently touched her face with the backs of his knuckles where she could feel a burn. "You were hurt."

"So were you."

That made him smile oddly. He dropped his hand, but took one of hers. His were long-fingered and, even with the dirt and worse, strong and capable. "This hurts?"

She glanced at her hand, where she hadn't noticed a slice. "No. It's okay. *I wasn't stabbed.*"

He laughed a short, abrupt sound. "No, you weren't stabbed. But now you see, don't you? Why you need to come—"

She stood on shaky legs and walked away. It was too soon after something horrible to start thinking or arguing.

'Come with me and I won't kill him.'

She shuddered at the memory. *I killed him instead, didn't I? Again.*

She walked to the stream on unsteady feet. Her right hand was covered in blood. More blood dripped past her elbow. She wanted to shower, but took her jacket off, then her sweater and threw them aside. Her long-sleeved T-shirt followed, leaving her in a black tank top. Faolan watched her but didn't speak. Neither did she. There wasn't anything to say. She fell to her knees by the stream and drove her hands in the icy cold water. She didn't mind the cold. *It feels like something, at least.*

She scrubbed her skin until all the traces of blood were gone.

The image remained of Dario's gray eyes, widening as she held the gory mess of his heart in her hand. The way she'd squeezed...

"Best not to think about it. The blood's all gone now. Faolan is fine."

She glanced at the boy. Their eyes met as if he'd been waiting for her. His hair was a mess and along his cheek another red mark, possibly where the Vampire had hit him, made her wince. *Dario. I would kill you all over again for that.*

Jamie squatted beside a body. He studied the man for a while. Then lifted the jacket, going through it, then the inside pockets of his shirt, then his pants. It was the disgusting rapist.

"What is he?"

"A Jackal." Jamie pulled something free and studied it.

"There are only a few, but a friend ran into some a few months ago. They were working with some Death Stalkers too, or something evil."

"He *was* evil." She shuddered.

Jamie nodded, concern etching lines on his face she'd not noticed before. His jaw was darker now, from being hurt more than needing to shave. She wet her discarded T-shirt and walked over to him, startling him.

He held up a hand, moving back from her. "What?"

"You're hurt too. Here." She dabbed at his jaw, following the line of a cut, down to his neck. She moved his shirt aside and found the stab wound, but, as he said, it was already healing. Wolves could do that. So could Vampires. Still, she wet the area and cleaned it as she had his face. He stayed perfectly still the entire time, as if he wasn't sure what to think of her.

What if he'd died? What if Faolan had died?

"Any other scrapes?"

"No."

She sat on her knees and met his gaze. His seemed baffled. *I confuse him?* "You could have killed them all without me."

He didn't respond. She didn't think there was much to say, so she rose to leave—until he caught her hand and held it. "Yes, but not before they would have found you and Faolan."

It was as close to an admission that she'd done well as she was likely to get from Jamie, she thought.

Good girl, now go get Faolan.

Did he recall that? She did. She held the memory close, wanting to cherish it.

He was very much the warrior. And now that she'd seen him, she knew that attitude was due to much more than being three hundred years old with old-fashioned values. He was stunning. So powerful she was certain, alone, he could have wiped the forest with them.

But was he more? His eyes were such an amazing shade of amber. She thought he had shocks of more of that color in his thick brown hair. His heavy brow was drawn down, and his lips tightly closed, as if he had something to say but didn't. No doubt it was to remind her that he'd said to stay hidden.

"Okay, I guess it was good then, me helping. Here." She brushed at his forehead, stopping anything else he was going to say. "You've got blood everywhere."

Faolan got up and came to them. Jamie watched her with a frown she couldn't decipher. *Does he think I'm a monster now, or still the weak woman?*

"What did you find on that gross guy?" She sat back on her feet, finished with Jamie. He was fine. The cut along his jaw was already healing, the other on his forehead also disappearing. She still wanted to touch him, assure herself he was still alive. But she couldn't find anything else to do for him.

"No ID, but he had a lot of cash."

"You took his money?"

"He won't need it. I also found this on the dark-haired woman." He held up something that caught the moonlight.

A necklace. She frowned and stopped it from spinning. *Forever* was inscribed on the back of an oval pendant.

"I've seen this before. On the—"

"Girl."

"Yes." She nodded, releasing the chain. "What does it mean?"

Jamie squinted, and his jaw flexed. "It means this attack was linked to what happened there. We've got to move. This was too easy."

"Too easy?" she spluttered, feeling sick again. "I just—" She glanced at Faolan, almost having said 'just killed for him'. "Why do they want you, Faolan?"

The boy shook his head sadly. "They always want people."

"Always?" She shared a concerned frown with Jamie, but when she went to ask Faolan what he'd meant, Jamie stilled her with a hand on her shoulder. The connection was electric, again, but warm, and somehow eased the sickness she still felt, and the fear.

Faolan had his head down, shoulders slumped, clearly still afraid, but more, maybe worried they'd leave him. "Yes. They always want the strong ones, the *pretty ones*."

"Well, they can't have you, can they? You're with us. So that means they will just have to get used to wanting something they'll never have. You."

Faolan sniffed and tilted his head to peek at her.

"They're gone now. We made sure of it," Jamie agreed. "No one is taking you from us. Okay?"

"Okay."

She sighed. When she did, Jamie gave her an odd frown. She got the feeling that as soon as they were alone, she would be drilled for answers she didn't have.

Like how I ripped those people's hearts out of their chests. I wonder if he'll still think I'm weak and defenseless now that he realizes I'm a monster.

Chapter Eight

Jamie helped Elsa onto the ledge. It led down to the town nestled in the foothills below them. "It's nearly dawn."

"I know."

"We should locate a room, but all the inns will be closed."

"I know."

He studied her making her way after Faolan and accepted that for now, *I know*, was all he was going to get. He'd tried to get her to smile several times, but each time his jokes had fallen on deaf ears. Not even Faolan had laughed.

Still, they were both alive. The boy subdued. Elsa quiet. He scented nothing on the air, but he hadn't before they'd been attacked either. He'd known cloaking could be done. Most Death Stalkers were experts at hiding themselves. *Cloaking* was what the pack called it. He thought it was something Elsa did very well. It had protected her in the past. He hadn't considered that Death Stalkers would be included in the craziness. Or that he'd be so distracted by a woman that nearly a dozen had snuck up on him.

Elsa was at the center of it all.

How such a new immortal, and one so small, and in so many ways ignorant of the dangers in their world could be so sought after disturbed him. *She* disturbed him. She'd come to stand beside him, instead of listening to him and hiding. She'd done it because she wasn't going to leave him. As if he needed her at his side.

If she'd stayed hidden with Faolan— He didn't want her in that position again. There were hundreds of positions he'd like to get her in. Most were with him on top, doing things to her that would make her sweaty and submissive to anything he could think up.

But he didn't do women like Elsa. The longer he spent with her the more he knew that. She confused the hell out of him. He was the kind of man who made up his mind, and did it. He planned, he followed through. He didn't plan, think on it, scratch it, come up with a new plan, discard it and…start all over again.

That wasn't him.

She turned him into that.

He focused on the woman driving his brain in circles. "Was this your first kill?"

It would explain the silence and the sickness she'd experienced. She'd ripped Black's heart out. And he'd been worried she'd think *him* a monster for how he'd destroyed those witches. *I only wish you'd burned them.* At the time all he'd known was relief that he hadn't disgusted her. Now he thought back on that and realized she'd meant it. When she killed, she killed. There was no coming back after your heart was ripped out.

Her small shoulders tensed. "I sense a place to sleep. I'll go there, you and Faolan —"

"We stay together."

That got a sniff, nothing more. No argument, no smart comeback, nothing.

She'd nearly made his heart explode when she'd walked up and started arguing with the Death Stalkers. Now, his heart clenched at the misery he could feel coming from her. She'd killed and she'd done it well, but he sensed that it horrified her.

"Why didn't you stay hidden?"

He got a glance over her shoulder at that, nothing more, before she continued on. "You were outnumbered."

"I was fucking fine," he snapped, irritated all over again.

Instead of giving him hell, she shrugged and sighed heavily, sounding tired. "It seemed like the thing to do."

"And killing Dario? Why did you do that?"

"It seemed like the thing to do."

They'd stopped on a cliff, overlooking a valley below them. The wind picked up, blowing her blonde hair. She tossed her head and reached up to push the remaining strands out of her eyes. Her hands were small and delicate, but he could still see her, beating the hell out of the redhead.

"There, I sense a place. Faolan? How about sleeping in a crypt? Sound like fun?" she called. "No? Okay, you can find a room in town." She pointed to the lights of a small village then moved her arm to the left. "But I'm going there."

He scanned the trees beneath them for whatever she was pointing at. He finally spotted the remains of what appeared to be some kind of estate. The house was in bad shape, but from this distance he could still recognize what once must have been an expansive property.

"We'll stay with you. Nothing will be open this early." He scented no one near, and better, no immortals within his range. The house might be a better bet. *I can protect it easier than a place in town.*

"Fine. Whatever you want." Elsa ruffled Faolan's hair, giving the boy a half smile. "Try not to get any dirtier."

"We'll go get fresh supplies, then see about the house."

She glanced at him, barely, and shrugged again. With that, she crouched and burst into mist. She always did that, as if she were taking off from her starting position the way a bird launched itself into the air. In a way, he guessed she was. Only they couldn't see her do it. He still tracked her through his other senses.

"I guess that means we're on our own for a few hours. Come on, she'll need food when she rises, and unless you're on the menu, that means we need some blood."

That got a brief dejected glance, nothing more. Jamie could relate. Without her the night suddenly seemed empty.

Elsa settled on the ground beside an old mausoleum. The marble and granite building was designed using pillars of Roman architecture thrown together with interwoven circles of thorns bursting with roses. Each flower was carved individually so that some appeared just about to bloom while others were simple buds and many more were fully opened roses in their prime. She could almost smell the rich scent of dew on the sweet pink petals.

The thought made her sigh. *How long since I've smelled dawn?*

Does it fucking matter? I killed. Again.

Elsa stared down at her hands and could still feel the warm wetness of bodies against her flesh. Still hear the echo of a heartbeat in her palm before she squeezed and burst the organ.

To stop the horrifying memories, she surveyed the rolling landscape spread out beneath her, like a patchwork quilt, and considered her options.

Run, now, away from the rising sun and sleep somewhere else.

Go to ground, here, where they will never be able to sense me.

Stay here, sleep and hope on the next rising everything will be okay.

She paused by the rickety cast iron gate. The house wasn't just breathtakingly creepy, it was an overgrown castle. Dark turrets rose high against the starlit sky like a fantasy story come to life.

There was a fourth option.

The trail from the crypt to the main house was muddy, with yellowed weeds striving for survival amid the rocky ground. She could imagine long ago, when it had been a pretty pebble-lined path through glorious gardens. She shook the thought off. *Think like an immortal who just barely escaped an attack. Survey your surroundings.* She didn't spot any footprints, but doubted an immortal would leave any. There was no sense of others here, but then there'd been no warning with the Death Stalkers, either. None at all with Nolan's *friends*.

My first kill. Did he regret hurting me?

She doubted it.

She passed shrubs that were overgrown mysteries, probably once giant dancing bears or unicorns, but now rose up nine foot tall, at least. She trailed her hand over the leaves, recalling how life used to be, before, when she'd not known how sickening people truly were.

The estate was large, but so neglected she felt sorry for it. Even the stone steps leading up to the arched doors were sliced through with cracks, where more weeds found purchase. Trees grew in the lawn, simply sprouting out of nowhere. She guessed, by the size of their trunks, that the house must have been lying here empty for at least a hundred years, if not longer.

This place was once beautiful and useful. I was once beautiful and useful as well. Now I'm still beautiful on the outside, but useless.

Unless I take that fourth option. Let the sun end it all. Goodbye nights, goodbye pain, goodbye struggle.

She sighed and tried the door, her thoughts darker tonight than any she could remember. The door surprised her. It was locked. Around the side was another that stood just ever so slightly ajar with only a small chain and lock to keep people out. Inside she could see the damage was extensive. Old leaves, twigs, and broken cutlery littered the floor, along with musty curtains and more linen that someone might have once thrown over the furniture to protect it.

Gaining entrance to a house, even an abandoned one, was tricky. She'd once entered a cabin, an empty one, much like this, and suffered pain like nothing else in her Vampire life. She'd made it outside, crawling inch by inch on her stomach as the nauseating agony ripped her to pieces.

An invitation had to be made, she'd learned. At least in some instances, others, she'd found didn't need them. She weighed the remembered pain with the curiosity she couldn't contain.

Pain is worth it. Besides, I hurt already.

Once she broke the chain, she took one step inside. Cautiously she took another.

Nothing. No pain, no agony, nothing. Somehow

disappointed, she shoved the door aside. It hit the wall and dislodged yellow-stained and peeling paint from the wall. Moonlight broke up the darkness with patches of silver light, revealing leaves and dirt everywhere.

She started walking, her footsteps echoing loudly amongst all the emptiness. Each room was the same. Deserted, neglected, but not damaged by people, just abandoned. There was no sign of anyone living here, not even vagabonds or homeless people. Sometimes those people lived where no one else could — except her.

To the back of the kitchen she found a staircase leading up. The wooden steps creaked in places but held her weight. Rooms upstairs were shut away, and when she opened one door, puffs of dust billowed up like clouds of smoke. It was surprisingly untouched, and like the kitchen, set up as if someone would return.

She kept walking, worrying her thoughts as she explored the silent mansion. Whoever had owned the place had either forgotten its existence, or didn't bother with it. But at one time it had been glamorous. There was even a room with a blue and gold ceiling and a parquet floor that reminded her of a ballroom. A double row of chandeliers hung intact and covered in cobwebs in the middle of the domed gold leaf ceiling.

She walked through and on to a side room. She stopped there, stunned to see a ballet studio. The ballet barres lined all four walls. The parquet floor was broken in places, much like the ballroom, but it was still an amazing room. There were pictures, tipped sideways, but of ballerinas from the nineteen-twenties, or earlier. She found a playbill for *Swan Lake* and another from *Der Idiot*. Both were in German and yellowed with age, but still remarkably beautiful. *Did we cross the border? Into Germany?*

Whoever had once owned this house must have loved the ballet. Or they had been ballet dancers. Maybe German ballet dancers.

She smiled faintly at that and trailed her hand down the

familiar wood of the barre. The feel made her throat tighten painfully. Her reflection caught her attention. Unlike the rumors she'd always heard about Vampires, she had always been able to see herself in a mirror. Maybe others couldn't. Her blonde hair was matted and dirty, no doubt from the fight. Her eyes were intense, like a wild animal's. Even her lips were different from when she'd been human, fuller, pinker, lovely.

Except everything beautiful and delicate about you hides a monster.

A monster that tears people's hearts out.

Standing there, she let that thought soak in, settling over the disgust she felt at the sight of herself. There was blood on her cheek, more on her dark jeans. She even spotted drops on her boots. With one more glance at the room, she walked out, shutting the door quietly before continuing back the way she had come through the house.

The pain in her throat grew. She broke into a run, bursting back out of the door she'd just come through. Her steps grew faster and faster until she was sprinting through the maze of towering shrubs. She brushed at tears that had no place in this harsh black and gray world she now lived in. Lethargy she always associated with the rising of the sun crippled her crazy dash, but she resisted the need for sleep.

Instead she wanted blood. The elemental, horrifying thirst was a reminder that she wasn't human. She wasn't a dancer. She wasn't Bobby's friend, or Tool and Masters' lead dancer. She wasn't a woman who could flirt with a sexy Lykae. She wasn't Faolan's protector.

She was something that should disgust them.

She was a Vampire.

She hunted through the rubble on one side of the crypt for what she needed. Her thoughts tore her up inside. But they also reminded her exactly why she kept away from people. *Can't care for someone. They die. Or they're taken away. Or they leave.*

Two rabbits bounded out of hiding. She caught one and

bit it on the neck. Drinking deeply from its rich, wild blood she stopped before she drained it. Captured the other when it broke for the bush to her left. This one she also set down, a little wobbly but still alive. It stared at her, its whiskers twitching, its odd, pink eyes wide, trying to decide if it should run, or examine her in horror.

Elsa made it easy. She crumpled to the ground. Fur, blood, and tears smeared a horrible mess on her face, she was certain, but she didn't care. It was hard enough trying to breathe past the sobs. She pressed her forehead to her knees and gripped the grass, tearing out sections of it.

I'm a monster. I've just bitten a bunny and wanted more. She choked back the sobs, but more followed.

"Oh, hell, this is *not* good."

She screamed, or half did, and scrambled back against the wall of the crypt, blinking to try to clear her eyes. All she managed to see was a man dressed like so many others in jeans and a hoodie, hands up as though to ease her or ward her off attacking him.

"Easy, easy, don't do that flying through me again. I'm Bryson."

"Go away!" Horrified, she covered her face. *Can't people just leave me alone?* He didn't leave. Tears, hot and fast, kept falling no matter that she now had an audience.

All the loneliness, the fear, the complete terror at times, the pretending she was fine, when really, truly she wasn't, simply burst free. It all just broke through the wall she'd built. The entire thing collapsed and wouldn't go back up.

"You know, I have to say, you surprise me. *This* surprises me, but that's only because, maybe, it should have happened long before now."

"How do...you know it...hasn't?" she sobbed. "I might do...this every single day... for all you fucking...know!"

"All right, okay, so maybe that's the case."

"Go *away!*"

"I don't think you should be alone right now. It sucks, but there you go. I'm staying at least until you go inside, away from the sun."

"Oh my fucking God! Will you...people just...stop? Just go...away. If I live or die... What is...it to you? I don't... even...*know* you!"

"Well, that's because you ran from me last night. I assure you, I am a gentleman. Certainly not willing to stand by and let a woman commit suicide because she's had a bad night."

"A...bad...night?" She squinted at him through the tears.

"Here, take this." He fluttered something against her arm. She went to swat at it and him, but ended up taking the handkerchief.

"Do you want to talk about it? Before he gets here? He went to town first. Shocking, I know, since he hasn't left your side, even when you hid away so well. But I can only assume he and the boy might want more than rabbit for dinner."

"Go away. All of you...can just fucking *go away*."

A sigh met her snarl and would have made her feel bad except she already felt bad.

"It's just me. After you had Aidan crash and burn, he left, and, well, Jaxon is...always up for a laugh, but he went home with Joey. So, it's just me."

She sniffed and wiped at more tears. She also drew her knees up and rested her forehead on them, refusing to meet his penetrating gaze. After several uncomfortable minutes of sitting there, knowing he was watching her, she finally asked, "What do you want?"

"I thought maybe you might need something, a handkerchief, shoulder to cry on, something like that."

"I just need to be left alone."

"Sadly that's not going to happen. It's the way of these things, encounters with someone that lead to another and another. You could go to ground, or, I suppose, let the sun kill you, but then what of the boy? And the wolf? If you go to ground, he'd probably dig you up. He nearly did last night."

120

"I heard him, he was just showing off he'd found me." She wiped her eyes and blew her nose on the handkerchief. "I'll keep this."

"Of course."

Bryson. The dry, crisp English accented reply finally got her to glance at him.

He was as big as she remembered. He'd settled down across from her, legs crossed at his ankles like he had all the time in the world. The black hoodie and jeans made it appear he'd just gotten done at the gym. He even had running shoes on.

"It will be dawn soon."

"I know," she snapped.

He tipped his head back and studied the sky. It was lightening up, but that bluish color that meant there was an hour until the sun broke above the horizon. "Can you stay alert past dawn?"

"I really don't want to discuss it."

"It?" He lowered his gaze to hers. "Ah, I see. Your abilities. Well, one thing is for certain, you are full of surprises. Have you killed before tonight?"

Astonished, she gaped at him, probably like a fish. She snapped her mouth shut, then immediately yelled at him. "You were there! Why didn't you *help*?"

"I was told to watch. Besides, Jamie was there and together you two did well. You didn't need me."

"It would have helped!"

"No doubt."

Again, shocked by his attitude, she considered what he'd said and not said. He didn't say he wouldn't have helped if they'd needed it. Her jaw hurt from where Melinda had scored more than one punch. She could have used some help but… *I survived. Someday I won't. Ten minutes ago I didn't want to.*

"Why were you told to watch?"

"The same as Jamie was, to see what you could do. Since you won't come in, and now won't talk to us even we ask politely, it was the only way. Although, Jamie didn't listen very well, did he?"

She didn't answer that, since she now had more to think about. Jamie was told to watch her. Not help her? Protect her? He seemed to think that was his mission—keeping her by his side, and safe.

I'm better on my own. Jamie wants things…I want. Not letting that happen. I need to move. And Faolan? What about him? "Do you know who the boy is?"

"No. Should I?"

She shook her head, avoiding his gaze. In the surreal world she lived in, this was the most bizarre situation so far. Bryson was anything but a sophisticated and sympathetic shoulder to cry on. He reminded her of a rugby player. One of those big, brawny men you hated to catch the ball if he were on the opposite team. He knew he was badass, because, well, he was.

Just like Jamie.

The thought of Jamie confused her and exhausted her. Jamie would show her things, she was certain she'd be addicted to from the first touch. But then what? He'd leave. It was there, in his gaze, the powerful lone wolf who never settled down.

"I'm tired."

Bryson nodded as if that made sense. "Go to sleep."

It wasn't that simple. He knew that, she could tell by the way he watched her, almost as if he were challenging her. He didn't care. That's why he didn't step in and help. He didn't care now either.

Does anyone?

"I assumed you'd picked this spot for the location." He patted the crypt behind him and smiled. "Prime property for a Vampire."

The statement, said in such crisp, polite terms, ignited a temper she didn't bother keeping contained. Bryson was ancient. If he wanted to end her life, or whatever this was, there wasn't much she could do. She imagined if he wanted, she'd even now be gone without even knowing he'd moved.

It pissed her off. Everything about her life now pissed her off.

"Fuck you, Bryson!" She shot to her feet and threw her arms out in an aggravation she couldn't contain. "I'm tired of sleeping in crypts with musty old dead people. I'm tired of drinking from…defenseless bunny…rabbits and… people who have no clue I've touched them!" She paused, but shoved her finger under his nose. "I'm tired of missing out on sunshine and iced tea and shopping with friends and…dancing. I'm tired of being on the run. I'm tired of all you people always showing up, just dropping in like I want to be examined by someone *else*, or introduced or evaluated to see if I can do *something* for *someone* I don't know and don't want to know! I don't want to do anything for anyone!"

She spun away from him, unable to stand the way he nodded as if it all made sense and she wasn't screaming at him.

"I just want to wake up each morning, not each *night*. I want to go the dance studio, and work hard, and bust my butt to be the best ballet dancer in the history of dance. Not… Not…" She spluttered to a halt not sure how to encapsulate all the misery. She had been a dancer with a life ahead of her. Then with one bite from a feral Vampire, she was this. "A monster who rips hearts out and sucks blood from…defenseless *bunnies*!"

By the time she was done, she was exhausted. Breathless and shocked, she stood, trying to catch her breath.

Bryson didn't say a word. She finally got the courage to peek at him and he was examining something on his palm. He finally sighed gustily and motioned for her to sit.

"Well, I hope you feel better."

She slid down the wall opposite him and drew her knees up to her chest, hugging them as she took stock. Actually she did feel better, in a sad, 'now I've said it and nothing

123

changed' way.

"Not really, but I guess."

"You don't have to actually sleep *inside* the crypt or a coffin. Anywhere the sun doesn't hit is the same."

"I know that."

"Ah, good then."

"You're English?"

"I'm older than England."

That was kind of sad. "Will you be here in the morning, I mean, at nightfall?"

"Oh Lord no. Jamie won't like that I was here to start with. But I will lessen the impact by not hanging around, after the two of us have a few words."

She frowned. "Don't hurt Faolan."

"I wouldn't dream of it. No worries for Jamie?"

"No."

Bryson quirked a black eyebrow. "He's that good, is he?"

"I don't know, but I don't think you're here to bash his head in."

"No, I suppose that wouldn't be a good thing to do. Have you met a witch named Circerran, sometimes called Trouble?"

She shook her head. "I've heard, though. Why? Please don't say she's on her way to this party because I am leaving when I rise. I want my old life back. Alone is better."

"Ah, I see. Well, if I were to give advice, I'd suggest you stay with the wolf, at least for now. It does seem as if you and Faolan have drawn some nasty attention. Wouldn't it be better to be prepared, in case next time you come up against something much more powerful than a few rag tag kidnappers?"

"Is that what they were?"

He shrugged and got up, groaning when he did. "I'm getting too old to sit on the cold ground." He offered her a hand and helped her up. "Whatever they were, you were their target, you and the boy. I suggest you think of the boy instead of turning away offers of help. Jamie is good, but he can only see what he's told. You might have to search outside of those parameters, Elsa. You are much more than a wolf."

"You're joking. I'm not a wolf...am I?"

"You're a Vampire. Now. If you are a wolf, ask yourself or, better, ask Jamie this — Why don't you know? Or, better, who were your parents, and where are they now?"

Stunned, she could only nod, too overwhelmed to think straight. "But I don't feel like a wolf."

"What does a wolf feel like, Elsa?"

"Not like me." She turned away, then stopped and turned back to face the tall Vampire. "I'd know if I was bitten by a wolf."

"You weren't bitten by a wolf. That kind of change," Bryson paused and studied the ground. "Not many survive that kind of bite. Only a few survive the Vampire, but the wolf bite is rumored to be excruciating."

That sank in slowly. Her bite had been agony like multiplied by millions. She shuddered at the memory. *Worse than that?*

"You were born a wolf, Elsa. At least that's what I believe."

"Which means I have parents who were also...Lykae?"

"Yes. At least one."

She hadn't known her parents. She had a vague memory of a woman. But it was more a dream now, rather than an actual image of a beautiful woman with blonde hair the color of the sun.

"Thank you. I'm sorry I...lost it, but thank you for listening."

He bowed at the waist, hand over his heart. "It was my pleasure. Go, the sun will rise in a few minutes. Best not to prove Jamie's opinion that you need looking after, am I right?"

She scoffed at that, but left him and went inside the darkness of the crypt, took the lid off the last sarcophagus in the long row and climbed in. Before she rearranged the lid back in place, she used the last of her energy to call her pillow. Head on that, she ignored her bedmate, a boney creature dressed in rags, and closed the lid, falling asleep almost before it settled.

Chapter Nine

"Stay there," Jamie ordered the boy.

Faolan nodded and crouched. It was his typical answer to the word 'stay'. It bothered Jamie, but for now he didn't correct the kid. He had said 'stay'.

"We have a guest."

Faolan nodded. "A Vampire."

"Yes. Bryson." Jamie watched as the Vampire stalked toward them as if he owned the house. It was daylight, just past noon. Jamie was surprised the man was up. Bryson kept to the shadows but he didn't seem bothered by the time. "It's a bit late, isn't it?"

"I was thinking early, but it's difficult to discuss such things with a night sleeper."

"A night sleeper?"

Bryson stopped at the table and eyed their supplies, then Jamie. "Well, you don't look like you've gotten much sleep during the night lately. Trying to keeping up with a Vampire, wolf?"

"What do you want?"

Instead of answering, Bryson smiled slightly and turned to the boy. "So, this is *Faolan*."

Faolan perked up to stare at Bryson. Bryson studied him much more intensely than Jamie liked. Faolan didn't seem to mind and examined the Vampire just as closely. If he could read Bryson's mind, he didn't indicate anything. Jamie hoped the boy didn't let on he could, if he could.

"What do you want, Bryson?" he asked *again*.

Bryson held out his hand to the boy, a chocolate bar on his palm. Faolan glanced at him for approval. Jamie gave him a nod. As quick as that, the boy grinned and took the candy. He *had* fed the child.

"How about a beer? I see you have a few."

Jamie tossed Bryson a Früh. The bottle landed perfectly in the Vampire's palm. He nodded, as if Jamie had been gracious. He wasn't. The beer was his favorite and he'd only purchased twelve. He'd wanted Elsa to try them, so he planned on only having one himself until she woke. Then see if she wouldn't drink the rest — perhaps get a little tipsy. Loosen up. Sit on his lap…

"Elsa will like this, its crisp, nice flavor. Always refreshing."

There was nothing to say to that, so Jamie watched Bryson hit the bottle on the edge of the table. The cap flew off. Faolan giggled, impressed. Jamie tossed the boy a 7-Up then opened his own beer. With his teeth. The temperature was still icy cold and the sweet taste was perfect.

"How long will you stay here?"

Jamie set his bottle down and took a seat. "Stay? We won't stay."

"It might not be a bad place. I checked the grounds and surrounding area. It's safe. Everyone has forgotten it exists. It's rumored to be haunted, but I don't sense any spirits. The former owner did kill his wife, though. Oddly enough, a ballerina."

Jamie ignored the talk and focused on what he wanted from Bryson. Answers. "You were there when Dario attacked."

"I was."

"Nice of you to help out."

"I didn't judge you needed any help. Seven mid-range-ability Death Stalkers, one highly trained Lykae. I thought you had it covered."

Bryson wasn't telling him nearly all that was going on. He'd been there. Jamie had only caught his scent *after*, but that meant nothing. Bryson was ancient. Jamie guessed near the same age as the Vampire King himself.

"Here, eat your burger. Then you can eat the candy." He had a vague idea real food should go before junk food. Faolan didn't seem to mind. He carefully wrapped the chocolate up in its foil and pocketed it in his new jacket. As soon as he was done, he opened his burger and started eating. Quickly, too, but that was also something Jamie thought typical of children.

"He's small."

"He's normal-sized," Jamie disagreed even though he thought the same. He'd purchased six burgers, fries, and two salads he thought Elsa might prefer. Grudgingly he sighed and tried to be polite. "Are you hungry?"

Bryson raised his eyebrows. "No, thank you. I appreciate it. Did you ask Elsa why Dario wanted her to come with him?"

"No."

Bryson sipped his beer. His sardonic expression said he wasn't finished. Jamie struggled not to throw the man out. He wasn't a talker. He'd always been a loner. Now he had a boy to care for, a woman who didn't seem to realize she also needed him, and now a visitor. *All in the space of a few days my life has become messy.* Elsa was proving that his worries concerning her were spot on. She was much more than he'd imagined. Harder to resist.

"She is...upset," he confessed.

"Ah, yes." Bryson pulled over an ancient, dust-covered chair, tested it, sat carefully and sighed. "Never know with these things. Yes, she was upset. The memories." Bryson sipped his beer and studied it, then Jamie. "They will return at the next waking. This, along with ripping two hearts out, having you doubt her every move, and running into more immortals in the past two nights than she probably has since turning, might be the cause of her being...*upset.*"

Jamie shifted on his chair. He didn't question her *every* move. She was so damn young. It was hard to believe she knew enough to defend herself. Until she'd ripped two hearts out of two immortals many years older—and stronger — than her.

"Or it could simply be you," Bryson tagged on, after another swallow. "This really is good. I've not had one in years. I think the last time —"

"What do you mean, it could be me?" Jamie set down his beer, ignored his burger and focused on Bryson with the single-mindedness he usually left to his latest target. He couldn't for the life of him think what he'd done that would have upset Elsa. He hadn't yelled at her for not listening to him. He hadn't shaken her and demanded that next time, if there was a next time, she would *never, ever* do such a thing again. He hadn't even forced her to give him real answers instead of her mumbled replies.

"Well..." Bryson sighed the word like a kettle releasing steam. His expression thoughtful, his gaze flickered from him to Faolan. "She'll stay for the boy, of course. Who wouldn't? Faolan, you're in some trouble, aren't you? I think, though, if I'm not mistaken, Jamie will make sure no one snatches you. Elsa, of course, will help, maybe even more than he can, but it's important you always listen to them."

It was sound advice. Possibly laced with some hits to Jamie, but he couldn't understand what those were. Again, he'd not even shouted at the woman. He thought once a day was enough. Plainly, he was within his rights to be more than a bit troubled by her behavior. She could have died. Whatever he'd done wasn't waiting until she rose. Bryson knew. He focused on the Vampire.

"Bryson." At Bryson's quizzical glance, Jamie couldn't control the growl. "Elsa."

"Oh, yes, Elsa and your lack of faith in her. Tell me something, Jamie. Are you certain she'd been on that cross for two nights? That would mean she'd been awake *and* unable to break free in direct view of the sun."

Obviously Alrick had shared his report with Aidan and Bryson. "She was missing when I returned —"

"Yes, Aidan and Alrick have discussed that. I'm asking

are you certain she hung there, in *broad daylight*, for a full day and two nights?"

Jamie fisted his hands. He was too close to this to see straight. *How could she have survived the sun? She couldn't.* "Fuck. She had to have been inside the house during the day."

Bryson shot Faolan a frown. "Was she? Was she inside the house, Faolan?"

Faolan set his burger down, chewing a huge mouthful, but shook his head. As soon as he swallowed enough to speak he said, "She was there one night, the night you saved her, Jamie. They brought her in right before dusk, then you arrived and..."

"Killed them." It felt right. But he was still missing something. *Think. Think. What was there?* Two witches slicing into Elsa. Blood dripping. Silky hair matted and dirty. The scent of her pain—a haze over his ability to think. His wolf snapping to the foe. Then dead witches, Elsa in his arms. There had to be more.

"How long was she on the cross?"

"Not long," Faolan whispered. "They were afraid of her and drained her first off, binding her too, while she slept." Faolan stopped. His eyes were suddenly too big in his small face. The color had leached from him so he was pale, but his eyes had glazed over, his focus on the past, not the present.

"Go on," Bryson urged.

"No, that's enough, Faolan." Jamie squeezed his small shoulder and kept his hand there. The boy shivered but gradually eased his tension.

"That's all," Faolan whispered. "All that happened. I couldn't help her."

"Of course not. You're too young. But you will someday." Jamie closed his eyes and hung his head. He'd thought she'd been there two nights, but she'd only been there one, and had woken, thinking he'd done those things to her and broken away, scared and hurt.

Why didn't I ask Faolan before? Why didn't I ask her before now?

"Jamie's right. You could do nothing. You're a child. But he did, so, now is a chance to do more. Tell us what else you remember. No matter how small. That, my boy, will be helping Elsa." Bryson tipped his beer at Faolan.

Jamie held his tongue and waited.

Faolan frowned fiercely as if he were trying to recall that night. "They were chanting over her. Like they had for the other...other girl. But this was different. It was like they had to hurry. Like someone else was coming, not you, someone who wanted her... For himself."

"Who? Did you see anyone else there? Before Elsa? On another night?" Jamie asked. It could have been Balrick... but he was imprisoned now.

Faolan nodded.

"Who, Faolan? Who did you see?"

"A...a man. A *Vampire*."

"A wolf and a Vamp?" he asked.

Faolan shook his head. "No, a Vampire. He always came and took the women, or he...did what he did to the other girl."

Stunned, Jamie shared a frown with Bryson.

"You're too close to see properly, Jamie. You need all the facts, you know that."

"Alrick isn't giving me all the *facts*." He kept the snarl out of his tone, barely. "Was it Black?"

A firm shake of his small head. "No."

"But you knew Black?" Jamie urged.

"Yes, he came often, but he served Samuel."

"Samuel?" Bryson repeated, lowering his beer.

"You know him?" Jamie asked.

"I have heard of a Vampire named Samuel, but he's been rumored to have fallen when we buried the House in Seattle."

Jamie nodded. "I was there. Nice touch, the park."

"It was Jaxon's idea," Bryson said dismissing it. "This other Vampire, he was tall? Elegantly dressed?"

Faolan fidgeted. "I didn't look at him. He scared me."

"Why? Did he hurt you?" Jamie asked, touching the boy's head.

"No. He hurt the girls, though, and left with them."

"Or killed them?" Bryson asked, again almost sharply.

Faolan nodded but there was a worried expression in his eyes. "Does he want Elsa?"

"He might, but he's not getting her," Jamie assured him. "Eat your burger. You're safe now. Elsa is safe now."

The boy nodded but picked at his food. Jamie focused on the issues.

"I studied the site," Bryson said. "That kind of ritual was done long ago. Some believed it could actually turn a Vampire back to human."

Stunned Jamie could only stare at Bryson. Elsa was beautiful—a Vampire, true, but that was part of who she was now. "Can it?"

"No. It also can't force...other, let's say, *latent* abilities forward. Not that she's lacking in those. It's fascinating what she can do because no one told her she can't."

"What do you mean?" Jamie took a large swallow of the beer. She was hurting. He hadn't needed Bryson to rub his nose in it. He could feel her unhappiness. It made him anxious. He wanted to check on her. But she was in a crypt, sleeping with a damn dead person.

He couldn't bear it. There was no reason for it. She'd walked through the house. She *knew* there were places to hide here, away from the sun. Part of him thought she'd gone to the crypt to reinforce that she was a Vampire, much as she spoke of *drinking* blood.

"She's done amazingly well. Ten years ago she was bitten and *survived*. A change is difficult." Bryson stared boldly at Jamie as if to challenge him that it wasn't. Jamie knew better. "She had to have suffered immeasurable pain. Alone, which seems to be the case, is...unheard of. Or isn't typical, shall I say? But clearly she survived, even without her maker."

"Isn't that good? Can't a Vampire control someone he bites?"

Bryson's light eyes flickered from gray to a darker shade of hazel. He didn't like Jamie prying. *Too the fuck bad.*

"Bryson."

"Yes." He sighed, but when Jamie eased his fists, murmured, "But also no."

"Explain," Jamie bit out between grinding his teeth. This was Elsa. He needed to know how to care for her. He gave an internal head shake. *Protect her.* The compassion in her eyes as she tended to his wounds. What would that be like, to have a woman... *care? Her, care about me?*

"It's not good because the change is *beyond* painful. It would have felt like her skin was being burned from the inside out. As if she'd been tossed in a fire and left there. Nothing would have alleviated the pain, *nothing*. Most go mad and that is one reason it's forbidden. They become feral, biting anything and anyone."

Jamie's heart clenched. He knew what Bryson meant, easily recalled—

"Elsa is the sanest person I've had the pleasure to speak with in some time, though." Bryson's expression turned amused. "She doesn't hold back her temper, though, does she?"

Jamie had just begun to relax again. He froze with his bottle halfway to his lips. The fondness, the warmth in Bryson's tone caused a growl to simmer in his chest, waiting to burst free. Carefully, he set down the bottle before he broke it in his fist. The Vampire was interested in Elsa? *Over my dead body.*

"What do you mean?"

"Oh, I'm sure you'll discover soon enough." He chuckled. "Enough said that she might appear at ease with her new existence, but if you scratch that surface, you're going to find out exactly why she has spent the last ten years alone." A laugh. Clearly impressed with Elsa.

Jamie's claws pierced his palms. His wolf snapped his

teeth.

"Odd, isn't it?" Bryson murmured, as if he wasn't the slightest bit aware that Jamie wanted to rip his head off. "If you think about it, she's had *offers*." He sipped his beer, frowning at the fire. "She's obviously run into both friendly and not so friendly immortals over those past ten years, but never once chosen to hook up with anyone." Another leisurely sip. "I'd have thought she would join something, at the least to be part of it, rather than be alone. I suppose the human tour was that, in a way. A show that allowed her to be a part of something she once knew. Odd that it wasn't traditional ballet, but rather something most in that world loathe. I mean, rock ballet?" Bryson laughed. "Stunning, absolutely stunning."

"She wants to be human," Faolan suddenly whispered.

Jamie swallowed the rage. The unfamiliar but dangerous jealousy riding him demanded that he rip Bryson's head off. Throw it at her feet and demand his reward—her. In his bed. Under him.

"I think," Faolan added, casting him a worried frown.

Jamie dug down, finding a place where he could calm his shit. The Vampire wasn't going to touch a hair on her head. *Breathe in. Breathe out. Breathe in. Breathe out. Don't kill the Vampire. He will never touch her. Never.*

"No. I don't think so, Faolan. I think she knows exactly what she is. A Vampire, and in her mind that means a monster." Bryson shrugged.

"She is wolf, like me," Faolan said, coming to Elsa's defense.

Bryson nodded. "True. She is like you. Strong." Turning to Jamie, the Vampire canted his head. "So, you're going to clean this place up? Move her so she wakes in a bed, rather than a coffin with some dead guy?"

Instead of snapping the man's neck for interfering, he shrugged.

"This place could be good if you cleaned it up a little, got some new sheets, aired out the bedrooms."

Jamie shook his head. "It's not far enough from where the attack—"

"There are no others after you. Those were already being watched, and were nearby. My guess is whoever called them sent them directly from the witch's house. It was easy to follow you from there, to where they found you."

"Then they can find us here."

"No, I set up a few blocks. It's safe enough. For now."

Jamie considered it. The place was defensible. With a few hours of hard work, he could have a room ready for her, a bathroom working and the kitchen cleaned. "Perhaps. But if they were sent, who sent them? Balrick is...tied up."

"He wasn't the only one out to change the world, Jamie. There is more insanity out there than there is reality. I'd give my left nut for a break from it all, but that's not happening any time soon. So suck it up, stay here. Circerran is on her way, or already at the witch's house. She'll come here after that. Perhaps she can reinforce this old place and make it secure for longer than what, a day, or two? Elsa's moved enough. Time for her to learn that running won't change that she's now part of our world."

Jamie laughed.

"What? You don't think my wisdom spot on?"

"I think"—Jamie paused to toss the Vampire another beer—"your wisdom sucks. I think Elsa is going to wake and hit the road as quick as she can." Not that he was allowing that.

Bryson nodded. "Of course. But that's your problem, not mine."

"It's not my problem," Jamie assured him. If Circerran could cast a few defensive spells, this place could be perfect. They could find out what was going on, live here, feel secure that nothing could get through... A plan took form.

Bryson tipped his beer at him and winked. "That, is where you're wrong. But I'll leave you to figure that one out. Thanks for the beers. Faolan, give some thought to letting Circerran take you and drop you off with Alrick, or perhaps Derrick and Samantha. Their boy is near your age. You two could do well together. But either way, the pack is probably where you're going to be the safest, especially when this pup gets an education."

Bryson laughed again, and with that, walked out, taking his beer with him.

Jamie studied Faolan, the room, and what Bryson had said. "Derrick is a good friend of mine. He does have a son. His mate is a good woman. They could watch you for a while, until we discover what is after you."

"I want to stay with you."

"Then you stay with me. For now." He stood and surveyed the house. "Let's see about getting this place cleaned up. Surprise Elsa with a real bed, instead of that crypt."

The Vampire thought Elsa was going to school him? The thought made Jamie smile. He was more than up for the challenge. As long as the Vampire realized no one else was going to hook up with her — ever.

Ever?

At least until I've had my fill.

The thought didn't soothe him. It caused the rush of rage and jealousy to bubble up like a too-spicy taco after no food for a week. But it was more at the idea of leaving her, ever, than letting someone else touch her. His wolf? Perhaps.

Chapter Ten

Elsa woke and everything wasn't as it should be. She surged to her feet, hands out and legs bunched, ready to get her the hell out of Dodge.

"Easy. I moved you. The coffin seemed to be overdoing it."

Jamie.

Jamie—memories flooded her brain, knocking her backwards. She gripped her head, trying to make sense of them all. Night-time. She'd woken, in pain. This had been the man holding her in his arms, close to his chest. She'd attacked, knocking him down. The smoke, the wind on her face, filled with the stench of blood and death and evil, along with pain from every pore had spurred her into action.

Another memory surged up and swallowed her, making her grip her head harder. The witches, their bodies still fresh with death. A scent of something else, a man on the wind... A man she knew. A man she hated.

"Settle down, you're safe."

She shook her head and forced the horror of painful memories back where they belonged.

Jamie. He'd saved her life—but she'd run from him because... *I thought he was Nolan.* In the dark, through the pain, she'd thought Nolan had come back from the dead. She'd run so fast she'd thought, just run, until she'd collapsed under a tree and passed out from lack of blood and her injuries. Her feet had been shredded, cut and bruised from the mountains and the rocks slicing them open. She'd hit her head, smacking it on a low tree branch when she'd leaped over a chasm.

"You're remembering?"

"I remember." She took a deep breath then another. "You saved me. I ran. I have no memory of how they got hold of me. I was in a room. I was safe. I didn't go to my hotel room. I was worried. I sensed someone drawing close so I found a new location. I was secure. I always have a spell to guard my sleep. I was safe."

"You weren't safe. Alone, you're *never* safe."

She glared at him for that. He was alone. "Where is your *pack*, then? Why are *you* alone?"

"I work better alone."

"So do I."

He tossed his dark hair out of his eyes and smirked. "Come down from the bed and maybe I'll buy that."

The fact that he had to tell her she was standing, fully clothed, on a bed, wasn't cool. Neither was standing on the bed in the first place. She walked to the edge and dropped to a sitting position. As she did, the room came into focus.

He'd cleaned. Even the sheets were new, not musty. She studied the floor, the walls, even the curtains. Everything was put to rights and smelled lemony. Yellow candles were set evenly around the room. The wooden furniture had been polished until it gleamed. Even the floors had been swept.

It didn't matter.

"I'm leaving. I'm better alone. I've always been — "

"Always is a long time." He walked over from where he'd been casually leaning on the wall, giving her distance, she could see, to deal with her memories, or so she didn't attack him again. *Why didn't I remember last night, when I slept with the mice?*

Doesn't matter. Nothing but leaving matters now.

"You're cool with being alone?" she asked instead of leaving.

He nodded, barely.

"Then don't shove that I like the same at me like it's

something bad."

"You're new to this world. You're either going to get snatched, or killed. You're going to have to accept that, and find safety within a group."

"I think you're wrong. I'm safer alone."

He sighed and suddenly got way, way too close. Right up against her. The bed was high so he was at eye level. It was interesting to face him at his level. Even more intriguing was the way her heart raced and her breath caught. *Am I falling for this arrogant wolf?*

"You agreed to see about helping me find who is after Faolan. Has that bargain changed because of one little attack?"

She searched his face, but he stared at her stonily. Little? She'd nearly been gutted. She'd killed. He'd killed.

"Where is Faolan?"

"Sleeping."

"Really?" She glanced at the windows, and realized Jamie must have found all the usable curtains and hung them up in here. Before he moved her, she assumed. She met his eyes again. He'd been watching her. It sent a thrill tingling along her spine. And lower.

"You're hungry. Didn't you drink?"

"That's not your business." It came out as a whisper because he lifted a hand and touched his long fingers to her jaw, tipping her head ever so gently. He smelled like pine, the sharp, fresh scent mingled with his warmth making her ache for something.

"You have a bruise still."

That required nothing from her, and she was grateful, because this close to him there were other things she began to notice. Things she'd noticed from the first but hadn't allowed her cognizant self to really, truly study. Now there was nothing stopping her. Jamie's hair was lighter than brown, more a sunburned chestnut. He wore it short, except in the front where it fell forward into his eyes. Her attention fell to his neck. His pulse beat strongly. *Of course.*

Everything about him was muscular. He was tall and lean, but packed and stacked. His feet were probably even strong. She knew his hands were...*but not with me.*

She noticed a dark line of a tattoo peeking at her from over his shoulder, coming up along his collarbone. The urge to see more of it was nearly overwhelming. Nearly as bad as the draw of his lips or neck, or pectorals, or...what he had beneath his broken-in jeans. *Would he be big? Long and thick, or short but wide all the way to the tip? Would I like the feel of him, sliding inside my body? Or would it be painful? Disappointing?*

"Elsa?"

"Mmm?"

He also smelled good. Clean, sharp, piney but...also musky, like a man. *Would he taste as wonderful as he smells?*

She got lightheaded just thinking about that.

He leaned one arm on the bedpost above his head. She bit her lip. *Not going to swoon over him.* But *Lordy,* he was...hot.

His veins rose along the curves and bulges of that arm, tempting her. She licked her bottom lip, already imagining the feel of his pulse. But it wasn't his blood she wanted — it was his taste in her mouth. *The salty essence of Jamie.* Such a controlled, confident man, what happened when that broke? When he was lost to a woman's touch? To her mouth and hands doing things she'd only dreamed of doing?

Can I even do those things to him?

"Elsa?"

She jerked her attention to his face. He was frowning. *Has he said my name more than once?*

"What?"

"I asked you if it hurt."

She blinked. His eyes were golden. *Lighter tonight?* "Does what hurt?"

"Your bruise." He leaned closer, forcing her to clench her fingers on the edge of the mattress. His hair fell in his left eye. She focused on that, noticing how it shimmered in the glow of candles he'd put by the bed. *Not touching it. Not pressing it back from his forehead.*

"No."

"Are you certain?" The deep timbre of his voice sent a shiver downward in a way that really was hot. All she could do was nod. His eyes flashed lighter. *Why does that make me giddy?* "Good. I was worried it might be broken."

Worried. Concerned for me and being nice…

"But you're tougher than you look," he added.

Is he going to kiss me? Yes! No! Oh, hell, I don't know.

He should decide because *I* can't. All he had to do was step an inch closer. Instead he stood there, searching her expression, until suddenly he did it. His lips softened, lifted and he smiled at her.

The impact dazzled. If he was handsome with his brooding, always serious demeanor, his smile was breathtaking. Perfect white teeth, a dimple in his cheek, eyes flashing with pleasure… *God help me, I want to kiss him.*

"Good, come on. We're going to have company."

She blinked. Her brain circled around the words, making sense slowly.

No kissing? "What?"

If Jamie had to guess, Elsa wanted something a lot more than he could give her right now.

Break furniture. He smiled, unable to stop himself. *She wants* sex. Sex until they were exhausted? Until he couldn't move… *Have I ever had sex like that?*

"We have company?" Her bemused expression made his grin grow. With it, her blush deepened. *What I'd give to know what she's thinking…*

"Well, we have to start searching for clues, remember?" And he was already starting. She was a puzzle. He'd once liked those. Tracking was a giant riddle. Elsa was proving impossible to understand, which intrigued him. *When was the last time I even cared enough about anyone to try and figure them out?*

His body was demanding sex. He'd come in here to check

on her — since it was time for her to wake. But he'd wanted to see if that teasing, hot woman would rise to the surface and rock his world too. His cock had anticipated action, even though he'd known no such thing would happen. Not with a witch on her way. Now it throbbed, wanting to know what the hell happened to that plan.

"Clues. Right." She appeared dazed.

Can't kiss her. Can't touch her. If I do... He fisted his hands, careful to appear relaxed otherwise. *Don't scare her.* He'd taken one look at her sleeping on the bed and known he'd wasn't going to chance touching her yet. He wanted her too badly. Needed things from her too desperately to be able to control his reaction. If she'd so much as indicated that she wanted sex, with a touch, a whisper, he'd have pinned her.

Not yet. No rushing her.

"Yeah, we need to head back to the witch's house, see what we missed. Alrick has Circerran and her mate, Jack, coming over to meet us."

She nodded, tucked her hair behind her ear then nodded again. "Okay. I'm ready."

Liar. She wanted him. He hoped. But even if she did, he wasn't certain she wanted what he want. *I can seduce her, slowly, into wanting what I want.*

The thought didn't sit well.

"Here." He helped her down, got a puzzled glance from her for it, and again experienced that shock when their hands touched.

She pulled away and straightened her long, blonde hair. A whiff of her floral-spiked scent carried to him. His erection swelled, his balls hardened and drew up, clearly ready for her. *I want to fuck her until she screams in pleasure. At the same time I want to hold her close and stroke her hair.* He shook his head. *She confuses me.* "Let's go. Circerran's a handful, but you'll be fine. Her bark is about as bad as her bite, but she'll calm it with you." Or he'd set her straight. The thought didn't even alarm him. Instead, as he thought it, he recognized it as the truth. Circerran might be the toughest witch of her world, but he wasn't allowing her to frighten Elsa.

Elsa nodded, still nervously playing with her hair.

"But first, I wanted to show you something." He didn't wait, but guided her down the hall and over to the ballet studio he'd been cleaning and repairing for the better part of the day. It still needed work, but he thought she would like what he'd done. "We can stay here, wait for a while, trying to figure out what's going on. While we do, I thought you'd like to…" He paused, unsure suddenly what he'd been thinking. What if she thought the studio was a stupid idea? All of a sudden it seemed that way to him.

Elsa caught his arm. He'd reached up to push the door open and paused, frozen there like a pussy. "What is it? Did you…?" She pushed open the door and gasped, turning to him in shocked pleasure. A rush of relief lasted only as long as a second because she cried out and hugged him quickly like she did Faolan, then released him to kick her boots off and walk around the room.

"It's amazing, Jamie. So amazing." She turned a circle and smiled at him. "Did you do this for me?"

"I thought you'd like to, you know, dance again." He watched her straighten her spine and posture, suddenly reminding him of all those ballet dancers he'd seen, but never really focused on. Ballet wasn't his thing. But Elsa, turning a circle, with her arms in a bow around her waist caught his breath. She went on tiptoe and lifted her leg up at an angle, spinning again with a laugh. "The floor is still broken, but I can help you."

"I can fix it. I found this as—"

"Shoes! Jamie, no boots on the floor."

He froze, one foot beyond the door. She scowled, pointing at his feet. He raised his eyebrows but kicked his boots off and walked over on his socks to where he'd found an old record player. "This. I found this."

She followed him and laughed happily. "Oh my. That is older than you, huh?"

"Watch it," he grumbled but it was a good grumble. "Here, see this?" He opened a hidden cabinet and she went to her knees in front of all the albums. "Think there's something in there you like?"

"I never wanted to dance ballet again. Not after," she whispered, but reached back and caught his hand. "Thank you. I think I can find something."

He didn't know what to say, so he waited. She released his hand, much to his disappointment, and picked out one record, placed it on the ancient spindle and set down the needle. Soft, soothing music filled the room, carrying perfectly. "It's an amazing sound, isn't it?"

"It's well built." He helped her up. "Show me something."

"Show you something? Like, a dance?" she asked in a disbelieving tone.

"Yeah, like a dance."

"You watched the show."

"Not live."

"You're impossible. I can't just dance ballet...now."

"Why not? Show me something, I don't know, one dance."

"From this?"

"Yes." At his simple response she flashed a smile then shooed him away to the other side of the room.

"Okay. Let me see..." She tilted her head and stared at him through the mirrors, but he could see her body beginning to take on the delicate poise on the posters. She looked like a ballet dancer, but in an oversized sweater that hung off one slim shoulder, and a pair of black pants. As he watched, she took a position with her hands at her sides in a circle, and her head held tipped up and straight ahead. With the music flowing louder, cresting, she began to move. Slowly at first, doing circles around the room, each one faster until with the music she flowed into a sudden leap and landed gracefully into another dip and sway, followed by more precise, flowing movements along the floor until with the last note she stopped, head bowed, arms at her sides again in a circle.

She was magnificent. He couldn't find the words. Couldn't think. Or breathe. If he'd wanted her before, now he ached to hold her. The music had been haunting, her dance sad and sweet. Her expressive face had been remote and tinged with sadness. When she finally lifted her face, breathless still, he was rocked by the sorrow etched on her beautiful features. He swallowed, unsure what to say to ease her.

"Elsa—"

"Jamie! Where the hell are you?" Jack bellowed up from downstairs. Elsa spooked, dropped her fangs and took up a position of defense. He quickly went to her and caught her hand to hold her still. Gods, she was lovely. Her eyes darkened when she was alarmed. Now they glowed, shifting from dark to light.

"That's Jack. It's okay." Not sure what else to say, he rested a hand on her lower back. "Your dance was beautiful, Elsa." She didn't respond, still breathless and he sensed, still hurting. "They can wait. Are you all right?"

"I'm fine. I need my boots." She walked away, pulling her boots on without a single glance in his direction. When he had his boots on and she was near him, he tipped her head up. Her eyes shimmered with unshed tears. "What is it? I don't want you—"

"It's nothing you would understand. Let's go, your friends, right?"

"Jamie!" Another bellow from Jack.

He didn't like it, but he guided her out of the room and urged her forward. She went, surprisingly subdued. He wouldn't understand? What wouldn't he understand?

"Well, you two took your time," Circerran muttered as soon as they walked into the main room. Jack stood from where he'd been sitting on the edge of the table. Circerran tossed her red hair over her shoulder and zeroed her green eyes in on him. She slid them to Elsa and pinned her with the same intense regard.

If Elsa was bothered by it, she didn't show it. His opinion of her went up. In his experience with the witch, she didn't

146

hold back saying whatever popped into her head. Neither did she temper her power. It radiated from her like a low buzz on the air. Elsa had to feel it, but she waited, silent, by his side.

"We weren't expecting you so soon." He guided Elsa to the table. She went forward, but there was reluctance.

"Bryson suggested we hurry before someone else decided to test your mettle." Circerran picked up a bottle of his beer, read the label and handed it to Jack. "You did pretty well, though, huh? Man, I wish I had seen you knock Aidan on his—"

"Cir," Jack murmured and pulled her up against him from behind.

Jamie blinked. The witch let him, even placed her hands over Jack's and rested back against him, briefly. They must have been gifted with mind speech because she moved away a second later with a laugh. "Just as long as you keep your fangs down, I think we'll be fine, you and I, Elsa."

Before Elsa could respond, Jack walked over. "Elsa, I'm Jack, and this is my wife Circerran. We're here to help out." Jack held out his hand—like a human man would—and, after a pause, Elsa shook it lightly. "I'm glad to meet you. I was only recently bitten and can tell you how impressed I am that you survived one at what? Twenty?"

"Something like that," she said in a subdued tone, then seemed to come to herself. "What exactly *are* you?"

Jack grinned, and the tough guy slipped, showing a warmer side to the ex-military. "I wonder that myself sometimes. We're still trying to figure it out, but I sense you're doing the same."

"Not really. I'm a just a Vampire."

Circerran laughed. "Good one. Right, so, you're *not just a Vampire*, but we'll drop your denial issues for later. Let's focus on the little episode in the woods, shall we? The first one," she tagged on when Elsa opened her mouth. "The hanging by cross one."

Elsa shrugged. "Not much to tell. They tried to mess with

me, he came along" — she flicked her hand at him briefly and ended with — "and he got me down. Here I am."

"Oh really?" Circerran walked over, eyes narrowing as she examined Elsa.

Jamie didn't like it. "Yes. It was pretty cut and dry." He put an arm out and pushed Elsa back so he could step forward. *Feels right. Keep her safe.* "Don't circle her."

Circerran's eyes landed on him, studied him, but he tolerated it.

"Jamie, uh, could you not," Elsa pushed at his arm and he pushed back. "Jamie?"

"It's okay, just interested in seeing her up close, but if that's the way it is…" Circerran smiled, not reassuring him in the least. *What am I doing?* Circerran settled next to Jack again, giving them space. He dropped his arm, realizing he was growling low in his throat. *What the hell is wrong with me?* Jack met his eyes and seemed to relax. *Not attacking me for growling at your woman?*

"Oh, man, you have got to let me watch when Alrick — "

"Are you actually here to *help*?" Elsa snapped. "Because so far you've only eaten the last of our takeout, and done something to make Jamie freak out."

Jamie cast her a double-take. He hadn't freaked out. If he had, the place would be destroyed and Jack would be bleeding. Elsa stared anywhere but at him.

"Sorry, sorry, really, it was too hard to resist." Circerran's gaze flickered over him, then on to Elsa. "Really, the chicken was excellent in fact. So, the cross. You don't remember anything?"

"I remember waking up, knocking Jamie out and running."

Jack whistled. Circerran blinked.

"It was more of a left hook out of nowhere than a knock-out," Jamie muttered. "She woke up, *freaked* out," he said pointedly, "and ran. I found her. We talked. Went back to the witches and found — "

"Another Vampire and a note that Jamie thinks means

something about me, but might be that other Vampire."

"Ah, the note. Can I see it?" Circerran sat down.

Jamie walked over and picked it up from the stack of papers he'd been going through.

"And where's this puppy of yours?" Circerran asked.

"Puppy?" Elsa muttered. Louder she said, "His name is Faolan and he's sleeping, since he's had a tough time of it lately."

Jamie thought Elsa kept the 'duh' off but it was there, ringing in the air around them.

"You named him?" Circerran was reading the letter, or doing something to the letter. "Growing attached already? He's probably not even house broken. No worries, you'll probably get him walking on two legs soon enough."

Is Circerran baiting Elsa?

Elsa's eyes flared wide. "Well, you managed, so I assume he can."

Circerran set the note down and leaned back in her chair.

Jamie glanced at Jack, but he was stony-eyed.

When Elsa didn't back down, Circerran lifted her eyebrows. "My, my, protective, are we?"

He wanted to wring Circerran's neck, but realized Elsa wasn't playing. She stared at Circerran with a steady, even gaze. *Like a wolf.*

His chest filled with pride. *Brave little wolf.*

"What did you learn from the note?" he asked, hoping to put an end to the pissing contest. Circerran ignored him. Elsa didn't blink.

He glanced at Jack, but he merely lifted his lips in a half smile.

The two women were like cats with a bowl of cream between them, sizing each other up to decide if they would fight or simply share.

"Circerran. What did you learn from the note?" he repeated.

She gave him a fleeting glace but sighed heavily, tapping the note with her fingers. "Not much. I've never seen

Balrick's handwriting, so I couldn't say if this is his. It could be speaking of Elsa, but it could be the other girl... I'll keep it, and make sure Alrick gets his hands on it. Now." She tapped her fingers once more, then stilled them. "The boy, Faolan. He wasn't kept in that shed full-time. He was only in there for a few hours at a time." Circerran shared a significant glance with Jack, who was silent and frowning. *Mind speaking?*

"How do you know?" Elsa asked, sitting straighter.

"I'm a witch."

Elsa snorted. "Yeah, well, *witch,* if you know so much, tell me, how long was he there on the property?"

Good question. If Faolan had only been there a week or two, perhaps he wasn't hurt too badly.

"A long time." Circerran turned her focus to him. "I'm surprised you missed that, wolf, but given the situation..." She studied him. "Maybe I'm not."

The situation? He was just about to tear into her when Elsa leaned forward.

"Jamie didn't miss anything. He got Faolan to come out, took his chains off." Elsa's eyes flickered lighter. "And he knew Faolan had been there a while."

He did? He shrugged when Circerran lifted a delicate eyebrow again. "It was obvious in how the boy acted," he clarified. "But he's not showing signs of trauma—" Her gaze moved from his, indicating that Faolan had suffered. "He's intelligent and he's eating, sleeping—all normal."

"For now."

"What does that mean?" Elsa demanded.

Circerran waved her hand dismissively. "Not important now—"

"Oh, I think it is."

"We have bigger—"

"You brought it up. Finish it."

He almost felt like the boy, when he and Elsa were going at it. Jack only gave a half smile, when he could tear his gaze off Elsa and Circerran. But when Jamie shook his head, and narrowed his eyes at Circerran, then Jack, the man got the picture. He hoped.

"Ladies, should we focus on one topic at a time?" Jack suggested.

Jamie exhaled, but kept it quiet. It wasn't that he wasn't enjoying the show, he was. Elsa made him proud. But it felt like he'd been dropped on a rollercoaster and was nearing the top of the drop. Only he wasn't certain with Circerran if the tracks were laid right or just fell off abruptly and killed them all.

"The boy is safe for now. Correct?" Jack went on.

"Yes. He's sleeping. We had a busy night, then a day." Jamie motioned for Elsa to lean back and relax. She gave him a flat stare, but reluctantly settled down. He rested his arm on the top of the chair, above her head. Maybe he imagined it, but she seemed to let out a relieved breath and ease closer to him.

"Right," Circerran muttered, then continued, "So we found where they were doing some interesting, shall we say, rituals. Not on that cross. That was there. Don't get me wrong, but beneath the house we found something much worse. Did you sense it?"

"The place stank of evil. Old evil, the kind serial killers dreamed of emulating. I've seen things, but this." Jamie shook his head at the memory of how malevolent the place had felt. "This was right off some horror movie script—if they were allowed to show such things."

Circerran surveyed him and nodded curtly. "It was. No network would be allowed to air what really went on there. No one wants to know such things."

Jack squeezed her shoulder, and after a moment, Circerran glanced at her mate, then to them. There was sadness in her eyes, and weariness. He'd always heard stories about the witch known as Trouble. All of them painted her as a tough, no-holds-barred witch who would skin a wolf as soon as say hello. The head of the Jade Coven wore authority the way Aidan did—with honor. Oh, there was a streak of mischief in her green eyes, no doubt about it, but she was doing well by her people. *And ours.* Aidan had gone to her for help more than once. He could do no less.

As long as she doesn't lay a hand on Elsa.

"The witches weren't running the show, Jamie. Vampires were, but…" Circerran rubbed her chin with her thumb and finally shook her head. "There was more. I fear the more."

"*Him,*" Elsa whispered. She swallowed audibly and brushed her arm against his. "Faolan said there was another man, a master. Maybe he's the one that left such a horrible feel to the place. It was there, even after Jamie killed the witches and burned the house."

"Right, and whoever that is" — Jack pointed to Elsa — "that's who we need to find."

Circerran sat forward and rested her elbows on the table. "All right, I'll take you to the witches' slaughterhouse, but I warn you, it's not a nice place. You two only scratched the surface."

Jamie didn't like it, but stood. *I'm taking Elsa into danger. She should never be in danger. Ever.* "We can't leave Faolan alone."

"No," Elsa said. "We can't take him either."

"I got it covered. He's sleeping, right? So we make sure he stays that way. Simple. Better, I'll make certain he's sleeping somewhere safe."

"What? You're going to move him?" Elsa asked. "He stays with us."

"Of course," Circerran said too quickly. "He stays with you, after. Now he's going to sleep like a babe at my house. Believe me, it's the safest place on Earth."

Elsa took his arm and seemed to want him to decide. Her blue eyes had never been so dark. He brushed her hair off her face. "Only until we return."

She nodded, but turned to the couple. "Only until we return."

"Trust us. No one is touching that boy again." There was a promise in Jack's firm tone. "If they want him, they're going to have to come through us, and that isn't happening."

"No it's not," Elsa muttered so low he was certain he was the only one that heard.

He smoothed a hand down her slim back, trying to reassure her. But even that brief contact helped his heart slow and his muscles relax. She leaned into him, surprising him but pleasing him in ways he couldn't understand.

Chapter Eleven

The dark forest around the witches' home surfaced, making Elsa's stomach roll.

"Here we are. Step out carefully," Circerran murmured behind them.

Jack took the lead, his broad shoulders back as he walked through the gate. Circerran had made the door appear out of thin air. A witch could do amazing things. Circerran, she guessed, could do anything.

Whatever Jack was, it was dangerous. Very, *very* dangerous. He wasn't a Vampire, exactly. But he wasn't a Lykae, either. It was like he was one, then the other, depending on something she didn't understand.

Am I like that? Both?

"Be ready," Jamie whispered at her elbow, and drew her into the clearing with him. She felt nothing, no tingle, no misty sensation, just one minute she was in the mansion's dining room, the next, standing in the grass outside the witches' house. Or, what was left of it.

"Good?" he asked.

She nodded, too worried that if she spoke, he'd hear how scared she was. His gaze was difficult to meet, but she did.

"You're doing fine. Stay next to me."

That was exactly what she was planning.

The place was just as frightening as it had been that first night. Only now she knew something else was buried under the destroyed house. The fire had done its work. The cross was only a blackened stump, the house left to a few stones for the chimney and a couple of pieces of furniture that had somehow escaped the flames. The Vampire's body was gone.

"We buried her closer to town," Circerran said. "She was pretty young. Bitten, not born Vampire."

Just like me.

"The witches, we tossed in a vat of acid," Circerran added.

Elsa ran her forearm over her eyes. *Why did I come here? Oh, right, proving how tough I am... Such a brilliant plan!*

Without having to check in on Jamie, she could feel his attention. She peeked over, and sure enough his gaze was pinned on her. He was dressed in another pair of worn-out black jeans that hugged his powerful thighs, paired up with his gray T-shirt, highlighting his chiseled muscles.

Yes, prove to the Neanderthal how brave I am. My plan was excellent...until we got here.

"They had a perimeter spell. I'm surprised you could break through it, actually, or should I say, I *was*." Circerran clucked her tongue.

Elsa trudged on, not getting Circerran's subtle digs at Jamie. It almost seemed as if the witch believed they were *together.*

"How long has this place been here?" Jack muttered. "Was the house ancient, Jamie?"

"It was old. My guess a few centuries. The mountains shelter it. If you didn't know where it was, you'd never find it. There're no roads, no trails. The ravine to the west is roughly two hundred feet from here and drops down four hundred. The south has that." He pointed to the cliffs Elsa could make out through the dense trees. "A river curves around and covers any other entrance. Along with the spells."

"A fortress." Jack kept walking until they were crunching through the debris of the house.

Circerran stopped inside, near the half tumbled-down chimney. "This is where we go down."

Jamie's muscles bulged as he helped Jack heave aside an enormous wooden door set in the charred flooring. She peeked over Jamie's brawny shoulder and bit her lip.

155

A black hole, steps leading down, and a whole lot of evil was basically a place she really didn't want to go, but for Faolan...

Jamie stood. Irises sparkling amber in the moonlight, he squinted at her. Gauging her fear, no doubt. "Still want to do this?"

Obviously, he thought she was going to chicken out. The stench of evil alone made her want to vomit, but she knew with this man there was only one answer. *If I don't act brave, he'll never believe I am.* "Of course, but if you want to stay up here, I can understand that..."

She thought Jack covered a laugh with a deep cough.

Jamie's frown deepened. "This is dangerous."

"Not right now, but it's gonna be worse below," Circerran warned. "I tried to clean some of it up, but...it's ancient."

"We also wanted to leave it, in case they used this site again," Jack warned. "We've set up a surprise if they do."

"I hope it's a deadly one," Elsa whispered.

"Oh, sweet feet, it is. Believe me I only *do* deadly with scum like this. Come on, it's better to just get it over with." Circerran went to walk down the steps but Jack stopped her with a hand on her arm. He murmured something to her, and the witch waited, as he went down first.

Stunned, Elsa glanced at Jamie and saw him dip his head and smile. "It's a man thing, isn't it?" she asked.

"Perhaps." He guided her down after Circerran. The witch was one of the most striking people Elsa had ever met. Red hair like most women only dreamed of possessing, green eyes the color of clover, straight from Ireland, and a body that was both tough and curvy enough to belong to a pin-up calendar girl. Top it all off with the fact that she was obviously deadly and Elsa felt like an afterthought.

What can I do to help these people? Nothing. Jamie alone broke through the spells, killed two witches and got me down, saved Faolan. I ran. Now I almost cry when I dance. What good am I?

"Through here." Circerran touched a dirt wall to the left of some rickety shelves. Elsa spotted jars of pickles and vegetables. The ordinary basement items made this place creepier. Even killers needed to eat, she supposed. She was starting to feel giddy, as if she'd been told moments before opening night on Broadway that she was now dancing the role of Juliet.

Jamie steadied her with a hand on her back. For some reason, it helped more than he'd ever know — because she'd never tell him. But just like in the forest, when she wanted to puke, the anxiety slipped away. Good thing, too, she thought a moment later as another dose of evil staggered her when a new room was revealed. She felt dizzy, but was pressed too close to Jamie to move. He still caught at her arm and steadied her.

"It's bad. This place —" Jamie half-sneezed. "It's..." Another, bigger sneeze.

"Disgusting," Jack supplied.

Jamie took a deep breath and narrowed his eyes. "Exactly. And it was hidden." He glanced up, then along the walls of the cellar. "Barracked by the spells?"

"That's our guess, yes. When you stormed to the rescue you killed the witches. The spells would have started unraveling then, but..." Circerran skimmed her hand along the wall. "These spells were placed here by a coven. That means they wouldn't have disappeared just with you killing two."

As she spoke, Circerran followed Jack inside. Emerald light spilled from Circerran's hands, casting the area in an odd, murky-green tint. Jamie urged her forward, his frown a formidable sign of his growing unease. She could feel his readiness for battle. Even above the evil simmering through the air, Jamie was a solid, powerful force at her back.

Taking courage from that, she stepped over the low threshold. Circerran moved aside, revealing what lay beyond. Elsa's gaze landed on an altar. She'd never seen such a thing in person, but there was nothing else the hip height block of stone could be. It was an enormous chunk of polished, black marble. Only it wasn't pure black. There were other darker stains along the sides and top of it. When she realized why, she couldn't move closer.

"Bloody hell," Jamie swore, glancing at her, then walked closer, leaving her behind.

She was cool with that. He studied the thing, getting closer than she ever wanted to. After a few seconds, he moved to the end. The clank of metal and a spill of light revealed cuffs. She shuddered and felt sicker.

"They bound them and killed them. Gutting them, or decapitating them." His gaze went over the other wall, studied something there she couldn't make out. With a low curse, he walked over and touched something. Gradually, as if he were reading the area the way a blind person would a book, he crouched down, tracing the stones with his hands. Every inch of him rippled with power.

"They abused them, too." He sounded as disgusted as she felt. Standing, he anchored his fists on his hips. "Shit. This is beyond sick. This is…"

"Horrifying," Elsa whispered.

"It is," Jack agreed. Circerran was silent, a pale presence that counterbalanced the evil. Jamie bent and picked something up and his frown deepened.

"Another pendant."

"We found more of those," Jack said.

"They were spelled at one time. They might be what draws him, or at the least warns him that they have something he wants."

"Balrick," Jamie spat the name like a profanity. "He was involved in this shit."

"We heard," Circerran said, her tone tired, but gentle. "When people fall, they fall deeper and deeper."

Jamie shook his head and stood, studying something else on the wall. He was good at this. Nothing seemed to escape him. Jack watched him, clear respect on his face. She thought he might be watching Jamie to learn as well. The thought made her chest feel warm and fuzzy with some kind of crazy emotion.

"I can't believe they hid this from me." Jamie followed a line of dried blood, or worse, on the floor.

"You were busy. Priorities are always safety first. Staying alive is better than digging around in something that might get you killed. What else can you tell us?" Jack asked.

Jamie grunted. It was so obviously a male sound of irritation and disapproval, she peeked over at Circerran. The witch winked, smiling. She was watching Jamie, arms crossed in her black leather jacket, letting Jamie do his thing. "He's good."

Elsa nodded, partially forgiving the woman for calling Faolan a puppy. She could admit, now, it was hilarious.

Jamie reached up and touched a hook. She couldn't for the life of her figure out what that was for, then decided she didn't want to know. They'd abused the people... she thought he meant...sexually. It sickened her. *Like the Vampire. Like they would have me?*

"There is a great deal of *him* here, but something else," he muttered.

"You can recognize his scent now?" Jack asked coming to stand right by Jamie.

Indicating a line of something on the wall to Jack, Jamie watched as the other man leaned in sniffing. "It's taking what you scent and unraveling it. Study it like a puzzle. Pull the scent you want out, each one if you have to, and figure them out. Know them."

"You do this when you track? Alrick told me you're the best tracker he's ever met."

Jamie shrugged that aside as if it was nothing to him. He'd crossed his arms while they spoke. The dark T-shirt pulled on his biceps. *Will his stomach be as hard as his arms?* For some reason, that made her lightheaded. "I like puzzles. Tracking is one big puzzle." The two men went over the wall inch by inch, before moving to the altar again.

"What else do you sense? Something you recognized?" Circerran asked.

Elsa thought Jamie wouldn't respond. He was so deep

into what he was doing, he muttered to himself. Finally, he grimaced and shook his head in frustration. "I'm not certain. It's...something. Whoever was here, at least one of them, I've run into before."

"Not Balrick?" Jack asked.

"No." Jamie shook his head firmly at that. "I can find no scent of him."

"He's still held up with the council. I don't sense he was ever down here." Circerran snorted. "He had other disgusting things to do."

Jack walked back over to Circerran, big, mean, and, she thought, ready to leave.

Wishful thinking?

"I thought you were the guy that killed him." Elsa remembered she'd heard that bit of gossip at a club. "A few months ago that was the talk of the town."

Jack rested an arm over Circerran's shoulders. *Just like Jamie had with me.* "I did. But he's hard to *keep* down. He's secure at the council."

"For now," Circerran muttered. "Done? This place is beyond sick. If no one triggers the trap within a few days, I'm cleansing it off the face of the Earth."

"Agreed," Elsa rushed to say, biting her lip after because Jamie walked over, a concerned frown on his handsome face. *Be brave. Be brave!*

"If we can find this man through this place, then we should leave it as it is." She half hoped he'd lean his arm on her, but he didn't. He stood close, though, which was good.

"He'll have other places." Circerran accessed the area. "Let's go."

"He will?" she asked, stunned by that.

"Yes," Jamie answered. "A creature like this won't be satisfied with only one place to feed his hunger. Come on, I've seen enough."

He guided her up, but went ahead of her when they drew closer to the top of the stairs. He turned and helped her up and over the debris as if she might fall and break. She let him, too shaken up by all this to keep up the brave act. *This is big. Much bigger than a simple – ha! – attack. If they have more places and they want Faolan.* Just the thought of the little guy made her sad.

"Did they... Did they hurt Faolan...like that, Jamie?"

Jamie froze, but squeezed her hand in his bigger, warmer one. "I don't know. I didn't sense him down there, Elsa. So he wasn't taken there."

"No, he wasn't taken down there. He was kept over there." Circerran pointed to the back of the house, where she could just make out something in the ground. She thought it was a tree trunk but as they walked over she realized it was a pipe. A chill shuddered down her spine.

A pipe meant air. An air hole in the ground? Goosebumps rushed her arms. "You're joking."

"Do I look like I make jokes about things like this?" Circerran snapped.

"Fuck." Jamie dropped her hand to walk over to the pipe. There wasn't a door she could see, and Jamie didn't seem to think there was one either. "How did they get him in and out?"

Circerran shrugged. "They could have spelled him in and out."

"It's a hole." Jack studied Jamie, then the ground. "Not bigger than a closet. We don't need to go down—"

"Fuck we don't," Jamie cursed. He'd fisted his hands so that his arms were corded with muscles. Eyes flickering, he glared at Circerran with enough pissed-off Jamie to make her step back. *He's protective of Faolan. Just like me.*

"Watch it, boy." Jack stepped closer to Jamie.

"*Boy?* Who's the youngster here, *pup*?" Jamie growled the word 'pup' and took a step until they were nose to nose.

Elsa's stomach dropped. If Jamie fought Jack, would Circerran step in? She felt her fangs tingle, ready to drop even as her heart sped up.

"If you want lover boy capable of doing more than whining in pain, you'd best calm him down," Circerran said as if she was discussing the weather.

For some reason, Elsa laughed. Her fangs stopped wanting to drop, too. "I'd suggest the same to you," Elsa said. "My bets are on Jamie wiping the floor with your *lover boy*."

For some reason Jamie turned just his head. His eyes had lightened, but flickered darker, then back. A whole different kind of shiver erupted down her body.

"Ease up," Circerran laughed. "I for one prefer my man unscathed. It makes things *nicer*."

Things. Elsa could think of a lot of 'things' to do with him, and every single one of them she guessed Jamie was more than capable of doing.

If I let him. Which if I am smart, I won't. How can I? If I do, I'm not going to be the same person after. Already I'm not – and I've had enough changes in my life.

Jamie wouldn't change it either, he'd ruin it.

There was one thing perfectly clear about Jamie – he wanted sex – hot, hard sex – but it was hard to tell if, after, he'd want more. And once he left? Life would suck even more. *If that was even possible.*

Chapter Twelve

Jamie paced the room, waiting for Elsa. Tonight had been revelation after revelation. Elsa was like a puzzle. Each piece slowly fitting into place, but he wasn't certain he could handle the end result.

Already, she stunned him at every turn.

Circerran, head of the Jade Coven, respected her. Said he was biting off more than he could chew. Jack, the newly turned wolf-Vamp studied Elsa with an appraising eye that, if not for the fact that he was mated, would have gotten him killed. Instead, Jamie had realized the man was accessing her potential use in the battle they constantly waged against the Death Stalkers.

Over my dead body.

Then there was Elsa. Standing in that cellar, watching him with her big, blue eyes. Standing up for him. Placing bets *on* him as if it was already money in the bank. That kind of shit, along with how damn hot she was, and how fucking scared she'd been but hiding it, did things to him.

She was driving him insane. The dance, her sadness, the killing, followed by more unhappiness, all of it swirled around him and each thing urged him to do something. Care for her. Hold her. Soothe her pain. Pin her to the bed. Make her cry in orgasm. Brush her tears aside. Anything and everything he could do, but basically, just *do* something.

The sound of her hit him a moment before her scent. For some damn reason it calmed him. His heart steadied out even as he picked up that hers had sped up.

"What are you doing?"

"Waiting for you." He turned, stunned to see her in a

pair of silk boxers and a pink tank top. She'd thrown a gray sweatshirt over it, but he knew with absolute certainty that she wore nothing else under that flimsy material. He'd only seen her in jeans or the black leggings, so the full exposure of her slim legs hit hard. So did the rounded globes of her plump breasts.

She tucked her sweatshirt closer and crossed her arms, hiding them. The memory remained. Good God, she was gorgeous.

"Why?"

That was a tough question. He rubbed the back of his neck, considering all the reasons why, and couldn't say even a tenth of them out loud—yet. "I wanted to see if you were all right after Circerran and Jack."

"Why wouldn't I be? Oh, right, I'm too fragile and weak to be all right after the big, bad immortals visited."

He raised his eyebrows at that. Surprised, he realized she was upset. *Why does that intrigue me?* He chose to sit for this one, sensing she was just getting started.

"Go on."

She was tapping her fingers on her arm, but stopped and gave him her steady stare. He grinned and watched her expression as it shifted to bemusement.

"You're odd. Really, really odd." She marched over to the bed, making a wide circle to avoid him. Then she climbed up, gifting him with a vision of her lovely bottom. Her ass was so damn pretty his thoughts blanked. *I want her that way, from behind, her head down, pinned to the bed as I make her beg to come.*

She sat, ending his fantasy. Biting her lip, she gathered a pillow on her lap and faced him hugging it. "I expected you to be downstairs, sharpening your sword, or calling in reinforcements."

"My sword is always ready," he added, unable not to. The jibe went right over her head. *Virgin. Gotta be why I am so screwed in my approach.*

"What are we supposed to do now? Wait here for...

what?"

"We wait here a few days to see what happens. If the trap is sprung and we catch this man, then you and Faolan don't have to worry any longer."

She studied him with narrowed eyes. *Is she considering letting me up on that bed? Is she strong enough to take what I want from her? Hours, days maybe of fucking while we wait on word?* In between eating and caring for Faolan. Recalling there was a boy here put a damper on his plans.

"I have a pack mate, Derrick, and his wife Samantha. They have a young boy. Faolan could go with them for a few days." Just until he got the first round of week-long sex out of the way. Then he could go slower, sneak in a bout or two, three of hard fast sex when the boy was busy.

She worried her lip. "And you think he will be safer?"

For some reason he felt like an ass when she asked that. "I think it would be safer," he finally muttered, but had to stand and walk over to her. "And it would give us some time."

Her blue eyes were lighter than ever. Glacier waters filled with thoughts he wished he could read. He stopped when they were inches apart. Her scent surrounded him. *Fresh, clean Elsa.*

She looked away and tucked her hair behind an ear. *Nervous?* "Why do I feel like you're not talking about searching for clues in that time?"

"Oh, but you're wrong." He tipped her head up with a finger under her chin. Her skin was so damn soft, he had to drop his hand or brush her hair back from where it'd fallen down along her face. "I *am* hunting for clues."

"Where? Here?"

"Absolutely." He closed that one-inch gap and heard her tiny gasp. Her arousal was the sweetest and most intoxicating scent he'd ever experienced. His muscles tensed tighter than a bow string. His body was fully erect, but it managed to grow harder. He wanted — *no, needed* — to taste her.

"What are you doing?"

Her breathy voice hit, adding another dose of excitement and torture down his shaft. If he didn't fuck her soon he was going lame. But just thinking that felt...wrong.

"I think you need to be kissed." As he said it, he felt the rightness of it. *Just a kiss. Maybe more, but no clothes off.*

"Is that right? And you're the man for the job?"

"I'm the *only* man for the job." The growl wasn't controllable. No one was touching her but him. No one was seeing her in her little cute PJs but him.

"We'll see about that."

He caught her nape and pulled her closer. Her irises sparkled darker, then lighter. She didn't deny him, though. Deep inside that felt — right. He pressed his lips to hers, suddenly wanting to give her a slow, seductive kiss. Heat exploded as her taste impacted with his questing tongue. She gasped and that electric snap of excitement he felt whenever he touched her detonated.

She fit him. She opened her thighs, allowing him in, and grabbed handfuls of his hair to tug him closer. Gods, she was a hot piece. A woman demanding what she wanted. He stroked along her tongue, showing her what he wanted with each thrust. He had no doubts, as the heat built between them, that if he slid his hand down to test her, she'd be wet. He could feel how hot she was, even between the layers of clothing and pillow separating them.

He had to touch her. Deepen the kiss. Make her come. Get her — *Wait. Slow down. Slow down.* He eased the kiss, not wanting to scare her. As he pulled up from her lips, she curled her hand around his neck and lifted up to keep on kissing him.

"Elsa, sweet," he managed to grate. He had to stop this, ease his needs slowly, not charge in full tilt and chance losing this... *Her.*

"Done already?" She drew him back down and kissed him this time. Her kiss was possibly the sweetest, hottest experience he'd ever had in his life. He'd kissed her, trying

166

to take as much as he could. She kissed him like she wanted to learn everything she could, to drive him wild. By the time she fell back, breathless and gazing up at him, he was ready to throw her down on the bed. "Still want to stop?"

"Fuck no. Woman," he growled. "I want to fuck you so bad I'm on fire, but you, little dancer, aren't ready for what I've got in mind."

Curiosity lit her eyes, then he thought a flash of anger lightened the blue. She lowered her lashes. "Is that so? Well…"

She trailed her fingers over his chest, watching what she did as she went lower. She stopped at his navel and he was glad of that, because any lower and she'd see exactly how honest he was being. Meeting his eyes again, she sighed, and eased back on her hands and stared up at him. "I guess we've had enough fun for the night, then."

Wait. What? She sat up and went to move away. He held her still with both hands on her rounded ass. It jostled her, but if it surprised her, she didn't show it. She pushed at his hands until he backed down. Then she crawled up on her knees.

"What are you doing?" he asked. Face to face, he could only stare. *Have her eyes ever been so light?*

"Me? I'm going to sleep. It's nearly dawn."

Stunned, he could only stare at her. "You're going to…"

"Sleep," she whispered and tapped his nose. "Next time, maybe you should decide what you want *before* you start something you can't finish."

"Oh, I can finish." He wrapped his arms around her and she fell against him. "Believe me, I can finish." His erection pressed to her leg as proof.

"Oh, I don't doubt it. With the right girl. Now stop."

With the right girl? She *was* the right girl. "You don't believe I want you?"

She shook her head. "Yes. No. You want. You don't want, want… Don't. It's enough to give a girl whiplash. Now, drop the macho act, and maybe, just *maybe* we'll see if *you* can keep up with me. But later. Right now I'm tired. I'm disillusioned with this world and now you. So…" She gazed pointedly at his chest, then down his arms, still holding her tightly.

He released her. Stepped back. Rubbed his neck. Blinked.

She was still there. Still hot and ready. Still beautiful and clearly…ready to box his ears.

For what? For saying she wasn't ready for fucking all night? *She isn't.* "You're serious."

"I am." She sat down on her knees. Folded her hands on her lap and held his gaze. Calm, beautiful beyond belief, and giving him a loud and clear 'no' he couldn't brush off.

His temper, built on days of frustration and want, plus an erection that was not going down, urged him on. "Elsa, I'm a *man*. I'm not a child. I fuck. You're a *virgin*. I can't be expected to think you're going to be able to give me a full run!"

"A full run." She tapped her lips.

He swore and turned around. *I need to shut my mouth.*

"You see, Jamie, what you're missing is this. You want sex, but this deal between us is strictly business. I don't *want* to mix the two. I told you this."

He tossed his hair out of his eyes and gave her another chance. "I know you did. You also told me if we did break the deal we'd break furniture. That kind of boasting is for children, Elsa. You're smaller than me. Newer to this. To fucking *sex!*"

"Isn't that an oxymoron? I mean, isn't *fucking* sex? Isn't that like saying a small dwarf?"

Stunned, he gave her his full attention. A blonde, beautiful, blue-eyed sensual woman stared back at him with all the knowledge to ruin a man's good sense they seemed to be born with. "Elsa —"

"Don't." She held up a hand, then used it to brush back her hair with a sigh. "I *am* a virgin. You're right, you figured it out. Good for you. But I guess what you can't figure out is what that actually *means*."

Hands on hips, he waited. He knew what it meant. She wasn't fucking ready to fuck! She didn't speak. Finally he had to. "And what does that mean?"

"Well, for one, I'm not a virgin because I haven't had offers. I mean, come on, Jamie. Open your eyes. I'm not exactly trailer trash. Second," she narrowed her eyes, probably because his mind was caught and circling around who to kill for offering to bed her. "Second, I don't want to have sex with you. I mean, you kiss very nicely, but you're not for me."

Doesn't want to have sex with me? Little liar. "You're aroused. You were before as well. I'm a wolf, I can—"

"Scent these things, yes, I know. Well, I don't screw every man who arouses me." She laughed. "If I did, I'd be walking with a limp."

His vision went hazy with red. Rage roared through him. *Other men had aroused her?*

"But that doesn't matter either. Not really." She nervously played with her pillow. *Am I scaring her now?* He battled the rage. *Figure her out. Find out what the hell you did wrong.*

"What does matter, then?" he grated. His head pounded from grinding his teeth. It was nothing compared to the throb of his shaft and tightness in his balls. He ached from head to toe for her and she *doesn't want me.*

"You don't want me," she said quietly.

Relief made his head spin. He laughed. "Oh, I want you."

"No, you don't."

"I think I'd know if I do." He gestured to his hips where he knew the clear outline of his shaft was pushing outward ready for her.

She dismissed his erection with a fleeting glance. "That just means you want to have *sex.*"

"Yes, exactly. With you!"

"With *anyone*. I'm no different than the countless other women you've been with, except"—she scooted up the bed, covered up and lay on her side—"for one thing."

"And that would be?"

"You're not going to fuck me and walk away because you're not going to fuck me at all." With that, she closed her eyes.

He stood there, stunned to his core. She sounded pretty fucking sure of that. *Not touch her?* His mind slowed, then sped up, tumbling over this new reality. *Not see her face when I bring her to pleasure. Not feel her soft thighs part for me or her body tighten around my shaft?*

"I'm exhausted. Can you blow out that candle by the door? It's not safe." She yawned and rolled onto her other side. "It's almost dawn anyway."

"Elsa, this is *not* how we end a conversation." He paced to the windows. Shifted them aside to see that it wasn't yet dawn. They had a good hour, longer maybe. He turned back. She hadn't moved. *Damn her, if anything this proves how childish she is!* She can argue all she wants, but shutting him out? Not talking to him about this? Childish!

"You just can't fall asleep. I never said I was going to fuck you. I *kissed* you. I didn't say a damn thing about anything else." *Not exactly true.* "Aren't you putting the cart before the horse? We can at least hitch up the damn team, can't we? Try them out. See if they work." He never said he was going to bed her and leave her. He didn't know what he was doing from one minute the next with her, how could she? "After we try this out. Give it a run." He laughed trying to tease her into talking. "Then you can go all possessive on me, if you want. I'm not some kind of man that goes around taking a girl's — Elsa, damn it, turn back around so we can discuss this!"

She didn't. *The brat.*

He went over to the bed, prepared to turn her over. But once there, he froze with his hand on her shoulder. *She's sleeping?*

All the pent-up anger, frustration and now sexual tension eased from him. He sat on the edge of the bed as if someone had cut the strings holding him up.

Sleeping. Unbelievable. And, for some damn reason, I'm not as angry as I should be.

Chapter Thirteen

"I think you've made Jamie very angry."

Elsa winced at the timid peek she got from Faolan. They were walking the grounds. Basically, that was what her nights had been filled with. Walking with Faolan. Because being near Jamie was difficult. He was either brooding over his computer, or being so loud 'fixing up the place' neither she nor Faolan wanted to be near him. Walking on eggshells didn't even come close to what it was like sharing a house — a mansion — with the man.

"I might have."

"Are you angry with him?"

"No. Yes. Maybe." She sighed. Jamie was complicated. She caught him staring at her from the windows when she was with Faolan. Sometimes, she found him waiting at the small hill near the cemetery for her when she returned from town. He always stalked off before she materialized. It was an odd kind of thing to do, but since the night when she'd busted him on his macho butt, he'd been like a bear with a thorn in his paw. Or a man so tightly wound he needed to let the steam out, or burn the house down.

Faolan kicked a pebble along the path.

She tried to think of what to say, but with all things Jamie, she couldn't. He wanted her for sex. That was flattering, but…then again, not. She'd been serious. Worse, her obsession for him hadn't lessened with seeing less of him. It was worse. She swore she could smell his tantalizing scent more now than when he was glued to her side. And it wasn't just his sexy Jamie scent she could pick up, it was his emotions — just *him* — everywhere she turned.

"He confuses me, Faolan. Worse, he doesn't respect me."

"What is respect?"

"It's when…" She considered her response. "It's when someone believes another person is worth something to them. Like, cares for them, and cares what they think or want. What they are…and likes them as they are, you know? Like, I like you. You're cute, funny, and you really are hilarious when you run on all fours. But more, it's you. I like you. I want what's best for you."

"Jamie wants what's best for you."

"Uh, no. He really only wants what *he* wants." *Sex. A fly by.*

"He's fixing up the house for you."

"What? He's doing that because…he's bored. He said he had nothing else to do." That wasn't exactly true. He had fixed up the dance studio, but since their fight, she'd not dared to go in there. The one time she'd asked him what he was doing, he'd turned to her, looked her dead in the eyes, then skimmed his amber gaze down her body, and back to her eyes. Then, in a deep voice, he'd muttered, "Got nothing else here to do with my time." With that, he'd turned back to tearing down a wall.

She'd learned to tiptoe around him after that. She wanted him more than anything in the world. If he so much as turned to her and said something, anything that indicated she was more than fun while on 'assignment', she would be all over him. She even had positions picked out. Wrapping her legs around his waist while he pounded into her was not the only one. Up there with that was pinning her to the wall and taking her hard and fast, standing up. God she could go on and on, but…not with him.

"He says he wants you to be happy here."

"When does he say this?' She'd never heard any such thing from him.

"When you're sleeping of course. Otherwise, he'd be angry. Maybe not angry any longer, but he can't figure out how to not be angry or how to tell you he's not angry now that he isn't."

She smiled. That was a lot of angry. "Uh, that makes no sense, kiddo."

"He made you angry. He got angry. Now he's unsure. He wants you happy, though."

"Happy." She stopped Faolan and pulled him to a bench near her favorite spot in the cemetery. "He talks about me?"

Faolan shrugged, smiled and sat nearer to her. "Sure. He always asks me what we do each night. He laughed when I told him about the bunnies you're keeping as pets. I didn't tell him you drank from them."

She grimaced. Both rabbits were scared to death of her, but she'd been bringing carrots and apple slices each night. Now they were waiting for her, half scared but also half hungry. "I don't drink from them."

"I told him that. He doesn't know you go get blood at the hospital."

"Don't tell him either." It was odd but ever since that first night, she felt uneasy at the thought of warm blood from a person. Now she misted into the hospital a few villages over and slipped inside, to where they kept unusable blood. It was quick, easy, and tasted like crap. But it avoided the oddness she experienced thinking of touching someone—a man—like that.

"I won't. But he really, really wants to know who you are drinking from… His wolf is not happy about you drinking from someone."

"His wolf?"

"Yes. His wolf is smart, and I think knows you don't drink from people, not now, but Jamie sometimes doesn't listen."

Where to start? Faolan was full of surprises. He was sitting, kicking his small feet out, appearing as if he hadn't a care in the world, while blowing hers. *Jamie does care, doesn't he?* "To his wolf? He doesn't listen to his wolf?"

"Yes."

She considered Faolan's downcast expression and tousled his hair, to get a grin. "You think too much. Be a kid. Stop

174

trying to match us up. He's not my type."

"He isn't?" Faolan stammered.

"Nope." *I'm lying to a boy and myself, aren't I?*

"I think he is," he countered, with a sunny grin, but when she didn't let up, his eyes grew worried again. "What will happen to me if you and Jamie don't fix this?"

"Fix this?"

"Be together."

"Oh, Faolan." She hugged him close and kissed his shiny hair. He smelled like apple blossoms and boy. "I will always be around. What does your wolf say?"

"My wolf doesn't talk to me. My wolf *guides* me."

He said that so seriously she studied his eyes. "What do you mean?"

Shrugging, he leaned against her, curling close so he could play with her hair. "My wolf helped me find you. And Jamie. When the witches made me pull you up, I didn't go back down. I stayed. I could tell my wolf knew someone would come. Jamie came. He saved you, then you both came for me."

Jamie's scent suddenly blew to her on a breeze. "Is that right?" *Speaking of the devil.* Her heart took off just at the sight of him. By now she had hoped she wouldn't get all giddy over him. She might as well have wished she'd been born four inches taller.

Faolan leaped up and raced to Jamie. To his credit he picked the boy up and laughed. "Yes. I knew you were coming. Were you sneaking up on us?"

"Why would I do that?" he grumbled and set Faolan down. "And why haven't you told me this before? These things are important."

Faolan laughed. "I don't know. You never asked me, I guess."

Had Jamie's gaze skimmed her, before he focused back on Faolan? He did appear...not so angry. Almost uneasy if that was possible.

"Elsa was going to show me something. Do you want to

come see?"

Jamie turned to her. "I brought you a sweater. It's getting cold."

"Thank you," she whispered, suddenly feeling out of her depth.

"What did you find? I checked the entire estate. It's safe. If I missed something—"

"No. It's not like that. I found a garden."

Jamie took that in, and appeared at a loss. He ducked his head and quickly met her eyes again, only briefly, before he nodded. She stayed still, unsure what to say or do. Jamie surveyed the cemetery, her, then Faolan. "A garden, huh? You've not seen it? I can't believe you've not found every inch of this place."

Faolan grinned, pleased with the compliment. "Nope. I haven't."

"It's not far. I found it last night before I went to town." *Since I haven't gone tonight.*

She thought Jamie tensed at that, but seemed to relax and nodded again.

"Here. You'd better put this on." He walked over before she could stop him and helped her into her sweater, warming her more with his body than with the cashmere. "Better?"

"Yes." She pulled the sweater closer. Bit her lip. *Show some appreciation! He's trying.* "Thank you, I was cold."

Surprising her, he grinned. It'd been so long since she'd seen it, she stood there, stunned. While she did, he lifted something and she dragged her eyes off him and spotted a beer in his hand. He had a cooler in his other. *More beer?*

"I also brought you one of these."

She shook her head. Drinking and Jamie… Probably not a good mix.

He opened his mouth to say something, thought better of it, then in a low tone, said, "I thought you'd like it…" He lowered the beer when she shook her head. Seeming disappointed, as if he'd failed again, he focused away from her, on the trees in the distance maybe. His expression troubled her.

"Is it cold? I like cold beer, you know, better than room temperature."

He hesitated. "Yes. I kept them chilled."

"Okay. Thank you. Just one, though, okay?"

A quick toss of the hair out of his eyes, and he smiled again. It didn't last. The brooding Jamie returned, but she still experienced warmth in her chest. He watched her sip it as if her reaction was vital.

It was wonderful. Crisp. Cool. "It's delicious." She read the label and widened her eyes. "German?"

"I like German beer. I noticed you did too. They make some of the best. Hard not to pick a good one."

"Well, I think this one is perfect." Turning to Faolan, she found him hunting through the shrubs, exploring the area as if he'd found a treasure chest. She caught him and tugged him playfully into a hug. "Want to go see that garden?"

His eyes went wide. "Yes."

"Take my hand, come on." She led him in past the huge shrubs and ducked under an overgrown tree. She'd walked the entire estate during her Jamie dilemma. This hidden place had shocked and pleased her. She hoped Jamie would like it and not think her silly. *Childish.*

A glance back showed Jamie following, eyeing the surroundings then her.

"*This* is the secret garden." She walked them a bit farther, then released Faolan.

The little garden was hidden by the shrubs, probably at one time locked with a door too. With the moon out the area was as clear as day, to her, except in gray, muted tones. Still, it was comforting. There was an amazingly clear pond on the left. Willow branches hung down, almost touching the surface. Overgrown cherry trees lined it on the other side.

"Wow! Jamie! Is that a little house? Like mine." Faolan raced off, running around more on two legs than before.

She laughed and glanced at Jamie to find him smiling as well at the boy's antics.

"Not like yours. That was a *shack*," Jamie growled the last. "This has…possibilities."

Did he sound interested in making this more? Like the house?

He turned in a circle, taking in the high shrubs, the large tree in the center and the tangled remains of a swing. A bench still sat under another tree, with a tipped-over table and what might have been a fountain. Chairs had also been left to the elements, along with the little shed. *Or maybe a cottage. A honeymoon home?* The walls were covered with ivy, but she thought it was white with a red tiled roof that slanted higher to the left where the chimney proudly rose. She could close her eyes and picture how pink roses would have climbed up along the sides. There would have been perennials of all shapes and colors lining the path, too.

"It just needs a little work."

She gaped at him. "Seriously? You want to fix this up?" *For me?*

His gaze landed on her with all the intensity he'd shown when he'd told her he had nothing else to do to keep him busy.

"If you want. I'm working on something else now." He walked toward her until they were inches apart. The amber of his eyes flickered, going from darker to lighter. It was the closest he'd come since he'd kissed her and told her she was too weak for what he wanted. "But for now, I want to investigate the table and chairs. I think those will be fine with a little work and a new coat of paint."

"You're serious."

He lifted his shoulders.

"I could do that," she offered. "I know how to paint."

A frown, then seeming to realize she was honest, he grinned. *Can't breathe.* "I bet you could."

She sighed like a sap. He was just turning away and cast her a double-take. "You surprise me all the time." He didn't sound as though he knew if that was bad or good.

She surprised *him*?

Without more, he walked over to the table.

She followed, soaking in the way his muscles worked under his worn jeans. *He has such a nice butt. And his back... solid. So... delicious. Is this Jamie telling me he wants more than sex? Is he fixing up the house for me? Why? I... We can't live here. Can we?*

"Are we going to make this place pretty, like before?" Faolan hunkered down next to Jamie as the table was given a thorough inspection. "It was once very pretty here."

"If Elsa wants to, we'll make this place prettier than it was before." She nodded, not sure what else to say. "It'll take a lot of work," he warned.

"I like work," she spluttered, then stopped. "But you'll have to show me how, you know, to make it all better."

He stood and anchored his hands on his lean hips. For some reason she got the impression his mind had turned... dirty. "I can show you everything you need to know to make it better."

Oh God, she just knew he meant a lot more than working on a garden. Her eyes dipped down to his hips without her giving them permission. The bulge there made it perfectly clear he was aroused. Very, *very* aroused or else... She lifted her eyes to his, seeing the challenge in his stare. *Is there more there as well?*

"Are you serious?"

At her question, his gaze pinned on her lips. "I've never been more serious. If you want me to, I'll show you everything you need to know."

Her breath caught again. At this rate she'd forget how to breathe, not that she needed to, but heck. She peeked at Faolan, but he was busy. Close enough to hear, though.

She couldn't stop the slow grin, and didn't want to. "Oh, I want you to, but are you certain you can handle me?"

Jamie's gaze turned slumberous. "If I can't, I'm certain you'll let me know."

"I am good at talking."

"As long as you promise me one thing," he murmured so low she had to strain to hear him.

"And what would that be?"

"Never fall asleep and leave me angry again."

She blinked. Grinned and ducked her head just like he did. "Oh, did I do that?"

"Yes." The growl sent a shiver of excitement to all the right places.

"Then don't disrespect me again, or underestimate what I can handle." She kept his intense gaze, but only because she knew, with Jamie, she had to or else she'd never have a chance of him listening to her. After making her legs so weak she was worried she'd faint, he finally gave a short nod.

"Fine, then we'll fix this place up and see what else we can work on." She hoped that meant somewhere with a bed, or at least a wall or couch because if she had to go one more night without Jamie's kiss, or his hands on her butt, or his body against hers, she might strangle him.

"Hooray! This will be fun! Right?" Faolan tugged on the swing, reminding her that adult fantasies like this were better left to when little boys went to bed.

"Oh, it'll be some kind of fun, buddy. Some kind of fun, but first, Elsa and I are going out to dinner."

She caught his arm. *Dinner?* "What? What will Faolan do?"

"He's getting a night with Jack and Derrick. They're on their way. I thought we'd head out in an hour. Is that good?"

Good? A dinner with Jamie in town. Alone.

She swallowed.

"Sure, sounds like fun."

Jamie didn't answer, but his eyes shimmered with enough heat to make her legs tremble. All of a sudden she wasn't certain she could wait an hour. *Oh, but I'm not missing it either. Hard work was always rewarded. Who knows, maybe I can show him a thing or two…*

Chapter Fourteen

An hour later, she walked outside. She had changed. Twenty times. Each outfit had seemed wrong. Until this one. She'd finally remembered she owned a black skirt. It clung to her hips and outlined her ass then stopped. Right under it.

Still, she wasn't worried. The key was just not to bend over.

She'd matched it with high-heeled, black leather boots she'd been dying to wear. They said hot, sexy, and *oh yeah*, out of your reach.

For a dash of who she really was, she'd shifted a tiny T-shirt that said, *'Smile if you stared long enough to read this'* in flowing script across her breasts.

Of course it was a V-neck and revealed the valley her breasts made, held up by her pink, silky bra. To tone it down, she wore the long cashmere sweater jacket he'd brought her. It hung down to above her knees. She'd take it off when she got to the restaurant.

Faolan was occupied. She'd avoided the room with the two big men teaching Faolan to throw a knife. They hadn't glanced at her, but she knew they'd sensed her walking by the room. Still, Faolan was safe. She hoped she was as well.

My first date. *What if this is just one more seduction to get me into sex? What if that is still all he wants?*

She found Jamie and halted her feet and her silly worries. "I am *not* getting on that."

He gave her another heart-stopping grin, revved the engine on a motorcycle that purred. His biceps bulged when he did it. In fact, his entire arm did. He met her eyes with a challenging gleam in his. Her breath caught when he simply sat there, giving her a head-to-toe inspection.

She waited. And waited. And...

He was teasing her.

"Nice legs. Now hop on."

Her heart did a nose dive at the compliment. "Not a chance."

"Don't be chicken."

She ignored him. Didn't stare at how unbelievably sexy he was, sitting on his big motorcycle. Or how his body was probably more than capable of driving her into orgasm—maybe even on the bike.

He narrowed his eyes and gave her a challenging stare. "Seriously. Don't be chicken. Come on, hop on. I promise to be gentle, since this is your first time."

Her eyes flew wide. She narrowed them on his wolfish grin and gave him the finger. Then misted away.

He laughed, sounding as if he'd anticipated that response. Before she'd reached tree level, he took off, the motorcycle *chewing* up the grass. It was unbelievably fast. He was obviously insane. It was clear he was into dangerous sports. The bike rose up on one wheel and he jumped it over a rock wall. Landed it perfectly on the opposite side, and kept going at a speed that really wasn't safe.

She shivered, even in her mist form. Such speed was fine in the grass, but what about concrete? Just the thought of the possible road rash made her nauseated.

"You won't ride a bike with me, but you'll fly like a bunch of smoke," he shouted.

She landed on a fence post a few hundred feet from him and materialized. He paused the bike next to her. "I am in full control." She shuddered when he raced in a circle around her. "You are not."

He was breathless and gorgeous when he stopped. She felt an answering smile tug at her lips.

"I would never hurt you. Come on, get on."

"First, I don't know if *that's* true." She kept the 'duh' off,

182

but it was implied. "And second, it would be impact with the road that would hurt me."

His frown returned. *Hooray!* Except, for some reason, his obvious displeasure now made her hot. *Baiting a bear. Baiting a bear.*

"I would *never* harm you or let anything else."

"*Never* is a long time, mister. I doubt you'll be around past Sunday. See if you can keep up." She concentrated and changed herself into a small barn owl. Catching an updraft, she soared high, watching Jamie, but more than pleased with herself.

She beat him to town, but only by cheating. A tree in his way, which she happened to knock down, inconvenienced him for, like, two seconds. Still, she needed a minute. Her mind was all out of sorts. *Baiting a bear and not sure I should...*

As casually as she could, she let the very polite waiter show her to a table. She mentioned she was waiting on a man, and ordered two glasses of wine, three steak dinners, and side dishes, considering how much he ate.

Until she saw him, she was fine.

He focused on her exclusively. For the space of a heartbeat, two, there was nothing else for her as well. The room disappeared. Her worries dissolved. Even her breath stopped.

Jamie. That was all she knew. Just him with his dark hair tousled over his forehead and amber eyes intense as he stalked to the table. He'd put on a dark button-down shirt that accentuated his muscled chest and arms. She wanted to rip the buttons off so she could lick him from his lean hips to his jaw line. When he reached the table, she finally remembered to breathe on a long, low sigh. Leaning over her, he blocked the light with the width of his shoulders. Right in her ear, he whispered, "*You* are a *very* bad girl."

Not missing this chance, she tugged him closer by his shirt. "And you are a very, *very* bad wolf. But I ordered you *two* steaks, so sit down." *Or drag me out of here and show me how bad you can be.* His eyes flickered from light to dark, mesmerizing her face? She shook her head internally. "Sit."

"I'm not a dog, sweet. I don't take orders." He bent closer until his warm face brushed along her cheek. He'd shaved. The roughness was still there, but now with a softer glide of tight, spicy-scented skin. God, he smelled good. Woodsy and Jamie. "How about a please?"

She swallowed. Not sure she wanted him to move or not. All she had to do was turn her head and there — *right there* — his neck would be. Perfect. Firm, warm skin she could sink her fangs into, sip, maybe drink a bit more, rub her hands over his chest. Test his taut muscles, maybe explore lower to see if he really was as hung as she imagined.

"Elsa." *Is that how my name sounds when growled?*

"Please?" she whispered, pretty proud her voice wasn't breathless.

He leant back and met her eyes, winked, then he flashed his grin. *God, if he kisses me I might just throw him down on the table and make a meal of him.* He made her wait, because yes, she wanted to know what he'd do next. Slowly, his gaze pinned on hers, he sat. Next to her. He also rested one arm on the back of her chair and other on the table to cage her in.

Who is this man and where is Jamie?

"Uh, wine?" She handed him his, avoiding his eyes.

"I'd love some. So, motorcycles." He took the wine, of course touching his fingers to hers, and sat back. Taking a sip he raised his eyebrows. "Good choice."

"It's France. I think they only have good choices."

He nodded serenely as if every ounce of her body wasn't on fire. "True. So, what's the fear of motorcycles?"

She shrugged. Swallowed. "I don't like them."

"Clearly."

The nice waiter appeared. Jamie didn't turn away but told him — in French — to bring another bottle, chilled, and make it four steaks. He asked for one to-go, with all the sides as an afterthought. She felt slightly better. *He orders everyone around, doesn't he?* The man bowed, left, and all the while,

Jamie focused on her.

Baiting the bear. Baiting the bear.

She swallowed her wine, drinking it down in one slow, steady gulp. No problem, he poured her more. She hadn't eaten yet, or had blood. Last night she'd picked at her food, and only sipped a few swallows of blood. Tonight she was hungry, but also needed to feed her blood thirst. And not on Jamie.

Jamie sipped his wine and coaxed her to sample a bit of bread. "It's good, right?"

"It's very good."

He smiled again, sending more confusion through her.

Apparently I've changed a rough and tough wolf, who never smiled, into a seductive and sneaky Don Juan.

"So, motorcycles."

Jamie finished another bite of the steak, amazed once again by Elsa. The dinner was the best plan he'd ever come up with. The owner had taken his money with a smile, and assured him he could have the place to himself. Already the staff was thin, the customers all but gone, and Elsa had eyes only for him.

She'd forgiven him. Once he'd gotten his head out of his ass and realized what he was doing wrong. Trying to get what she obviously didn't dish out to everyone.

Her.

She'd stayed. He'd half worried she'd wake and run. She hadn't. So she'd already given him something she hadn't given anyone else.

Her time.

"This is a decent steak."

She smiled after she swallowed her sip of wine. "It's delicious. Admit it."

He conceded a nod. "What is that?" She had gotten him steak, potatoes, a creamy soup with asparagus and herbs. She had a steak, some kind of vegetable au gratin—a creamy whipped something, and the same soup. Salad lay in a bowl between them. Bread sat on a trencher. A cheese plate had arrived. Even butter was presented in a crystal bowl. All of it was nibbled, tested, tried while she talked to him about things he'd never considered before. The way the food tasted, how many varieties of wine they had, how the room was decorated much like the mansion had once been. All of it was...interesting.

"Here, try. It's delicious, too." She lifted her fork, holding it up expectantly.

Gods, what he wanted to feed her—have her feed him. If she knew she'd be back in owl, mist, or wolf form a million miles away from him.

He took the bite. Parmesan and...something garlic and pepper hit his mouth.

It was delicious. Creamy, cheese, pasta, he guessed.

She nodded and smiled. "Good, right?"

"If you're not finishing it, I will." He smiled when she rolled her eyes. "It's delicious. Mac and cheese on crack."

She spluttered and covered her mouth. "Jamie, you are crazy."

He was. How was he going to keep his hands off her? *Why should he keep his hands off her? Easy, because she made it clear she was not interested in me—unless I wanted more.*

"Excuse me." She put her napkin on the table and smiled. "I need to go to the ladies' room."

He scooted back and stood. She did as well, removing the long, flowing black sweater jacket. Without his direct orders, his eyes pinned on lush cleavage, then focused on the lettering on the top. His grin cut across his face and he laughed. *Damn her.*

He knew Elsa. He knew she could call whatever the hell she had to wear from wherever she kept her stash of clothes...

No one else was reading that damn—

"You like, huh?" She met his eyes, winked and got past him.

His gaze shot to her ass. Barely covered. Skirt so short it

was impossible not to watch in anticipation each flex and bunch in case he got a preview. She walked — *fuck that* — she flowed across the floor as if she'd been born in high heels.

Virgin. *Who cared? She wore that skirt for me.* Those boots were going to stay on when he took her. And that tiny skirt that barely covered her assets was going to be kept on too, at least around her waist.

I have this in hand.

Seduction was the name of this plan. Seduce her, keep her safe. She'd fall into his arms, realize she liked sex with *him* and he could work on convincing her to stay at the compound. Then, he could...go back to tracking. Visit in between missions.

He rubbed his chest, frowning at that idea. Ten minutes later he still felt unease at his new strategy. This was possible. The mansion was safe for a few more days. *Get a sense of things, see if—*

He caught her scent. Everything would have to work out, he decided as soon as she came into view. If anyone else was in the room, she didn't notice. He noticed she didn't. So the cleaning crew could live, but he was not letting her wear something—

She smiled and lifted her finger to her mouth, biting it as she approached. Did her gaze dip down to his hips?

His erection, suffering from neglect, pulsed heavier. He'd been too busy fixing up the house to take care of business. Then, he'd not wanted to. Elsa was right there. When he found release he wanted it to be with her.

Now?

He wished he'd taken the two minutes.

Managing to pull her chair out, he also swallowed a groan at how good she smelled. His chair nearly fell backwards. He caught it, sat, got his arm back around her, and settled closer. *Breathe in. Breathe out. Easy.*

She pushed a finger against his chest. He leaned in. Instead of pressing him back *she* moved closer. "You were smiling."

His lips curled. He dipped his eyes down and exhaled.

Her breasts were…dazzling. "I still am."

She laughed and reached up, surprising him by laying her hand on the side of his face. He groaned, but covered it with a cough. *She has more control over me than I do.* She went to pull away, but he covered her hand and brought it to his lips to kiss her palm.

"I think I'll be smiling for a while, now," he murmured, dipping his eyes to have another long look at her. *Does she have pink or rosy nipples?* They were budded, clearly liking his attention. He lifted his eyes and smiled again. "It's an amazing view."

She laughed and shook her head. "You're crazy. You know, I always hated my…mmm…chest."

He swallowed. Sat back. Examined her expression. Stunned, he realized she was being serious. "Why the fuck would you — ?"

"Jamie, did you know swearing wasn't actually *necessary* all the time?"

Surprised again he squinted at her, considered her flashing eyes to see if she was teasing, and modified his response. "Why would you hate your body?" *It's perfect.*

"Well, I was raised in the ballet. Not taught, you know, like in lessons after school twice a week." She peeked at him. He nodded, but had no idea what she was talking about. "My adopted parents were ballet dancers. *Both* of them." She said that seriously, as if it meant something. "Anyway, I practiced ballet *every* day. All day on holidays, weekends. Then I hit puberty." She sighed as if saying she'd reached old age, and lost out on a dream.

"And?" He was curious. As a man he'd always liked to solve things. Before he'd been bitten he'd been a warrior, but he'd also made things. He'd enjoyed it, he remembered. Elsa was a puzzle. A living, breathing, smoking hot one he ached to figure out.

"Well, you know," she muttered and lifted a shoulder. Her breasts rose and fell under her tiny T-shirt.

He tipped her head up. "I really don't. Go on."

She rolled her eyes. "I got breasts."

He was about to say and how nice they were too, but sensed that wasn't the point. Thinking about his limited experience with ballet he tried to picture her as one. She would be stunning. Like a princess.

"Jamie, prima ballerinas don't have, well, breasts. Not... my size breasts. Which is totally unfair. I really don't have," she paused and laughed. "I don't have *big* breasts," she whispered. "It's just that my ribs are small."

He was lost on her talking about breasts. Even if her face turned rosy it was the most amazing conversation he'd ever had. *Did women worry about these things?* He studied her body. She was perfectly proportioned. Stunning. "You're perfect. They must have been insane. It wasn't like you couldn't dance. I assume you didn't use them in your routines."

She spluttered on her sip of wine and coughed.

"Hell, sorry, here." He handed her water.

"Jamie, seriously?" She squinted at him. "Are you... trying to make me feel good, or...comparing me to all your other women?"

"What? Where do you get these ideas?" Pissed all over again, he sat back and stared at her. *Why would she think such a thing?* He was here with her now, wasn't he?

She turned her head and stared down at her plate, moving food around with a frown.

I just raised my voice. He glanced around, but other than the cleaning staff, they had the place to themselves. Next to him, Elsa was quiet, back to tolerating him like she had the past few nights. *What to say?* "I wasn't comparing you to anyone. I think you're shaped beautifully."

That seemed to sink in slowly, and when it did he got a sparkling smile, then a frown. Her face was flushed, maybe from the wine, but maybe because the topic made her uncomfortable. *Hadn't anyone ever complimented her before?*

"Well, anyway, that was sweet..."

He canted his head. Was she...running a tally on him? A

good Jamie and bad Jamie? He blinked as the idea settled. She *had* cast him several glances when he'd said the wrong thing. The look in her eyes had been that of a woman being proven right. '*I don't want you because you only want sex.*'

Her words made more sense. Adding the other night up with now, he realized she was testing him, trying him out, wasn't she? To see if he wanted *her*, not just to get laid. *Or maybe to see if I'm good enough to win the prize.*

"Elsa." He picked at her plate, liking her food better than his. *Because she's touched it?* "I don't eat dinner with a woman very often." *At all.* "I'm used to dealing with men. I'm going to say what I think. Always will, but if I say something you take the wrong way, it's better to…" He considered what to say, unsure how to put words to what he meant.

She sipped her wine, licking a drop of red from her pink lips. Gods, how he wanted to do the same. She set the glass down and studied it, then him. "Ask you and not jump to conclusions?"

He sighed. "Exactly." She could see reason. The other night she'd been tired, as she'd said, disillusioned and he must have said something that upset her.

"I just did and you growled at me."

He froze, a forkful of her pasta at his lips. He ate it, considering that it was there, and thought on that. *I did go for angry before I thought to ask what she meant. Just as guilty as her?* "I am not comparing you to other women. I was simply telling you that I think you dealt with some fuckwits — idiots — and you're perfect. Anyone that can't see that is a fu —"

She covered his mouth and leaned her forehead to his shoulder. She sighed. Her breath was sweet, and scented with wine. "Yes. A fuckwit. Nice. Thank you, and in the future, if we have another dinner, or a meal, and you say something and I question you, don't growl. I'm just curious about you."

She lifted her head at that. Her gaze moved over his face, then landed on his throat. She'd done that before, and the rush he felt was electric. Sexual. *If she drinks from me…*

"Okay?" She met his eyes again. Hers were so blue he had to swallow before he could respond.

"Okay. You can ask me anything," he said, then remembered grumbling at her in the forest when she'd started questioning him on tracking. "But first, go on about these fu — this ballet. Did you have to just stop?"

She smiled and poured him more wine, handing it to him after. "No, but I wanted something I couldn't have. I also felt like I disappointed my…mom and dad." Adopted mom and dad she meant. "I mean, there went all those years and years of broken toes, busted ankles, pulled tendons…and dreams." The last came out softly. "I mean I still danced. I was good, too. I love it. Or I did. But I would never be a prima, not with my shape and I'm a little short, too. Contemporary fit for a while. But I guess that's gone now too."

Broken toes? Busted ankles? Dancers were pretty fragile-looking creatures.

"So." She shook her head and smiled too brightly. Sipping her wine, she eyed him over the rim, then lowered her glass as he raised his. They clicked glasses and he watched her lips as she took another small sip. "At least *someone* at the table likes them."

He nearly choked on his swallow of wine. She wasn't really joking, she sounded like she forced the comment. "I like them very much." He took her small hand and brushed his thumb over her knuckles. She let him, even seemed soothed by it. He could see it in the darkness that spilled from her eyes. He knew what she left behind. It was a dream. "You could still dance." He had in fact replaced the entire floor of the studio for her as a surprise for later.

"Yes, I suppose so, but not on stage. The other night." She dropped her gaze to her plate. "Ballet just makes me sad right now. Maybe later it won't."

He agreed but kept silent on his opinion. "I wanted to be a blacksmith. Never wanted to be a warrior. It was making things. The way heated metal could change, and you could move it, working it into something else. It fascinated me. I would work for days on one piece that was no bigger than your hand. Trying my best to get it just right. I like difficult tasks, though," he reminded her, setting her hand down with one last touch of her skin. *Like her.* "So being a warrior fit, I suppose."

She either ignored his hit toward her being difficult, or didn't catch it. Her eyes lit up with the lighter blues. "You were a warrior? You still *are* a warrior. It's in every line. Plus you order everyone around."

He spluttered on his wine. *He* ordered everyone around? Well, if he did, it didn't include her. "Is that right?"

"Well, yes, of course you do. But a blacksmith," she touched his hand now. Traced the lines of his tendons, then turned it over to examine the palm. His hands were rough, calloused from sword work and just years of work. She seemed to like it, though. She rubbed the tips of her fingers over the ridges, then pressed her hand down flat and laughed at how much bigger his was than hers. His chest thudded painfully. "You are so big. Every part of you, built for your life, I guess." She met his gaze. He caught his breath at how the light reflected on her creamy skin and made her eyes sparkle. "Do you still work with metal?"

"No. I gave that up." *A long time ago. When I was human too.* "It wasn't possible, with the wars back then. We were always busy trying to survive. Now? I can't imagine there is a need for my skills in the forge."

She seemed to ponder that with a cute little frown. She tucked her hair behind an ear and tilted her head to gaze at his face. He would have paid a fortune to know what she was thinking. "Wars. It must have been...difficult living then. Do you like it better now?"

Difficult question. Did he? He liked hot showers. He liked softer beds, but often found them too...big. He liked easy access to nourishing food. But he missed... His eyes fell on Elsa and her sweet curves and small hands. *Delicate.* He missed protecting someone.

"I like it now." Especially, he wanted to say, now with her beside him. "More wine?"

A glowing smile. "Are you trying to get me drunk and take advantage of me?"

He decided to answer her truthfully. "No. I'll seduce you, but never take something you don't offer."

She blinked. A slow smile lifted her lips, sparkled in her eyes. "You really are too confident for your own good. Why do you think you'll be so successful?"

He liked this. Sparring with her. He could almost feel at ease with her, knowing if he did say something that upset her, she'd let him know. He just had to not get upset with her if she did. *Like the other night.*

"Well, you're very beautiful. I have been told I'm charming."

She burst into laughter, covered her mouth, eyes round and shook her head.

He frowned. At one time he had been called charming. He thought. "I'm not charming then?"

"Oh, you are, of course you are." *Lying?* She giggled then held her breath. Let it out on a sigh and blushing said, "I just think of fairy tales when I think 'charming' and you." She tapped his chest. "You are not a fairy tale prince. You're more a rogue. A scoundrel."

Heat hit his neck. In that moment, he wanted to be a prince. Not be this rough around the edges warrior who kept blowing it with her. A scoundrel.

"But you are very nice when you try."

When he tried?

"What you've been doing to the house... It's amazing."

More heat hit his neck. "I wanted it to be nice." *For you.*

"Why? Did you...buy it?"

He didn't want to answer that, unsure even why he had but nodded.

"Oh, Jamie. I can't believe it. That's..." She trailed off and studied his face. "Great. You've already done so much. It'll

193

be nice when you're done."

"I guess I still like fixing things," he admitted.

"Yes, well, you must not rest at all. Even the bathrooms are…clean. I can't imagine how long all that took you. Did you sleep? Ever?"

In the bed, next to you. He poured her more wine, sipped his after. "The water isn't hot."

She dismissed that with a wave of her hand. "We can boil it. Well, I mean, you can… I mean, if you stay. It's probably best if I go…"

Did she sound like that wasn't what she wanted? "I thought we decided to stay. A few days to see if the trap springs."

"Yes, there's that." She tucked her hair behind her ear. *Nervous?*

"I can get the water running hot if we had a hot water heater that worked. Maybe from this century."

"True." She relaxed somewhat and nibbled on a piece of bread. "You never told me why you like to ride that motorcycle. Not really. You're a speed freak? You love danger?"

"I like a fast ride." A hard ride. He wanted to make them both sweaty and so tired they couldn't move a muscle. "A motorcycle is as close to running as we can get. Our wolf can outrace a car, if we're hard pressed. But a motorcycle… It's the wind in my face. The power of it under me. It's all of that, but really, it all boils down to liking a fast, hard ride."

"Really?" she whispered studying his lips. *Does she want another kiss? Or know how much I want one?* "Mmm, I can't see the draw."

He bit his tongue. Her words *were* getting slightly slurred. In the last five minutes alone she'd finished her glass and half of another. *Nerves?* He leaned in, caught her knee in his hand and said, "Jealous?"

Her heart rate jumped. "From what?" Her breath smelled like wine and sweet Elsa. It occurred to him that he'd not yet kissed her tonight. Her warm skin burned his palm and there was no way her mouth wouldn't sear his lips.

194

"My motorcycle, but don't be."

She blinked.

"I'd love to take you for a ride, too. How about now?" He stood and helped her to her feet. She swayed, caught at his shirt and stared up at him with a bemused expression.

"I think you mean that in a very, *very* naughty way."

Heart pounding, he didn't have the words. She was so damn beautiful. So soft. Her skin so smooth and warm. Even her irises were tender with something when she teased him, something that made his throat feel tight even as his body swelled harder. He fought the expanding erection, but hell, no woman on Earth impacted him like Elsa. Never would either, he began to worry.

She took a step, then another and stopped. He walked right into her back. His cock, already in misery, gave him a shudder at the base warning him to get her naked. "Jamie! I think the staff is sleeping!"

He breathed in against her neck. She smelled so right. "I paid them to let us stay later."

"Oh," she whispered, leaning back into him so he got the full impact of her rounded bottom pressing to his shaft. *Jesus!* Sweat flooded his skin. "That was very thoughtful."

She had to feel his erection. He couldn't have hidden his need even if he'd wanted to. With his size, he always had to go slow — at first. *With Elsa I have to go slow even now.* He bit down on his cheek to remind himself once again that she was a virgin.

"You're fascinating when you're this Jamie." She giggled and pushed away, weaving her way to the door.

This Jamie? He caught up to her, got her outside and to the bike but once there her giggles ended. She stiffened and pulled back. He held tight to her tiny waist and stroked her hip.

"Come on. No more running. Be brave."

She turned to stare at him. "That is the silliest thing you have ever said. And let me tell you…" She rolled on her high heels. He held her carefully to his chest. "You've said some doozies. But brave? *I* am *not* brave." She pressed a hand to her chest and sighed. "Yes, sad, I know. Disappointing yes, but..." Her eyes flew wide. "Am I... Am I...*drunk*?"

He cradled her by her hips so she stood still. "A tad. So no shifting, misting, or...mice." Horror filled her expression. "You're stuck with me, and my bike."

She pulled free and turned away, stalking off — wobbly — with a clear plan. He hijacked her plan and turned her around, stroked her slim arms. "I only had a few glasses of wine. It's safe. I never wreck. It's a dirt road."

"It's a *motorcycle*! No."

"Yes. I won't let anything happen—"

She straightened, tugged her skirt into place. He hadn't realized that the tiny thing had moved but apparently it wasn't covering enough now. "I am not— Oh God!"

Immediately worried, he took a deep breath, testing the air for an enemy. Nothing. "What?"

"I have to *drink*, that's what. I can't be... I can't be *drunk with you*!"

"I thought you went off and handled that already," he snapped, unable to keep the anger out of his tone.

She tossed her hair.

"Elsa?" Hope bloomed in his chest.

"I didn't. I haven't been able to for some reason!" she cried, throwing her hands up. "But tonight I need to..." She wavered on her feet, then caught herself. Hand to her forehead she winced. "Oh God, this is *so* bad."

He scratched his jaw. She hadn't been drinking? Hadn't been able to... *Kill two birds?*

If she drank from him, she would feel even more beholden to him. If she drank...she would climax. He fucking knew he would. There were stories. A million stories about Vampires and their bites. Most Lykae hated the idea, scorned it, but he wasn't fooled. One of his oldest friends, Ranger, was one happy male and there was no chance he'd let Star drink from anyone other than him.

"You aren't drunk, just tipsy. Here." He picked her up.

She let out a little scream, cute as hell, and threw her arms around his neck. She weighed nothing. He had to stare down at her just to be certain he was actually holding *all* of her. She was there, a perfect fit. So light, so amazingly beautiful, his heart steadied at how right she felt in his arms. He might not be a prince from those fairy tales, but she felt like a princess in his arms.

"What are you doing?" She frowned.

"Just so you don't fall on those heels." Silky hair caressed his arm and he felt such a rightness in his chest he couldn't move. She felt…like his.

"I never fall on heels." She sniffed but sounded distracted. *Staring at my neck?* She made a little humming sound and her fang peeked out, nibbling her plump bottom lip. Holy fuck. She was thirsty. Sweat coated his forehead. Dripping down his back. It was cool out. And this was his idea. *Seduce her?* He could barely get her out of the parking lot.

"How about you face me, not the road? Would that be better?"

"But…" She peered up at him, squinting as if she couldn't see him properly. "I won't see the road?"

"Right. That's the idea. Just look at me."

"Just look at *you*," she whispered, sounding as if she liked that idea. *She likes the way I look?* "Okay, but if you wreck, I *will* kick your ass." Her hot breath had his shaft tensing. He battled it back down. As soon as he could walk, two things occurred to him.

One— He'd have her on his lap, facing him, which meant she would be flush with his hard-on.

Two— He had to drive that way.

I can do this.

Doubts filled him. Just the idea of her not being happy made him cringe. Tonight had showed him all he could have if he just did this right. Figure her out. Win a place in her life. He could do this, drive them home.

She nuzzled his throat, purring when she did. *What the fuck am I doing? Just get her home. To the estate, tuck her in, kiss her once, or maybe twice. Go jack off all night.*

Deal.

He got on his bike, still holding her, and twisted her around to face him. "Elsa?"

She fell against him, laughing when she did. Arms around his neck, she leaned into him. He didn't have to slide her closer until her panties were pressed to his groin—the angle of the bike did it for him.

He slammed his eyes shut. *Fucked. I'm so fucked.* She will hate me.

"Jamie?" she whispered in his ear. "Are you certain you can do this?"

Hell fucking no I'm not. "Just need a minute," he grated, gathering handfuls of her silky hair. *Have to catch my breath.*

"Oh, even your neck is hard. But not here." She nuzzled his ear, sending a shot of something he never knew existed down his spine. He grabbed the bike, afraid to hold her as tight as he suddenly needed. "So soft. Is it the only part of you not all hard?"

He managed a sound she took for an answer.

A mischievous twinkle lit her blue eyes, and she leaned in until their lips were almost touching, her breasts right up to his chest.

He could *feel* her nipples hardening against his chest.

"Or, if you want, I can show you something." She pressed her lips to his and slowly slid those little hands down his torso, going arrow-straight for his erection.

Fuck. He wanted to let her. *Needed* to let her.

He gently caught her hands. Pulled her back and made her open her eyes. "Elsa, baby, you want to feel what you do to me?"

She smiled. "Oh… What *I* do to you?" Tugging at her hands, she leaned in and bit his bottom lip. Shocks of pleasure rip corded through him. "I want to do very bad things to you, Jamie O'Connor."

The plan? Fuck the plan, there are no plans in battle. Just survive. "Sweet, if you don't stop—"

"Shhh — don't do that."

"What?"

"Order me about. Threaten me. Tell me, 'If you don't do this.'" She mocked his voice and laughed, delighted with herself, then leaned in and stroked her hands up his chest and around his neck. "Kiss me instead."

"Elsa, I want to kiss you."

"Good." She nodded.

"But do you want to, or does the wine, does it want you to?"

"Wine makes you bolder, but..." Again, another frown and sway on his lap. He caught her by her rounded bottom. Lowered her, easing her legs over his. She seemed to go along with the adjustment. He waited but she didn't move. He sighed in relief, until with a soft wine scented Elsa sigh, she scooted closer. He glanced down. Big mistake. Plush, rounded breasts pressed together to create a valley he wanted to drive his cock between, or lick, bite, hell, just touch. Each breath made them quiver. "I thought *you* were going to kiss me."

He jerked his head back up. Locked his hungry gaze on her lips. "I want to."

"Then *do*." She pressed closer again. The pink curves of her lips were so close he could smell her cherry lip gloss. "Or maybe I should..." She pressed her lips to his, flicking her tongue out to taste the corner of his mouth. Heat stroked his body. He felt on fire. Another flick, another lick, another soft kiss. He refused to move, didn't pull her close, didn't breathe. *How have I lived without this? Without...kisses like butterfly wings.*

With a light, sweet breath, she lifted her head and stared, dreamy-eyed, at him. "Did you like my kiss?"

He nodded, unsure what to say.

"Oh," she breathed and kissed him once more. "My first date ending with a kiss. I'm glad it was you, Jamie."

Fuck. Fuck. Fuck.

I'll rip the head off anyone else that thinks of having you.

199

He wanted her so damn bad the handlebars of the bike bent under his grip.

"It was better than I dreamed. Now…" She sat up and exhaled, making those amazing breasts rise up right under his nose. His mouth watered. "Why are you sooooo—hard and, oh my God, so full of"—she slid her hands lower, then thankfully back up—"of yourself? Wreck and I. Will. Kick. Your. Ass. Got it?" Her grin was contagious.

He swallowed his desire and found his voice. "I got it." He started the bike and gunned it. "Hold tight," he managed.

Two seconds into the drive his third and most fatal flaw to his brilliant strategy hit hard. .

She lifted her arms, wrapped them around his head and began licking his neck. Her hair flew all around them. "Jamie, oh God, your smell is *so* good."

He nearly lost the road. He desperately gained control, used a leg for the turn and kept them from toppling.

"Elsa, almost home. Can you—?"

"Oh, Jamie…is that your…*erection*? Oh my God, it feels like one of those big flashlights. I want to see it."

Fucked.

"Can't. Driving. Soon."

"Oh." She rolled her hips, licking—as if she couldn't stop herself—his neck. "I made you this way?" She laughed. "And I thought your chest was hard." She leaned down and he thought tried to see his erection. It wasn't hard to miss. Her hair flew in his face. He jerked his head to dislodge most of it. "I wondered about it. What you would look like. Will I like the feel of it? I wonder if I will, or will I be disappointed?"

Disappointed? "Elsa, sweetheart, arms around my neck." *She's thought about my cock?* He had to let go of the bike and move her long hair off his face. She tossed it over one shoulder and met his eyes. Hers were still unsteady, hazy with the wine he'd poured her. "You really do want me, don't you? I'm not sure we should wait. You're more than ready…"

"Elsa." He had to concentrate on the road, tight turn, the mansion up ahead.

Elsa began to rock. His vision went black.

"Elsa, sweetheart, you can't do that!" He grabbed her around the waist, kept control of the bike one-armed and tried to stop her from grinding onto his cock.

"Will you come for me?" She shimmed right out of his hand. Back onto his shaft, clearly made for him. "If I do this, I think I will. It feels *so* good."

He blinked. Sweat dripped down his face, stinging his eyes, but he couldn't respond, couldn't see the road. He caught at both handlebars, handled the next turn and didn't crash. Elsa handled him much easier. She moved as if she was born knowing how to make a man come. If he didn't know better, he'd believe the cunning female had put him in this position on purpose.

"Elsa, can you wait, maybe two minutes? Maybe—ah!" She pressed down hard with her pelvis and flung her head back, grinding, grinding, grinding. Breasts right below his nose, sweet-smelling blonde hair flying around him. He knew the only barrier to claiming her was the silk of her panties and his damn jeans.

The road vanished. She found a short, fast rhythm that hit the spot under the flared hood. Locked, loaded and ready to fire. *Cannot come. Cannot wreck. Get her home. Lay her down. Climax. Success.*

An impossible battle plan.

She cried out, tensed and suddenly ducked down, meeting his gaze, blocking the road with her stunning blue eyes and wild, blowing hair. She was bold and breathless. God help him, she was going to come.

As if in slow motion, he watched. Fangs sharp, she panted against his lips. Then, with a small moan leaned in, blowing his mind with a hungry kiss. Everything but her vanished. Her mouth was hot. Silky golden hair spilled all around him. A sharp spike of pain, then his world went insane. He bucked up into her core, pressing her down by his grip on her small waist.

Wait! No, not thrusting. Not holding her down. Holding the bike.

"Elsa!"

He lost control. The world turned upside down.

Elsa pierced his neck. Pleasure swallowed him whole. Black dots swarmed his vision. With a rumbled growl, he clutched her close to his chest and had enough sense to roll. They impacted with something — *who the fuck cares?* — but he took the brunt of the fall. Elsa held on to him like a cat with her last meal. He held her just as tightly. *Yes! Mine!*

Possession surged between them. He caught her ass in his hands. He kneaded the supple flesh the way he'd longed and thrust between her thighs, hearing her moans in his neck as she climaxed harder. His thrusts turned frenzied. He twisted so he was on top. Then he gave her harder surges when her body shuddered.

With a rush the world went still. He hung there in her arms, caught in his own trap. She trembled under him, still caught in an orgasm, legs locked around his hips.

His back arched, and, he gripped her tight, holding her closer as his climax detonated.

"Elsa!" he shouted to the heavens. "That's it, girl, that's it, you're making me fucking come!"

Mindlessly, he bent his head to suck on her shoulder as his seed burst from him. Each ejaculation was better than the last, building higher each time. Her skin was soft, warm, and luscious. Needing more, he tore at her skirt, shoving it to the side. Silken, wet flesh met his seeking fingers. He groaned, growing weak with the delicious stimulation against his fingers as he shuddered with each pulse of release.

With a sob of passion, Elsa broke her bite. Tossed her head and withered against him. He couldn't stop the shallow pumps of his hips, couldn't hold back the groans of satisfaction at how hard he was grinding down against her body, or how wet she was for him.

"Oh God, yes!" She lifted her chest, her breasts quivering under him as she lost herself in another climax.

Stunned, he gaped down at her. *Need to give her more.* He lowered his head and bit down on the slender expanse of her tender shoulder. Her taste filled his mouth. His cock swelled harder, stunning him as he hit another climax.

"Ja...mie..." She stuttered his name, rocking hard under him in her passion. *Again. Give her everything. Give her all you can.* He needed to hear it again. *My name.* He released his bite.

"Say it again, sweetheart. Who's giving you this?"

Her eyes opened, half-lidded still, with shimmering desire deepening the color of her irises. He pressed his fingers to her plump flesh and pinched her clit ever so gently, rubbing it with his thumb when she cried out. Within moments, she was thrashing under him, lifting her hips and twisting, seeking more. *Hot baby, such a hot baby.*

"Jamie!" He felt her climax through his fingers, savored it and gentled his petting.

Muscles rigid, he gave one more desperate flex of his hips as another jet of seed pulsed. Boneless, he sank down on top of her and tried to catch his breath.

She continued to shiver, showing him how much he'd pleasured her with every slight inhalation of her breath. He savored it, treasuring it, and her. Her first climax. *Climaxes.*

His chest felt full. Even as the world came back into focus, he knew he'd never be the same again. He'd never come so hard in his life. Never heard such passion from a woman. Felt such heat. He kissed her throat, sliding his lips down to taste where he'd bitten her.

My little virgin is going to flip her lid.

He lifted his lips in a smile at the thought. More than ready, he kissed her temple, nuzzled her tender neck and held her hands above her head.

"So beautiful, Elsa."

She slowly relaxed under him. Calm. Complacent. Sweet even, then in the midst of licking his collarbone and possibly her way back up his neck, she stiffened.

He held his breath.

Time slipped by slowly enough for him to register that he still had one hand on her bare pussy, savoring the slickness of her flesh. She still had her legs spread wide for his thighs.

That all changed. She tensed, closed her thighs, or tried to. His hips were pressed up between her legs possessively.

"Oh God!" She shoved at him, tried to wiggle away, but he wasn't a fool. He kept her right where she was.

"It's okay. Sweetheart, it's okay. Shh — calm down."

She gasped. He lifted his head. She sucked in a breath — held it. He met her eyes. They were rounded, shocked, sober — a bit — and slowly shimmering with anger. She was miffed. More than a little.

"You are so beautiful when you come."

The plan was to calm her. To show her how wonderful she was. How much he thought of her. It was a misfire to the extent that even he got it. A second *before* she launched him into the air. He landed against the ground and took what felt like a whole body punch. Too late, he also understood that maybe a virgin wouldn't appreciate being drunk, having an orgasm, and wrecking a bike.

Plan? Fail. Didn't get her home. Didn't tuck her in with a kiss. Didn't go jack off…

Instead, he had come so hard he was soaked. His jeans creamed. Not just come, but climaxed twice. *I didn't know that was possible.*

He gained his feet. Held his hands up. Watched her narrow her eyes. Her skirt was askew, her hair wild and her shirt slipped off one beautiful shoulder. He'd ripped it?

She looked well sated, if not madder than hell.

"You're okay. I'm okay. It was nothing. I lost control. You're so fucking…so…"

She screamed. Fisted her hands at her sides and let loose a holy roller of a yell. Seemingly satisfied, she pinned those flickering eyes on him and stalked closer. Every inch of her said he was going to get his heart ripped out. He found himself stepping back.

"Elsa, sweetheart, calm the hell down."

She didn't. If anything she strode faster.

"I'm not kidding you. You are overreacting and if you attack me you will be sorry. I won't hold back, sweet cheeks. I will not hold—"

"You got me drunk! You put me on that! Facing you," she cried. "You knew I hadn't had blood. You knew I would want it. You wrecked! We could have *died*!"

He nodded.

She stopped abruptly, expression startled. "You're agreeing with me?"

"I did wreck, but we weren't going to die. I did *not* get you drunk."

"Like hell you didn't!"

"Okay, maybe to loosen you up, but not to take advantage of you. I had to get you on the bike. It seemed like a good idea at the time to have you facing me, and not the road."

"Why would *that* be a good *idea*?" she shouted.

He let her catch her breath, and when she wasn't ready to hyperventilate, he said, "Because I wanted you to have fun and feel safe. I thought the road would scare you, going by so fast."

She blinked.

He took a chance and lowered his hands. She didn't attack. He took a step closer. "You were strung out, tired from the week. I could tell you were unhappy. I wanted you to have some fun, but I was trying to get us home without wrecking." *Climax in my arms. From me.*

"So you thought an orgasm while driving a high powered machine that could kill us would help?"

He had to wonder if Elsa wasn't the most sarcastic person he had ever met. *Probably.* But her scathing tone reminded him of that score card. *Did I just make her throw that away?*

"Up until I met you, I thought I could manage a machine like that through a snowstorm with a bigfoot hot on my trail. I could drive a machine like that blindfolded." He stepped closer. Her eyes flashed brighter, sparkling in the light of the moon. "One kiss on my neck, with you sitting flush in my arms, and I found out I was wrong."

Her expressive eyes narrowed. He didn't know what else to say. He surely couldn't tell her she was his, *damn it,* and if she was hot, and needy, he was going to be the only one seeing to that fire. He also couldn't admit he had seduced her, gotten her drunk, and taken her on his bike in the hopes that she would want to stay. *With me.*

I have nothing to give her. No home. No jewels. No stability. Nothing a woman craves.

When did I decide to keep her?

How can I let her go?

She blew out a weary breath, and turned her side to him, crossing her arms. "I still think I should kick your ass."

He touched her cheek with the backs of his knuckles. "I bet you do. We need to go find the takeout. I think it flew overhead."

She lowered her head in her hands. "I'm not happy with you. Can you leave me alone for a while?"

Not happy with me? He had wanted a nice night. A dinner. And a kiss… She'd given him so much more. He touched her hands and she lowered them. "You can have anything you want. I'll go find the food. I wanted to fix the water tonight. Then you can take a bath, if you want. Or if I don't fix it, I can heat water."

"Thank you. I'm fine. Vampires clean off without water."

Reminding him again? She turned before he could say more. He let her. There was more here. Something he was missing. She walked easily over the uneven ground in her high heels. She was so small and alone. He rubbed his chest. He wished suddenly he was the kind of man who could give her comfort, but after tonight, and what he'd done, he wasn't sure he could be. *I need her to want to stay.*

I thought my plan was solid.

A solid fail.

Chapter Fifteen

Elsa walked toward the house.

Jamie.

We have to talk.

Her body still felt unlike her own. She wasn't sure what was more addictive. The orgasms. Or the taste of his blood. The heavy, warm spice made her wonder what the hell she'd been drinking all these years. He tasted like home.

But what he did to her body...or what she did *with* his body... Sinful.

I got drunk! I told him things. Her cheeks flamed as the memory of how she'd compared the size of his penis to *a flashlight.* What a moron he must think her. *Obviously, I turn into Chatty Cathy with enough wine.* Who knew? And why wasn't there a warning label? *Vampires get drunk on wine.*

Maybe anyone does with three bottles.

She sighed and kicked a shrub.

Love is like war... Crazy. *That means I need to go back in there and win this time. Leaving is easier...* The mere thought made her feel panicked. *Be honest, if you never saw Jamie again how would you feel?*

Devastated. No more kisses? Crazy. No more...of him? *I haven't even gotten him naked, or watched him touch himself. Leave now?*

If I leave now...

She started off again, too anxious to stand still. She tried to work it out before she ran into him but alone, she only had half the story. First kiss and first orgasm don't equal happy ever after. *But he wants me. That erection proved that, his words after, his sweetness... He wants me!*

She froze mid-step. *He wants me to stay. He wants me here. I could…stay. Get to know him. See if…I'm the one?* Back to square one. He'd know. He's old! So wise, so smart, so much the *elder…*

But what if he doesn't know because he's never experienced it?
She stopped again.

How does one know? Maybe it's a slower thing, maybe… I am the one. And here I am, being stupid worrying over what he thinks and feels. There's only one way to find out.

Stop running.

Feeling immensely better, she took off again, starting to run as she neared the house. Until, with a suddenness that almost landed her on her butt, she ran straight into Jamie.

"Jamie!"

"Damn, are you all right?" He cradled her elbows frowning at her in concern. "Elsa?"

"I thought you were inside."

"I was. I know you wanted to be alone, but it's cold out." He handed her a sweater. "We forgot your sweater at the restaurant."

"Jamie," she sighed feeling like a jerk.

"I know. I said I'd give you time, I'm not—"

"It's not that. Thanks," she said, suddenly shy. "I was cold."

Silence descended like a curtain on the final act. She toed the ground and hugged the sweater to her chest. Jamie didn't move, but since she didn't lift her head, she wasn't sure what he was doing. She thought staring at her. Suddenly it was too much. *Be brave.* She met his gaze. "I'm sorry I got upset with you. Dinner was nice."

He blinked, crossed his arms slowly and bent his head, rocking on his feet a little oddly.

"I mean, crashing and all that, that wasn't fun, but I did have a nice time. I said things that…I shouldn't have—"

"I poured you too much wine. I didn't mean to get you drunk," he said with a wince. "Maybe just loosen you up."

"You loosened me up all right, and my tongue."

He laughed and nodded. "You can get me drunk next time, I've heard I talk a lot."

"You do?" She felt a bubble of happiness burst free from the worry. "I mean, I won't. Get you drunk I mean…" There wasn't much to say after that.

He nodded as if she'd said something interesting. "You must be tired. Do you want to go inside? Rest?"

She sighed, so relieved he was being nice about this, she couldn't hide it. "Yes. I'm exhausted."

"Come on, I'll make sure you don't run into anything else." He took her arm and tucked it through his like a gentleman. He'd cleaned up, she noticed, and changed his clothes. "In the morning, I'll make this up to you."

She felt heat warm her cheeks. *If he sleeps with me… Does he mean…?*

"Here you are, be careful." He guided her inside and to the staircase. He brushed at her cheek and his gaze centered on her mouth. "I'm sorry I got you drunk, Elsa."

"It was still a good first date," she dared to whisper, then turned and raced up the stairs. *Maybe he does want me. Maybe he just needs to know how good it can be, with me.*

Chapter Sixteen

"There you go, try that again," Jamie called, watching Faolan throw the knife and hit the dead center of the target. "Good. Real good."

He was good too. Derrick had been impressed. Jamie could see why. Within half an hour, Faolan could hit the red mark with every single throw. Now he was dead center each time.

He was just about to throw again, the last throw Jamie decided, when something shuddered through the mansion.

"Foalan!" Jamie called the boy to him. "Hide. Now. Here, while I check on Elsa." Jamie shoved the frightened boy under the table and handed him two knives. "Use these only if you have to, but don't hesitate. Hide otherwise."

"I will." Eyes wide, he moved into the darker shadows under the table and his scent slowly eased from the room.

"Good boy. Stay." Jamie raced up the stairs, taking them two at a time in his rush to reach Elsa. This was not the wake-up he'd promised himself. The thought raced through his mind as he turned at the landing and crashed right into her. "Elsa. Shit, I'm sorry. Elsa?" He pulled her up and saw she was laughing, but also holding her mouth. He'd bloodied her lip. "Shit, I—"

"That wasn't the wake-up I was hoping for."

He growled. Obviously she was fine. *Gods, she fits me. Even thinks like me.* "I was thinking the same fucking thing. Come on." He half dragged, half guided her down the stairs and raced with her to the table where he'd left Faolan. They'd made a family room of sorts in this main dining room, either by default or because it was closest to the stairs. "Faolan, stay hidden."

"He's good," she said breathlessly. "I can barely sense him. But what do we do?"

"We wait." Whoever had triggered the alarms was either gone, or they were that good at hiding themselves that he couldn't detect them.

"Wait? Why wait? That's not—"

"Trust me, just once," he said quickly, snapping his sword into place, but checking on her. "Elsa."

"Yeah, yeah, trust you." She rubbed her hands on her legs. "You should know by now I do. I mean, you wrecked a bike with me on it and gave me my first orgasm. Do you think I let just anyone do that?"

The switch in topic got his full attention when he was certain it shouldn't have. "I don't know, do you?"

"Jerk!" She hit him on the chest then gasped like she'd bruised her hand. "That hurt. And no, I don't. For your information, Mr. Macho, I do *not* sleep around. Can you say the same?"

He grinned and didn't bother to hide it. "I'm a—"

"If you say guy I won't have sex with you. Ever."

He paused and shook his head. Women were the strangest creatures on Earth. They were in possible danger, and now, when his mind should be focused on that, she wanted to define whatever the hell was going on between them. Last night she'd quietly gone to sleep. After apologizing to him. Of all the things Elsa had done that was the strangest. He'd lain next to her, watching her until he'd fallen asleep too. Since he'd woken all he'd wanted to do was go up and check on her. Hell if he knew what that meant, and now wasn't the time.

"There is someone here and you want to talk about this now?" She must think he was going to fuck her and leave her. A chill rushed his spine, since that was exactly what he'd once planned. Well, nothing with her went according to a plan. But that was what he normally did with women.

"No. Of course not." She sniffed and turned her back on

him. "I don't want to talk to you at all when you act like —"

He caught her arm and turned her. "What does that fuck—?"

"Stop swearing in front of Faolan."

"You're talking fu—sex in front of Faolan!"

She smacked him again, open-handed this time, on the chest again. "I was not. You were!"

"Woman." He dragged her closer so he could whisper in her ear. "If I had the time right now to set you straight, I wouldn't be talking in the first place. I'm sorry we wrecked the bike last night but I'll be damned if I'll lie and tell you I'm sorry about anything else that happened. Now, get ready. Whoever it is should be here by now."

"What—?"

"Just focus. What do you sense?" he asked, sensing nothing at all. No scent, no sense of danger, nothing.

"I…" She scanned the room, focusing on the darkness beyond the doorway, then the windows. She reached up and moved her hair out of her eyes, but her focus was on whatever she was looking for. "I don't feel anything. What does that mean?"

He didn't want to guess, but tensed when something caught his attention. Then it was gone. A scent, something familiar, now…gone.

"What is going on?" Circerran and Jack slipped in behind them, through a door the witch built in the air. She used a hushed tone, but after the absolute silence it was loud.

"We don't know. I'm going to find out, though. Stay here." He gripped Elsa's cold hand and got her attention on him. "For once, just do—"

"—what you say. Got it," Elsa said. "I was actually doing what you wanted, before, so…"

He checked her eyes, and she was being honest. Not waiting, he took off at a jog, Jack at his side.

"What was it?" Jack asked.

"There was a scent, coming from the back, but it was gone before I could identify it."

Jack kept up with him as they did a complete sweep of the back of the house. They went out of the door Elsa had broken the first night, then on to the kitchen.

"Still nothing?" Jack asked.

Jamie shook his head. There should be something.

"That's not good, right?"

"That's seriously not good. If someone is hiding, like Elsa does, then he could be anywhere," Jamie related quickly. There was much Jack didn't know. He was new to this world, newer than Elsa even. Tougher, sure, but newer. "Just be ready. If he can do that, he might still be here."

"I try to always be ready."

They covered the rest of the lower level and found nothing. Jamie sent Jack upstairs while he did a perimeter check outside. By the time he got nearer to the house it was fully dark. He'd found nothing except an uneasy feeling by the odd gate at the front of the house. He studied that again as he drew near. He still couldn't pinpoint anything to hold on to, so he knelt in the dirt and brushed aside the grass at the base. There in French script he thought he found a word.

"What is it?"

He jumped. "Damn it, Elsa—"

She had the nerve to laugh and pat him on the head. "Oh, did I startle the big, mighty warrior?"

Holy fuck. He hauled her by her perfect ass right up to him and pulled her down on his knee to kiss her. She laughed and tossed her head so all he got was a taste of her neck, which was fine. He held her tighter and rolled her to the ground. She squealed.

"Hush." He slid right between her lush thighs as if he belonged. "You really need to listen to me."

"Oh, I listen, I just don't take orders."

"Elsa—"

She wrapped her legs around his hips and arched up, stopping him in mid-retort. It was all he could do to hold the side of her face gently as he tasted her lips. He wanted her, wanted to take her right then and there. It wasn't a full moon. But he guessed it was close enough. Danger was a distant thing. The alarm, the people waiting in the house, all of that receded into the background as she moaned softly at the first drag of his tongue along hers.

She might as well have said 'fuck me'. It worked the same. He pressed his hand down between them, this time not wasting a moment. He cupped her through her jeans and rubbed the seam against her until she broke the kiss with a shocked gasp. *Bingo.* He didn't stop the pressure, but carefully pressed right where he'd made her gasp. At the same time he sucked along the column of her throat. She wasn't a fuck. She wasn't the type of woman he found to relieve the boredom and strain of his life. She was…

"Elsa."

Her lips were open, wet and beckoning him but he watched as her eyes lost focus and she began to tremble in his arms.

"Come for me, let me hear you come," he whispered gently, pressing against her clit a bit firmer.

"Jamie!" She mouthed the word, but she might as well have shouted it. She trembled, her lush breasts quivering under his nose. He dipped down to lick along the mounded flesh. Another gasp and her legs fell open, shuddering as he held her.

Sounds began to register past the pounding of his heart. *People. House. Danger.* All of it rushed back to his consciousness, as did the length of painful need his erection had become. It ached. Actually, it hurt like he'd used it to hammer nails all day.

"We have company, sweetheart," he said quietly when she startled. He caressed her face, holding her still so he could kiss her lips. His body required more, much, *much* more.

"Jamie?"

"Yeah?" He breathed against her cheek, not ready to end the moment.

"What about…well, what about this?" She curled her hand around his shaft, finding the head pretty damn easily too. "What about you?"

"This." He took her hand and pulled it back up between them and kissed it. "Will wait. You, woman, need to know this isn't some quick one-nighter."

"No?" she challenged.

He grinned. Footsteps were coming nearer and they belonged to Jack.

"No."

He lifted her up and stood, keeping her in his arms and his mouth over hers to quiet the gasp of surprise. He was rocked to the soles of his boots at how out of control he'd let this get between them. *We're in danger and I just about fucked her.*

"But right now we need to see what the—what's going on. Agreed?" He set her down slowly, savoring the painful slide of her body along his erection.

"Okay."

"Damn if all it takes is giving you an orgasm to get you to agree I'm doing that more often."

She tossed her head to stare back at him in disbelief. "I can't believe you just said that! You really are—"

"—amazing."

She gave him a slow, sexy smile that zipped along muscles that were already worked up to full capacity. "You were."

He didn't know what to do with that, so he shook his head and tried to clear it. She took a few deep breaths, as if trying to calm what was building between them too.

"What were you…? I mean…" She breathed deeply a few times, then said, "What were you doing before you pounced on me?"

"You needed to be *pounced* on."

"I might want to be pounced on again, too, but not in front of—"

"Jack, I think I found something." He stepped in front of her. He still couldn't believe he'd been so distracted by her he'd dropped his guard. At least he'd retained some amount of sanity and kept their clothes on. "Here, at the post. It's French, *por toujours,* but it means forever. Just like—"

" —the pendants. But what does that mean? Is this house connected?" Elsa scanned the area as if, suddenly, it was as horrifying as the witches' house.

"It can't be." Jack stopped near them.

"First rule of your new world should have been *anything* is possible. I've been over every inch of the place. I've never scented danger, but it's here. Or it *was* here." Jamie drew in a deep breath. The unease he'd felt earlier was gone. *Does that mean the danger with it?* "Bryson said that a woman was killed here, a ballerina, by her husband. Elsa is a ballerina. This is here." He pointed to the same scroll-worked words *forever.* "We're not that far from the witches' house. It's all too close. Nothing is coincidence."

Elsa put her hand in his, clearly not happy and needing reassurance, because she also leaned into him. She was still warm and soft from her orgasm, but she was trembling and not in the way he liked.

"There's a connection. There *has* to be. But that doesn't mean it's centered on me, Jamie," she argued.

Jack shook his head. "Well, it sure looks to be circling the wagons around you and the boy. We set this alarm not thinking we'd need it. You needed it."

Elsa pressed her lips together. She was frightened, but he could see she still wasn't buying that she was the one being hunted.

The thought of either of them being hurt panicked him. But with her here it was proving too difficult to focus. *Look what happened, even in the midst of danger.* If she were with the pack, he could make sure she was safe, and keep her away, until after the full moon, at least.

He'd be able to see clearer. The moon pulled him toward her. The urge to claim her was growing worse each night. What would happen when it rose? Would he lose his wolf and...harm her?

"Do you still sense something?"

Jamie shook his head, more to clear it than to answer. "No. But there's something here, something I'm missing." He focused on Elsa. Because she was there, his brain seemed to stop functioning. If she so much as smelled a tiny bit aroused, forget it, he was lost. It would be better if she were safe with the pack.

"Let's go see if Cir missed something too or she found something," Jack muttered.

Elsa nodded, going along with Jack. Jamie walked a bit slower behind them, worrying now that she might fight him as hard on leaving as she had on staying.

Chapter Seventeen

"I've got to go wash up," Elsa said, when she had Faolan tucked in.

"No hot water yet," he muttered. "Tomorrow, I'll get that worked out."

"Why? Are we really staying here?"

He gave her an odd frown, almost like before—meaning before the kisses, before the, God help her, orgasms.

"No. I think it might be best if we moved to the pack, let this settle for a day or so. Then see what happens."

"I don't know, I mean, Circerran and Jack said we were okay here. I don't like to be around too many—"

"—immortals. I know. But you have the pack all wrong. It's not like they are in everyone's business. It's a big estate with more acreage than you can imagine. There are cottages if you want one. Some people live at the main stronghold, but most don't."

She smiled and thought about it. "Where do you live?"

"I don't really live anywhere." He glanced away. "I have a room at the stronghold."

"Really?" She studied the floor as she headed to the bathroom. He'd cleaned the wood until it shone. "That's kinda sad."

"Not really. I move around a lot."

"Right, I know that. So…" He'd walked closer, but stopped at the doorway, leaning a shoulder against the wall. "You'd be there too, and we'd just wait?" An uncomfortable silence, which she took for a no, then he met her eyes again. *Yep, for sure a no.* She turned and cut him off. "Nope, not going. I told you I'd help with Faolan and I still will, but I won't be going to the stronghold. I don't belong there."

"Just think on it. It's safer—"

"Not without you." She was shocked she'd said that out loud. Her face grew hot.

He grimaced and shook his head, as if she were being silly.

"Look, I'm used to tracking. It's what I do. But I do it alone. I'm not trying to be harsh," he said, taking her hand, or trying to. She pulled away. "Elsa, I'm not trying to do anything but figure out what's going on. Haven't you ever needed to figure something out and needed to be alone to do it?"

She nodded, because yes, he'd allowed her that last night. But he was still talking about leaving her with his pack. *Leaving me. Am I more than a one-nighter? Really? If I am, why does he want to drop me?*

Because maybe he wants two nights, or a whole bunch of hook-ups, but you're not his mate. The thought had her stomach aching. Worse, it sounded...right. It fit. *God, it's like he's in an arranged marriage, and I'm just someone to waste time with... until he finds his mate.*

"So you understand what I mean?"

She nodded again, because she did. She interfered with his work, but when he wasn't working, that was cool, they could mess around. *But can I? Mess around with Jamie O'Connor?*

"I have to go wash up. My face feels dirty."

"Elsa." He pulled her to a stop and there it was—the banked passion he'd kept on hold since she'd met him. Was she strong enough to take it, and make this about what she wanted, on her terms? *If he wants to leave it's going to hurt.*

So leave him first, and make it hurt less.

She blinked as the idea took hold. All this time, she'd been worrying over what this was between them, and each time she'd come to a full stop because... *I don't think I'm his.* So what if she wasn't? If he wanted her, and she wanted him... What good was holding out for the one? What if the one never showed up?

But have sex with Jamie O'Connor, then leave before he does?

Can I do that?

"I think your face is pretty clean."

She laughed. "Was that a compliment?"

The relief on his face was crystal clear.

Can I put this on my terms not his?

He backed her into the bedroom he'd cleaned. Where they'd almost had sex because he'd wanted a quickie. It seemed like years ago, not just a few days. But in that time she'd grown closer to him. Even when he was being the wounded bear, she had learned more about him. Now he felt familiar, but not at the same time. *I've never seen him naked.* The way he stared at her now, though, she felt the rush of desire rise up and something brave, daring, and even demanding surface. *He should be mine. He can be.*

If only for a night.

"I want you." He said it so brashly. As if to scare her off.

"I want you too."

He didn't laugh, but there was a hint of a smile on his handsome face before he drew closer and moved her to the bed. She rested a hand on his chest, and felt the beat of his heart against her palm. He was breathing steadily, but there wasn't going to be any stopping now. Even if the alarm sounded, or Jack and Cir walked in, the man facing her now was determined, and primed.

"Sure you're ready?" he asked.

"You sure you are?"

The next second she was flat on her back, Jamie on top of her. He settled his hips between hers, and all thoughts but how much she wanted him disappeared. She pulled his head down by a handful of hair and kissed him. He groaned into it, like she felt he should, and groaned even louder when she lifted her hips and meshed her body to his. The length of his erection inflamed her, making things happen in her body that startled her, but were so good she moaned into the kiss. She needed naked, but more, she needed *him* naked.

"Fuck me, Jamie."

"God damn, woman. Hasn't anyone ever warned you not to talk like that to a man?" He wrapped his arms around her, and tugged her hair in his hand to pull her head back. It felt so good, she wrapped her legs around his lean hips and ground against the substantial package trapped under his jeans.

Jamie was hung.

And she enjoyed every inch he shoved against her. Unlike the disgusting feel of the rabid Jackal, Jamie was wanted, *oh so wanted* and more, he was *needed*. He grew harder and she knew when he filled her, she was going to at the least know she was alive. Maybe being careful when they got to that point would be wise, but for now, she wanted him wild.

"Does it look like I care?" She tugged and got enough space to twist so she was on top. Wild, open-mouthed kisses followed. His mouth was hot, his tongue strong as he stroked it along hers. She dove in, tasting him as deeply as possible, until their teeth clashed and she was breathless. It was beyond wonderful. It was fucking, but with their mouths. It took every ounce of her concentration because she needed more, wanted it all.

He gave her more.

With a sudden jerk, she found herself on her back, Jamie covering her with his heavy, hot body. She couldn't get enough of him. A wild, purely satisfied part of her felt him grow, stiffening in preparation as she stroked all over him. Everywhere she could reach, she touched, under his shirt, down the back of his jeans to squeeze his silky, firm ass, up his shoulders, along his biceps as he held himself over her on his elbows. But he didn't stop kissing her, not once. He used his tongue along hers, dominating the kiss in a rhythm he matched with his hips. Each time he ground down on her pussy, sparks seemed to fly.

It devastated her. She wanted, no she absolutely *had* to

have him do that, but with the substantial erection he'd shoved firmly between her legs as far inside her as possible.

She caressed his toned stomach and got hold of his belt. At her touch, he lifted a fraction, allowing her room, but didn't stop kissing her. He did gather her hair in his hands and tug, making her arch her neck. The kiss broke, but his lips on her jaw then hotly kissing a path down her throat made up for it. She was too busy anyway. She got the belt open, the buttons on his jeans undone, but when she shoved her hand inside there wasn't enough room to pull what she needed out.

He was so big it was impossible. Just getting her hands on him was enough—for now. She measured the length of him, and grew wet just at the size of his shaft. He was thick, the hard flesh covered with a thin layer of satiny skin she held tightly and rubbed, so it moved up and down. His groans grew deeper. *Yes!*

"Damn, baby," he growled, pulling up just enough to stare down at her. She bit her lip at the need in his eyes. A rush of pleasure made her gasp and arch her back, wanting what she saw in his golden gaze. "Fuck me, that's it, Elsa. Get wild."

Wild? She was on fire, so hot for him she felt like she was hurting from the lack of him filling her. She slowed and eased her other hand down his stomach, torturing him a bit with a long caress meant to tease him. He tensed and his breathing grew harder, then with a roughness she craved, but didn't know it until he hauled her mouth to his, he kissed her. It was as good as the other kisses, those sexy battles that ended with him controlling the thrust and drag so all she had to do was savor every second of the ride.

She got his buttons open, but couldn't manage to pull what he had where she needed it—specifically, out of his jeans.

"Here, let me." He laughed at her attempts and reached down, doing something that allowed his erection rose up and out, landing on her skin with a heat that made her insane with want. She drew his head down and bit his lip, sucking it after, but wanted to remind him that laughing wasn't nice.

He tossed her onto her stomach for it, and her jeans tugged down, then over her ass. With a deep, erotic growl, he bent one knee up and shoved his hard erection against her. The head surged along her vagina, hot, heavy and oh so thick, she fisted the sheets.

"Jamie!"

"Fuck, you're wet." He pulled up but returned to breathe hotly in her ear, his naked chest settling on her back. Her shirt was shoved up, uncomfortable but she didn't care. All she cared about was him, now, penetrating her and riding her until nothing else mattered but this.

She moaned as he pushed forward, feeling the head fully for the first time stretching her, as he pushed. *So good.* It was beyond erotic. She pressed back against his size, wanting more of him.

"Let me in, Elsa."

"Jamie!"

"This is fucking, Elsa. I'm not going to go easy on you. Not going to hold back and not going to stop until you tell me to." He held himself there, just the tip spreading her, his hot chest to her back, his thighs shoved to hers, and his head by hers, breathing hotly against her neck and ear.

"I haven't. Don't stop!"

He laughed again and she arched her head and bit down on his biceps.

"Ah, fuck. I warned you. We can stop now."

"Oh, no we can't." She moved her knee, braced herself and shoved backward and managed to lodge him inside to a painful degree. She clenched the sheets and gritted her teeth, too far gone now to stop, as she pressed back harder.

"God damn, sweetheart," Jamie gritted. "So tight, here, let me or I'm gonna lose control." He took hold of her hips. She tested his control, couldn't move. Excitement and need mixed to a degree that had her moaning.

"No. Fuck me, Jamie." There was *no* controlling this. She surged forward on her arms then pushed back just as hard, taking more of his painful size this time.

"I warned you." Jamie tightened his hands, until she couldn't move, and at the same time, he pressed her down, one knee still bent. A warning growl vibrated through her, the only warning before he started fucking her.

"Jamie!" It was as wild as the kiss. He didn't go slowly. He didn't hold back. He shafted into her until the bed was smashing into the wall. Their bodies slapped together even louder. And each time he smacked his hips to her butt, his cock burrowed deeper and deeper to the sound of his rough growls of pleasure.

The fit was tight. She felt every hard inch, every swell and curve of him and loved it.

The pleasure grew, building until she couldn't stand it any longer and screamed into the bedding. Jamie bent lower over her and breathed into her nape, wet, hot breaths that made her climax reach a peak and hover there. He whispered how sexy she was, how wickedly perfect she felt around him, and how he was going to make her scream. Her mouth opened, but no sound came out, no breath left her as he continued to pump and pump until, suddenly, it happened.

She climaxed.

Nothing compared to it. She was filled, could clench down and ripple along Jamie as her body began to shudder in reaction. Her first orgasm, while being fucked, hit hard. It took her breath and captured it. Her thighs shivered, her arms trembled, and she screamed.

Jamie nudged her head, finding her lips and seared her mouth with an open-mouthed kiss. At the same time he kept her impaled until she could feel his sac brushing the front of her pussy. She couldn't catch her breath, couldn't seem to remember she didn't need to, since she was a Vampire. Nothing mattered, nothing existed outside of Jamie.

We're one. One body, one breath, one.

The pleasure detonated again before the first climax had slowed. She convulsed, tensing and easing, tensing and easing in ecstasy.

Jamie drew back, breaking the kiss with a shout. "Oh, fuck yeah! That's it, girl, that's it, gonna come for you."

His erection stiffened inside her, growing impossibly bigger. Then, with an out-of-control bout of thrusting that scooted her up the bed, he bit down on her nape.

Heat flooded her womb. Something wild broke free inside her. Something she'd never known she held, buried deep within. She felt whole. Complete. She relished his bite, his cock, and savored both with low moans and lusty thrusts of her hips.

On top of her, Jamie shook with the force of his pleasure, making her tremble in turn. The way he held her down so tightly, with his arms around her arms and head, the fact that her jeans were shoved down past her butt, and his bite on the back of her neck pinning her in place, all collided. Without thought, she stopped kissing his forearm he'd planted near her lips and instead sank her fangs in, drawing on his blood. Sweet, intoxicating Jamie flooded her.

Jamie broke his bite. "Fuck, fuck, *fuck*, yes, woman!" He surged into her, still hard, still able to fulfill more of what she wanted. "Do that while I do you again, Elsa baby."

She sucked harder, drawing on his blood, not too much for fear he'd pass out and this would be over, but enough to make him groan in pleasure. She wanted him to *do* her again. She wanted more until she couldn't lift a finger. Until she couldn't remember what a monster she was.

She released her bite and shoved back into him. Jamie grabbed hold of her hips and took over with a growl. He pumped into her, creating that fast, hard, frenzied tempo she needed — again.

By the time he'd emptied himself two more glorious times, she was higher than any kite had ever flown. His blood tingled down her throat. His seed trickled along her thigh. And his body was heavy, hot and breathless, on top of hers. *Feels right.* Only she wanted more of him, more of this, more of it all. *Can't leave him. Never letting him go.*

"Again."

"Holy fuck, Elsa." He groaned, but his penis, still lodged so perfectly inside her, stiffened, growing bigger and longer as he breathed against her neck. It was so thrilling, tremors weakened her. Sweat-slick skin slid along her back, meshing them perfectly.

Shocking her, he pulled free, but reassured her by immediately turning her over and tearing her jeans and boots off. He was still in his jeans, but what mattered was out and hanging low and heavy from his hips.

She took hold of him, thrilled to hear him groan heavily. Both hands didn't cover him, and one wouldn't go around him. The flesh was velvet over stiff, brown steel, enormously thick from the tip to where it nestled in a tawny bed of soft pubic hair. The rounded head split like a peach, but was warm, and still glistened enticingly from their wild sex. She traced down the column, learning the rounded grooves and weight of him in her hands.

He didn't let her play for long. He pressed her back, by crawling up between her thighs, and settled his cock on her pussy, shifting to lodge it right where she wanted. He groaned as he thrust forward, but with the one surge he impaled her perfectly. He seemed to agree to the perfection. He stopped there, eyes on her face, shimmering amber down at her.

"So damn soft and ready."

"Jamie," she whispered.

"Gotta have you again." With a heavy groan, he fell onto her. She eagerly shifted her legs around his hot sides and back so she could wrap them around his waist. The kisses turned frantic within moments, as did the hard smack of his body impacting with hers. This position dragged his heavy erection past her clit in ways the other had not. She skimmed his skin, dragging her nails over his muscles, and lifted her hips to meet his thrusts. The brown disks of his nipples drew her attention and she sucked on the small points, loving his deeper groan and faster, harder pace. All too soon she was biting his shoulder, needing to feel the pulse of another climax so badly she couldn't bear it.

"Jamie."

At her sob, he lunged deep, pushing her legs onto his shoulders. She arched her neck and cried out louder when he tore her shirt up and over her breasts.

"Give me these beauties. Show me what you can do, Elsa."

What I can do?

She fell apart. At the first hot feel of his mouth around her nipple, she lost the option to scream in pleasure, because it exploded, kidnapping her breath and trapping her much as he had her, pinned down and at his mercy.

He didn't stop. He kept on, thrusting and leaving hard, stinging kisses on her sensitive flesh until his rhythm grew wilder and he groaned heavily. Then, he rose higher on his arms and captured her mouth for a passionate kiss. She felt him stiffen, then with a deep growl, he pumped his body harder, coming with such urgency she fisted the sheets to stop herself from clawing him in her own excitement. His climax drove her crazy. She wanted for it to never end. As long as he fucked her, there was a break from everything because, in his arms, there wasn't room to think. There wasn't time to worry, or be concerned that she was spreading her legs for a man she might have to leave. Nothing but him, and more of what he gave her, mattered.

He collapsed on her for a brief moment, sucking along her neck and to her ear, then groaned as she tightened on his penis. "Another round?" he mumbled.

"Yes. More."

"Un-fucking-believe-able." He surged upward, apparently also ready for more, but this time, she had a feeling he was going to make it the last. She only hoped that meant the last for the night and not the last, period.

Don't want to leave this behind. Him behind.

Chapter Eighteen

Jamie pulled his erection almost free from Elsa's tight, sweet heat then thrust back in, growling and clenching his fists in her silky, tangled hair. He flexed his hips backward, watching every glistening inch slide free and the way her pink sex kissed the tip. She was wet with excitement and from the loads of cum he'd spurted, but damn, she was tight.

She wasn't a 'lie on the bed and take it' kind of girl. She moved under him and stroked every inch of him she could reach. She drove him nuts with sudden bites. And God help him, the addictive draws on his blood. Every time she did that, he swore his body was going to burst with pleasure. The sensations didn't stop at his hips, but raced along every nerve ending until his toes were curled and he swore his hair stood on end. If she'd licked her way down to his cock and suddenly told him she could hold her breath for hours, he wouldn't have been more blown away.

She didn't talk, though, or make loud noises, or do all those over-the-top sounds some women made. Elsa made a sound only if he hit her just right, or he didn't. She sobbed, or she gasped, or she laughed but she did it all only when she *felt*.

She felt a lot. He made sure of it.

Any other woman would have stopped him after the second go. He got the feeling Elsa would have *let* him stop, but walked away one hell of a disappointed and unsatisfied woman.

He wasn't going to let her down. Not a chance. By the time the full moon hit, he was going to have her ready for every possible position they could think of, plus any more that came to mind. She'd never have to ask for more, because he'd always make sure to give her all she wanted, just to hear that sweet sound of her pleasure.

The thought made him stiffen, the pre-warning that she'd done it again, made him lose his control. He was a man who could fuck for hours *without* coming. He'd been fucking her for hours, but had come more times than he could count. It was addictive. Everything about her, from her skin to her hair to her soft, warm, tight pussy, and especially her lips, was off the normal sex experience for him. He didn't have to hold back, she sure the hell wouldn't let him. Just the reality of that had sweat trailing down his back as he powered his hips back and forth, working his cock so she cried out a little louder each time.

The build-up to climax tingled along his spine, warning him that time was of the essence. He tipped her to the side and pushed her legs to her chest, driving into her pussy, so he could sample her lips and her bouncing beauties while he took hold of her rounded bottom. The plump perfection of her breasts was only topped by the most gorgeous set of nipples a woman had ever owned. Each was a pearl of hard, pink, sensitive flesh that he could sample for hours. He tracked the bounce of one and caught it, sucking hard so the little nub was pressed tightly to the roof of his mouth.

Elsa gasped, arched her neck and clenched on his cock in another orgasm.

Each one of her climaxes filled his chest with a warm, tight sensation, as if he'd done something right with her. *Finally.*

She clenched his hair in her fist and pulled, to add to the fire she already had going on in his groin. His balls were drawn up, tight and hard. Sweat drenched his flesh. His heart raced. His arms were trembling with strain, but nothing short of a horde of Death Stalkers could stop him from pleasuring her.

He lifted from her breasts and surged forward, thrusting to his completion, but really tempting her to bite him again on the chest. She did, hard enough to make his balls prickle in warning, then blow. He dug his toes into the bedding, groaning at the ecstasy. Something under them cracked, but he couldn't have cared less. The sensations grew more intense rather than less, until his arms gave out and he fell onto her, shuddering so hard the bed shook and whatever broke, dropped them a few inches. She didn't loosen her bite. She sucked harder, slipping her hands down his back to cup his ass to keep him in place.

Only when she'd wrung every ounce of strength out of him did she slip her fangs from his chest and lick the spot. She might as well have licked his cock. It stiffened, more than ready for attention, but he wasn't. He rolled off, groaning as his muscles went loose as noodles. The only muscle that wasn't rose up hard and ready along his navel.

Elsa seemed to think that a challenge. She lifted up, ripped her shirt and bra off and climbed on.

"Again?" She settled on his lap, sitting her perfect pussy right on top of his cock. The ultra-soft skin of her inner thighs stroked along his hips, while she leaned forward, perching her small hands on his chest. *Jesus, she is beautiful.* "I think we broke the bed, but let's see if we can't do some real damage."

He couldn't believe the anticipation in her voice and couldn't say no either. Not when his cock was hard and missed the warmth of her sucking him in. She laughed and bent to kiss him, lifting her gorgeous ass in the air as she did. He rubbed his hands down her back to take handfuls of the rounded lush curves. She had an ass that fit his hands perfectly, plump but toned, and satiny-smooth.

"I think I've worn you out. Need some of those blue pills?"

"Woman." He laughed and squeezed her butt. "It's your turn to do some work. Ride me."

"Oh." She widened her eyes and reached between her breasts and slowly past her stomach to where he waited at her pussy. Her grip stunned his senses, especially when she stroked him up and down, over the crown, then under that sensitive hood. "Are you certain?"

"Elsa."

She smiled as she licked along his lips, outlining them with her pink tongue. It seemed to satisfy her to no end when he thrust into her hand impatiently. She sucked on his bottom lip, smiling after she released him then kissed him as deeply as she could. Coming up for air, she smiled down at him.

"Elsa—"

"Are you certain you want more, Jamie?"

"Doesn't it feel like I'm certain?" He lifted her with his hips. Her breasts bounced and she nearly fell off. He carefully caught her arm and steadied her.

"All right, all right!" She laughed and he sat her back down. "But I'm not going to go easy on you. Not going to hold back and not going to stop until you tell me to."

Parroting his own warning back at him shouldn't have made him laugh, but it did. He rose to wrap his arms around her and press his chest to hers, unable to hold in the laughter. Until she pressed her hands to the side of his face and held him there as she kissed him again. Everything else fell to the background. She kissed him as if she never wanted to stop, as if this was much, much more than fucking.

He knew it was for him. He wasn't certain what she was thinking. Was this something more or just wishful thinking on his part?

At the sudden worry, he took over the kiss, unable to stand it any longer. Her breasts plumped up against him, teasing him as he wrapped his arms around her. Her smooth, toned body was familiar to him now as if he'd made love to her for years, not hours. The way she caught her breath, or gasped, or bit her bottom lip—everything she did caught and held him closer to her than anyone else in this world.

When he released her she was breathless and glowing. "You kiss beautifully."

It was a funny thing to say to a man, but he didn't laugh. She meant that, and for some reason that strengthened the bond he felt building between them.

"Show me what you've got, woman." He fell back down, taking her with him and his cock slipped along her pussy in the process. "Ride me."

She reached down and handled him well, drawing the head right to where he wanted, then pressed back. She didn't stop there, but held him down firmly with a hand on his chest, and lifted onto her knees, her breasts swaying like two perfect peaches right above his nose as she began pumping up and down on his cock. Her stomach was lean, grooved with a line down the center, but still womanly soft in all the right places. Her ribs drew his attention when she lifted her hand to her face and bit on her palm as she swiveled her hips. He caressed them, marveling at the feel of her warm skin.

"Holy hell." He'd been fucked before. He was man enough to admit he liked to be in charge. But sometimes a man wanted to watch a woman gain her own orgasm just with his cock and whatever she wanted to do with it. This was nothing like that.

Elsa dropped her hand and smoothed it slowly over his chest, biting her lip, the bottom one, with a fang peeking out at him, reminding him how damn good it felt to have her drink from him. She had her head to the side, her hair swinging in time with her movements. Her breasts jutted, the nipples pink and perfect. He spotted marks from his mouth on both, especially near the underside of one, where he'd bitten down during a wild climax. Each pump of her hips was coupled with a low moan and a harder, firmer drive at the end of each thrust, so she hit his thighs with her rounded ass.

It was like nothing he'd ever seen before. The closer she grew to her orgasm, the more she leaned forward, until each thrust on his cock brought her chest sliding along his and her open mouth inches from his. He could barely keep still. It was impossible not to touch her, rub his hands over the smooth rippling muscles of her gorgeous skin as she fucked him.

She gasped and stiffened, tightening on him, then began going faster, harder, more urgently on him as she drew closer to her climax. Suddenly she clenched, jerking and shuddering. Even her legs trembled. He caught her and held her in place. Her eyes radiated such ecstasy, he got lost in them.

The intensity grew until, unable to stop himself, he rose and plastered her to him, fucking into her with rapid, desperate drives of his hips as they fell back down together. He bit her on the shoulder, unable to contain the rapture without her taste in his mouth. She gasped his name on a moan. He heard the need and stiffened and rolled her onto her back so he could pump into her harder and give her what she needed.

When he could breathe again, he made to move, certain he was too heavy for her, but she stopped him with a hand on the back of his head.

"Don't move," she whispered, tightening her grip on his hair.

"I don't know if I can."

She was silent, then she pressed a kiss to his shoulder. After the workout she'd given him it was sweet. For some reason he pressed one to her shoulder and rolled, pulling her with him. It'd been forever since he'd slept, or felt like it.

"Rest. I'll see about giving you more later."

Instead of laughing, she curled up in his arms and positioned herself so she was as close as possible. He brought her leg up, between his, and her head down to his chest. *Sleep. Certainly she could do that for a few hours.*

Then he'd see about letting her know that the only solution to her being safe was to go with Faolan to the pack. There, she'd be protected. She didn't want it, but she had to understand it was for the best. She'd been amazing tonight, but during a full moon, a wolf was always more aggressive. He'd learned to shy away from sex during those times.

With her, he was certain, even if he might want to have her on the full moon more than anything else in this world, he shouldn't. *Look at tonight. I just took her repeatedly, when this was her first sexual experience. I barely felt her virginity slip away. What will I do when the moon is full?*

She has to go to the pack. Keep her with them, get busy then go to her as soon as the full moon is over.

For some reason, as he thought it, his gut clenched. He ignored the sensation and settled his head closer to hers. He was a loner, not equipped to take care of a woman. She'd be better, safer with the pack.

Then why does it make me want to pull her in even closer?

No answer came, but he wrapped his arm around her head and drew her small body as close to his as possible. She sighed against his chest, the feeling so right he brushed another kiss to her sweet-smelling hair and settled over her.

I'll figure it out in the morning – evening. When we wake.

Chapter Nineteen

Elsa woke alone. It was still night outside, but the bed was empty. Well used, but now cold and silent.

Jamie. She could scent him, nearby but on the phone. She moved off the bed, and on bare feet, walked to the door he'd left ajar.

"No, that works. She'll be ready. The boy, too. No, I won't be coming with them. The pack can take care of them better than anyone. Now that this mission is finally over, I can concentrate on what I was supposed to be doing."

What he was supposed to be doing? She walked back to the bed, suddenly numb all over. *So this had been a pit stop mission until the next real one?*

Don't jump to conclusions. Let him explain.

She dressed, calling whatever she could remember from her flat in London. As soon as she pulled the fresh jeans and T-shirt on, she walked downstairs, still feeling numb. Her inner thighs were tender, but other than a few beautiful marks on her shoulder and love bites on her breast, it was like any other night. Like last night — *Jamie making love to me so sweetly, so wildly* — never happened.

Can't leave him. Can't leave him. Don't panic. Don't panic. It meant something. He was so tender. So amazing...

"Elsa, there you are," Jamie said in greeting, turning back to his packing immediately after. "There's food on the table."

Faolan raced up and hugged her.

"Going somewhere?" she asked, hoping that he wouldn't keep to his plan or that there was a reason for it. *I just need a reason. Maybe a reason for it.*

235

"Yeah. I know you were against going to the pack, but someone is coming to collect you and Faolan. I want you to go with them. It's safer. At least for a few nights."

Her heart sank, aching so badly it felt as if he'd sliced it first, then dropped it to her toes. *He's leaving. Lone wolf. Better off by himself. A tracker.* "And you are going with us?" she asked, as casually as she could.

His shoulders stiffened, but he didn't turn to face her. "I have a job they want me to do. We let this sit for a day or two. See what we're missing. It's safer for Faolan."

Elsa studied Jamie's profile, all he would give her. He was tense. The warm, thoughtful lover from last night was gone. Even the knuckle-dragger had disappeared. He turned to give Faolan a glance. The boy smiled, but it didn't last long.

"Is that what you think, Faolan? You'll be safer there?" she asked.

Faolan frowned and shrugged. "I don't know, Elsa."

"He will be, trust me," Jamie said, zipping up packs and shoving more things in side pockets. He really was busy. *He's had his fuck, now he has to run.*

"What about all the work you did here? Will you still live here?" *Will you want me to come and stay too?*

"Not sure. Last night we had a visitor—"

"You're not sure of that. Even Circerran and Jack weren't."

"I sensed someone. So did you."

"And? We were fine. This is the place to be. Here. I can help. I have before. I can again." *Please, Jamie, don't do this. Don't make this a quickie. Don't make me mean so little.*

He tensed but didn't respond.

She turned away, unable to stare at his profile any longer. *He won't even glance at me?* Faolan anxiously watched them, clearly catching that things were back to not okay. She experienced another slice of pain in her chest.

"The pack is safer, Elsa. Why can't you see that?"

"I guess I can't. Sorry."

"Sorry? For what?"

I let this happen. This rising, she'd hoped to wake up to

warm kisses and Jamie hot and heavy on top of her. Dreams. *I can't believe I let myself dream when right there the reality was always right there. He was always on this course. Always going to go, so grow up, face it, and either deal with it, or let him go.*

"Faolan, can you go get me my sweater? I think it's upstairs." She tousled his hair. *I'll see him again. Once I'm over Jamie, I'll find a place, maybe get Circerran to protect it with spells and have Faolan live with me.*

Faolan smiled and raced up the stairs. She turned to Jamie. Anger and hurt were toxic emotions. She studied his stiff shoulders, and something else occurred to her, making her even angrier. *He regrets last night. I'm one of those women men screw, then are embarrassed to have to deal with after.*

"I'm sorry because I see I was wrong."

"It's for the best this way," he said, still sounding distracted. "You don't have to say you're sorry."

It was too much. She placed trembling hands on her hips. "I'm not saying I'm sorry because I think going to your fucking pack is right, you stupid fuckwit! I'm sorry that *fucking* you has suddenly made you *fucking* unable to not only think properly but *fucking* listen properly. I'm leaving. On my *fucking* own, just like you, it appears."

He threw his bag onto the chair with a thunderous expression at the first use of *fucking* out of the bedroom. She didn't care.

"What the fuck is wrong with you? You can't stay by yourself! It's clear to everyone but you."

"Sorry, but I don't think you know *everyone*." *Gain control, don't let him see you cry.* "I really have told you this several times. You should keep up."

"I have a job—"

"Liar. You don't have a *job*! We're not done with this one!"

His face went hard as stone—maybe screaming at him wasn't the best move on her part. But it *hurt*. The more he talked, the more it hurt.

"I have to find a missing friend, Elsa, but that doesn't mean I'll stay gone."

It was too little, and too late, and much too awkward. "Whatever, I won't be here."

"Elsa, you just need to calm down and listen. You can't act like a child any—"

"God, what is it about people starting sentences with my name and following it with stupidity? I don't want your opinion, your advice, or you!" She wasn't going to be able to hold back the tears much longer.

His gaze darkened ominously. "God damn it, you are not safe alone. You aren't safe, *period*. We had sex, Elsa. It doesn't change that you need *protected*."

"I can protect myself!"

"Only a child talks like that!"

"You would know! At least I don't have little toys I put on a shelf to keep them safe. *I live*. It's more than I can say about you! Go track that puzzle and see if you can figure it out!"

"Elsa," he grated, clearly trying to rein in his temper.

She turned away, heartsick at the way he was tossing her aside. She'd said she'd stay until he got Faolan picked up. So in a way he *had* kept his side. She'd said they'd break things. They'd broken the bed. *So, I kept my side of the deal.*

"We've completed our bargain. The boy is all set." *Deny it, Jamie. Deny it!*

He stared at her as if she was being unreasonable. Arms crossed, head half down, glowering at her. Nothing more was said, though.

So it is goodbye. I will not cry.

She'd flattered herself that he'd used the boy to get close to her. Well, that had worked, hadn't it? He'd gotten closer than any other man. She'd almost thought he *was* fixing this place up for her. Score one for team Jamie. He got the virgin after all.

She stood taller. "Goodbye, Jamie O'Connor. Tell Faolan I'll see him soon."

She was proud that she hadn't inserted a 'fucking' between O and Connor. She'd wanted to. She misted and shot through the ceiling. She wished she could be back in her London flat, miles away from him and whoever he'd called to come *pick her up*.

A sudden dizziness, along with a sick sensation like she'd fallen from a height and suddenly she was standing in her bedroom.

"Oh shit."

She stared around, because this *was* her home. And she'd been in France seconds before.

The shock was hard to take. The complete lack of Jamie — his handsome rugged face, his scent, his muscled chest, his stubborn, arrogant butt sending her off like some kind of child — anything and everything *Jamie* — was missing here.

But *something* was here — something that didn't belong.

Tensing her muscles to mist away, she suddenly heard a voice from her worst nightmares. She froze.

"My, my, you are a busy girl, aren't you? No, no, no, none of that. I think you should *stay*, my dear. And to think, I thought I'd lost you."

She fisted her hands. That was all she was allowed. Nothing else worked. Every muscle in her body refused to listen, to obey anything she directed as the man who'd taken her dreams and her life, and gave her this misery, pushed open her bedroom door and walked in.

Samuel.

"Missed me, did you?"

My maker.

Chapter Twenty

"Say that again?" Alrick said. The quiet way he spoke, and punctuated each word, only drilled into Jamie what a fool he'd been. If the rapid, near world record heartbeat wasn't proof enough. That and the cold, chilling panic caused by his fuck-up.

Elsa, what the hell? Why did you fucking leave without letting me pull my head out of my ass?

"She isn't here. She isn't nearby either. She disappeared."

Faolan watched him like a lost puppy. Jamie could relate. He'd been focused on getting Elsa safe. On not listening to her, because if he had, he would have pulled her into his arms and kissed her. *She'd been here, right here, with me, and I couldn't make her see what I really wanted.*

Maybe because I didn't know what the fuck I wanted.

"How?"

Jamie considered that. How many love songs wailed on and on about not knowing what you had until it was gone? Too many. They were all true. *Every fucking one of them.*

But I did know. I was trying to protect her – from me and whoever else was after her. I should have trusted her, should have known no matter what, I'd never hurt her. Full moon or no moon, he'd never cause her harm. *As soon as I get her back, I'm never letting her go.*

"Jamie?"

"I think she shifted."

Alrick cursed. "I thought you said she couldn't do that."

"She hadn't before. She did now." All it took was really, really wanting as far away from him as she could possibly get. *She thinks I fucked her and was just dumping her, walking away.*

Her eyes, the dull hurt... He rubbed his face. *How am I going to make this up to her? How do men make shit like this up? It's not like I forgot her birthday. I fucked her and she believed I was leaving her.*

Because you were!

Alrick sighed. "Samantha and Derrick will be there in an hour, tops. They've offered their home to the boy."

Stunned to lose not only Elsa, but now Faolan, Jamie gripped the edge of the table and hung his head. *I've fucked this up. Now I have to fix it or live with the results.*

I can't lose them both. I can't lose either of them.

I'm fixing this. I don't know how, but I'm fixing this. She's mine. She's mine!

"Jamie?"

"Yeah, I heard you. I want Faolan with me, but for now, it might be safer to let him stay with them for the time being."

"You want—what the hell do you know about raising a boy? A *Lykae* boy?"

Faolan walked over and slipped his hand into Jamie's, watching him that way he had, that way that made Jamie think about a home, with the boy running outside in the yard, playing ball with him as Elsa watched. *Dreams. How did dreams sneak in on me?*

"I can figure it out. If he wants to stay with me."

Faolan leaned his head on Jamie's stomach, and slowly snaked his arms around his waist. Jamie stood for a second, unsure what to do. Elsa would have hugged him. He hugged the boy with one arm just like she'd have done. "I can learn to take care of him. He's not a babe. He can tell me what he needs."

"Sure, and the sun is going to rise in the west. You're a tracker. I thought you wanted to go back out, find Vik—"

"I changed my mind."

"You changed—Jamie, tell me you didn't... Tell me you didn't do to Elsa what I am beginning to think you did."

He'd done Elsa every way she'd allowed, every way she

wanted, and was going to do her again, as soon as he found her pretty little ass. After he explained she was staying with him. After he made sure she knew that the next time she had doubts about him, to give him a five second warning to shape up *before* she shipped out.

Temper. She has a temper. *Bryson, that fucking Vampire must have had it directed at him.* The thought pissed him off. He wanted to be the only man she shouted at.

Suddenly he remembered something else. Blood. She would need to drink and she *would* drink, too. From men. He barely kept the growl from his throat. No way was he letting her get near enough to another man to drink from him.

What the hell am I thinking? What if she enjoyed sex with drinking and now she's out there, hunting for both again?

Over my dead body. She's mine.

"Boy, you have lost your mind. If you think I'm letting you—"

"Elsa and I need to talk. I think she's in London. I need to go. We need to get a train or a plane so we can get there. Text Derrick. Have him meet me in London instead. Got it?"

"Jamie, I swear to God if you touched one hair on her—"

"What? I can't hear you? Alrick, you're breaking up." He muffled the phone with his shirt sleeve and motioned Faolan to grab his bag. Jamie shouldered his and ended the rant Alrick was giving him by hanging up. "He's pissed and I might get in deep trouble, so don't do that to him when you grow up."

"I won't."

The quick, serious answer cracked Jamie up. The panic was edging back enough for him to think. She was in London. He could feel the direction, knew she had a place there, and nothing and no one was going to stop him from finding her.

She's mine. My mate. If it took her leaving for me to know that, then I'll explain it to her. But no one is keeping her away from me.

Least of all his king.

Chapter Twenty-One

"Well, well, well, you *have* been busy, haven't you?"

Sickened by the sound of that voice, Elsa simply stood, unable to move. The man who had bitten her and changed her life walked into her bedroom.

Samuel.

Tall, elegantly dressed, handsome with the classical features of a millionaire playboy, Samuel smiled, eyeing her with an ownership he didn't deserve.

"You really have done well. Perhaps not with the company you keep," he said, leisurely reaching out to lift a piece of her hair. He brought it to his face and took a deep breath. "Although, it's nothing I can't mend."

She wanted to jerk away from him, to insist that he not touch her with his creepy hands, to scream and most importantly mist away as far as she could go. Instead, she stood there, much like the rabbit had when she'd released it. *Terrified.*

"Now, before we make any mistakes, let's make our situation clear. You've survived. That means you're strong. More, you're beautiful and remarkably talented. All of which makes my decision even more right." He brushed his fingers along her collarbone, and the revulsion she experienced threatened to double her over. Instead, she stood there. He slipped her hair over her right shoulder and brought something out from his pocket, and placed it on her neck, latching it so that the cool metal of the chain rested on her skin. "He'll be pleased, I think."

He? He who? And if Samuel was disgusting who was *he?*

"There, that wasn't so bad, was it?" he murmured behind

her ear. "Now, let us leave this place. I think you will be a nice addition to my collection, a very *nice* addition. You might even think back fondly on me when you realize this was always your better option." He pressed her back against his body, letting her know without having to ask exactly what that meant.

God help her now, because when she tried to shift, to mist, to lift a finger, she couldn't. She couldn't even open her mouth to scream, not even when he placed his mouth to her neck and wrapped his arms around her.

The bedroom disappeared, and the 'dropping out of an airplane' sensation hit, indicating that he was shifting her — but to where, she didn't know. A room, correction, basement with cages met her when the world took shape again.

"Now, first you have to stay here, while I do some business, but soon enough," Samuel said, "we'll begin your training."

He opened one cage and shoved her inside. "Be a good girl and sit."

She immediately sat on the floor, cross-legged and docile, but inside she screamed. Her body didn't respond. Even worse, she saw the enjoyment her obedience gave Samuel. His smile grew wider, and he nodded. "Very good. Now, stay right there."

A second, no more, and he was gone, leaving her in the dark, without a clue how to break whatever power he had over her.

Jamie, you're right. No one is safe. Especially me.

"She's not there." Jamie studied the windows of Elsa's flat. Faolan tugged his sleeve, suddenly drawing his attention away from the problem. She should be here. He'd come straight from France, barely stopping, only for as long as it took to get the damn ticket for the crossing to London from the mainland. Each second without her felt like hours and now she wasn't here.

Faolan tugged his arm. "Jamie!"

"What is it, Faolan? Are you hungry? We can pick up something after —"

"No. Elsa. She's in trouble. Big trouble. *He* has her."

A pit of something dark and bottomless felt as if it opened in his stomach. "Who? Who is he?"

"Samuel."

"Fucking son of a bitch!" He turned and nailed the street light with a punch that made the metal crunch under his fist. "This is why she should have listened to me!" He paced to the corner then back again, doing it several times more before he could tame his reaction. *She's alone, and now in trouble. Unprotected.*

"She was hurt. You hurt her."

Stunned, Jamie turned to the boy. "I never hurt Elsa, Faolan. I never will."

Faolan frowned, reminding him of Elsa when she confronted him. "You did. You were going to drop us."

Elsa had thrown that at him, but he'd ignored her. *If I'd just talked to her —*

"She was right, wasn't she?" Faolan challenged.

"She was wrong! I wasn't—"

"I heard you on the phone. She heard you on the phone. You were going to leave us both and go after your missing friend."

Truth — but for about half an hour of insanity. "Faolan, a man is entitled to mess up once in a while and not have his life ripped to pieces for it."

From the way Faolan blinked at him, he guessed that didn't satisfy the boy. "But you *really* messed up."

"Yes, I know."

"Really, *really* messed up. She's hurt and angry. Very angry with you. You should always want her near you."

"I got the picture, boy. Now, how do you know? That this sick son of — this Vampire was here?" Jamie took a deep breath, more to calm down than to scent for a Vampire, but he got a faint taste of Elsa on the breeze. She was angry with him. He didn't care. She could beat on him as much as she wanted. Hell, he'd give her boxing gloves to do it so she didn't hurt her hand, as long as she promised next time, to give him a warning before she just disappeared. She'd warned him if he brought up the witches, she'd leave. He'd listened. She'd warned him if he'd said he was a guy, she'd not have sex with him. He'd zipped his lips. She should have remembered, and warned him.

He hung his head and stared at his hands. He'd touched her with these hands just hours ago. *When will I ever be able to feel her hand in mine again?* Last time he'd hunted her, he'd not had her scent so clearly.

It was nearly dawn, that time when she always seemed to slow down, and sometimes become silent. Brooding, perhaps, on what life had given her. A life filled with nights.

"He was here, there," Faolan gestured to the windows. "Waiting on her."

"Let's go. Come on." Jamie dodged a car and crossed the street, assured that Faolan was right behind him.

"They aren't here," Faolan said breathlessly at the top of the stairs.

"I know. But people leave clues. We'll use those."

"We need to hurry."

Jamie opened the door easily because it wasn't locked. He stepped inside her house. It was much the same as when he'd found it before. Everything in its place, since that seemed to be Elsa's style. She even had her shoes organized on a shelf by the door.

"Here, follow me." He walked to the living room, scenting more than her here, something else… Something familiar. Frowning, he crouched near the sofa and examined the dark olive cushions. He'd sat here, waiting for her like some kind of sick freak. Jamie stood and walked to the kitchen, opening the refrigerator. It was empty and clean, only bottled water and juices in boxes. Samuel had touched this. Studied the cabinets, and touched her dishes.

In the bathroom he found more of the man's scent, on her

brush, and again among her cosmetics and perfumes.

The last place Jamie ventured was her bedroom. He'd been here before of course, but back then Elsa had been a mission, not...Elsa. The bed was made, the soft gray and white checkered comforter smooth, and the buttery yellow blanket at the foot of the bed folded as neatly as it had been all those months before. Even her yellow pillows were nicely arranged. Samuel had touched them, though, and beside her nightstand, the man had sat on her bed.

"I know this scent."

Faolan had followed him silently, watching but not saying anything as Jamie prowled.

"Who is it?"

"I don't know." Jamie growled and headed back to the living area, sitting on her couch to try to jar his memory. It was there, somewhere in his head. He knew this scent, had run into this man before — this Vampire before. *Think. Think!*

"Fuck!" He shot to his feet. *David.* The weak, barely changed Vampire in Seattle. That was who had been here. He'd also been in that fucking cellar. "That son of a bitch!"

"You remember?"

Jamie tamed his temper and recalled that swearing in front of kids was probably a bad example.

"I know him." He studied the boy and came to a decision. "I want you here. No, don't argue. This is dangerous, Faolan." He had a feeling more was going on here than it seemed, too. But if he could find David, he'd find the Vampire who had his woman.

"I can help. I'm strong. I can help with her, don't leave me, Jamie. I can help."

Elsa had said the same. He'd hurt her by not believing in her. Now she was in danger. *So am I, every fucking day. We're immortals. The boy, Elsa, me. Life is going to always be dangerous no matter what we do.*

"I can help, Jamie."

"You remember how she taught you to hide, Faolan?"

248

"Yes."

"When we locate her, you're going to hide. Got it? Hide her as well, if… If you have to." If she was hurt. If she was unable to. *Elsa hold on. I'm on my way.*

He paused, considering what would happen when he had her again. His wolf was pacing, becoming harder to control. "After we find her, we might need—"

"Time alone."

He nodded, not about to get into what that meant. Or hoped it meant. Even if she made him sleep on the floor for the next ten years, he wasn't leaving her side.

"Maybe we should call Bryson?"

"Bryson." He considered it, then the boy. It was a solid idea. When dealing with Vampires, it was best to have one around. "I'll make the call. Come on, we're walking until he can give us a lift to Seattle. And I'm warning you, if I sense it's bad, you're hiding, you got it?"

"Yes, Jamie."

"Good." At least someone listened to him. If he got Elsa back, he was going to listen to her, but he was also going to sit her down and explain a few things. Like how much she never, ever needed to leave to get her point across. He'd accept he'd fucked up and she would accept that springing a disappearing act on him was not in the cards. Not now that he'd realized she was his.

Just hold on, Elsa. Just hold on.

Chapter Twenty-Two

It felt like forever before Elsa heard Samuel's footsteps on the stairs. Or at least she hoped it was him, and not whoever the other *he* was. It had been hours. Her legs ached, her butt completely numb from sitting for so long. Even the complete blackness of the basement was now a light gray. She wished she could close her eyes and not be here, because here was straight out of some kind of horrifying headline.

The cell she was in had bedding. Sort of. A dirty, smelly once-upon-a-time white blanket tossed on a wire-framed bed with the metal box springs showing. The mattress was another disgusting piece of garbage dragged out of a trash bin. That was all she could see, since she couldn't turn her head. It was enough. At her feet, there was a chain, which led to the wall. She could just barely make out how it hung there, high in the center of the wall.

No doubt this was where he kept his collection. The thought made her sick. The evil of the place made her sick. The thought of him made her sick. Everything had her stomach rolling.

The chill in the basement was wet, as if the place flooded often, giving it a musty smell along with a coldness that seeped into her bones. It had to be past dawn, but she couldn't sleep, wasn't even tired in fact.

He didn't tell me I could sleep, is that why?

The door opened and Samuel stood there, light behind him, framing him in painful brightness. She blinked and tried once again to move.

Just a finger. Just a finger.

Nothing. Nothing at all responded for her.

"Ah, such a good girl." He'd taken his jacket off and wore only his dress slacks and a button-down shirt. In his hand he held a glass of something, whiskey she thought. He lifted it and sipped from it, watching her. "Go to your knees."

She didn't think she could, not after so long on her butt, but she did, rising as if he owned her body, not her. It hurt terribly, but she didn't waver.

"Open your mouth."

Her mouth opened. It was humiliating. Worse, he seemed to enjoy that it was. She tried to hide in her mind, but it was all too real, after hours of nothing but darkness and silence.

"Wider," he murmured and opened the cage door.

A cold sweat of fear blanketed her skin and she struggled with her body at the same time as her mouth stretched wider for him.

"Close your eyes and tilt your head back."

The action was immediate. Her fear escalated, especially when he touched her lip with his finger, tracing her mouth, then stroked up her face to her hair. The only sound in the room was his breathing, which increased and grew louder as she knelt there, mouth open wide, her knees aching and her head tilted for him.

"Such a pretty girl." The compliment was gently spoken. The slap to the face wasn't. It was loud, hard, and it stung.

"Don't move."

She jerked from the blow. He gripped her hair and poured the liquid down her throat, making her choke and swallow the burning whiskey. Another slap to the face, harder still, then another when she choked, and most of the liquid spewed out of her mouth. He drowned her with more, much more than he'd had in the glass. He kept on, smacking her face and holding her head back hard enough to bend her backwards. When she thought she couldn't survive another second, he let go.

"Don't move." He ran his finger over her mouth. She was breathless. Her face ached, burned as badly as her throat, but she still felt like vomiting at his gentle touch on her lips.

"Open your eyes."

She did. He stood over her, eyes glowing like chips of green ice, watching her. Waiting on her, she realized. Hatred, an emotion she'd had for him all along, but never focused on, rose and choked her harder than the whiskey. She was breathless, gasping, and even though she wanted to strike at him, or not move at all so he didn't gain the satisfaction of seeing her struggle, she knew she'd do neither.

He ran his hand over her mouth again and brought it to his lips. There was blood on his finger—her blood. He sucked the tip in his mouth and cleaned it with his tongue. Before she could comprehend what he would do next, he jerked her upright by her hair, ripped her shirt wide open and sank his teeth in her left breast. The pain was horrible. It sickened her to the point of needing to cry out, but she held it in, somehow finding the strength to refuse giving him what he wanted.

It didn't seem to matter. He drew on her so painfully she wanted to scream. Instead, she hung there as he rutted his hips against her, clearly getting off on her pain as he drank his fill. The world began to go dark.

Before it faded completely he pulled his mouth away to groan out his release. She thought she heard him say, "You will be mine first, in every way. Only then can he have you."

I will never be yours. Never!

Chapter Twenty-Three

Jamie finished explaining what he wanted, but Bryson just stood there, staring at him. "Did you hear me?"

"Yes, I heard you. You fucked up. Elsa left you. Her maker, Samuel, has her. What I want to know is why should I take you with me? I can deal with this alone."

Something like relief, followed quickly by pissed off, kidnapped him. He punched Bryson in the nose and bent him backwards over the nearest car. "No one deals with this but me. Understood?"

Bryson casually reached up and touched his lip, running his tongue along his teeth. "Jamie, get off me before I grow upset."

"I go. You can take me or I go without you." He tightened his hands on Bryson's jacket.

"As far as I know the fastest way to Seattle is going to take you eighteen hours. I can be there in one minute. Now, get off."

Jamie dropped his hold and backed away, but only a foot. The night misted steady rain down on them, but he barely felt it. The need to go to Elsa, to find her, was beating at him too hard for anything else to matter. She was on that cross again, but no matter how hard he ran, he couldn't close the distance to reach her. Bryson could help him. Bryson stepped inside Elsa's house and, within seconds, recognized the scent of the Vampire he called Samuel.

"I need you —"

"Yes, obviously you do. I say you need more than just me. This is getting complicated, which means another web of illusions set up to trap the unexpected. Samuel, for example, is not intelligent enough to pull something like this off—alone. The man is narcissistic and a lecher but he's not smart enough upstairs to recall his brain below the belt isn't running the show."

All the blood felt as if it had drained from Jamie, as if he'd slit his wrists and was on the cusp of entering heaven or hell. Whichever would take him, he supposed. "If he touched—"

"Oh, he's touched her. Get that straight," Bryson snapped. "And make sure it doesn't matter when you get her back."

"Doesn't matter? I'll kill the bastard, I'll rip—"

"Yes, yes, that is necessary, of course. But make sure it doesn't change your feelings for Elsa."

Jamie fisted his hands at his hips and stared at Bryson. "Are you suggesting I wouldn't want to have her if that son of a bitch touched her?"

"I was. Yes."

"What is wrong with you? Why would that change one hair on her head? If she's hurt, I'll help her heal. Nothing another man does changes that."

"Good. Now, we need to decide what to do."

"What? We go to Seattle. I find him and end his fucking life." It seemed easy to him. "I just need you to take me to Seattle, Bryson. Now would be best."

"And the boy?" Bryson asked.

Bryson jumped from topic to topic like a frog chasing after a fly.

"He goes. He knows what to do, but he stays with me." Jamie had already called Derrick and suffered through the dressing down he'd gotten for not being where he was supposed to be, then waited while Derrick let him know what a dumbass he was for losing Elsa. But it'd been worth it. Derrick and Samantha were ready to fetch Faolan if things went wrong. He'd sent them the picture of Elsa and Faolan from when he'd bought her dinner. Samantha had assured him she could reach Seattle in seconds. Jamie had already booked a hotel and sent that to them, so he knew the boy was well secured no matter what went down. It was all ready.

Except he was here, and Elsa was *there*.

Please, please be there.

"I'm calling Samantha, she'll take me." Jamie pulled out his phone.

"Derrick won't let her within a mile of Samuel. Not if he's smart and he's one very intelligent man. Now you, did the cunning gene skip you? Think like a wolf."

"Bryson."

"We need to hurry, Bryson," Faolan said, cutting Bryson off from whatever else he was going to say.

The big Vampire sighed and nodded. "I was just warming up, kid. Someday you'll understand."

"He messed up, but his life doesn't have to be ripped to shreds." Jamie widened his eyes at his own words repeated from a kid, but it seemed to work on Bryson.

"Right. Well, this is your one fucking 'get out of the dog house free' ticket."

"Don't swear in front of the boy," Jamie growled.

Bryson clearly thought he'd lost his mind. "Sorry, Faolan, he's right."

"It's okay." Faolan smiled politely.

To Jamie, Bryson said, "You need to stand closer if I'm going to shift you both. I'll take you together. Otherwise, I have to leave the boy alone and I'm guessing you don't want that."

"Can you? Shift us both?"

"Of course." Bryson took hold of his forearm and Faolan's small hand. "It's daylight in Seattle, so we go to a place I have."

"Then she's sleeping?" Jamie was stunned. He'd not thought of that, but he should have. If it was nearly dawn here, it would be mid-morning there. "It's nearly five here, what time is it there?'

"Nearly eleven. Now you're thinking like a wolf."

"Damn it, Bryson, she's in trouble! We need to go. Surely

she's okay. He wanted her for a damn reason, not to let her burn in the sun. Let's go!" Samuel wanted her for sex. The thought screwed his head up and twisted his gut. *If the bastard hurt her...* Just the thought of her being wounded that way made him ill, and crazed, so he shut it off and focused. "We need to go."

Bryson gave him a nod, but it was a short and a too-hesitant one. It didn't reassure Jamie that the sick fuck hadn't taken her to just kill her. "Hold on."

The world disappeared, and all he felt was Bryson's grip, then, with a dizzy rush, he was standing in a room lined with books. A library, or...elegant study. "This is your home?"

"One of them."

Jamie gave Faolan a quick check. He grinned, clearly excited about the shift.

"You managed that well." Bryson walked to the giant hearth. It lit, Jamie assumed on Bryson's command. The blaze grew until it lit the room with its soft glow. "Lots of wolves can't handle the shift."

"I have other things on my mind right now than worrying over a shift. Where are we?" The place was out of the past, complete with candles, and he sensed no electricity whatsoever.

"About ten minutes from Seattle. Can you sense her?"

Jamie concentrated, breathing in deeply, and the relief he experienced was only fleeting, because her scent was faint, and difficult to pinpoint, then vanished.

"I do, but it's weak." She was alive, though. She *had* to be alive.

"Good. I don't sense Samuel, but he was always good at hiding. We thought he was dead, burned when we destroyed the House here. It appears he's more resilient than we gave him credit for." Bryson settled onto a chair and sighed. "We have to wait, at least until dusk. If you scent her, then she's alive."

"I can't wait until dusk. I'm going *now*."

"You won't find him or her. If he has her, and he hid from me, *and* Aidan" — Bryson pressed his fingertips together in a steeple and studied Jamie—"then he's got one the one thing we didn't consider—an extremely good ability to hide. I can sense Vampires as well as you can scent them, and I can't locate him. It could mean he has a spell, or he's that careful, or that's his ability."

"It doesn't matter how careful he is, I'm going to rip his spine out and feed it to him."

"I see. So you'll go alone, hunting for him?"

"I will. Faolan, come." Jamie headed for the door, hearing Bryson sigh behind him.

"Vampires have protections, guardians that watch their homes when they sleep."

"Do you?" he asked, at the door, turning to see Bryson nod.

"Of course. This entire place is a protection of sorts. You may come and go, but when it's dusk and you still haven't found her, I'll find you. Until then, get the boy something to eat and let him rest."

"I don't need to rest," Faolan said immediately. "We have to find her, before it's too late."

"Too late?" Jamie asked, suddenly not liking Faolan's fear. "Too late for what, Faolan?"

Instead of answering, he focused on Bryson. "He knows."

"Bryson?"

"Does that child read minds?" Bryson said it casually, but the tone was threatening enough to make Jamie step in front of the boy. Bryson rose to his feet and the friendly, slightly annoying Vampire who tolerated Jamie slipped away. "Boy, come here."

"He's not—"

Faolan surprised him by walking toward Bryson. "It's okay, Jamie. Bryson won't hurt me. I didn't read your mind. I heard your thoughts, your worries over the other man."

Jamie watched Bryson touch Faolan's forehead, lightly but still, the hand was huge, as big as the boy's head, nearly.

257

"Careful, Bryson."

"Of course."

"Samuel's scent was in France. In that cellar, but you think he answers to someone else?"

"Ah, you are something, aren't you?" Bryson murmured, ignoring Jamie's question. He ruffled the boy's hair and finally answered. "I do. If that man still rules Samuel then we need to move fast. I'll go see what I can discover."

"Do you think this man is Samuel's master? The one we were hunting for in Europe?"

"I'm beginning to."

Jamie studied the idea, testing it for merit. It could be, and really, at this point he had to believe anything was possible. "How are you connecting the dots?"

"It's a rumor, nothing you would have heard, but I tend to believe most rumors, until I know for a fact they aren't true. A few years ago, before we arrived in the States, we heard of the damage the House in this town was causing, but when we arrived, it wasn't the House, but the Coven, or, more specifically, one man, called *Master*, who was at the center of the corruption."

Jamie digested that. "What kind of corruption?"

"Women missing, boys, girls, some adult men," Bryson said with a heavy sigh. "He went for strong immortals, even humans. Rumors spread that he wanted the 'glowing ones.' Immortals or humans with powerful spirits are often called glowing ones in the oldest of legends. Virgins as well, of course. We thought he had been destroyed, but..." Bryson cast a worried glance at Faolan. "He and Samuel were up to something. Samuel is powerful, don't get me wrong. He was on the top of his food chain, ancient, with some history that dates back to our roots. If someone else is calling the shots, and not him, then that someone is much more powerful than we realized."

Jamie accepted that. Nothing was ever simple. It'd taken him months to find Elsa, and less than a week to fall in love with her.

"You got the details on the witches' dungeon?"

Bryson nodded. "It fits what we discovered here, in Seattle. There's more. The charms. Those are new, but" — Bryson winced and shook his head — "they are also familiar. In the past we found other things, small tokens near the bodies, but the writing was always in French."

"*Pour toujours.*"

"Right. Jack mentioned the gate at the mansion. I thought it was coincidence, then I remembered there are none. Something about the murder there bothered me. A woman died, but her husband claimed he didn't kill her. He denied he'd hanged her, right up to his own death, twenty years later, and he still denied it then. He claimed spirits took her, tortured her, then killed her while he was forced to watch."

Jamie digested that, feeling sicker. If he were forced to watch such a thing...

"How did he die? Old age?"

"No. He was found hanged, his entrails spilling from a slice through his stomach, wearing his ballet costume from the couple's performance of *Romeo and Juliet.*"

"It just gets worse and worse, doesn't it?" Jamie asked. Only as he said it, he recalled Elsa's smile when he'd sampled her pasta. She'd glowed with happiness and filled him with the same. Or the way Faolan had stared up at him eagerly when he'd said he'd fix up the secret garden.

"It does. But then there are bright spots that make you remember you're alive." Bryson tousled the boy's hair again and Faolan smiled.

It was true. Elsa made his life brighter. So did Faolan. He'd trade his life for either of theirs. Easily, too. He met Bryson's steady gaze and nodded.

"We find Samuel, and then we find this...Master. I'm not leaving anyone behind who might hunt her down again, Bryson." He raised his hand when the Vampire moved to argue. "Is he a warlock?"

"He could be, we never learned what he was. There were just rumors about the Coven, no more. But the coven here traces its roots to France, Jamie."

"Then this is much easier than you think, Vampire. It's a full circle. This is where it began. This where it will end. With me killing Samuel, then his master."

"It's never that easy, boy and you know it. But you have my help. We should have seen that this was done properly the first time," Bryson muttered. "Now we will."

"No offense, Bryson, but you've helped enough just getting me here. It's daylight out. How will you help?"

Bryson laughed, and pushed a torch to the side. A wall rolled back to reveal a hidden passageway. "I'll use the tunnels, of course."

Faolan grinned, shaking the hair out of his eyes, and peered inside.

"There's more to Seattle than what you see on the horizon, Jamie. Just search for her, while I see what I can find. I might have to call Aidan in on this."

Jamie nodded. "Call whoever you have to. I want her safe. No one, not Samuel, and certainly not his master, will keep her away from me."

"I suggest repeating that to her, when you reach her. I also suggest you go to the seedier side of Seattle to start that search."

"I'm going where I found Samuel before. If I can't find him, then I know another Vampire that *can*."

"Ah, now you're thinking like a wolf, boy."

Chapter Twenty-Four

A bedroom with long, red velvet drapes, black walls, elegant furniture, and an enormous fireplace, under an even bigger portrait of a woman, met Elsa when she woke. She must have made a sound because Samuel walked over, his bare feet silent on the marble floor.

"Ah, yes, I see you're a late sleeper. Interesting."

He had another glass of whiskey in his hands, but unlike the night before, he'd ditched the clothes and wore only Calvin Klein white boxer briefs. His body was pale, but toned, his abs tight and hard, but every ounce of him disgusted her. Most especially, she hated that he was blatantly aroused under the white cotton.

She felt herself gag, but nothing came out.

"Come now, on your knees."

At the command, she rose to her knees, shaking a little as she did. She wavered and he caught her head, taking hold of her hair again, like he had last night to hold her still. His gaze flickered over her face, then down to her exposed breasts. The fabric of his boxers grew tighter, outlining his penis as it stiffened.

Instead of more orders, he dragged her to her feet, again with the grip on her hair. He didn't bite her, but stared at her face, seemingly pleased with what he saw, if the smile meant happiness. It seemed more like gloating.

"Let's find something more appropriate for you to wear, shall we?" He released her and walked to a wall, pushing something so that the wall opened, revealing a brightly lit room. "Come, I will need to find something to fit you."

She walked, but it wasn't because she wanted to, or even

said to her legs, "Move." It was wooden and forced. *Stop. Stop. Stop!*

The screams didn't help, neither did her thinking as hard as she could to turn or lift her hand or anything. Just like the night before, she was unable to control her body.

"Ah, here." He held up a sexy black dress with one hand, and pulled out lingerie, the kind that strapped on, and buttoned, and hooked a woman in until she looked like a blow-up doll...or a courtesan. She felt sick. Last night all he'd done was drink from her and get off doing it. Tonight, she knew he'd allow no such thing.

"Here, take these. There." He turned to the rows of shoes and boots. She held the clothing to her exposed chest, hiding her breasts in a feeble attempt to feel normal.

"And these." He picked out a tall pair of black boots. They were impossibly high-heeled and the top of each boot would reach to her upper thighs.

"With that ass you need these. Ballet. What a wonderful way to sculpt a body to perfection." With boots in hand, he walked to a bench set in the center of the walk-in closet. Row upon row of clothing filled the cabinets. Surely enough to dress her, or whoever else he had in his collection, for years. He set the boots down and picked something else out from a drawer.

He straightened, and staring at her, he tilted his head. Sipping his whiskey, he strode over. He gave her a disdainful sneer, then tossed the clothing on the floor, behind him, near the bench. He fondled one breast, then the other, sipping his drink as he did. A chain with a familiar medallion swung from the hand he touched her with. He paused and pulled the chain over her breast, twisting it so the metal slid along her flesh, and caught on her nipple. All the while he continued to sip his drink. Leisurely, he wrapped the chain around her, pulling it tighter and tighter so the point of her entire areola was trapped and pinched by the silver.

Seemingly thrilled by that, he bent and sucked her hard

262

enough to make it hurt. He didn't bite her, but the threat was there because he let his fangs drop. Pulling up, he released the tight binding and studied her face. Whatever he saw made his eyes flare with something sick.

"Don't move." He walked away, glass in hand, opening another cabinet, filled with things that made her stomach tense and fear trap her tighter than his complete control. Sexual toys, whips, cuffs, odd metal rods and leather of all colors and sizes lined the wall. He reached up and picked a thick, black leather collar off a shelf. He replaced it and picked up the one next to it, a smaller, but no less disgusting collar.

He finished his drink and set it down, before coming back to her. She trembled, but the fear was unstoppable. The things he could do to her... She fought the restraints on her mind, but nothing, not one inch of her would listen.

"I want this on your neck, as a reminder," he breathed, settling it on her. He buckled it tight, and breathed against her throat. "You'll be my bitch for a long time, but the things I will teach you." Meshing his hips to hers, he ground against her, making that sick feeling increase to the point she had to swallow or spew. He was erect, his penis hard and ready.

"Soon, you won't need this." He gripped the collar and pulled her closer. "Or my orders." He squeezed her breast hard enough to leave bruises. "But until then, take those filthy clothes off." He shoved her back even as he ordered her. She hit the wall, cracking her head hard. He held her there by the collar. "Nod, so I know how eager you are to suck my dick."

He dropped his hand only after she nodded, amazed that she could do that. She attempted to shift, but nothing happened. Misting got the same response.

"Take your clothes off. Let me see you."

She began removing her shirt, hands trembling, but obeying his commands, not hers. As soon as she was naked, he took her clothes and dropped them into some kind of hamper or dumb waiter built into the wall. After, he studied her, and all she could do was stand there, not even breathe or blink.

"Amazing. Now, dress. Slowly." He walked over and sat, legs spread so that he could watch every move she made as he began stroking his cock through his boxers. She stopped seeing him. Instead she turned inward, too afraid to do more. She concentrated on winning her body back, even as she hooked the silky stockings to the garters and smoothed the ultra-soft material up her thigh.

Just one finger. Just one finger.

By the time she had the bra, panties, stockings, and garters on, he was breathing hard, clearly enjoying the show. She picked up the dress, still compelled to put it on. It slipped over her head and down her body to right under her ass, while it barely covered her breasts. The lace of the bra was entirely visible. No doubt she could pass for a high priced whore.

If she so much as bent at the waist, just slightly, her ass would be exposed. But since he'd already had that view, she bent, picking up one impossible boot, slipped it on, then zipped it up the side. The next went on just as easily, but when she lifted her leg to the bench and bent to zip it, he stopped her.

"Stop. Don't move." She was horrified to see him walking toward her with his penis jutting out. She slammed her eyes shut and prayed.

Please, please, please, not rape. Not rape. Not rape.

"I can make you want it. Beg for it." He touched her shoulder with his clammy hands. His disgusting erection brushed the back of her thigh. The panties were no barrier to what he wanted. Each cheek of her ass was clearly exposed, with only black, sheer gauze between them.

He toyed with the edge of one side of her panties, sliding his finger up and down, while he rubbed the head of his cock along her inner thigh. Revolted, she couldn't do anything but pose there like some plastic blow-up doll.

Please, no, no, no, I don't want it. I don't want it.

Featherlight, he brushed his fingers down her spine, then on to her ass again, with a possessiveness he should know he didn't deserve. She felt sick, a vertigo as if she might fall any second from the top of the highest building without a safety net, hit hard.

I'm going to pass out.

"You don't believe me. But you will." The deepening of his voice scared her. So did the sudden, hard, direct slap of his hand on her bare butt. "A woman like you needs this, don't you? A lesson to show you that your ass is mine to do whatever I want with." He brought his hand down harder and harder, clearly trying to humiliate her. The grip on her hair tugged her head up, each punishing blow to her ass making him breathe harder and harder. By the time she was in real pain, he groaned, a sickening sound, not like Jamie's at all, but she knew what was coming.

Jamie. Think of Jamie. His gentle touch, his rough words, but tender, passionate lovemaking, how he kissed and made my toes curl long before he ever found his own release. Think of that brooding expression. Remember his kindness. How it felt to have him touch me. Him.

The image of Jamie grew, filling in with details she'd shored away without conscious thought. His brief smile when she told him he'd need blue pills to keep up. The way he'd shared her passion, his gaze locked with hers as she climaxed. The way he'd touched her jaw, like she mattered, *truly* mattered, when she'd been bruised.

Samuel savagely yanked her hair. She was certain he'd ripped it out at the roots. But he held her like that, staring into her eyes breathlessly, searching for something, she imagined, but what it was, he didn't find because he tightened his fist and sneered.

"First, you're going to suck my cock because I want it."

A shove and she was on her knees with a painful crack of kneecaps on marble floor. Still with the death grip on her hair, he brought his penis up against her face, shoving it along her cheek. His dick wasn't big, but it was bent at an angle and stiff. The mushroomed cap was a sick, pale color that he rubbed against her with each of his rough thrusts.

"I can make you beg to suck me off, Elsa. That dog you rutted with will be nothing but a memory. I can make you want me. Want me so bad you can't stop yourself from crawling to me wherever I am, to get your mouth on my cock." Each word seemed to turn him on even more. Slick pre-cum slid along her face and she truly did gag.

No. Not even if you keep me here until I'm a thousand.

Even as she thought it, she knew it was true.

Jamie, why did I leave? Why didn't I stay and slap you silly for being so...stupid! Talk to you. Make you explain!

She would crawl on broken glass to be with Jamie, but this monster would never make her *want* him. The certainty of that strengthened her. Something inside snapped, frightening her. At first. Until she took a deep breath and realized it was the first since Samuel had walked into her bedroom back in London.

I'm free? She wiggled her fingers just to be certain.

She didn't think, she bit — hard — right down on Samuel's disgusting penis, so hard she swore her teeth met right through the wimpy sized thing.

Samuel screamed.

It wasn't good enough. She also grabbed a handful of his gross, low-hanging sac and squeezed the pale, clammy flesh. The paralyzing woodenness of her muscles had disappeared, and she took full advantage of that, by twisting the handful.

Samuel didn't seem to know what to do besides scream bloody murder and try to desperately shove her away, crying like a baby and staggering like a drunkard.

She let go. She also spit out his nasty taste and wiped her mouth of his foul, disgusting scent. She rose to her feet and quickly nailed him between his legs with her knee, even as he cupped himself, sobbing raggedly.

"Ballet did more than make this body, stupid. It also

made me strong."

He fell to his knees and she brought her leg up again, hitting him right under the chin so his teeth snapped shut. She held him by his greasy black hair so he couldn't get away.

"You sick, disgusting fuckwit! I will *never* want you. Who would? You slimy, sick bastard! I will never want a pathetic sick-o who can't hold a candle to a real man like Jamie. You call him a dog? That, you sick pervert, is you."

"You can't do this to me!" he gasped, spitting blood past his lips.

"Oh, but, you slimy creep, I can." She dragged him closer, so he could see how much she was doing this to him. "I am so sick of immortals. So sick of what you did to me. And now you come into my home, into my *place* and can enter without being invited, then force me to strip for you, you disgusting fuck. I was just getting used to being a Vampire, too."

"You can't do this. I forbid you to do this."

She misted her hand, shoved in his chest and slid her fingers around his heart and watched his eyes grow rounder before he screamed, throwing his head back and blubbing. More blood spewed from his mouth.

"It hurts like a bitch, I bet. Don't worry. I am going to enjoy ripping your heart out. And you know what else?"

"Don't do this. I forbid you to do this!"

"You scream like a girl." She slowly made her hand whole and squeezed much harder than she had his balls. "I hope you rot in hell for an eternity, you stupid motherfucker."

His eyes went wide, so wide she was surprised they didn't pop out.

She held on and pulled, ripping his still-beating heart out. His eyes dimmed, slowly extinguishing the person he had been, and turned him into nothing more than a dead, pathetic man who got off on hurting people. She threw his heart onto the floor. It slid along the marble and hit the wall with a wet sound.

Revulsion tried to take over, but she kicked Samuel's sorry butt when he went down, which helped keep the nausea at bay.

"Fucking piece of shit."

It took whole minutes for her to accept that she was free. More to accept that he was gone. *Her maker. Samuel.* No last name. Just like every other immortal she'd met. Except Jamie.

Jamie O'Connor.

What am I going to do, now?

She laughed, sounding insane even to herself. Her clothes were…gone. Her hand was covered in blood—again—and it was near dawn. This place was just as not happening for a sleep-over either. *Jamie. I want Jamie.*

Just go. Just get out.

Instead of running, she walked on the high heels to the door, and noticed a bathroom. She made it there before she dry-heaved over the porcelain bowl. After, she picked up soap and scrubbed her face and even lathered up her mouth. It stung and tasted horrible, but it wiped away his foul taste.

By the time she was satisfied, her face was raw from scouring. She straightened and avoided looking at herself, instead she walked out into the super-creepy bedroom. It wasn't dawn yet. She had a few hours, at the most, but when she pulled the curtain aside, it was just barely dark. *Dusk? How can that be?* It felt like hours since she'd woken on the floor. *I always know what time it is…*

The Seattle skyline met her gaze, stunning her even more. *It all started here.* She glanced behind her shoulder, knowing it had almost ended here too. Samuel's bare foot proved it hadn't.

Why hadn't it?

He'd said something about wanting *him.* Just remembering that made her sick, but she also remembered she'd realized she never would want him.

An image of the man she *did* want, Jamie with his brooding

frown and dark hair, filled her mind. *I thought of Jamie, how I only wanted him, the stupid jerk.*

She focused back on the city. *I used to live here. I used to call this home.*

It wasn't any longer. She didn't want to go to London. Not after finding Samuel there. France was out for several reasons. One being she hadn't forgiven Jamie yet.

Dropping the curtain, she gazed at the material for a moment as she stiffened her resolve then turned and headed for the door. "Doesn't matter. I'm out of here."

Maybe I'll figure out what I'm going to do with the rest of my... immortality, along the way. Enough hiding, enough running, I've got to accept this, me, and let the past go.

At the door, she paused, a sudden thought rising above the chaos.

If I don't go see Jamie, then I will be running. Confront him and lay it down nice and simple like so even he can get it. Might be humiliating if he doesn't want me, but... I won't know if I don't try.

Decided, she headed out, not expecting to barrel into the one person she needed a little more time to figure out how to talk to, before she actually *talked* to him.

Chapter Twenty-Five

"Jamie!" Elsa stared at his handsome face, so shocked all she could do was blink.

"Woman, what the fuck are you wearing?"

It wasn't a *'hello, I'm so sorry'*, or *'hello, I'm fucking glad to see you'*, but it didn't matter. Because as soon as he spoke, he wrapped his arms around her, cradling her to his chest as if he never wanted to let her go. With a low sound he tightened his arms and pressed his head to hers.

"Doesn't matter. Don't want to know. Don't care. You're here, alive, and whole. That's what matters. You're staying with me. From now on, Elsa. With *me*."

"Okay."

"We're not going to argue about it, you're not better alone—" He pulled back to stare down at her. "Wait, what?"

"I said, okay."

He scanned her face then, with a wince, crushed her in his arms again. "I've been searching the city for you. You weren't *here*, I was just *here*, on this street. Then your scent surfaced, strong and so damn sweet. Just showed up outta nowhere." He tightened his arms and pressed a kiss to her forehead, then her cheek. "I got here as soon as I could. I didn't mean what I said, I just wanted you safe. You're safe. Now you're going to stay with me. Together we can figure this out. But you're staying with *me*."

Jamie babbling was the last thing she'd ever thought she'd witness. But he was. She didn't know what to say, not that he gave her time.

"I got here as soon as I could. As soon as I could," he repeated. He exhaled, then drew a deep breath, burying his face against her neck. "You scared the shit out of me. I thought I'd lost you."

"Uh, thanks. I was enjoying the moment."

"What moment?" He lifted his head and that hint of a smile lifted his lips.

"You, realizing you love me."

For some reason those arms of steel turned to even tougher metal, and she was crushed up against his warmth and the wonderful Jamie scent. It wasn't the 'I love you' most women wanted, but for her, the silent death grip was enough.

She hugged him tighter too, her heart overflowing with such warmth she never wanted to leave his side again. *This is where I belong. With this man. Gotta tell him.* "I thought I'd never see you again. Never be able to tell you I just needed some time to think, maybe teach you a lesson that you needed me," she whispered against his chest. "I was so frightened, Jamie. All I wanted was you. Only *you*. You were right, I'm not strong. I was so wrong—"

"Elsa, I wasn't right. I was wrong. You are strong," he said firmly. Meeting her eyes he smiled. "But I'm glad you still want me. Believe me, Elsa. The next time, warn me." He shook her by the shoulders gently. "Tell me, if I do this or that you will leave. I won't do it. Whatever it is, I swear to God, I'll stop. But you have to tell me. And you have to promise not to disappear again, eh?"

He shook her slightly again when all she did was stare at him open-mouthed. She snapped her mouth closed. "Okay. I promise."

"Good. But I'm not letting you go. You belong with me." Another shake, and a firm hold on her upper arms. "I mean that, woman. With *me*."

There wasn't a thing to say to that, so she pressed up against him and nodded.

"We both came to save you." At the sound of Faolan's voice at her elbow, she gasped and realized he was there too. Jamie didn't release her but Faolan hugged them with his small arms and buried his face against her side. "But you saved yourself."

"Well, if you three are done with the hellos, we should get going inside."

At Bryson's familiar voice, she stiffened and felt a blush heat her face. "Bryson is here?" she whispered, suddenly shy.

"Yes, and I do *not* want that moth— I don't want him seeing this," Jamie muttered, loosening his grip enough to stare down at her. "Fu—Elsa what—?"

"Are you trying not to swear?" she asked quietly.

He grimaced. "It's not good for the boy to hear."

She smiled and kissed him, then wrapped her arms around his neck and *really* kissed him. He returned the kiss, and took over, erasing everything but him. When he was done, she brushed his hair off his eyes. His amber gaze glowed with something she hoped was the same thing she felt. *Love.*

"True. Swearing is not good, but neither is taking him to a Vampire's home."

"Right, but— Why do you taste like soap?" He grimaced and raised his hand to wipe at his mouth, but froze, wrist up against his lips. "Did that son of—?"

"No. I didn't. He didn't, I mean. I'm fine."

Jamie's eyes narrowed and he slowly dropped his arm, his gaze dropping too. The low-cut dress, the boots, the expanse of her upper thighs, all got his attention before he focused back on her face, examining that as thoroughly. He reached up and brushed his thumb over her bottom lip. There was a small sting there, possibly from the night before.

"Elsa."

She shivered at the sudden intensity in his body. He'd been like that before, when they'd faced the Death Stalkers. He reached behind his back and pulled out his sword, snapping it into place, and tried to get past her through the door. She clung to his arm, and was dragged a few steps forward before he realized it.

"I'm going to kill the motherfucker."

"Jamie!"

"Elsa, I need to go inside."

She grabbed his arm again. "No, please, don't go in there. I killed him."

Jamie's eyes narrowed almost as if he doubted that, but he nodded tightly. "I still need to go inside."

"Jamie's right. We need to go inside." Bryson glanced around meaningfully. She followed his gaze. There were empty cars parked along the street, some of the houses were lit up and she could scent people nearby, walking and even hear them talking, but no other immortals were near. "We shouldn't be out here talking."

"We can't walk away without examining the scene," Jamie added.

"I don't want you in there." She didn't want him seeing... Samuel, but Jamie took her hand in his tenderly. Jamie showing her such kindness was more wonderful than the silly dreams she'd held on to of becoming human again. "Please, I don't want you to see—"

He cupped the side of her face. "There's nothing that's going to change how I feel for you, Elsa. Nothing that—"

"Sick freak."

He nodded. "Right, nothing that sick freak could do that would end what I feel, here." He pressed her hand to his chest. "Nothing, Elsa."

She wavered. He was so sincere, so solemn when he said that, as serious as he'd ever been, explaining to her that being alone wasn't safe. She still didn't like it. Going in there was going to be as disgusting as being there in the first place. But she saw in Jamie's eyes he wanted to, more, he felt they should. "We should?"

He nodded. "We should. Be brave once more. I'm right here."

"I know, but..." She bit her lip. "He didn't rape me."

She'd meant it to reassure him, but it seemed to do the

opposite. His eyes turned whiskey bright. He scanned her face, then her clothes, clearly not reassured. She thought he even growled.

"He was going to, you know that, but no, he didn't. I… killed him. He cried like a baby," she added, trying to get him to snap out of his frozen state. "He screamed like a girl, too."

"Elsa," he breathed, somewhat relieved, she sensed. He caressed her arm until he had her hand again, and pulled her into a gentle hug.

"I wasn't sure what your angle was there, but scaring the hell out of him seemed to work," Bryson said, as he passed them. "Shall we?"

"Elsa." Jamie dipped his head and leaned it on hers. "Can you change your clothes?"

Warmth hit her cheeks. *Why hadn't I thought of that?* For the life of her she couldn't think of a single piece of her clothing, not with Jamie right there, watching her. He still didn't believe her that she'd not been raped. "I told you that he didn't—"

"Most women say that, on their own, if it happens, a mental knee jerk reaction when faced with the man they are involved with, I believe," Bryson commented. "Come on, Faolan, let's go inside and give them some—"

"No!" She pulled away from Jamie and took Faolan's small hand. "You can't go in there."

Faolan's eyes widened and he paled under his tan.

"He can't stay out here," Jamie said. "He is strong. Like you. He's safer—"

"With us," she finished, exhaling the panic out in a long sigh. "I don't want him inside the bedroom, then."

Jamie's jaw flexed and his biceps bulged, no doubt from fisting his hands until his knuckles cracked.

She petted his chest, and concentrated on him. "I'll change." She smiled, and for some reason, a tear leaked out, the last thing she expected. "I just can't think of anything I own…"

"Those baby-blue jeans, the soft ones, and the white T-shirt you had on, the black sweater over it, with your boots and leather jacket from the first night."

"You remember all that?"

He stepped closer so he could kiss her behind her ear and whisper, "I remember *everything*."

She nodded and smiled a bit more. It was wobbly but things had gotten intense. *Jamie loves me.*

Jamie stood straighter and brushed the tear aside. "You remember the outfit?"

"Yes."

"Let's throw this trash away."

She filled her mind with the images of the clothes and removed the ones she had on with the same thought. The old clothes settled on her, soft, warm and smelling of Jamie. She leaned into him and he hugged her. Her face was pressed where it should be, against his heart, not near his neck, because of ten inch heels.

"I hate this stupid life, but not you. You make up for it all."

He laughed a short, surprised sound. His grin was worth more than any applause she'd ever earned.

"You have no idea how glad I am to hear that. Now, are you ready to go inside? It's starting to rain." He kissed her forehead, and lifted his jacket to cover her head. "Come on, be brave a little longer."

They went inside, past the front door and Faolan grinned at her, clearly excited to be here. For the life of her, she couldn't understand why, but supposed it was a boy thing. Jamie had dressed him better. He wore an olive green jacket, military style, with a black T-shirt, hers she thought, under a red and black checkered shirt and darker green cargo pants, with her Adidas running shoes. His hair was tousled but his eyes were bright, happy.

"You did well with him," she said to Jamie.

Jamie shrugged but smiled. "I did what you would do, or what I thought you would do."

She took his hand in hers again when he started to move. "Just don't think the worst, in here."

"Elsa, I won't."

"What do you want, I mean, to find?"

"Everything. Clues. It's not Samuel, sweetheart. It's someone else that we need to find."

She remembered now, what Samuel had said about having her first.

"*Him*. Samuel said he was taking me to…him." She felt sick with fear all over again. Shivering she tried to be brave, something that Jamie seemed to believe she could be.

For him, I can be brave. Just a little longer.

Chapter Twenty-Six

Jamie touched Elsa's cold face. He couldn't stop touching her. She was alive. Not only alive, but whole and unharmed. Samuel hadn't taken her spirit and broken it. He hadn't raped her. Bryson may believe that he had, since she'd offered that he hadn't, but Jamie knew she spoke the truth. He thought she always would, especially when it came to the harder things. Like this.

"He won't get you. We'll make sure of it. But I need to see this place. There might be clues here."

"Okay. Faolan, stay here, right here." She pointed to a bench near the door, one of those people put for you to take your boots off at. Faolan gave him a hopeful half-smile, but Jamie nodded to the bench.

"It's best. Eat some of those packs of jerky. We're going to be busy from now on until this is over."

"Jamie, he can't go with us to hunt a creature that Samuel was answering to." He heard the worry in her voice and stroked her back softly.

"No, he can't. But he's been helpful and he can stay with us until we leave here. I asked a friend to watch over him. They have a boy, but I don't want him to stay there full-time. I want him to be with us."

"Oh."

"Is that okay?" he asked, not sure what she thought.

She hugged his arm and nodded, brushing at her face as she turned away. "That's a good idea."

"Elsa." He caught her hand and pulled her closer so he could see the tears she was trying to hide. Bryson had gone upstairs and Faolan was busy with the phone he'd gotten him. Jamie could hear the video game, but really all he could see was Elsa's blue eyes shimmering with tears. They broke past her thick lashes and fell, unchecked, down her cheeks. "Elsa. Talk to me. What's wrong?"

"It's nothing. It's everything. I... This is going to be okay? I mean, Jamie, Samuel was going to take me to...to him. I think the man who did those horrible things in France."

He tightened his grip carefully on small arms. "That man isn't getting his hands on you, Elsa. This is going to be okay. I just need to see what's here then we can go. If you want to stay with Faolan—"

"No, we go together."

He agreed. "Together then. Stay by my side." He let her lead the way, sure he wasn't going to like what he found. He'd barely gotten his heart rate back to normal after searching and not finding her for hours. After that one brief scent of her, he'd thought he'd lost her for good. It had worn at him, beating him at every step. It hadn't helped that Bryson had begun to worry and Faolan had grown quieter and quieter.

But now, he had her with him, only the stress was still there, like a heavy rock on his chest, making it impossible to breathe.

"Here, it was in here," she whispered.

Bryson walked out of a smaller room to the side of the room they entered. A bedroom. But built like the set of some porn flick from the eighties. Red curtains, black walls, gold trim, it was extravagant and made his skin crawl.

The Vampire's face was chalky white and he held up a hand. "Believe me, you'll sleep easier if you don't go in there, and take my advice, don't piss Elsa off. Ever."

Jamie growled. "Bryson—"

"He's right." She hugged her arms around her middle.

Bryson grimaced and hurried to say, "Elsa, I didn't mean to say what you did was wrong. You did exactly the right thing."

She held up a hand, another shaky smile on her pale lips.

"It's okay, I'm okay. I'll stay here, you do your thing."

"Are you sure?" Jamie asked.

"Yes. It has to be done, so do it. But hurry, if you can."

"I will." He gave the bedroom a once-over, sickened by the black walls and russet drapes. Even the bed was nauseating. He found chains at the head and foot of it. Clearly the bastard played with his victims. But these weren't pink and fluffy, these were the caliber meant to hurt whoever was wearing them. The scent of sex hung heavily in the air, stale and layered with fear. It covered the sheets, the floor, even the walls.

This is where he raped his women. And men.

He caught Bryson's eye and nodded. "Like France."

"Yes."

In the bathroom behind a wall, he found more items that made his skin crawl. Bondage devices no store ever sold. He shut the cabinet and headed to the room where Bryson had been. Elsa didn't stop him, but he could tell she was keeping her focus on the view out of the window, not on what he was doing.

Inside he found Samuel—the man who'd claimed to be David. Elsa had ripped his heart from his chest, leaving a gaping hole. Blood had spread in an enormous pool under him. His body was sprawled backwards, one leg at an angle, his hands flung up by his head. His boxers were bloody and, after Jamie crouched near him, he knew why. Elsa had bitten his penis. It was deep, too and it wasn't fangs. She'd simply bitten him—hard enough to paralyze the man.

"He was saying things I didn't like. I turned my head and bit down. I think my teeth met."

"I think you're right. So you washed your mouth out?" The soap now made complete sense.

"Yes. It seemed like the thing to do."

"I bet it was." There was more whiskey in here, the scent coming from the body, he realized. Elsa's scent was strong here, too, terror the primal emotion, but anger was there as well.

"You broke his control. How did you do that?" He examined a tattoo on the inside of Samuel's wrist. A large silver watch partly covered it, but when Jamie shifted the metal up, the full tattoo became clearer. It resembled a coat of arms. A dark cross in the middle, with the border worked in faded blue with the once yellow fleur-de-lis.

"I thought of you."

Jamie dropped the Vampire's arm and stood. He wanted to wash, but held off to study Elsa's frown. "You thought of me?"

She had walked over to the wall of clothing, not touching anything, and not standing too near the blood or the body.

"He wanted..." She nodded to the man and winced. Samuel had apparently wanted a blow job. "He said I'd want it, I'd want him." A laugh that spoke of frayed nerves then she rushed on. "But I would *never* want that with him." She focused on the body for a little longer, then shuddered and met his eyes. "I only wanted you. Maybe to slap you on the back of the head for saying what you said, but still, I only want you."

He held her before she finished, relieved she still had enough spunk to find humor. "Next time, smack me, don't leave."

"I hope there isn't a next time."

He kissed her hair. "There will be."

"You two ready?" Bryson asked. "I can't believe you can stomach this."

Elsa blinked and quickly wiped at her eyes.

"We're done for the night," Jamie said, steadying her.

"No, I can help, we can—"

"We can take a break. One night won't change things."

"It might. He left and he went somewhere, when he left me in the basement. He went to *him*... I think. What if *he* is expecting me tonight?"

Jamie cursed, but only in a whisper. "He'd better like disappointment because he is never getting you," Jamie said sternly. "You need to rest."

280

"I *need* to be safe."

He didn't like it. Worse, he didn't like the sudden dive his stomach did at the thought of someone who controlled Samuel, ever touching her.

"She's right, the quicker we can finish this, the safer she will be." Bryson settled a hand on his shoulder. "She's fine. Let her show you the basement. It can't be as bad as this."

"I thought it was," she said. "He nearly drowned me with whiskey. Seriously, I never want to drink whiskey again."

His heart felt as if it'd been crushed in his chest. "Elsa—"

"Let's just go. I'm afraid and that makes me want to run. But I'm done running." She took his hand, easing the panic somewhat. He scanned her face to see if she was okay, but she stood on tiptoes and brushed a kiss to his lips. "I'm okay."

"All right, we check the basement then we go. You need rest more than we need answers." He paused to touch her cheek where there was a slight pinkness near her mouth. She was going to protest about resting, but he stopped her. "I need to know you're safe, even if it's just for a few hours before we go back out."

"Okay."

The one word dug at his heart, but he smoothed her hair back off her face then guided her out of the room. She stopped at the front door.

"What is it?"

"Ah, I don't know where the basement is…"

"I do," Faolan said, pocketing his phone and standing. "It's over there, behind that door."

"How do you know, Faolan?" Elsa asked, letting Jamie guide her to the door near the kitchen.

"It's evil. Like him, and like the witches."

Like France, he meant. Jamie tensed, but turned the knob, opened the door and walked down the steps into the basement. It was evil. Like France, like the basement they'd found hidden under the burnt house. The stench of blood and fear was coupled with the scent of sex—and, more recently, whiskey.

He found the cell Elsa had been in and crouched near the bars. It was a small four-by-four space. She'd sat there, in the middle, for long enough that he could sense it strongly. Hours. She hadn't lain down, though and he wondered why. A drop of something caught his eye and he reached in, touching the rusty stain and brought it to his nose. Her scent. Her blood. There were more drops by the first and farther away, by the wall, as if the bastard had struck her and her head had turned to the side, spilling drops on the ground and wall.

He stood, having seen enough. "I wish I'd been a few minutes earlier. I would have helped you kill him. Slowly."

She squeezed his hand and more tears shimmered in her eyes.

"He hurt you."

"He tried. Is this where he took other women?"

"Yes." He debated telling her more, but finally said, "And boys. Men, women, boys, and young girls. Just like the basement in France."

She covered her mouth with both hands. "Oh God. I think I'm going to be sick. Some of those clothes… They were for dressing boys up and small…children."

"There's a lot of missing people in the world," he said gently. "You did a good thing, killing him."

She nodded, but he could tell she'd had enough.

"Come on." He led her to the stairs, and was about to follow when a long object under a cloth caught his eye. "I'll be right there." She went on up and he walked to the wall under a rickety shelf filled with small jars and metal coffee cans.

He lifted the rag slowly. A short, thick, double-edged sword, used for killing at close range, called a *braquemard* by the French, which was also slang for cock, lay on the table. It was unsheathed. Dried blood stained the metal where the grip met the blade. Otherwise the metal was spotlessly clean and well kept.

He shoved the rest of the cloth aside. Hooks of several different sizes and designs, along with chains, were neatly organized like the tools on a doctor's tray. All of them were made of dark metal, either because they used some local metalsmith or they wanted them to resemble older work.

More chains were hanging in the cell Elsa had been in. A hook, with the frayed ends of rope, snagged on the tip hung above his head and to the left. He touched the fibers and scented death on them. Someone had been hung here recently, and died. Before they did, though, someone else had had sex, or at the least masturbated.

He crouched under the hook and scented the strong evidence of blood and semen. Worse, he recognized the stench of entrails, as if someone had been gutted. Water had been used to clean the floor. He found a hose and faucet on the wall.

But what did they do with the bodies?

A furnace stood in the darkest recesses of the basement.

He got up and walked over, not liking what buzzed around in his head. He unlatched the metal door and swung it out. Ash filled the thing to at least six inches deep. Nowadays, people used central heat and air. He glanced up and saw that no pipes were directly linked to the old wood-burning furnace. No water, no air, just one larger tube directly from the furnace upward. Going to where, he'd bet, there was a fireplace in the Vampire's room.

A serial killer Vampire. Or a serial killer's assistant?

The stench in here wasn't all Samuel. It was someone else as well. And it was years and years' worth of them both. Their sickness was deep, strong enough that if Jamie got within a mile of the source, he'd know it.

He shut the furnace, more disgusted with this world than ever. Humans were monsters just as much as any immortal. They sodomized boys. They killed little girls. They kept women as dogs on a leash. Immortals were just as horrifying, but to think an immortal was preying on human and immortal, using them sexually, and murdering them to cover it up... It was sickening, in a world that he already knew was filled with horror.

Upstairs, Elsa sat close to Faolan, learning his game, by the sound of it. As soon as he walked through the door, she rose and came to him, touching his chest like she had earlier.

"You found something."

He covered her hand with his. "I'm not sure. But we can go now. What do you think, Bryson?" he asked, suddenly weary of it all. It'd been over two days since he'd slept. The lack was catching up to him. "Is it safe to break for now, and start again tomorrow night?"

"Yes. We've all done enough for now. Besides, I need to meet with Aidan. I called Circerran."

"She and Jack both saw the basement in France. They'll want to go over this one as well."

"I'll tell them. Jack will be a good man to have on hand," Bryson added, glancing at Elsa, then, oddly enough, down at the boy. Jamie put his hand on Faolan's shoulder and Bryson lifted his gaze to Jamie's again.

Elsa rested her head on his chest, reminding him that she was quickly dwindling.

"We won't stay in the city." He wanted her safe, away from this.

"Stay at my place," Bryson offered. "I won't be there, and even if I do return home, it's huge. You know the way. Go there. In the lower level there are bedrooms. Each has a natural hot spring."

"Thanks, it's a nice offer, Bryson, but—"

"Take it. Elsa, you need to rest. Convince him. I have a feeling we'll all need to be rested before this is over."

"What do you think, Jamie?" She lifted her head to watch his face, letting him make the decision. She'd done that before, but he'd been so caught up in everything going on, or going wrong, he'd not realized how much she did trust him. Which made failing her much worse.

"If you're okay with his place, it's close." He brushed her

heavy, silky hair off her face, so ready to have her in his arms again his hand trembled.

"Do you have food?" she asked Bryson, as if that would be a negative. Jamie smiled and hugged her closer. She would be fine.

Bryson gave her an offended frown. "Of course. And blood. It's bagged, but I have a feeling you won't need that." He saluted Jamie and tousled Faolan's hair, giving the boy another candy bar. "Kid, get some rest, you look like hell."

With that he was gone.

"Really, he shouldn't talk like that to you. What was he thinking?" Elsa muttered to Faolan.

"He always curses, Elsa." Faolan yawned.

Elsa laughed and turned to him. "Maybe he is tired, Jamie. Can we go to Bryson's? I think it will be safe."

"It is." Jamie got them both out of the house as quickly as he could and to the car. He opened Elsa's door, and she slid in with a sigh. Faolan was already climbing in the back. As soon as he got in the too-small sports car, Elsa let out a relieved-sounding sigh.

"I was worried. I thought now, something will happen and you'd be gone."

"I'm not going anywhere." He'd been thinking the same thing, as soon as Bryson had left. He started the car. "I thought the same thing, but about you."

"You did not."

He laughed at her quick denial. "I did. You scare me." He took her hand and kissed it before he glanced in the back to check on Faolan.

"He's already half asleep," Elsa murmured.

"He helped today. We'll let him rest, but hey." Jamie laughed and took his jacket off to cover the boy. "Here, don't fall asleep, or I'll have to carry you to your room."

He got a mumbled something as a response, nothing more.

"He's so cute," Elsa whispered in his ear. "And much

braver than me." There was such feeling in her voice when she said that, he knew no matter what, the boy would stay with them. "I thought you weren't scared of anything." She brushed a kiss to his jaw again.

He leaned over so he could kiss her quickly on the lips. "Everyone fears something. How about we get to the house and rest?"

"That sounds wonderful, but... Maybe we could also do a bit more?"

His smile threatened to remain the rest of the night. "Anything you want. I won't even need you to do any work," he promised, earning a laugh from her before she snuggled up against his arm.

"We'll see about that."

Chapter Twenty-Seven

Jamie found the rooms Bryson had spoken of and laid the boy down on a large king-sized bed, took his shoes off and covered him, without Faolan waking. Elsa had already gone ahead to the room down the hall and across the corridor. The Vampire must have had a dozen rooms, for what Jamie wasn't certain, but the luxurious home made him uneasy.

Would Elsa want something like this?

He worried that thought, along with what he actually owned, until he opened the door to their room and found Elsa on the floor, back to the bed, her knees drawn up to her chest, crying.

"Elsa." He reached her quickly and picked her up and sat with her in his arms, on his lap. "Elsa."

She turned in his arms and hugged his neck, crying softly against his chest. The bed, the bedroom, everything disappeared and all that mattered was this woman in his arms. *How did I miss this? How did I not know she was mine?*

He stroked her back, holding her close but not as hard as he wanted. She shook with her tears but he let her cry, trying to comfort her as best he could.

"Elsa, it's going to be okay. I'm going to make sure of it. You have to believe that." He laughed past the pain he experienced seeing her hurting. He kissed her forehead. "There's nothing on this planet that matters more to me than you. I don't have this," he gestured to the room, "but if you want this, I will get it for you."

"This?" She sounded tearful still, but confused.

He dared to tip her face up so he could kiss her wet lips. "A house like this. I have a room at the compound, a closet with some clothes, weapons, stuff like that. But if you want this, I'll get it for you."

"I want *you*."

"You have me."

She shook her head and pushed against his chest, straddling him in her frustration when he didn't release her right away.

"No. No I don't. You aren't mine. You would be drooling all over me, and eventually you'll leave me for…for…your mate!" She hit him on the chest with her small fist, and when he got his brain working, all he could do was laugh, which made her hit him repeatedly and scream a little.

He tossed her onto her back and caught her hands, kissing one then the other. "Elsa, you *are* my mate. You are mine. Just as I am yours."

She froze in mid-struggle, eyes wide, then pulled her hand free and hit him again, trying to get away as much as she had before. He let her, confused but willing to let her explain. Only she got to the headboard, and, breathless, stayed on her knees glaring at him.

"What? You're going to have to speak. I don't read thoughts. I don't understand women, and if you don't explain it, I won't be able to either."

"You are *not* my mate! You would know. I might be new to all this"—she flung her hands out and growled in frustration—"but I know about mates."

"Oh?" He sat back amused, for now, but also intrigued. "What do you know about mates?"

"Jamie, you're pissing me—"

"—off. I know. I don't know why, though. Look, sweetheart, I am not trying to piss you off, that was actually my idea of letting you know you and I are going to live for the rest of eternity together. So, you obviously don't sense it. And I'll be completely honest, I didn't know what it was, when I did sense it."

She threw her hands up. "That is not possible. Wolves… They know. They *know*!"

He nodded, which didn't seem to calm her at all.

"Then you agree? You're *lying* to me?" Her voice broke on the words.

"Enough! I have never lied to you—okay, okay, once, damn it!" he shouted, when she tried to crawl off the bed. He caught her, manned up to the mini fist fight and let her exhaust herself hitting him on the chest. When she was breathless and clearly done, he kissed her fists.

"It's terrible, Jamie. It's like loving a man who you know will have to marry this other woman because he has to and there—"

He turned her head and kissed her, tried to make it gentle, but ended up toppling her onto her back and driving his tongue along hers in such urgent need he shook with it. She twisted away far too soon, and he kissed her jaw then behind her ear.

"You love me."

She sucked in a painful breath and he turned her head, immediately. "No one is ever going to replace you. *No one,*" he growled. Her eyes turned steady and she slowly relaxed. "I sense you. I know you're mine. It was one reason I tried to remove you so I couldn't hurt you... I worried." He paused and pulled her up, so he could face her as he spoke. "I felt it, but didn't know what it was, just that as the moon reached its fullest point, I didn't trust myself near you. I worried I'd harm you." He whispered the last and touched her soft cheek.

"You would never hurt me. I might hurt you."

He smiled, but it was painful. "Elsa, I wasn't born a wolf. At times I don't understand what I'm feeling or what I'm doing. It might not be...safe for you."

She widened her eyes and sat back more on her feet, staring at him. "You weren't born a wolf."

It wasn't a question, but he shook his head. "No. I was bitten on a battlefield. My brother as well. I survived because Aidan found me. We never located my brother."

"You weren't born a wolf."

289

"No. I wasn't." He waited, there was a lot going on inside her head, but he wasn't a mind reader. "What is it?"

Suddenly she smiled, the bright flash of sunshine he couldn't live without, then she flung herself so hard at him he toppled backwards. She hugged him and kissed his face, smiling so big he couldn't follow the rapid change from crying, to anger, to now happiness.

"That's good?"

"Yes." She stopped and pulled up to sit on his hips. "This is good. It means..." She tilted her head and rubbed her hands over his chest. Her hair fell like a waterfall of golden silk around them. "We're a lot alike."

He laughed. "Baby, we aren't anything alike. You're beautiful, graceful and...you have a temper."

"You shouted at me. And you're graceful."

He had shouted. "I only raised my voice because you weren't listening."

"Saying raised your voice means the same as shouting, Jamie. And I was listening, I just..." She sighed heavily and brushed a tear. "I do love you. I'm sorry I hit you. I'm sorry I didn't give you time to explain back in France. I wish I had."

He sat up, adjusting her so she straddled him. "You don't hit hard, and besides, I wasn't thinking. Or I was. I was thinking about you, Elsa. I never want to harm you. This," he touched his chest, "this worries me. I don't want to—"

"Hurt me. I know, so you won't." She shrugged.

"It's not that easy. During the full moon I sometimes don't know what I'm doing."

"It's a full moon tonight, Jamie."

He stiffened, suddenly realizing she was right. He analyzed his need for her, and it was there, an urgent pulse along his flesh, but so was the need to secure her, which he realized meant soothing her.

"Got you, didn't I?" Her grin was perfect. He laughed and drew her in, and she sighed into his neck. "I hope that means you are going to do something about this." She rocked on his erection and bit down on his jaw, lightly but with a sudden desire he realized she'd been holding back, just as he had been.

"Baby, we're going to do something about this." He assured her, pressing her lush ass down so her body was even closer to his. "Do you feel something, an urge to make love, that's hard to resist?"

"With you? Always." She laughed, blushing a pretty pink.

His chest felt full. He cradled her closer. "You know what I mean. An instinctual need?"

She tilted her head and her hair brushed along his arms. "I have always…felt something. Are you saying that was… my wolf?"

"It could be."

"Well, if so, I guess we both don't listen very well." She frowned slightly, then widened her blue eyes. "That first time, when you touched me—"

"And it was a shock?"

She nodded.

He caressed her cheek. "I don't know, but I do know I'm never letting you go, Elsa. This is where you belong, baby."

Her gaze turned tender, the way it did for Faolan, and now him. "Will we…mate tonight?"

"Elsa," he groaned, feeling that tingle along his cock he always experienced before he came. She was needy, wet already he knew, for him. He could smell it, and more, he could sense it as if she'd walked naked in the room to get his attention. She needed him. After what she'd gone through, he guessed she needed to be loved. By her man.

"Well, there is more than just this, isn't there?" she whispered, rocking along his hips. The pleasure grew, making him sweat. "Jamie?"

"Yes." *Words. Ancient words that they could say.*

"Oh, God, you're close to coming, aren't you?" she teased, biting him again. "Just from the thought of being stuck with me for the rest of your life?"

"Elsa." He got control, but only because he toppled her

to her back again and got some space for his body to slow down. When he had pulled back from the edge, he saw her watching him, a smile on her face as she waited.

"I like that I can do that." He groaned and stiffened all over because she reached down and fondled his cock. "You missed me?"

"Hell yes."

"It was only one night."

"Two. You left, then tonight."

"Tonight isn't over."

"No, it's just begun," he cautioned and lifted up, then off the bed. She sat and frowned at him. "Come here."

"You are so bossy," she whispered, but crawled over.

He reached out and touched her cheek again. "I am? I want this to be special."

"It will be. Come to bed."

"I was thinking we'd start in there." He gestured to the hot spring he could sense behind the door, and she smiled, clearly pleased.

"Our second time."

He laughed. "Sweetheart, this is more like our tenth, but you can be assured, it won't be our last. And, Elsa, it's going to be a mating we'll always remember. I only wish I could get you flowers, and bring you to—"

"I have you. You're all I need, Jamie. You're home now. You." She was eye level this way, and she leaned forward and kissed him, wrapping her arms around his neck as she did. It was a quick, hot kiss compared to others they'd shared. She moved back and seemed to like what she did to him because she smiled. "Go make sure it's ready. I'll... get undressed and be there in a minute." He frowned, but when he opened his mouth she placed a finger against his lips. "It's a woman thing."

The rush he got from that wasn't rational, but he knew no matter how long she took, he'd be waiting for her. Still, he bit down on that slender finger and at her shocked gasp, he hoped *excited* gasp, he pulled her to him and kissed her soft lips once more.

"All right then, one minute."

I'm nervous.

There was no rational reason for it. She'd already done things with Jamie O'Connor she hadn't known, until she'd done them, *could* be done. He'd seen every inch of her and yet...

This is different. What if he sees something he doesn't like? Worse, what if I do something he doesn't like? She wished she could postpone this, just for a day, until she could go shopping and find some sexy lingerie to make him crazy.

In the end she washed her face, again. Brushed her teeth, yes being a Vampire helped with that stuff, but even after several minutes of brushing and flossing, she was still an anxious mess.

Be brave.

She shed her clothes, and taking a deep breath, pushed open the door. The room was amazing. Carved out of rock, the natural-looking pool of steaming water stunned her. But more than the room, more than the soft music of a waterfall coming from the back of the pool, Jamie stole her breath.

He groaned loudly and that sound drew her complete, utter attention. The water rose to halfway up his muscled stomach, leaving him visible from there up. What she saw made her knees weak. He was stunning. Already wet with drops of water, his skin was tight, muscled and bronzed from the sun. It took her moments to take him in. The intensity in his golden eyes, the complete focus on her, and slowly the fact that one of his arms was resting on the back of the pool, while the other was underwater, moving rhythmically.

There were no words. The impact of him stroking off to the sight of her blew her insecurities right out of her head.

She walked to him and each step brought her closer, but she sensed it was bringing him closer as well. When she reached the side of the pool, she stepped over the edge and slowly lowered herself into the heated water.

Jamie groaned deeper, tensing his chest muscles and his arm muscles bulged.

"Oh God, you are so beautiful," she whispered.

Water sloshed over the edge as he captured her in his arms and kissed her. It was an amazing kiss, just like all the others, but this one was urgent, desperate and she opened for him, giving him everything he wanted. He guided her hand to his erection, and, groaning deeper, he closed her hand around the thick head. She stroked down the warm, velvety flesh, caught in such excitement she couldn't seem to kiss or touch enough of him.

Seconds of tantalizing touching and Jamie pulled her free from his erection and guided her legs open so he could position her. She stopped him with a hand on his chest, and watching his face, moved downward. There was one thing she'd not done to Jamie O'Connor. One thing she'd wondered about, and wanted, needed somehow. It didn't make sense but she let her desires run, trusting that he wasn't going to complain.

"Elsa —"

"I want to."

He dragged her up by gripping her face, and kissed her with so much passion that she almost changed her mind. Obviously he liked that idea, though, so she knew exactly what she was going to do. *I'm going to pleasure my man.* She was released just as fast as he'd grabbed her and he scanned her face.

"I *want* to."

A slow, stunned smile blossomed on his handsome face and he closed his eyes, opening them right after as he sat back and tried to lift out of the water.

"No. Like this."

"Baby, just how are you going to do that? You'd have to hold your breath."

She settled a kiss to his hard chest. "Jamie. I don't *have* to breathe."

For some reason he froze and all his delicious muscles tensed that way they did when he was going to explode in action, typically fighting action. She rose to meet his eyes. His expression turned from stunned to slap happy.

"Damn. I can't be this lucky."

She took that as permission to begin.

"I hope you never forget that, either, Jamie O'Connor." She went under, kissing the tip of his erection first, then slid her mouth from the tip to the rough patch of hair nestling his tight sac. She felt him groan, more than heard him. More excited than ever, she took measure and sucked back up the underside of every inch of him, stunned by his size all over again. Not willing to wait, she pulled the stalk down and sucked him in, thrilled at the first taste of his musky manliness. The head was soft, yet still hard, just as the length of him was. She stroked her hands firmly up and down, aware that he was groaning heavily. Unable to take too much, she concentrated on making sure what she could handle was given as much attention as she could, before she tried to go deeper.

Jamie grabbed her hair, but unlike Samuel, Jamie was careful, and if she had to guess, holding on for dear life. She concentrated on a spot under the flared head, savoring the texture and warm taste of him. Jamie began to subtly thrust his hips. It wasn't deep or even, she thought, conscious, but it was telling. It also lit her up like the fourth of July. She was so in tune with his growing excitement that she managed more of him when she twisted her head just a little. She did it again, surviving the gag reflex, because she thought Jamie had shouted something. His other hand landed on her head and he tried to pull her off.

She spluttered to the surface. "What?"

He looked like a wreck—in pain—tensed and bulging muscles along every inch of him. "I'm gonna come."

"Good." She ducked back under, found the warm stalk of flesh waiting. She sucked down the head, moving her mouth faster when she heard him yell. He did it again and she slipped back up, added both hands around the middle of his erection, as far as she could go, then started a hard, fast stroking and sucking. Jamie roared. *Could anything be more exciting? Watching him again…*

All too soon, Jamie grabbed hold of her head and started thrusting for real, in that way she knew was going to be the end. Her own body sizzled with heat. An ache built between her thighs, circling around her empty, untouched pussy.

Just when her jaw began to ache, Jamie's thighs trembled. His hold on her hair turned to a death grip. His erection went super-hard, so wide she couldn't handle much of him. She used her hands instead, while she sucked softly, faster and faster. *Come for me. I'm going to make him come for me.*

She thought he yelled again. He tightened his hands in her hair, and seconds later, warm, salty cum burst from the tip. She tried to swallow, spilled most out of her mouth. He pressed deeper. She felt the next blast go down easier, and the next. All the while, he trembled and kneaded her head with shaky hands. Even his rock-hard thighs shook.

It was more fun than anything else she'd ever done. Better, she knew she could do this to him any time she wanted. She gently slid him from such a deep position and he tensed his hands in her hair. She took that as a sign to go slowly. She tried, but he was still so hard, still so delicious in her mouth. She got another burst of cum for playing with him and forgot that breathing wasn't necessary when she swallowed. Water rushed into her nose and she choked, coughing and laughing as Jamie pulled her up out of the water.

"Elsa, shit, did I hurt you, are you…? Are you laughing?"

She nodded, coughing up more water and maybe something else as well. Jamie groaned and pulled her into his arms. "That was life-changing."

"It was?" She peeked at him through her hair. He pushed the wet mess aside and stared at her for so long she grew embarrassed. "I didn't do it right? I tried. I mean, well, you know—"

"You were a virgin. That night. You gave me your virginity. Now you give me this."

She nodded, unsure of the sudden change in him, but certain of one thing. "Fuck me, Jamie."

His face darkened to a deep copper and his eyes glowed. "I'm going to make love to you for the rest of the night. Until you can't utter those words ever again," he said, making it sound like a vow.

"What? Why?"

"Because you won't need to tell me." He kissed her forehead. "I'll make sure you don't need to. And for the record here, baby, that was the only blow job I ever want. Always, just like that," he murmured.

"Well, we'll have to get a hot springs then."

He laughed and stroked her body, making her hotter. "You don't believe me, but it's true. Sappy, sure, but that's what you do to me, turn me into a sappy, lovesick pup, eh?"

She laughed at the image and got kissed for it. He didn't stop with her lips. "My turn."

"Oh, God, your turn?" He settled her over the edge of the pool and laid her back, widening her thighs as he did so he could slip between them. "Oh, yes. Your turn."

At the first lick she was certain life had completely sucked before Jamie. After her first orgasm under his skilled tongue, she knew it. He didn't stop there, either, more than ready to make his promise a reality.

She didn't mind. In fact she begged him to stop, only because she wanted him inside her so badly she ached. He didn't make her wait long, but drove her to a devastating orgasm within minutes. He joined her then began all over again.

"I love you, Jamie."

"Baby, you own my soul," Jamie whispered, teaching her more things she knew would fill their lives with absolutely no time to worry over monsters, sick perverts, or anyone else but each other.

Chapter Twenty-Eight

"Are you certain of this, Elsa?" Jamie asked.

"Are you?" she asked, touching his face with her fingertips.

He took her hand and kissed each slender finger. "I am. I don't want to rush you. We can wait."

"For what? To see if you throw your dirty laundry on the floor or snore too loud? How will that change this?" She touched her breast then his chest. "I want you. Do you—?"

"—want you? Until there isn't room for anything but you. You helped me find my heart, and now, you hold it."

"Oh, Jamie," she whispered. "That was so perfect."

He cleared his throat at that, and focused on what he was trying to say. "The pack, the mission, hell, keeping you safe, all that falls to the side, and all I can think of is you. I'm not certain that is good."

"It's good." She nodded repeatedly and squeezed his hand.

He grinned and had to admit he felt the same. She was like him in so many ways it boggled his mind. Half the time they finished each other's sentences. Elsa fit him. She'd told him when he'd worried over the earth-shattering blow job that it had been more fun than anything else she'd ever done. *Fun.* As if he was fun. He didn't feel fun. He felt raw, exposed, but still wanting to be closer to her.

"I'm not a good man, Elsa. I've done things," he began, suddenly recalling that a mating often exposed the couple's minds to one another. "I've killed. Many times, simply because I was told."

She considered that and him. "I've killed." She shifted the

covers over her breasts where the silk sheet had slipped. "And not just Samuel," she rushed to say when he frowned. "And those Vampires in the forest weren't my first kill either. I once killed...someone else."

"Elsa, whoever you killed, you killed because you needed to, no other reason. Survival, yes?"

She winced and turned away. It was the first time since she'd walked to him in the hot pools that she'd done that. He waited, not willing to rush her. If she wanted to tell him this, she would.

"It was, but... It was, I mean that was why—"

"You have always stayed alone."

"Yes." She stared at him and her eyes filled with shimmering tears. "I thought he was a good guy. A nice man. A...wolf, like you."

He pulled her closer so she could rest in his arms and let him curl around her, unable to stand her crying. He kissed her hair and she shifted so she could face him. More tears, a trail of them, leaked from her blue eyes, but he brushed them away.

"It's hard to kill. The first one is always the hardest, and stays with us the longest."

"Do you remember your first kill?" she asked, after a while of letting him soothe her.

"Not really, but I remember one and it's always stayed with me. Even through these years of being a wolf, I've never forgotten. Sometimes it happens like that, I think. Up until him, I had only fought men, men trying to kill me and in the desperate battle to survive, sometimes you don't have time to process what you've done." She seemed to relax as he spoke, so he continued. "For me, though, the first kill I remember was a boy—not a man, a young boy."

"A boy? Like Faolan?"

"No, perhaps ten and six."

"That's a man, Jamie."

"No, baby, it's not." He kissed her mouth then, rested his head on his hand to stare down at her lovely face. "You

remember that I told you I was changed, not born a wolf?"
She nodded. "I was a soldier, during a time when we used
swords still and very few of us had muskets. We were
traveling from —"

"Wait. Is this America?"

"No. This was in Egypt."

"What were you doing there?"

"I was in a war. Napoleon. Have you heard of him?" he
teased.

She snorted. "A little. Go on."

"It was there, in a desert, that we were attacked by a
group of men. They'd been sent after us when someone in
our group had...slept with one of their women."

"Oh? Who did that?"

"My brother."

"Oh..."

Jamie shrugged. "He was thoughtless, and often got
us into situations where we barely survived. This time,
though... They attacked at night. I was fighting off a few of
them, when I broke free and turned, striking before I could
see who I faced. It was the boy."

The sound of his saber taking that child's future from him
still haunted Jamie's dreams. The complete shock on the
young man's face, and the tears that had filled his almond
eyes, even the rattling sound his last breath made as it left
him. It was all there, as if it had just happened.

"He died quickly, but I've never forgotten, and for a
while, I couldn't forgive myself or my brother. We were
bitten a few years after that and I lost my brother, still angry
at him for that boy's life."

"Oh, Jamie." She rose and hugged him, holding him as
if he were fragile. Such tenderness from her was given so
easily, so often too. She'd cleaned his wounds as carefully.
He rested his head on her slender shoulder and kissed her
satin skin.

"It was long ago, but what I wanted to say was you killed.
And I have as well. We live through these things, and go

on. Before this is over, we will kill again, too."

"I know but that is different."

He lifted his head and saw her bite her lip. "And this man you killed, this wolf, he didn't deserve his death?"

She ducked her head and sighed. "You ask such hard questions."

He laughed and lay back down on the bed. She followed and rested her chin on his chest. "You should rest. We can—"

"No. Before we do, I did kill him because he deserved it. He tricked me, and tried to rape me, and force me to take vows I wasn't going to take. *Ever.*"

At the word rape, he tensed, not pleased to hear such words, so casually spoken, from her.

"He was a Death Stalker. One of the ones with a tattoo. He'd covered his up, of course. Maybe it helped him get more women. I don't know. He was suave, charismatic and...nice when I hadn't spoken to any other immortals before. He was...a liar, though. A fake. He was evil. Just as Samuel was, just as this monster is. I... They caught me outside the pub I'd met him at, after I'd turned him down. He'd offered to let me join him."

"And this is why you were so resistant to joining me."

"Yes. Nolan. He scared me, he was so—"

Jamie stopped her with a hand on hers and sat up, drawing her with him.

She startled and frowned. "What?"

"Nolan. A wolf. That looked like me."

She nodded. "Jamie? What is it?"

Nolan. Charismatic. Always a ladies' man, always getting what he wanted, or...taking it, Jamie had worried. He'd never caught Nolan but he'd begun to fear leaving his brother alone for too long. Women who had been friendly with him would shy away in fear the next time he saw them, running away sometimes when Nolan arrived. "Nolan."

"Jamie, you're scaring me."

He focused on Elsa and saw that she was white as a ghost.

"No, it's okay. It's okay." There had to be another answer. Had to be.

"Oh God." She scooted away, eyes wide, and nearly fell off the bed. She caught herself and pulled farther away when he tried to help her. "Your brother. What was his name, Jamie?"

"Elsa, baby, come here, you're overreacting—"

"Overreacting? Tell me I didn't kill your brother!"

He couldn't think, and when he didn't respond, she covered her mouth in horror and backed away from him. He did the only thing he could think of, he caught her before she could do something crazy, and held her small shoulders in his hands.

"I want you as my woman. Now, forever, and fucking always." He kissed her and breathed in her scent, giving her his. "With this breath, with this body, with this heart, I freely bond myself to you for all of eternity."

She gasped, but didn't make a move otherwise.

"Now say it back to me."

"Jamie—"

"I want you as mine—"

"I want you. Now, forever." She sniffed and tears fell, but he manned up and didn't break the connection he could feel building.

"Always."

"Always."

She hesitated, then pulled his head down and kissed him, doing what he'd done, and something between them started to grow, building ties he wanted, so he could bind himself to her forever.

"With this breath, and body, and heart," she whispered.

He covered her hand she'd placed on his heart and touched hers as well. Her eyes pinned him in place, the blue so light he could see his reflection staring back at him.

"Go on," he urged.

"I freely bond myself to you for all of eternity," she said brokenly.

As soon as the words left her mouth, he pulled her close and staggered to keep his bearings as those webs of connection flared wider. Her warmth and love surrounded him. She held him there, and he wasn't sure if she whispered his name out loud or in his mind, but the amazement in her tone, along with her love, a deep, steady beat he didn't deserve, captured and held him.

"I'd die for this woman."

"Jamie! Don't think such things."

He dove deeper in her mind, letting her see the worst of him, all of his sins and past mistakes, his life since he'd turned—everything was exposed to her. Tentatively, she explored, as if still afraid. At the memory of Nolan, she tried to pull away.

"No, look deeper, baby."

"But, Jamie!"

He felt more sorrow from her, but gradually she shared his worries, his fears over his brother. Just as slowly, she let the memories of what Nolan had done to her play out for him. He couldn't help but gather her closer. She was so small, so delicate, but had been so brave.

"I was terrified. Only you would think I was brave."

"Bravery is not never fearing, baby. It's fearing and still surviving by any means necessary."

As he held her, she finally relaxed and opened herself even more.

He saw how close she'd been to dying, again. Saw how Nolan had thrown her against a wall then hit her until she was dizzy and couldn't see straight. Saw how his brother had shoved her over a table and ripped at her clothes. Saw how Elsa had fought back, gaining her freedom by being stronger, and more frightened than she ever had in her life.

She bloodied Nolan, and his brother had flown into a rage, hurting her again and managing to nearly strangle her. Elsa had been close to losing consciousness when she'd shoved at Nolan, misted and been caught again, but this time with her hand inside Nolan. She'd pulled free, not realizing what she'd done until he'd fallen on her, crushing her under his weight. The other men had run, afraid of her as she rose to her feet.

"You did the right thing. The only thing. If you hadn't…" He cupped either side of her face and held her still and forced her to meet his eyes. "If you hadn't, I wouldn't have you now. You would be dead, Elsa. Nolan picked his path. He had the same opportunities I had, but never took them. He always went the easy way. All too often, that was the wrong way. I lost him over three hundred years ago. He was dead to me then, sweetheart. I only wish he had died and spared you such pain."

"I'm still sorry. So sorry I killed him."

"I am too, only because this haunted you for so long. We were meant for each other. Maybe we were meant to heal each other, eh?"

"And love each other."

He gazed into her pretty blue eyes and leaned closer, so they were forehead to forehead.

"Yes. I love you. Nothing will change that because I see you. I think I always have seen you, ever since I started hunting for you, I guess."

Finally he sensed her relaxing, accepting what he'd said. He tightened his arms and picked her up, smiling when she caught at his neck. "I think it's time to rest."

"I think you're right." *"But you're still worried. Why are you worried about Alrick? I'm not. Who cares what he thinks?"*

"Ah, fuck."

"You really think a lot of swears. Do you think Faolan sees them? I wonder – wait. You think…Balrick…" "Oh, no way is he my father. No freaking way." She pulled away to stare wide-eyed at him.

"Uh, baby, can you *undig* your claws from my shoulder? It might be true, but it might not be. It doesn't matter." He set her down on the bed and nodded toward the covers. "Come on, I'm tired. I haven't slept in days and I had a workout already. All this thinking isn't good for you. Let it rest."

She sat up straighter. "I can't rest. Not now."

"And worrying about it will somehow make it better?"

He got the impression of her flipping him off through their bond and laughed. He also tugged her under the covers, and next to him. "Rest. Sleep just a few hours. We can do that. I love you. You love me. We're a—"

"Do not do the Barney thing. How do you even know that song?"

Laughing, he settled more comfortably around her, turning her so her lovely ass was to his hips and his arms around her, and his head near hers. "I watch TV."

"In this century?"

"Maybe. Sleep."

He didn't think she would, but she surprised him by turning, rearranging them, and curling up close to his chest with a happy sounding sigh. "I'm going to sleep. But wake me if anything happens." "*Anything.*"

"*Baby, you'll be the first to know, after me, if anything happens. Sleep.*"

"*Okay, but then I want to try something.*"

An image of her going under the covers and her mouth watering in anticipation stunned him. Can I be this lucky?

"*Yes, as long as you understand that Balrick is not my father.*"

"*Sweetheart, even if he was the sperm donor, he is never going to be your father. He's not a part of you.*"

"*How do you know? What if I'm like him?*"

He brushed a kiss to her hair and tipped her head up. "You're mine. My mate. My life. You're not evil. Only that mouth of yours and I love that, along with your ideas. Now, tell me you understand."

She nibbled her lip, scanning his face. He smiled. "*You can read my thoughts.*"

"I love your face. I understand. I'm not evil. But, Jamie…" She pressed a hand to his chest. "But, Jamie, I don't even know for certain I have a wolf."

"That's where you're wrong," he murmured. "Slow your

worry, let me show you."

Her eyes glowed lighter blue and she smiled. "Show me?"

"Yes. Here." He took her hand and settled it on his heart. "Breathe with me. Match my heartbeat."

She frowned adorably, but did as he asked. When she was calm, he dove back into the wonders of her beautiful mind. He bypassed the memories of her years of training, amazed by all the work she had put in to be such a good dancer. Struck again by how difficult it had been, much like sword training, with broken bones, bashed muscles and pulled tendons. He went back further, to where she had stored a memory of a golden-haired woman.

"Here. See this?"

"My mother?"

There were tears in her mind-speech, but he gripped her hand in his. *"Yes. Now, go deeper, see this?"* He revealed something else, something warm and strong, something bright and comforting. *"This is your wolf. This is mine."*

As he slowed his consciousness, he revealed the sharp, bright energy of his wolf, the essence of his connection, like a line that linked him to his center. To that line was now Elsa, and deeper, her wolf.

"Oh! But... But I know this. I...know this." She seemed to open an area she'd hidden from him, a painful one—her adopted parents' death. That warm, strong essence had comforted her. Then again, when she'd been bitten, it had guided her to a safe location, and had shown her how to hide.

Elsa blinked open her eyes and he cradled her face in his hands. "You are so fucking unbelievable. I doubted you at every turn. Thought you weak, but you aren't, baby. You aren't. You're strong.'

"I'm not. You make me strong. She makes me strong, but, Jamie"—she ducked her head and played with his hand—"I sometimes just want you to hold me tight and tell me it's all okay. Even if it's a lie."

He tipped her head up and kissed her brow. "Then I

will, but being scared doesn't mean you aren't brave, Elsa. It's overcoming your fear, and fighting on, surviving, that makes you strong, baby. Believe me."

She blinked and that quizzical frown eased into a smile. "I like you like this, being the nice Jamie."

He growled. "I thought you'd forgiven me."

"I have. I simply meant, I love you, I guess." She smoothed her hand up his chest and to his face. "I want you happy, too. Will you be? With me? I can't go out in the sun, I don't know how to track. I don't even —"

"Are you backing out of this? Because it's a done deal, woman." He caught her to his chest and laughed at her astonished gasp. "I like nights. I like being right next to you. You are a good tracker, and I'll train you... If you —"

"Oh, Jamie! Really?" She pulled away and studied his eyes, as if not trusting him.

"If you want, I will. I didn't want you to think I was being pushy. And I don't have to track —"

"I want to." She said it so quickly he lifted his eyebrows. She blushed a pretty pink. "I mean, if you want to."

He fell back, taking her with him. She curled up and rested her chin on his chest. "I want to. When this is over, and we're safe, I'll prove it. Until then —"

"I'll sleep in your arms and wake in your arms."

He got the memory of her waking alone, cold and scared, when he'd been on the phone.

"Never again. I'll wake you with a kiss. I promise."

She settled closer, kissing his chest once more, and sighed. Through the new bond, she sent him a warm burst of her love. Could life possibly get better? He turned so he could enclose her with his arms and legs. Once he had her where he knew every inch of her was warmed by him, he sensed her drifting off, happy thoughts filling her head, all surrounded by him. He smiled, enjoying how much she thought of him. Then, slowly, as if his body realized it had found home, he eased into a sleep filled with contentment.

Chapter Twenty-Nine

"So, we're going to ride around town all night? And this is called hunting?"

Jamie shoved the car into fifth, trying to avoid the distraction of his beautiful woman sitting next to him. *His.* She was his. The novelty wasn't wearing off, possibly ever. He'd never had a thing of his own, nothing outside of a few weapons, a room with the pack, and some clothes he stored in the closet there.

Now I have a mate who loves me. She thinks I'm better than a prince in those stories, because I'm a scoundrel and a prince.

"Or a prince-scoundrel. I can't decide. But I liked Tangled *better than* Cinderella.*"

"I thought we decided not to pry?"

"You broadcast." "Plus, I love how pleased you are with my thinking. Now, I'll stop, I promise, if you'll explain why we are driving around Seattle."

He cast her a dubious frown, but she appeared sincere. He actually didn't mind her being in his mind. It was odd, but he wanted that connection as much as he wanted or needed to touch her—constantly. "We're hunting for someone who I hope can lead us to whoever is behind this."

"Oh."

She said that faintly, as if the memory stirred up things she didn't like. They'd had their break from all this, but it had hung over him like an enemy at his back. She reached over and covered his hand, and he realized he'd tightened his grip again. He let go to hold her hand instead.

"I don't have much either. I mean, a flat in London I never want to see again..."

He laughed. "You're better at reading my mind. Watch it, I'll catch up."

"I know you will. You're sneaky. Besides, I like the house in France. What's wrong with it?"

"Do you?" He felt her happiness through the bond, and relaxed. *"We fix it up and fill it with stuff."*

"Okay. What are we doing out here driving around?"

She made it sound insane to get out of bed. He agreed. He would have stayed in bed forever if he could have. She'd woken him—thrilling the hell out of him with another blow job. The 'practice' had made him realize that, not only was she imaginative, but giving. So much so that he'd come hard enough to break the headboard. A man could die happy with a woman who wanted to make sure he got his pleasure, as she explained when he could see straight again. Then he'd tossed her onto her front and made love to her until she'd begged him to let her come. Only then did he give her orgasm after orgasm. He might have even worn her out.

"You wish."

"I never wish. I want. You. All the time, but now…"

"I want to find someone I saw when I was in Seattle that last time."

He shared an image and she nodded. "Vampire?"

"Yes. Bryson should be here by now, so that's why we're running in circles." He'd heard from Bryson several times during the day, which pointed to the Vampire not taking his own advice and resting. Not that he'd let Elsa rest.

"I've had plenty of time to rest and I'll have centuries more, I'm sure."

Immortality had never settled well with him. Now he worried he'd not have enough time with her.

"We'll have ages to get fed up with each other."

"I can't see that happening any time soon. You don't snore."

"Of course not."

"You could have," he said aloud, switching to speech because the problem with mind speech was that he always wanted more. He couldn't imagine not always wanting more either.

"You know, we could get a room, and wait for him. Or we could have stayed at his place, and waited for his text like he suggested."

It wasn't the first time she'd indicated that staying in bed—or anywhere else but here—was a better option. "Elsa, if I get a room with you, we aren't getting anything done but you."

"I'm okay with that. Did I complain last night? I didn't hear you grumbling. You say that like it's a bad thing. I think it's brilliant."

He laughed. *What do I do with that?*

"I'm new to this sex thing. You might be tired of it, but I'm—"

"Woman. Hold your tongue. Tired of it? Did I look tired of it? Didn't I just make your toes curl not an hour ago?"

"Well, yes, but..." She shrugged, and the tiny strap holding her camisole up over the satin barely-there bra slid down. It was like the call of the wild. He nodded to the strap.

"Your shirt."

"Is still on. I'm wondering why."

The comment got a smile, but he refused to give in. If they got a room, he was going to—

"Fuck! There he is."

"I'm glad you didn't swear like this in front of Faolan the entire time."

Not about to admit that he did slip once in a while, since he had tried to modify his language, he pulled the car over with a squeal of tires. The abruptness tossed Elsa into him. He caught her with a stiff arm up against the dash. "Sorry. There he is."

"That guy? He's so old and...creepy."

"He is. Stay in the car." He opened the door and ran to where the man was talking to a prostitute smoking a cigarette. Behind him, the car door opened, shut and Elsa ran after him. He didn't mind-speak to her, only because she already gave off a frustrated vibe at his attitude. She seemed to think he was sometimes a Neanderthal. The thought made him smile. But he would gladly let her call him that and worse, if she'd just have listened and stayed in the car.

It was a good thing he'd left Faolan at Bryson's because no doubt the boy would have followed her lead, not his.

"Damn it, does stay—"

"I didn't like *him* telling me to stay. I don't like *you* doing it either." He got a *freezing* cold blast through their link, and, oddly enough, an image of a blanket on the floor.

He halted so fast she barreled into him, again. He caught her. "Shit. Elsa, I never—"

"Focus. What do you want from him because he is— Oh, he's running."

Jamie spun and took off.

"Follow me and stay close."

He caught the man at an alley a block down from where he'd left the car. Growling, he yanked the Vampire by the throat and held him up high against the wall. "Why did you run?"

"You were chasing me!"

"Jamie, he won't be able to, oh, never mind he doesn't need to breathe."

He spared her a two-second glance. She shrugged and smiled. "Sorry, go on."

If this was how they were going to work together, he had serious doubts he'd ever get anything done outside of *her*. He turned back to the wheezing Vampire. "You have some information I want."

"Me?"

"I think you can let him down a little, don't you?" Elsa said. "He's pretty harmless. Aren't you?"

"I am *totally* harmless. Really!" He squealed the last when Jamie lifted him higher. The bloodlust coming off the man was scented with drugs, human drugs. Crack. Pieces of long, thin blond hair, unwashed of course, fell in his watery gray eyes. There was grease on his face and on the patches of whiskers dotting his chin and jaw. He was pathetic.

Jamie lowered him until his feet touched the ground. "Don't mist. You see this woman? If you mist, she will find you and tear your heart out of your chest with her bare hand. You got that?"

The Vampire stared, wild-eyed, from him to Elsa. She was to his left, but from his peripheral vision he could see her smile. The frost melted a little through their link.

"True. Samuel learned the hard way not to fuck with me."

The language sent a shiver of something close to joy down his back. A woman should cuss, not so he could, but because in this world they lived in, it was toughness, not niceness that got you through.

"You're... You're the one that got away from him."

"She got away, huh?" Jamie shoved the guy right back up the wall.

"Jamie..." "What's your name?" Elsa murmured, coming up on his left. He dropped the man so he stumbled.

"His name is David Daniel Rockwell the third," Bryson called. Jamie peered over Elsa's head. Bryson stood by a blood red BMW. "He's useless. If he'd been someone who could tell us anything, he'd never have been left behind by his House."

"I have my uses," David said drawing himself up. "You just never saw them."

"No one saw them, especially the people you killed from behind, or while they slept," Bryson muttered.

"Oh, God, that's horrible." She stepped away from the man. "And you smell like...drugs. Are you high? Can we get high?" she asked Bryson.

"High? If we do enough of anything we can fly."

She laughed.

Jamie didn't.

"Are you jealous of Bryson?" She sent him an astonished laugh, then what felt like a hug through their bond, clearly

happy that he didn't like her laughing at Bryson's humor.

He couldn't deny his jealousy, though. "*You like him.*"

"*I like you better. I also love you.*" She stepped closer, which sent one of those sappy shivers of happiness down his back. He thought she hooked her finger in his belt loop. "*And you like my breasts.*"

He would have spluttered a denial, but she had seen his mind, so he took it like any man would. "*Obviously. I'm pretty interested in that lovely arse, too.*"

"*Arse?*" She gave him a happy laugh through the bond, but pulled his hair too. She also moved so he was between her and Bryson.

"My, you two were busy, weren't you?" Bryson murmured, with way too much of a knowing smirk as he walked up. He refocused on David, so Jamie let it slide. "What do you know about Elsa, David? That would be helpful information. Aidan might not have me bring you in if you have something helpful."

"In?" David cried. "I've done nothing. I've done nothing, it was all lies. You—"

"Answer the fucking question before I have your heart at my feet." Jamie drew him closer, so he could see how serious he was about that. The man's eyes widened and the ring of blood around the irises grew fainter. He stared from him, to Bryson then to Elsa. His gaze pinned there too long, Jamie thought, but then it was back on him.

Bloodshot eyes wide, he answered, "Okay, okay. Samuel, he was told to change her, you know?"

Jamie moved his head back a fraction, disgusted by the man's breath. Even his teeth were rotted and brown. "And?" he demanded when David gaped at him.

"He did it, but he wanted her. She somehow got away, though. Left. He tore the town up searching for her. Then Aidan came and Samuel hid. He is good at hiding. *He* taught him to hide."

"*Was*. He's dead," Elsa said.

"He?" Jamie growled right on top of Elsa. "Who is he?"

At the question David spluttered and backed away, or tried to. He hit the wall and shook his head. Jamie grabbed hold of his neck and shoved him upward again.

"I warned you. If you try to mist I will kill you. Now answer the bloody question. Who is *he*?"

David squeezed his eyes shut and began blubbering like a babe.

"Jamie?" she whispered. "You're strangling him again. I think we should have gotten a room," she added in a lower whisper. "You seem tense."

She might have been right. His mind wasn't working like it should. But there were other ways to relieve the tension, he just hadn't told her that yet. Fighting was one of them.

"Answer." Jamie relaxed his grip, but only slightly. "Or I will beat the shit out of you, then you'll answer."

Bryson clucked his tongue. "David, you're not making this wolf very happy. I can't say I'm impressed with your usefulness either. Shall we dispose of him?"

David started making gargling sounds. "No, wait. I am useful, Bryson. You know that. I have things. I know things."

"Then tell us, because Jamie really wants to kill you. So if I were you, I'd say whatever I could to get out of here."

David blinked and nodded. "Yes, yes, I will. I will. I can be helpful. I can."

"Give me a name. Who was in charge of Samuel?" Jamie asked.

"I don't know his name, real name. He goes by…Master. I just know Samuel, he wanted her real bad." He motioned to Elsa. "He wanted her. He has a collection, you see. He liked pretty things, at least at first, but he shared when he was finished, too, like a good friend, before we took them to…to him. You know what I mean?"

A chill shivered down Jamie's back. He knew exactly what David meant. It sickened him. A man was given more strength than a woman to protect her. If she deemed him someone she wanted to give more to, then he was blessed.

But never should a man take what wasn't offered freely. *Never.* But it happened. His brother had almost done such a thing to Elsa. She'd escaped, but many innocents did not. It was one reason he'd become a tracker — to take out those kinds of immortals, and to help his friends, his pack.

"Jamie." Elsa touched his back, alerting him that, once again, he'd grabbed hold of the man. At least this time he hadn't strangled him, merely ripped his shirt. "*I got it. I hate men like this.*"

"*That's because you're a good man.*" The complete conviction in her voice warmed him.

"Ah, shall I?" Bryson said, moving forward.

Jamie stepped back next to Elsa. Immediately, she took his hand in both of hers. "He's disgusting," she whispered against his arm.

"We need him," he reminded her. She nodded.

"So, Samuel was a good friend, then, was he?" Bryson asked.

"Yes, yes, a good friend." David's eyes darted to him then glued back on Bryson.

"He took you with him to meet all his other friends, did he?"

"Of course, I was an important man to him. I was always someone he could count on. He gave me things. He looked after me, helped me stay alive."

"Ah, a good friend then." Bryson lifted a finger when David opened his mouth. "Tell me something, David. Do you want to live?"

The Vampire's eyes grew rounder. He nodded quickly, his head wobbling and his lips loose and open. Fear radiated from him, along with the stench of decay.

"Show us where he met these people. Then, maybe *I* will be your new friend, and maybe *I* will help keep you alive."

David nodded, harder this time.

"Good boy, David. Very good," Bryson said, leading the Vampire out of the alley.

"He *really* is disgusting, Jamie."

He took Elsa's hand in his. "I know, but if he leads us to whoever set this manhunt after you, then we can end this right here."

"What if we never can? If it's always like this? With someone always after me?"

He cradled the side of her face, knowing now what the darker blue meant. She was worried—about being a burden, he thought. "Then, they'll have to get through me, to get to you."

She smiled and he knew he'd just said the right thing. "Or through us both. I do a mean heart pulling out thing."

He laughed and slung his arm over her small shoulders. She fit him. "You think so, huh?"

"Sure, besides"—she jangled the car keys—"I didn't leave the car running in this neighborhood while I raced off after a sick Vampire. So I'll be useful."

"You're something all right." He hugged her closer and kissed her silky hair. But he refrained from telling her that if she'd listened to him, then he wouldn't have been leaving the car running in this neighborhood. "Just stay by my side."

She smiled. *"Always was the deal, right?"*

"Correct. Always, sweetheart, now get that pretty arse in the car so we can find this bastard and end this bullshit. We need to start on that dream house."

"What dream house?"

"The one I've been fixing for you."

"Oh, that dream house."

This wasn't going to be easy, taking her into something dangerous. *I'm doing it, though.* Not because there was no other option, but because she loved and trusted him.

That kind of crazy simply made him sure he wasn't going to lose her. He ducked down and breathed in her scent again, feeling her happiness easing into him.

She's mine. Not losing her.

Chapter Thirty

Elsa thought Bryson was being very sweet, but trying to hide it. Jamie didn't see it that way, she could tell, but she couldn't help the sappy smile she got whenever the two of them got into a sparring match. David, though, he made her uneasy.

"Is it more than your reaction to meeting a stranger?"

"I'm not certain."

Jamie caught her hand and gently kissed her palm. His gaze was filled with concern. Now that they had shared such intimacy, she could see how he held things in — mostly behind that brooding expression. She loved him so much it hurt. *All those love songs, and this is what they mean.* "Let me know if you feel threatened by him, Elsa. Anything at all, like what you experienced with other wrong immortals."

"I will."

Seemingly satisfied with that, he smiled. She leaned over and kissed him. *"I love you."*

His smile grew and the amber in his eyes shimmered. "I love you, too."

The light changed and someone honked behind them. Jamie glared at them. It was so cute, she sighed. *Sap. I'm a sap.*

They'd been following Bryson through town. She wasn't certain, but she thought they might be approaching the big cemetery on the hill, near where she used to live as a child.

"This is it?" she asked, sitting straighter. The strap to her camisole slid down her arm and Jamie reached over, gently pulling it back up on her shoulder. Immediately, every inch of her remembered how his hands felt on her body. Over *all* of her. Deep inside where he'd staked a claim, she tensed her muscles, easily recalling his body filling hers.

"Don't," he growled, then shocked her by taking her face in his hands and kissing her. It was quick, but when he released her, she was dizzy. "I suggest you put a shirt on over that, because every time that falls down your arm, I am inches from laying you back in that seat and making love to you."

"I like that idea—"

Jamie growled. He did that more now. She loved it. "Later. Right now we have something else to do, remember?"

She reluctantly agreed. They were usually on the same wavelength, but not this time. She wanted to hide. If they did, maybe in two, three years, or maybe longer, this would all be gone. But Jamie was even more determined to find whoever this Master was and end his existence. She trusted that he knew best, especially with going after trouble, not running from it. The connection she felt with Jamie helped. It eased her, every time she almost panicked, into calming down. He was simply so strong, so sure that nothing would harm her when she was with him, that she believed him. *Maybe because you've seen him fight.*

That could be a big part of it. Jamie was...amazing.

Up ahead, Bryson slowed by the entrance to the cemetery she remembered. "This is near where I grew up."

"Yeah, I noticed that. There are no coincidences," he muttered, but she heard. She also agreed. "Stay close to me, and if anything at all appears wrong, shift away. I can get out just as fast, but you should go immediately." She opened her mouth to protest. "Wait for me here, besides, I'm always going to be right here." He tapped her on the forehead. "Wait at the car. I'll come and then we'll run, okay?"

She wasn't sure she believed him, until he leaned closer and kissed her. Drawing back just a little, he met her eyes. "Trust me. I'm not losing this for some macho move on my part."

"Good, no knuckle dragging allowed." She hugged his head and kissed his silky hair. She also tested the bond, reassured that there he was, right *there*. She just had to think on him, and he was warm, strong, and all hers. "Not until we get alone and you can do all the work, okay?"

He laughed. "Deal. Now, come on. There's no one here, other than us."

"And a cemetery full of ghosts," she grumbled, but let him go and dragged her sweater jacket out of the bag at her feet. He opened her door and waited while she shoved her arms into warm wool.

Bryson walked up with David lurking behind him as she got out of the car.

"It's safe. I sense no one. Yet," Bryson said. "It might not remain that way."

Jamie growled a few curses.

The empty rows of tombstones were creepy enough without Bryson saying that. "It's like no one has been here in a long while," she whispered, wrapping the sweater tighter around her.

"What do you mean?" Jamie said, stopping her from following Bryson. Bryson turned back and studied her too.

She wasn't sure.

"Go on, trust your instincts, Elsa," Jamie urged. *'What is it?'*

"Well, I'm not sure." She studied the ghostly shapes of tombstones leading up the hill where a mausoleum stood. "It reminds me of that night, when the alarms went off?"

"Yes." Jamie drew in a deep breath. "I agree. It's...lacking scent."

"Right, that's what I do," she whispered. "When I hide, Jamie, that's what I do."

Jamie took her hand and warmed it between his. "That's also what you are teaching Faolan to do."

"Exactly, but this... This is big. If you know what to search for, you can tell where someone is hiding," she tried to explain.

Bryson frowned. "What do you mean?"

"When I hid from you, Jamie, how did you know where I was?"

"Your scent."

"No." She laughed and tugged his hand. "I don't think so. I think you saw where I *wasn't,* and that's how you found me, that first night."

"In the trees?" Through their link she could feel him remembering that first awake encounter. His memories of the cross were blurred with panic and anger—toward the witches. She tried not to pry, but he was much better at staying out of her mind than she was at leaving his. He'd thought her beautiful, even then, he'd been unable to take his eyes off her. His memory of her was...wonderful. Embarrassing, but wonderful all the same.

"You thought I was beautiful even then?"

"Sweetheart, you captured my heart the first time I saw your picture. It just took me a while to figure it out."

"I like how...open you are telling me these things." She hugged him around the middle. "Not that I give you a choice." She felt his laugh through their bond and through his chest.

"In the trees?" Bryson repeated. "You two have a story, don't you? But right now, what does this mean, Elsa. Is he here, now?"

"No."

At her immediate response all three men frowned.

"I think he'd be..." She thought about it. "He'd be different. Darkness within nothingness. I don't think he can hide from us so easily. At least if we know what to look for."

"And we know what to look for?" Bryson asked.

"Jamie does," she said confidently.

Jamie raised his eyebrows.

"You do. You found that mark on the post in France. You found me. You found Faolan—"

"You found him first."

"I don't know if that's true. You could always find

me, even when I was hiding. Think, how did you know something was wrong that night in the mansion?" She sent him a soft dose of her love and trust. He grumbled but studied her thoughts.

"It's the nothingness, true, but more. With you" — he paused to squeeze her hand — "it's a clean, fresh feeling you can't mask with shadows. But with this... It's the complete opposite. But it's not something I can track to the source, because it's too broad." He scanned her face, then the cemetery. "But it's there, in that."

Bryson nodded and walked over to where David sulked in the shadows of an enormous oak tree. "Is that the place, David?"

"Yes," David said hesitantly.

"We should go," David added, hugging his hands under his armpits while he bounced on his feet. "I should go."

"I don't think so. You come with us. Then, if we find what we need, you and I will have a long talk. Until then, you're with us," Bryson warned. "Is this the right place?"

"Yes. That's where I met them," David whispered.

"Right, and the creepy whispering will help how?" she asked.

"It won't," Bryson said loudly. "Death Stalkers are like this, they hide with nothingness. The ones you ran into are from a faction of Death Stalkers we thought we'd disbanded a while back. I still believe that to be the case. But every army has stragglers and deserters."

"Not all of them had the mark," Jamie agreed. "The woman."

"With the medallion," Elsa remembered with a chill. The night was getting toward that time when the moon would be the highest, but with the cloud cover, it was missing. Not even the stars shone down to lighten the shadows. "She didn't have the tattoo."

"True, but she had the necklace, and maybe that means something more than we ever realized." Bryson headed for the dark buildings.

Jamie followed, pulling her along. "Stay close, always on my left."

"Okay." Jamie remained a warm, strong presence at her side. "I planned on sticking to you like glue."

He smiled, relieved, she thought. He kissed her again, but it was all too brief. *We might not survive this.* The thought made her skin crawl with fear. *We will. We have to. I can't lose Jamie, not now that this life is beginning to be a…life.*

"You're not losing me. And I'm not letting you go."

"Lead the way, David," Bryson said at the entrance. "I'm interested more than ever to meet your new friends."

Elsa winced. "I'm really not, are you?" she whispered to Jamie.

"Not at all, but if this is linked, we have to follow it. When you hunt, you always follow the trail." He brushed one more kiss to her lips and met her eyes. *"Ready?"* She nodded. That seemed to be all he needed. He kept her hand and walked beside her to the crypt. "I avoid these places."

"You do? I spend most of my days hanging out in one."

He grunted at that. "Not any longer."

"I can't believe you've never been in a crypt."

"I've been in more than a few, and I got you out of one, if you remember? But I don't go hunting among the dead. It's usually live targets we go after." He made her wait as Bryson tested a few coffins by shoving the lids off and scanning the insides. She guessed they were empty of Vampires, because he moved on each time. She began to worry what would happen if he *did* find one, but they made it through the wide corridor without a discovery.

"Calm down."

She focused back on Jamie. He was tense, every inch of his body hard with muscles she guessed he was tightening at every little sound, because he was worried about her.

"This way," Bryson called, barely visible in the dimness. "There's a passage." A sound of rock rubbing rock echoed off the walls. She covered her ears, appalled by the noise. Near her she sensed something. Jamie caught her hand.

"What?"

"There, I thought something was there." She pointed to the stone wall closest to them. Jamie left her to investigate. She checked behind them, and quickly around, but found nothing more than dark rotten-smelling walls and stone coffins with their lids half turned from Bryson's investigation. "This place is wrong, Jamie."

"Yeah, it is. Come on."

Another thud of something heavy falling made her grip Jamie's sleeve. His firm hold on her hand reassured her. Bryson said something too low to make out. At the same time, Jamie ushered her forward. Light suddenly blazed as if someone had set fire to a thousand candles. It didn't diminish the creepiness of the place. Shadows lengthened into sinister ghouls that clung to the corners. Bryson had shoved aside a wall to reveal a hidden room.

"I can't do that."

"If you tried you might be surprised," Jamie said, still holding her hand in his stronger one.

It was sweet. So was the complete reversal on trusting her to be strong enough to go with him on this. He moved ahead of her slightly, edging into the room, but stopping her just back from the entrance. His vibe was worried, more for her than anything else, but still he was trying. It just might take a bit more time to ease him into accepting her being along. She was cool with that, because she needed more time to get used to walking toward danger and not away.

"*You're okay?*"

She rubbed his chest. "*I am, but this is…wrong.*" He tensed, agreeing with her, she felt, then he stopped. "What is it?" she whispered.

"It's another altar," Jamie growled. "I don't want you here."

"I don't want *you* here either."

"There are more of the necklaces. Both in English and French," Bryson muttered in an angry tone.

Jamie scanned her face and her thoughts. His handsome

features had never seemed so chiseled from stone, but now, through her connection, she knew it was his way of weighing his options. There weren't any. If she left, he would as well. She kept that firmly in mind. Finally, jaw clenched until it bulged, he nodded and guided her forward. She got her first real look at what they'd found. Her stomach flipped and churned.

Chains, stained and ugly, hung from the blackened walls. Farther in, blood-red candles surrounded an old stone altar, just like the one in France. This one wasn't as tainted with blood, but maybe that was because it was newer.

The sudden buzz of a phone made her gasp and half mist before Jamie grabbed her closer to his side.

"*Stay.*" Out loud he said, "Phone, nothing more." He pulled his cell out and his gaze flickered. "Circerran. Let me fill her in on where we are." But as he spoke, the phone stopped ringing. Silence filled the space again.

"Good idea, because I think she'll want to see this." Bryson pulled a tapestry aside and revealed some kind of ancient characters chiseled into the stone.

She covered her mouth, realizing that there had been a similar, much older piece hanging in France. "There was a wall hanging like that—"

"—in France. I know. We fucking missed it!" Jamie rubbed his eyes with the heels of his hands. "Not focused. I'm not fucking focused—"

"Jamie, if you say because of me, you're sleeping on the floor. We can't see everything. No one can. But we can get Circerran here, and let her read this and see if it is a clue. Okay?"

He'd jerked to halt at her threat and stood, head down, fists on his hips. It was difficult not to shrink back from him when he was this angry, but she knew he'd never hurt her. "*Jamie.*"

"*Elsa, this is dangerous. And I'm not focused.*"

"Jamie, please." The croissant and coffee they'd shared in bed grew to a heavy lump in her stomach, ready to come back up. "Just trust me, okay? I trust you. Trust *me*."

He caught her in a quick hug and nodded. "I do trust you. We can't see everything, but I'm not used to missing so much, Elsa."

"I'm sorry —"

"Don't be." He dropped his arms as the phone started ringing again. Without saying hello he snapped, "We've found something. Yes. I'll send the location. We're across from the gate, directly up a hill with the biggest of the crypts. Let Jack lead. Right." He turned to the side listening, and she shivered, watching him open his mouth then shut it.

"She's tough sometimes, but she'll be here," Bryson said at her elbow.

"Is that... Is that blood?" she whispered, pointing to the altar. David stood to the left of the door, hands under his armpits again, crouched over as if someone had hit him in the stomach. She watched him glance from the altar to her, and back as if his eyes couldn't stay still for long.

"Yes, it's blood." Bryson sounded disgusted. "Sacrifices were made here. I'm guessing nearing the hundreds if not higher than that. I need to see the place in France. There's something we're missing. This seems almost too flamboyant. Staged like some macabre show."

"It's not a show I want in on." She shivered again and noticed David watching her. "Did you help them with this?"

"No, no, not me." He shook his head and began rocking on his feet. "This was only for him and a few of his... favorites." His gaze bounced off her, then back to the altar, then back to her and off it went again.

"Is there another place like this, David?" she asked.

Jamie settled close to her and took her hand.

"I don't know. I don't know," David whispered, becoming more agitated. "We should leave."

"Why? Is this place watched? Will we draw this man here?" Bryson asked.

David shrank down on the wall, stooped and unresponsive at Bryson's questions. She squeezed Jamie's hand, worried now more than ever.

"This place… It's like a barrow, an ancient burial mound," Bryson said, examining a shelf littered with more of the medallions and candles but also different shaped metal and glass jars. Old ones, the kind that people took time to craft, not mayonnaise jars. She doubted they were filled with nails or preserved peaches, though.

Bryson picked one blue glass jar up and lifted the lid. "These seem to be…trinkets." He put the jar back down and turned away, his expression intense with anger. "Something to remind them of their kills."

"Like a serial killer?" she whispered.

Bryson hesitated but nodded. "When we kill this being, the world will rejoice."

Jamie walked over to a table by the altar and picked up a knife, using it to flip something over. "When was the Gold Rush? 1848?"

"I believe so, why?" Bryson asked, walking over. "It lasted several years…" He bent to examine what Jamie had found. She followed. Even David came closer to see.

"Jamie?" she whispered.

"Look."

There, under the blood splatters, was a newspaper clipping with the heading, *Gold Mine Found San Francisco*.

"Does this mean we go to California?" she asked.

Jamie snorted then glanced at her. "Not likely. That means this place has been in use at least that long. The newspaper was laid down here, maybe to catch the blood."

It hadn't done a very good job. The table was stained nearly black. It was as if someone had washed the room in it.

Footsteps followed by a "Yo, Jamie, it's Jack and Cir," preceded Jack, then Circerran into the room.

"Holy Danu." Circerran halted at the door, freezing so quickly Jack took a step, then seemed to realize his wife wasn't by his side. Circerran's green eyes were wide. Her face was always pale, but it seemed to get white as a ghost. "This place is…"

"Evil," Elsa said.

Circerran's gaze snapped to hers, but the beautiful witch nodded. "Agreed. We need to burn this place to the ground."

It was the last thing Elsa heard—before a blast shook the room. Dust billowed down a moment before she was shoved backwards by Jamie. Her entire world shifted—as if she'd caused it—only she hadn't. All she could do was hold on tightly to Jamie's arm and hope that, wherever they ended up, they would survive.

Chapter Thirty-One

Jamie got hold of Elsa and held on. She clung to him. Along their bond, he felt her terror. He experienced a deep, wrenching sensation as if someone was trying to snatch her right out of his arms. He held on tighter.

That odd sensation of missing something that was hiding grew like a black stain of ink on his vision. He knew no matter what else was happening that the man they sought was here.

Elsa had said he'd known where she was because of the nothingness she left behind. She was partially right. He'd known she was there because of the wrongness — a smudge on the tapestry that was the forest — that stood out. In a sense, by hiding she'd become visible to his wolf.

This time, the smudge was bigger. Out of it stepped a man. Circerran shrieked and Bryson attacked, sword raised. Jack launched himself at the figure from the other side. Both hit the black mist and…were gone. Circerran called Jack's name, then his and Elsa's but he didn't respond — Elsa wouldn't let him.

"Don't think. Don't move. Don't breathe. You're a shadow. Shadow and mist, Jamie."

"You're hiding us."

"I am."

"Sweetheart, I need to help them."

She surrounded him with angry Elsa vibes that reminded him of when she'd smacked him on the back of the head. *"Easy, easy, that's my brain, sweetheart."*

"No doubting me. We'll help them, just let him step out of the freaky black tar pit, okay?"

"You're brilliant."

"Shhh."

He stilled his thoughts, letting Elsa lead as he waited. Light flooded all around them. Circerran swore loudly. Jack shouted her name. Wind blew and Jamie felt the Earth move. Moments of holding his breath and he heard Jack and Circerran—he hoped—land near him. *Bryson?* He couldn't tell if the big Vampire was there or not.

"Now?"

"Oh yes, now!"

As if saying that released them, a room appeared around him. He drew his sword, snapping it into place as he rushed toward the men trying to tackle Circerran down onto an altar. Jack was chained but still fighting with all he had left—his teeth and claws. Bryson was nowhere to be seen. Neither was David.

He let that go and fell into the battle. First he freed Jack, slicing through the chains with one blow, and quickly turned to catch one of the robed men by his throat. He crushed his head against the room's massive stone wall and dropped him.

Elsa shot something silver and sharp past his head, and he heard the impact of the knife in someone. He turned and kicked the bastard in the chest and drove his sword into his throat, twisting it after so that the man died.

Jack freed Circerran. The couple were nearly out of sight under the flood of black-cloaked figures.

It wasn't them Jamie focused on. It was the man across from him, on a balcony, overlooking the macabre scene with apparent glee.

"Oh, the absolute perfection of it all," he sang. "Fight, fight as hard as you can, whore, it will only make the ending sweeter."

"Did you just call me a *whore*?" Circerran's voice broke on 'whore'.

Jamie caught Elsa to him, keeping her back and to his left, away from his sword.

"We need to kill *him*." She pointed at the man on the dais.

"Sweetheart, believe me, I got that message."

"*Sorry!*"

"*Don't say that unless you get hurt. Then say it. But don't get hurt.*"

"*I'm trying. How about we help Cir?*"

The crowd of robed figures parted and there, across from him, he saw something that made his heart feel as if it had stopped.

"Faolan!" Elsa's cry echoed in his head, drilling into his brain that he'd not been seeing things. The boy was here, and in trouble. Even as he realized it, he picked up Faolan's unique scent.

Faolan was on the dais, behind and to the right of the group of men there. He stood on his tiptoes, his face bright red and his chin up. Around his neck was a noose. All they had to do was kick the chair he stood on and the boy would fall to his death. His little body was bare from the neck down to his hips where they'd put a pair of silk pants on him. Faolan's lean, muscled boy's chest was heaving with each breath.

"Jamie." Elsa pulled at his hand, dragging him back, when he went forward without conscious thought.

"I have to get to him."

"*Of course you do, but not that way. Look, what do you see?*"

Near Foalan sat a man with black, straight hair, long enough that it reached past his chin where he wore a short beard. He was dressed in a satin shirt, but it was his erect penis that caught Jamie's attention. It tented the fabric of his pants in a sickening display. Elsa gagged when she also noticed.

"*Elsa!*"

"*Please. Look!*"

Two men stood on either side of the silk-robed man. Another hovered behind them, almost a shadow in the candlelit room. One man kept reaching out and touching Faolan's leg, sliding his hand up the boy's crotch and back down. But it was the man hovering that he concentrated on. The Master.

"*I see. I see enough to know they are all dead.*"

"*Good. Go. I will be fine. Go and save him, Jamie, like you did me on that cross.*"

"You come with me. No more alone. Together. To wolf, Elsa." Her blue eyes flashed. He sent her all the love he felt for her and let her hand go, only when she nodded. As soon as she did, he didn't wait for her to obey him, he shifted, taking his wolf form and attacking anyone that stood between him and Faolan.

Elsa burst into a wolf by his side. More, she was *her* wolf, embracing the link he'd shown her last evening, with such trust he wanted to howl. She ripped two men to pieces on her way to the dais. But it was Faolan both their wolves were set on. When she drew closer, Jamie brushed his shoulder to hers, then nudged her head with his, even as he started running. He gained the dais with one jump. The one in the chair dressed in silk died first.

Jamie ripped his throat out.

Elsa attacked the one who'd touched Faolan, biting and tearing the man to bits.

Jamie dropped his wolf and rushed the last man near Faolan. Wiser than his friend, he avoided Jamie and kicked the chair.

"Jamie!" Elsa's scream made it clear she was back to her human form as well.

Faolan's eyes rounded then he closed them as he fell abruptly. Jamie dove and caught him before the rope could tighten.

"Jamie!" Elsa's scream warned him as sharp pain dug into his side. He held on to the boy and lifted him as high as he could.

The man behind him rammed the knife in deeper. "Bastard, I'll see you die under the knife after I feed you your balls!"

Jamie jerked his head back, connecting with something

solid. The man cried out and stumbled backwards. *Now. Faolan, down, kill the last man. Keep her safe.*

Jamie jerked the rope off the hook and dropped Faolan at his feet. He nearly went down as well, oddly dizzy. *Kill the man. One more.*

"Jamie!" Elsa's cry warned him in time to shake his head and swing around, prepared to kill. Elsa was there. One of the robed men, his black hair disheveled, his nose bleeding, and eyes wide, faced her. But he wasn't attacking. He stood stunned, as if he were frozen in place.

"You *disgusting* pig! If I could, I'd feed *you* your balls. But you don't have any!" Even as she yelled, Jamie sensed pain through the bond. He lunged for them, but was just in time to see her shove her hand into the man's chest and rip his heart out. She flung it down and immediately her gaze sought his. He thought she swayed on her feet. "He was disgusting," she whispered. Her eyes were too big in her pale face. Her lips chalky white, and a sense of her blocking him — something he didn't realize she could do — filtered to him.

"He was." He walked carefully toward her. Elsa's eyes went wide and her gaze landed over his shoulder. He turned, grabbed the man trying to sneak up on him and tossed him over his shoulder. He landed on his feet, but just as Jamie raised his hand to end his life, Elsa's hand emerged from his stomach. The man screamed and Elsa pulled her hand back with a wet sound. Eyes wide, he dropped to Jamie's feet like a falling tree.

Elsa gripped her stomach and doubled over.

"Elsa!" Jamie dove for her, catching her. From behind he sensed one more of the bastards coming up. He twisted, catching the blow from a short sword against his shoulder blades.

Jack landed next to him with a thud, flinging a man off, but Jamie slipped and landed hard on his side. Elsa's head made an awful crack on the floor and she went limp. *'Elsa!'*

When she didn't respond, or open her eyes, he shoved her

hands away from her stomach. Blood stained her clothing. He tore at her sweater and her camisole to see a long gash from a blade.

Jamie lost his cool. He surged to his feet and backhanded the first robed figure who tried to come at him right across the face, throwing him into the wall. He grabbed handfuls of greasy hair and knew with absolute certainty that this was the man he had hunted. This was the Master. He'd hidden in the shadows on the dais. He'd been the presence hiding in the crypt when they'd entered. The wrongness Elsa had sensed at the house.

"That's him," Circerran confirmed.

It was all Jamie needed. He threw the black-haired bastard down and punched him, landing blow after blow to his head until he heard something snap. Even then he kept on, punishing the man for all the lives he'd taken, all the families he'd destroyed, and all the hopes he'd crushed. For Elsa's fear and her torture. For Faolan and the horrible things he'd had to endure in his small life. For his own dreams and how they'd been ripped from him. He didn't stop until a familiar scent hovered close and a hand he knew could help him remember the good in this world touched his shoulder.

"He's gone now, Jamie," Faolan whispered.

Sucking in a lungful of air, Jamie nodded. He was done. Under him the man was no more. He'd never hurt anyone ever again.

"He can't hurt Elsa now."

"Or you," Jamie breathed, catching the boy's hand. He met Faolan's worried brown eyes and breathlessly pulled him closer. "Or you. He's gone. He's better forgotten, here, where no one ever will remember that he lived."

Faolan hesitated, but nodded slightly. His neck was burned from the rope and there were fresh bruises on his face.

"He's right. I think you sent him to hell, but just to be certain…" Jack held a hand out and Jamie took it, gaining his feet with difficulty. "I say we let Cir send him there, just in case he needs a guide."

"I'm on it." Circerran raised her hands and began to murmur something even as a green glow slowly crept along her fingers and palms.

"Elsa?"

He didn't spot her at first, until Faolan tugged him forward and there she was, on her side, where he'd left her. She was still and too silent, and he experienced a rush of fear, until through the bond they shared, he sensed her still there, safe, but unconscious, or just beginning to surface. He landed on his knees by her without a memory of moving. Cradling her head to his chest he brushed her blonde hair off her face as gently as he could. His hand shook so he had to move slowly, but she stayed limp in his arms. "Elsa?"

"Elsa?"

She stirred, then lifted her hand to rub her forehead and blinked open her eyes, then closed them tight. She smiled weakly, but didn't open her eyes again. "I hurt my head?"

"Yes."

"And my…side?"

"Yes."

"But they're all—"

"—dead. Even the Master."

She winced and tested her stomach. Her blue eyes were still filled with worry, but she slowly seemed to realize it was over. When she did, it began to register with him as well.

"It's over." He brushed a kiss to her knuckles. "It's over."

"It's over… I never thought that anything would feel so good… But it's over. That feels good," she whispered. *"Now we can start our lives. Right?"*

"Baby, we're going to continue our lives. This bastard wasn't ever going to stop us."

Tenderness filled her blue eyes, the kind only she could give. His heart slowed, and warmth filled him. Love, he knew, from her.

"Yes, Jamie beat him to a pulp," Faolan assured her,

touching her arm to get her attention.

She squeezed the boy's small hand. Her worry over them lessened, easing her enough to lay softly against his chest.

"He's fine, Elsa. He's strong."

"God, he could have been —"

"Don't, baby. He's fine, be proud of him. He's strong."

"I am." There were tears in her mind speech, but to her credit she hid them from the boy. She reached out and ruffled his hair, pushing it off his eyes. "He's a tough guy, isn't he? Pretty good to have around, you know? In a fight."

Faolan giggled and tossed his hair out of his eyes. "I think so."

"Can we burn him too? And spread the ashes over all seven continents?" she whispered, tugging his sleeve. "I really want him dead, Jamie."

He cradled her closer, feeling his heartbeat slow even more as her scent filled him with peace. Against his chest she curled her hand in his shirt and sighed.

"Anything you want, baby. Anything you want," he assured her.

"Hey, I already got that covered. He's ash, and believe me when I say he can't come back from that." Circerran grinned and crouched by them. "Man, you two... Glad you finally tied the knot. Does Alrick know? Because I have a feeling that will be fun to watch."

"Alrick can suck eggs for all I care," Elsa grumbled. "I don't want to see anyone, no offense, Cir, for a long, long while."

Jack laughed and Circerran nodded, clearly not offended. "I bet."

Elsa joined them, but carefully, he thought. She moved to sit up and he helped her. Then couldn't stop himself and crushed her to him, pulling the boy in too. Happiness filled him. He would have lifted her up and swung her around if she didn't warn him she might vomit on him if he did.

"I will let you later, though."

"Will you?"

"Anything you want, Jamie. We did it."

"We did it."

She sat up straighter, staring around. "How did we get here?" she asked. "And Faolan? I thought you were safely tucked away at Bryson's house." Her eyes flew wide. "Oh, no, where is Bryson?"

"I don't know. We lost him," Cir answered. She squinted off into the distance and shook her head. "He's okay. That other Vampire was hurt, but they managed to get out alive."

"So they were...led down a rabbit hole too?" Jack asked.

"Yes. That crypt." Circerran stared at Jack.

"They mind-speak."

He kissed Elsa on the forehead. She toyed with his shirt, seeming to need to touch him as much as he needed to touch her. *'Yes.'* Suddenly he was tired, beyond exhausted and the stench of a battlefield was no place for her or the boy.

"We can settle all this later. For now, I need to get my family out of here." Jamie lifted Elsa up in his arms. She wrapped her arms around his neck and kissed him on the jaw.

"Yes. Let's get out of here, Jamie. I never want to see this place again."

"Right." He nodded to Faolan to get moving. He paused, looked around and back at Faolan, then down at Elsa. "Just where the hel—? Where are we?"

Elsa laughed and Faolan did the same, hugging him pretty hard for a small boy. Circerran joined in, muttering between laughs how he took the cake. Even Jack chuckled. Finally he did as well. With Elsa, and Faolan, did it matter where he was? They were together. Soon enough, they'd be together in their mansion, rebuilding a garden.

"I love you, Elsa."

"Oh, Jamie. I love you too." She sent him a burst of images, mostly of him, in ways he'd never thought of himself, all from her memory, and all tinged with the warm, tender feelings she had for him.

"You own my heart, Elsa. All of me."

"I promise to take good care of it too." She laughed through the bond and he joined her, but also added, *"Forever."*

"Forever. Mmm, maybe we should use something else? For an eternity? A millennium? Until the cows come home?"

He kissed her. What else was there to do? When he did, she shivered and wrapped her arms around his head. Distantly he heard Faolan tell Circerran and Jack they might need some alone time, but if Elsa heard, she didn't deny it. Life *could* be this good. Now it *would* be.

Running Scared

Excerpt

Chapter One

There has to be some kind of mistake.

The MapQuest directions sat on the truck seat next to Lacey, outlining that this was the right exit. She hadn't accidentally decided to take a wrong turn. Besides, there weren't any decisions in her life right now, only directions. She smiled at the thought. Yeah, her attempts at making colossal, life-changing decisions had landed her here, in the middle of nowhere, with no one and nothing around her.

Well, not exactly nothing. There were mountains everywhere. Huge, monstrous mountains, like the kind you could see on the travel channel seconds before some giant paw-waving, open-mouthed, roaring grizzly ate the cameraman.

Oh, yeah, this had to be some kind of mistake. Lacey needed the beach. And people. At this point, she'd settle for a pizza from her favourite beach shack. To hell with anyone else. She needed out of this truck, she realised, surprising herself with a broken mini-sob.

There wasn't a car in sight when she pulled her truck off the turn lane and stopped a few hundred yards onto the cracked asphalt of the old highway.

Two fumbles at jerking the door handle open, and she jumped down, the map in her hand. Blue sky, a cold November breeze, clean air and mountains filled her senses immediately. One deep breath, two, and half the tension simmering along her skin disappeared. Not the unease, though. The breeze felt different from home. Smelt different. Was different.

This has to be a mistake.

She rubbed her hand through her hair at the thought. Yeah, sure, this had to be a mistake, right? Wrong. Throughout this mess, she'd kept thinking that any time now she'd wake up, that this couldn't be happening, that there had to be some kind of freaking mistake. Life couldn't turn from normal to horrible in the blink of an eye. A decision to go outside a club trying to avoid a creepy guy couldn't destroy everything she'd worked so hard to build.

But, yeah, one look at the rugged, wilderness reminded her that, yeah, one thoughtless decision had ripped her life to shreds.

If she could reverse time, she'd — what? If she'd known that by leaving the bar she'd witness a mob hit, would she have taken her chances with the creepy guy? Probably not.

So here she was, standing on the side of a road on what looked like some crazy Wild West movie set.

Reality sucked. Delusions worked so much better — at least for about ten seconds. Lacey hadn't witnessed a murder. She hadn't been beaten to within an inch of losing her life. She hadn't spent months in a hospital trying to breathe on her own. She hadn't been forced to testify against some of the nastiest criminals in the world. She hadn't been left out to dry like this, forced to move, alone, to a place so remote and far from normal she might as well have been on another planet.

She was used to people, sunshine that smelled like the ocean...heck, music and noise, for God's sake. She was used to delis filled with adorable little old Italian men, smiling at her and asking about her day. She was used to Jewish bakeries with bagels that she'd get up at seven for on a Sunday morning. She was used to coffee shops brewing wicked espresso by the cup. She was used to nice people. Beaches. Safety.

The landscape facing her she was not used to. Big open grasslands, lined with the brilliant colours of fall foliage. Yellow and burnt cinnamon, deep green pines next to the white bark of some other kind of tree — beech or aspen, she didn't know — all created a wildly beautiful picture.

The view gave her the creeps. Maybe she was afraid of wide-open spaces. Agoraphobia was a possibility.

Humour bubbled up and she rubbed her face with both hands. The map crumpled a little, reminding her of the brutal reality of her new life. She was running scared. Nothing was going to change that. Not standing here, not staring off at the mountains, nothing.

So many regrets washed over her. Tears stung her eyes — she felt like they were clogging her throat. Lacey fought them and ignored the deep hollow pit in her stomach.

She needed a plan. Action washed all the turmoil aside — always had. She'd always filled her life with action. Being forced to sit in a truck for days on end had driven her slightly insane, no doubt.

The real estate office in Troy couldn't be too far. She'd find that, then her home, and see her new address for the next... Ah, God, who knew how long she'd be here?

Forever?

And didn't that thought put a huge dollop of pity into her pity-party sundae? Two blinks and the tears held off, so she focused on the mountains. The peaks looked white, possibly ten feet deep in snow by now. She could hike up to that snow; feel the cold on her face, maybe trail run along the ridges and ravines? They would be a challenge. Something to do. Later, maybe, after she'd settled in.

A truck slowed behind her, bringing the heartbeat she'd settled down to normal skyrocketing. What felt like ice water flooded her veins, while goosebumps beaded along her arms and a huge whoosh of adrenaline raced through her veins. The FBI agents had been clear: do not act anything but normal. What that meant, really, after all she'd endured, was a bit unclear. She didn't feel normal in her own skin, let alone here in this wilderness. Besides, she doubted she would look normal to a small western town filled with redneck cowboys. She was a beach babe, had always been one, and didn't think the changes of hair and scenery were going to make a difference.

Truck doors closed and she turned to face two guys — two cowboys, she corrected herself, taking in their jeans, rough looking tan jackets, scuffed boots and dusty black cowboy hats. Both walked over, and she panicked. What was she supposed to say?

They don't look Russian. The thought ran a frantic circle in her mind, followed by, what does a Russian hitman actually look like? God, did he have to be Russian? Or even a he? A humorous hysteria built up, but she took a deep breath and clenched her hand around the map. She steeled herself not to take a step backward as both men walked right up, almost breaking her bubble of personal space.

"Miss, can we help ya out?"

More books from
Billi Jean

Can a woman learn to trust her heart enough to give her dream another chance?

*When he's faced with a woman he can't forget, can he trust
that with her touch, he can finally hold on to love?*

About the Author

Billi Jean

Billi Jean was born in California but didn't stay put for long. She's lived in New York, Indiana, Missouri, Arizona, Colorado, Florida, Massachusetts and Vermont. She's lived in and worked from ranches to beach-side coffee shops to the woods in western Massachusetts. Now living and working in China, she continues to write for Totally Bound Publishing.

Billi Jean has been writing since high school when she couldn't wait for Robert Jordan to write his Wheel of Time series faster. As an adult, she still finds herself drawn to fantasy-adventure stories, but with an erotic romance flair. Her books are extremely hot, with a focus on strong characters that are shoved into fast-paced adventures. Her unique style of incredible journeys infused with hot passion leave her fans hoping for more.

Billi Jean loves to hear from readers. You can find contact information, website details and an author profile page at https://www.totallybound.com/

Home of Erotic Romance

www.ingramcontent.com/pod-product-compliance
Lightning Source LLC
Chambersburg PA
CBHW020211260626
47156CB00002B/331